Advance praise for *Sister Chicas*, by Lisa Alvarado, Ann Hagman Cardinal, and Jane Alberdeston Coralin

"*Sister Chicas* is an exquisite project, set in the steaming streets of multicultural Chicago, with multivoiced Latina characters that ring true as well as smart. Latinos are a diverse and complicated people. These three gifted writers have produced a unique and unforgettable single novel. Bravo."

—Luis J. Rodriguez, Author of *Music of the Mill*,
a novel, and *My Nature Is Hunger*, poems

"I wish I could invite Taina, Leni, and Graciela, those funny and lively Sister Chicas, to my kitchen table. They'd start confiding and laughing about their *familias*, clothes, and, of course, boys. Like real sisters, they'd share what matters to them, honoring their Latino culture, writing from the heart—each one becoming a beautiful unique *mujer*. ¡Maravilloso!"

—Pat Mora, award-winning author of poetry, nonfiction, children's books,
and the acclaimed memoir, *House of Houses*

"Think *Ya-Ya Sisterhood* crossed with *How the Garcia Girls Lost Their Accent* and you'll have some idea of just what a treat this delightful novel is. Narrated by the three main characters in each young woman's strong, clear voice, the novel offers a compelling and perceptive look at what it means to grow up as a Latina woman in contemporary America. The authors thoughtfully provide a useful glossary of Spanish words and phrases.... These extras in the novel make it ideal for an extended book club discussion.... It's an engaging introduction to Latina culture for non-Latinos and I would imagine an appealing, even comforting text for young Hispanic women who seek authentic images of themselves in a well-written novel."

—Merri Rosenberg for Education Update

W9-BXW-248

SISTER CHICAS

A Novel

LISA ALVARADO,
ANN HAGMAN CARDINAL, AND
JANE ALBERDESTON CORALIN

NEW AMERICAN LIBRARY

New American Library
Published by New American Library, a division of
Penguin Group (USA) Inc., 375 Hudson Street, New York, New York 10014, USA
Penguin Group (Canada), 90 Eglinton Avenue East, Suite 700, Toronto,
Ontario M4P 2Y3, Canada (a division of Pearson Penguin Canada Inc.)
Penguin Books Ltd., 80 Strand, London WC2R 0RL, England
Penguin Ireland, 25 St. Stephen's Green, Dublin 2,
Ireland (a division of Penguin Books Ltd.)
Penguin Group (Australia), 250 Camberwell Road, Camberwell, Victoria 3124,
Australia (a division of Pearson Australia Group Pty. Ltd.)
Penguin Books India Pvt. Ltd., 11 Community Centre, Panchsheel Park,
New Delhi - 110 017, India
Penguin Group (NZ), cnr Airborne and Rosedale Roads, Albany,
Auckland 1310, New Zealand (a division of Pearson New Zealand Ltd.)
Penguin Books (South Africa) (Pty.) Ltd., 24 Sturdee Avenue,
Rosebank, Johannesburg 2196, South Africa

Penguin Books Ltd., Registered Offices:
80 Strand, London WC2R 0RL, England

First published by New American Library,
a division of Penguin Group (USA) Inc.

First Printing, April 2006
10 9 8 7 6 5 4 3 2

NEW AMERICAN LIBRARY and logo are trademarks of Penguin Group (USA) Inc.

LIBRARY OF CONGRESS CATALOGING-IN-PUBLICATION DATA

Alvarado, Lisa.
    Sister Chicas / Lisa Alvarado, Ann Hagman Cardinal, Jane Alberdeston Coralin.
      p. cm.
    ISBN 0-451-21770-5
    1. Hispanic American teenage girls—Fiction. I. Cardinal, Ann Hagman. II. Coralin, Jane
Alberdeston. III. Title.
    PS3601.L866S57 2006
    813'.6—dc22   2005029694

Set in Berkley Book
Designed by Patrice Sheridan

Printed in the United States of America

PUBLISHER'S NOTE
This is a work of fiction. Names, characters, places, and incidents either are the product of
the authors' imaginations or are used fictitiously, and any resemblance to actual persons, living or dead, business establishments, events, or locales is entirely coincidental.
    The publisher does not have any control over and does not assume any responsibility for
author or third-party Web sites or their content.

For all the sisters who came before me.
For the girls we were, to the girls we still are.
For the *comadres, y otras chicas* whose stories shine like diamonds,
whose talents are legion, whose love knows no bounds . . .
Mil gracias for smoothing my path,
for feeding my soul, for lighting my way.

For Gregory, for being there each and every day,
for sharing the writer's life.

And for you *Mamá*, always in my heart.
I wrote this story for you.

— LISA ALVARADO

✧✧✧✧✧

For my son, Carlos, and husband, Doug,
for their love, patience, and unerring belief in me.

For my real-life Sister Chicas and coauthors,
Jane and Lisa, brilliant writers,
bonded sisters, and invaluable friends.

And for Elena Dávila Hagman, who I wish could have lived to see
my Latina blood rise to the surface in such
dramatic and public fashion.
Tu vives en mis pensamientos, Mami.

— ANN HAGMAN CARDINAL

✧✧✧✧✧

I owe my heart and all its stories
to my *mami* Aida and my *abuela* Juanita Santalis.

— JANE ALBERDESTON CORALIN

✧✧✧✧✧

THE AUTHORS WOULD LIKE TO THANK
THE FOLLOWING *HERMANAS Y*
HERMANOS FOR THEIR SUPPORT:

*O*ur editor and honorary Sister Chica, Kara Cesare, for understanding our vision and being able to see the potential in half a book. Our agent, Nicholas Ellison, a.k.a. *El Capitán*, for his unwavering faith and support, and Sarah Dickman for her patience and tender loving care to working authors. Fellow novelist Thomas Christopher Greene for his encouragement and for not thinking of writing as a competitive sport. Our first enthusiastic young readers, Elena "Leni" Hagman, Meredith Finch, and Peter Hagman. Gregory McCain, for going the extra mile with the kind of feedback that put flesh on the bones. Marcela Landres, for opening the door through which we walked. Luis Rodriguez, Maureen Seaton, Rosalind Cummings-Yates, and Pat Mora, who understand that generosity is a living thing borne out by action. Roberto Tijerina for the gift of *la idioma*. We thank friends and artists Rebecca Villarreal, Maria Mazziotti Gillan, Thomas Absher, Sarah Meselson, Anne Connor, Bernice Mennis, Kyle Cushman, and Tara Mahady for their everlasting love and support. To Lambda Legal and the Midwest Regional Office, Union Institute and University, and Binghamton University for keeping body and soul together and understanding the artist's journey.

And finally, our gratitude to Isabel Allende, Sandra Cisneros, Ana Castillo, Elena Poniatowska, Julia Alvarez, Judith Ortiz Cofer, Julia de Burgos, Gloria Anzaldúa, and Esmeralda Santiago—for stoking the fire that lit our imaginations.

TAINA

I'm waiting for the bus, the 56, and here it comes, barreling down Milwaukee Avenue, a half a block away from my house. Everybody else takes the train, which is just as close, but I promised *Mami*. She thinks it's too dangerous for someone my age to ride the blue line alone. I honestly don't see the difference. But she's my mother—what can a fourteen-year-old do but obey her mother? Once a week, I take the fifty-six to meet two-thirds of the Sister Chicas, Leni and Graciela, at El Rinconcito del Sabor, a restaurant near Logan Square. Every time we walk in, the proprietor drops what he's doing and escorts us señoritas to a reserved corner table. Don Ramiro is a *caballero* through and through. Even though Leni rolls her Siouxsie-and-the-Banshees kohl-outlined eyes when her chair is pulled out for her, I know she secretly enjoys his attention. He brings Graciela her steaming cup of *café con leche*—just the way she likes it. Me? Well, when I ask for a glass of tamarind juice, Don Ramiro pours it into a champagne flute. Can it get better than that?

If my mother found out I was frequenting El Rinconcito, she'd probably say I was bringing bad luck to her restaurant, Cafetín El Yunque, which sits at the intersection of Division, Ashland, and Milwaukee. My mother and I live in the apartment above it. My first day of school at Whitney, she jumped, her pink hair rollers bouncing down onto her forehead. "What a perfect opportunity to get El Yunque's name out in the community!" she said, rushing to her purse, pulling out the business card where a big palm tree waved next to the cursive *Cafetin El Yunque*—the Paradise of Chicago.

"Tell people, Taina." She pushed the card into the front zipper of my book bag.

"*Sí, Mami,* as soon as I can." I groaned.

"Promise?"

"*Te lo prometo,*" I mumbled back. To my mother, promises mean complete and total loyalty. I promise to work in the restaurant three nights a week. I promise to wear the lacy señorita bra she gave me for my birthday. I promise to eat malanga root every week because it's good for me. I promise to introduce all my friends to her. I promise to not eat at Taco Bell. Actually, my friends Leni and Graciela follow along with her on that one.

"That stuff's cardboard covered in watery salsa!" Leni complained. "Plus, you aid and abet those corporate monsters every time you walk in that joint. I won't be a 'walking ad' for that crap."

"Actually, Leni's right, *mi* Taina. Just think about the stereotyping. They used a Chihuahua to represent the cultural face of the Mexican people. *Por favor.*" Graciela always lengthens out the *favor* part of her *por favor*. It's when her *Latinidad* comes out the strongest. Her words curl out of her mouth like the lyrics of the *canciones del amor* that float out of Don Ramiro's radio every evening.

Thursdays around four o'clock, I head out to meet my Sister Chicas at El Rinconcito. I wave good-bye to Ramon and Lupe, El Yunque's waiters who are just starting their shift. "She's going to see her *novio,*" they childishly call after me as I rush out El Yunque's door and book to Milwaukee to wait for the fifty-six. From her perch, a desk in the back near the bustling kitchen, *Mami* frowns at their taunting. But I know she's smiling inside. Of the two waiters, she adores Ramon most. His father works the deli counter at Fritz's, a butcher shop two streets down from our place. Yesterday afternoon, as I pleated the polyester table napkins into the fancy peacock tails my mother loves, she whispered like a schoolgirl into my ear, "What do you think of Ramon?"

"What do you mean?" Though one stubborn napkin did not want to keep its folds, I did not stop what I was doing to look at her. I knew exactly what she was asking.

"I mean, what do you think of Ramon? He's a good Puerto Rican boy," *Mami* offered, her voice rising as if asking a question. "Just like the boys back home. Why don't we invite him for dinner?"

"*Mami*, he's nice but I don't . . . I don't like him that way." Inside my head burst with the memory of another boy's face, my first love's wondrous smile, the way his laughter made a spot on the small of my back whirl.

"What way is that? I'm only talking about dinner, not marriage! *Dios mio, hija. Qué exajerada.*"

Leni and Graciela know my mother. And they know why I blindly do everything she tells me to do, but what can I do about it? She's my mother. You do what your *Mami* tells you, even if that means sleeping with a silk cap on your head every night. Even if that means wearing every bit of clothing she buys for you. Never mind that it's always something you don't like. But sometimes you beg anyway for that simple, printless, unembroidered, sequin-free sweater—something black, gray, fitted, and plain. Everything she thinks is all wrong for you. Loving your mother means doing everything she wants, especially when it comes to your hair.

Once a month, *Mami* drives me to Rosa's Beauty, where Sol Maria coats my hair with Dark and Lovely no-lye relaxer till my scalp feels like it's about to peel off. While Sol Maria pulls on every strand of my hair to make it straighter and straighter, she talks with everyone in the room, sharing bits of gossip, new or old, with the customers shuffling in and out the door, a cloud of hairspray floating over their heads.

By the end of the visit, I am always physically and mentally exhausted, with a crick in my neck, my collar soaking wet, and my scalp covered in second-degree burns. To my mother's delight and my horror, my natural curl has been chemically ironed straight. While she pays the seventy-five dollars for the all-day visit, *Mami* will glow with pride. She will gush over my transformation, while all the Dominican and Puerto Rican *salonistas* call me "*Chinita*," little Chinese girl, warning me to not let too much time pass until the next visit to "the beauty." If you ask me, it's a little like telling a prisoner to not go too far out in the yard. Even if I wanted to escape, I couldn't.

I've been writing a poem about my sacrificial visits to Rosa's, hoping that it's good enough to print in the *Monitor*'s poetry column, but it still has some kinks that need to be ironed out. Ha. Pun intended.

ROSA'S BEAUTY
It was a ritual
one Saturday a month
storm or shine, broke or not
Mami would drive me to Rosa's Beauty.
It was like walking into your girlfriend's house,
Rosa's, with its lime-green tile floor,
slippery with black hair clippings
under a forest of high-heeled, flip-flopped women,
spitting fire in Dominican Spanish,
frying-pan hot, *ají* in each word
room aflame with their lipstick
all talking the same ~~gossip~~ *bochinche*.
Five hours amid smoke and ash
lotions and dyes tinting the air
scissors and mouths moving
to any ~~salsa~~ mambo radio tune
and by then my head was burning alive
with the power of the relaxer
unable to wash it out,
ruin a girl's reputation for looking good right
and good. There we were, on our way
to be called *chinitas*,
~~relax~~ straighten out kinks
we couldn't correct in our everyday.
Couldn't make family better or bring fathers back home
but we could look real nice like real Puerto Rican girls
    should.

How am I going to tell Leni and Graciela about my mother's crazy plan? I mean, they know *Mami*. They've been up close and personal with her special brand of insanity. The first time they came to my house, *Mami* rushed them to her walk-in closet. In record time she had them trying on her *tacones,* three-inch skinny high heels, the kind that force your toes into the tiny tip; the kind that keep podiatrists in the money. Grachi was so polite, but I could see the surprise in her eyes. (That's what I call Graciela— Grachi, though I'm not sure she likes it. She's not the kind that appreciates any sort of cutesy nickname.) For Leni, *Mami* had a whopper: a prissy pink pullover. Wait—it gets worse. There were poodles sewn onto the chest.

"Ay, girls, I am so happy you like these clothes. Maybe you can teach my only daughter to like them. One day, Taina, you're going to ask yourself why you didn't listen to your mother," she said, shaking a long ruby-painted fingernail at me. How I felt for the Sister Chicas: Graciela cradling her sensible shoes while perched on the black high heels, and Leni's spiked purple punk hair clashing against the pink pullover. I could just imagine Leni's tattoo *de rosas* punching through the pullover's cotton blend in rebellion.

I loved my mother, but things were always this way. This very morning she got me riled up, catching me while I was buttering my toast by the kitchen window, the morning streaming in on its own vehicle of light, settling down on a circle of cracked Formica.

"*Corazón,* in two months you will be fifteen, you know. I have been thinking that you should have a *quinceañera.*"

Momentarily choking on a corner of my burned toast, I whisked my body around to my mother, who stood framed in the kitchen doorway, smoothing her hands with Jergens. I couldn't believe I'd heard what I'd just heard. "*Mami,* noooo. We can't have a big party. We just moved here. It's too soon."

"*¿Y qúe?* I know people I can invite. And you have many friends from that school, don't you? Elena and Graciela will love the idea."

"It's Leni, not Elena. And *Mami,* I don't want a *quinceañera.* You remember what happened to Leti's father."

Leon Feria, a friend of my mother's family, planned a year in advance for his daughter Leti's *quinceañera,* renting the largest and priciest hall in the Caribe Hilton. His family thought it was a strange and uncommonly impractical thing for Sr. Feria to do, considering that he earned his money working for Goya Foods as a quality-assurance manager; he wasn't exactly rolling in it. But as everybody knows—people talk. And talk they did. Mrs. Santos told Dona Vicky, who told her daughter Alejandra, who told my mother that Sr. Feria, with his shoes in hand, sneaked out of his house at night to do all night bookkeeping in a hotel's back room. He worked tirelessly, saving almost every dollar for his little girl's birthday party. His wife, *Mami*'s friend Dania Feria, confided in my mother that her husband wasn't sleeping well but that she didn't know why. "Just look at the bags under his eyes. Do you think he has a *novia?*" Mrs. Feria asked *Mami* tearfully. My mother, unusually silent, kept the rumor to herself. "Ay, no, *amor,*" I heard my mother console, "he's probably just working too hard. Give him some time." Still, I wondered why he never told his wife the truth, letting her worry like that for no reason. Maybe he was just too macho. In December, *Mami* and I received a silver-embossed invitation to the Iglesia del Primero Sanctuario, the church Leti Feria received her communion in, the church she would reaffirm her faith in, the church her father hoped she'd marry in.

The night of the big fiesta, as we walked the red-carpet stairway to the banquet hall, all the guests' mouths dropped to the floor. Caterers served a five-course meal to three hundred guests surrounded by crystal stemware, yellow and white roses, and silk duponi tablecloths. Why do I know the tablecloths were made of silk duponi? Only because the women at our table could not help repeating, "It's duponi! Silk duponi!" every five minutes or so. Around two in the morning, the bar ran out of mojito mix and the guests ate the last morsel of the wedding-size *tres leches* cakes from my aunt's famous La Deliciosa Bakery. Sr. Feria sat at the head table, a smile plastered on his face, watching his family and friends unbuckle their belt buckles and throw off their high heels.

Watching the butter on my toast melt away, the kitchen's one fluorescent blinking annoyingly, I turned to my mother, hoping to win my argument. "It's too much money, *Mami.*"

But *Mami* was nunfazed. "Ay, Taina, you don't have to worry about that. I'll worry about the cost. Anyway, it's a perfect way to introduce you to Chicago. And to save money, we could have it here in the restaurant, our El Yunque! I can just picture it . . . can't you? We'll do an ocean scene with shells and mermaids and little boats. Ay, it will be so beautiful. I'll dress the window with fishing nets and flowers, and we'll *iluminar* the whole room with white and blue Christmas lights. All the city will come to just look at it. *Chiquita,* talk to your friends about it. They will love the idea."

"No, they won't, *Mami.*"

"*¡Por favor!* Enough of this nonsense. I am proud to say that your grandmother, *mi madre que está en el cielo,* gave me one, and her mother before her gave her daughter the same, even though times were tough and money was tight. It's a *tradición, nena.* And this mother will not break with tradition." With a final "Humpf," *Mami* turned on her thin high heel and clicked into the hall, leaving the soft scent of Maja perfume behind her.

What am I going to do? I really think this is the first time in my life I've wanted to disobey my mother. But it is useless to argue with her. When *Papi* was still around, he would whisper to me after arguing with my mother, an ear-to-ear grin on his face: "Don't spit into the air; it will fall back down on you." I was not willing to spit on myself so early in the morning. So I'm on the way now to see the girls to tell them . . . to tell them . . . What will I tell them? That my mother is planning a very expensive circus and they will be hired clowns dressed in ugly pink taffeta?

❖ ❖ ❖ ❖ ❖

The 56/Milwaukee careens to another stop. Funny how I now know this route like the back of my hand. It is the bus I take every Thursday to meet the Sister Chicas. And it is the bus where I met Yusef for the first time—Yusef, my first love.

A mother had climbed on board, her screeching son clinging to her waist. Her kid's face was splotched the kind of beet red that kids turn when they've been crying for a very long time. His mother was flustered, blond hair tousled around her face as if she'd been caught in a tornado. She fumbled in her pocket for change, and dropped several coins against the rubber mat. The people crowding onto the bus behind her rolled their eyes, nudged each other knowingly, and whispered about badly behaved children and irresponsible mothers. My anger crept under my fingernails; I closed my fist against it. I know that if Graciela were there she would have already sacrificed her seat and helped the woman pick up her change. But Graciela wasn't anywhere around. So I decided: *I'll do it.* I moved forward, felt my calf muscles tense as I began to stand in the aisle, inching toward the frazzled mother. As I straightened my body out like a new tree limb, I felt the telltale breeze of another person stealing my seat brush past me.

Just then, right in front of me, just as I was nearing her, a guy swiftly moved in front of me. He bent at the waist and plucked each coin from the floor, handing them to her in a grand poetic gesture of chivalry. He looked my age, maybe a year or two older. He was tall to my five-one, and though he was slightly turned away from my point of view, I could tell he was all grin. *There's just something about him,* I thought, staring. *Stop staring. Stop.* But I couldn't help myself. He was beautifully long in his tan wide-wale corduroys that met paint-splattered black work boots.

The mother with the banshee baby thanked him with an embarrassed grunt and pushed past both of us down the aisle. He didn't seem fazed by her response. We were alone—as much as we could be during morning rush hour on city transportation. "Hi," he said, and I felt all the chemically straightened hairs on the back of my head crinkle with excitement. Everyone but him and me had a seat, our bodies listing with the bus's rhythm. He moved toward the center of the bus, clutching the steel rail above his head, coming closer to me, close enough for me to notice his dreads touching the tunnel of his black turtleneck, the hair whispering over the tight knit. I imagined the locks met the soft valley of the nape of his neck, cotton-puffed out like a halo. *Did I answer his hello?* Dios mío, *I can't remember! Is it too late now? Yes, I can't say it now, ten minutes later. He already must think I'm an* idiota. I *am an* idiota. *Taina, close your mouth—you've missed your stop, a voice in my head that sounded just like* Mami's *startled me out of my reverie.* ¡Cara!

I squeezed past him, whispering, "Driver . . . Driver . . ." But the driver wasn't answering; instead, he pointed wearily to the sign above my head: PLEASE DO NOT DISTURB THE DRIVER. HE IS CONCENTRATING ON YOUR SAFETY. The fifty-six bounced away, crossed Fullerton, and loomed toward the corner of Milwaukee and Kedzie. The grinner touched my shoulder.

"Miss your stop?"

He looked down at me with another one of his award-winning, Crest-strip smiles. His voice was made of sugar cubes. I nodded at his question, my head snapping up and down like a little girl saying yes to candy, my words muted by the prettiness of his face, the angle of his nose a long slope toward full dogwood lips. I felt a poem coming on.

"Uh, yes. I mean, no. I . . . can get off at the next stip. Stop. The next stop."

"Your papers are slipping out of your arms." I looked down and there they were, two hundred eight-by-five-inch card-stock flyers sliding out of my notebook toward the bus's tire-rubber floor. I pinched my elbows against them, but it was no use; my fate had already been decided.

"Let me," the stranger whispered, catching the mustard-yellow sheets from underneath my loosened clasp, collecting them in his strong . . . paint-splattered hands. At that point the bus lurched, a whale turning into the ocean of asphalt. It was movielike, the longest second of my fourteen-year-old life, my bones moving back and forth in the aisle like a trapeze artist over an awestruck crowd. In the clockwork movement of one second to another, that sweet knight in shining fell onto the stressed-out damsel. This was so very Harlequin romance, not that I'm complaining. Thinking back, the fall should have hurt my butt, my back, my elbow, but I don't remember feeling anything but my heart pitter-pattering against my rib cage. God, more clichés? I don't remember seeing any of the passengers' faces looming over the spectacle. I remember only his face, smooth velvet, leaning over me, his half-grin showing me he was both amused and embarrassed. But I was one more than that. I was in love.

Various oohs and aahs ribboned through the length of the bus, though they were not reserved for us. He and I were laid out on the bus's rubber runway, flyers splashed around us like a yellow brick road. At that moment, my plain Mary Jane flats felt like ruby slippers. I didn't usually feel pretty, but there was something in Yusef's glimmering eyes that told me he saw me differently from any other boy who had ever looked at me sideways. Not that they ever did.

Back in Puerto Rico, *Mami* kept a close watch on my social life—okay, as much as a preteen Guzman living in Puerto Rico is allowed a social life. Even until a year before we moved to Chicago, *Mami* never let me out of her sight. She was the only mother to chaperone school events—though no teacher requested volunteer chaperones. *Mami* would stand guard, sitting cross-legged in a metal chair. "No slow dancing, Taina," she would warn, her stern face inundated with disco strobe lights. It didn't matter anyway—the boys didn't want to dance with me.

Mami wanted to make sure I didn't turn out like her brother's daughter Linda, whom she always called a delinquent. Linda was sixteen when her parents discovered she'd been sneaking out of her window at night to meet her boyfriend, Steve, a U.S. Army private from Fort Buchanan. It took a long time for *la familia* Guzman to find out what they were doing: They would rent a room at the hot-pink Escondido Motel near the base. Linda and her secret soldier would spend the entire night together. Following them one night, Linda's father, Mario, busted in the frail plank door and pulled Linda away from Steve; he yanked her so hard and fast, a blue bruise clung to her forearm for almost two weeks. See, it wasn't so much that her parents discovered the romance, but that they couldn't keep the truth back quickly enough from the entire upscale San Patricio neighborhood they lived in. Soon the truth spread from house to house like a brushfire; everyone who was everyone gossiped about the whole mess like old women picking *gandules* on their backdoor step. The whole mix of streets knew that Linda's future had already been matched to Eduardo Salvatore, a pencil-thin Argentine whose father owned a textile factory in Humacao. With her secretly dating what Uncle Mario called "a *yanqui* nobody," Linda had dashed her parents' hopes to the Caribbean Sea.

Soon, every so-called self-respecting parent of the Guzman clan ordered their daughters to stay away from Linda. She was the family's new black sheep. Weird, huh? I was only ten at the time, but to this day nobody even dares to whisper Linda's name in the open air. Still, some things get out. The last thing I'd heard about Linda was that she was working as a dentist's assistant somewhere near Washington, DC.

I wasn't thinking about Linda or my *Mami* those ten stops between falling to the fifty-six bus floor and watching Yusef scribble his phone number on one of my mother's flyers. I wasn't thinking at all, really, but stupidly ogling him. I knew he was saying things I should have been listening intently to, and honestly, I want to believe I was listening intently and responding intelligently to Yusef's questions, but at this moment I can't remember exactly what we talked about, what he said, what I said. I mean, this moment was the first time in my life I'd felt these . . . feelings. You know the kind—the quivering knees, buzzing brain, cartwheel stomach. When I was standing so close to him on the bus, all the hairs of my arms stood at attention. At one moment, when he was talking, he put his hand on mine, and I thought for sure I'd faint. I know how that sounds: faint? Who am I—Jane Eyre?

Still, I didn't understand what was happening to me; it seemed my whole body was working under an assumed name. Sure, the girls in gym class giggled nonstop about boys and crushes, but I never knew what they were talking about. Boys weren't like this; boys weren't like Yusef—they didn't smile at you, unless they were about to do something mean. The boys I knew certainly never tried to rescue me from falling to the floor. And believe me, I've fallen a lot. No, *boys* don't act like this. Only men were gentlemen, *caballeros*. Men like my father, who (at least, until before he left us) opened doors and called girls "ladies." He was a lot like the men in guayaberas who sat outside the bodegas in Mayagüez, sipping *café con leche* out of Styrofoam cups. Whenever my mother passed them by, they always tipped their finely crafted straw *pavonas* toward her. My mother, her hips in a natural sway, would demurely turn and smile. "Smile only with your lips," she would whisper to me once inside the store. Though I never understood why I wasn't supposed to smile with my teeth showing, I knew that around those men I never stammered or clammed up. I never got what my father used to call potato-salad brains. But around Yusef, wow, I wasn't just potato salad: I was mush.

"You should get off here," Yusef said, pointing to the next stop. Part of me, the mush part, was happy to see the bus careen toward the curb. All I know was I made it out of the fifty-six bus waving like a giddy schoolgirl, a plaster-of-paris grin on my face, my stomach in my throat, knee bones quivering like Jell-O pudding. Happily, I clutched his telephone number in my fist.

✧　✧　✧　✧

The first time I called Yusef, I had to sneak behind El Yunque, near the trash bins where the cooks lit up during their cigarette breaks. It took a week's worth of summoning enough courage to press those numbers, but I really wanted to hear his voice. I could smell the scent of Camels and cooking grease on the public phone's receiver as I pressed it close. I didn't want anyone to hear me say, "Hi, Yusef, it's me, the girl on the bus. Well, the girl who fell on the floor of the bus. Um, the one holding the yellow fever— I mean, flyers." Listen to me—bubbling like a mountain spring.

"Taina? Wow. I was starting to think you were a figment of my imagination. I don't know, maybe I'm still dreaming."

"Should I pinch you?" *Oh, God,* I thought, *where did that come from?!*

"Well, if you want to pinch me, you have to see me."

Dizzy, I pressed the plastic receiver to my ear as if it were a conch shell. His flirting was a rug being pulled out from under my feet. My free hand trembling against the cool brick restaurant wall, the rough mortar scratching my palms, I tried hard to be cute. Nothing. *What a dud.*

"Taina? Are you there? Hello?"

"Yeah, sorry, I'm here."

"So where are you calling me from?"

"Outside my mom's restaurant," I whispered, though I was not sure why. I was alone in the alleyway; my mother's kitchen seemed so far away.

"You don't have a phone in your house?" Yusef asked.

"No, I mean, yes, of course, we have a phone. Upstairs. I just have more privacy here."

"Outside? Mmmm. Keeping your admirers a secret?" He laughed. My Keds shuffled back and forth nervously. He continued playfully. "Well, Taina, I don't mind if you call me from a telephone booth—as long as you ain't Superman."

I meant to laugh but instead it came out like a cough. "Sscha."

"All right, all right, I get the point. No more ribbing."

I couldn't keep my grin back. I sighed. "Good, 'cause I don't have much of a break left." I imagined him smiling on the other line.

"Girl, you're smiling right now, aren't you? Just to let you know—I've been smiling since I picked up the phone."

"Really?" *Really?* Couldn't I come up with something more intelligent than that? What was wrong with me?

"Yes. Really. Thinking about you makes me feel good."

I didn't know what to say. Well, that wasn't true. I knew what I wanted to say. But my mouth was frozen. I was suffering from hypothermia.

"Okay. So you're not big on sharing, huh?"

"Sharing?" *Uh-oh.* Something green caught itself in my throat, and the word *sharing* creaked out like the voice of a ten-year-old boy in the middle of puberty. *God, I wish Leni were here,* I thought. *She could tell me what to say next.*

"You know, Taina, if flirting were a muscle, I'd have pulled mine about three minutes ago."

And then the miraculous happened. It was like the seas parted or the sky opened up and cats and dogs rained down on my head. The vise that was my mouth loosened; my jaw unclenched itself, and suddenly words like bottle rockets exploded between my teeth and flew out of my mouth. There was nothing I could do to stop them:

"You don't have to work too hard with me, Yusef. I already like you."

Even if Grachi or Leni asked me, I don't believe I could have explained it.

✧ ✧ ✧ ✧ ✧

Okay, focus, Taina. One dilemma at a time. The girls must already be waiting for me at El Rinconcito. How am I going to tell Leni and Graciela about Mami's *dumb, dumb, dumb new project? Okay—this is how I'll break the news to them:*

"Girls, *Mami's* planning a hostile takeover of my life. I'm running to the hills for freedom. Anyone with me?"

Of course, there's no way I can run away. I'm scheduled to work the register at El Yunque after school tomorrow. If I keep this up, I'm going to go loony tunes. I'm stuck. I need my Sister Chicas to help me out with this one.

2

Graciela

Thursday afternoon. Blue October sky—it's sunny, but it's the kind of pale, distant light that tells you the summer's over. Perfect day so far. I'm on time—4:05 by the clock in the window of the bank on the other side of Logan Boulevard. I've got the commute down now, grabbing the subway at the Racine/University of Illinois stop by 3:25. I'm a freshman at UIC, honors English lit and early childhood education—not so bad for an eighteen-year-old from Pilsen, you know? I've settled into my class routine, and so far it's been a pretty smooth transition. Well, smooth except for one or two glitches—a couple of people in the admissions office complimented me on speaking English so well, even though I was born here, and in my Composition 101 class, someone's mouth fell open when I told them I'd already read *Romeo and Juliet* my junior year of high school. Overall, though, it's been amazing.

I know I'm lucky, with opportunities other kids from the neighborhood haven't had. It's important to me, to my family, that I contribute to *mi comunidad, mi gente,* offer something to people who have less. Between my own classes, tutoring in the community outreach program at Casa Aztlán, and my part-time job at Librería Tzintzuntzán, I'm busy, but that's okay. Busy is good.

Besides, I'd never miss my Thursday-afternoon appointment with my girls, *mis* Sister Chicas.

I'll have a long commute later; it'll probably take me at least forty-five minutes, since it's always a wait to catch the train after rush hour's over. Leni's also got a way to go to get back home, all the way to her mother's glass-and-steel condo overlooking the Lincoln Park running path and the lakefront. Usually she'll just call a cab—let's just say her "allowance" is generous, really, really generous. Taina is about fifteen minutes away by bus, which works best, since she's the youngest and should be closer to home.

Tonight's the one night I miss dinner at home, but my parents understand. They trust me; they're proud of me, too. Believe me, the feeling's mutual. After all, *Mamá y Papá* are my heroes, my role models. I know how much they gave up, how much they sacrificed to give me a decent life, a decent education. It's important that I give something back to them, honor who they are, what their example has been. When I finish school, I plan on getting a teaching certificate and teaching English, maybe even at Benito Juarez in the neighborhood.

You see, they were both professors of literature in Morelia, their hometown, not that far from D.F.—that's Mexico City's nickname if you didn't already know. It's touching when you hear them talk about it. They were friends in high school who ended up at college together, sharing the same major. Classical literature, by the way. My favorite photo of them shows them bright eyed, serious, holding hands, and having what looks like a very important conversation.

In the picture, *Mamá*'s hair is shoulder-length, just like it is today, her olive skin smooth. Since then, time has sketched laugh lines in her beautiful face, crinkles at the mouth and the corners of her eyes that she shares with *mi Papá*. And there's *Papá*, muscular but thin, tall by Mexican standards. He's a little heavier now, but it suits him. He still has the same head of wavy hair, coal black in the photo, that's salt-and-pepper these days. Every time I see that photo past and present merge; then and now, they are beautiful, strong, and proud.

After winning appointments to Universidad Nacional Autónoma de México, the national university, *Papá* moved to DF first, then *Mamá* a year later. My parents laugh when they tell the story, saying how young they were, how romantic. Student activists on campus, they organized support for land and water rights for farmers on the border. They paid dearly for their principles: The university forced them to resign for what was called "inappropriate conduct."

After a year or so of just getting by, tutoring what *Papá* called *hijos de la indolencia*, friends here helped them get green cards, and they came north. Once they made their way to Chicago, my *tío Ruben* helped them apply for citizenship, and I was born not too long after that. My mother had a difficult pregnancy with me; there were serious complications during delivery. It made their dream of a large family one that never came true.

When I was five, I remember *Mamá* pregnant and going to the hospital, and coming home with just *Papá* and empty arms, and both of them so very, very quiet. I guess there were other miscarriages before that, too, but I was too young to know what was happening. My parents never really talk about it, which is unusual for us, because we've always talked about a lot of things—most things, really.

Anyway, after about a year of *Mamá y Papá* working in restaurants, new friends of the family got them jobs at an electronics factory, and for the last twenty years they've been the most literate, best-educated assembly line inspectors of radio and cell phone components. It's a union job with benefits, but they've both worked years of overtime to make sure I had a good education and the things they thought really mattered. We shop for clothes at resale stores, buy groceries with coupons and sale papers, and drive used cars. But our home has always been filled with *música tradicional y literatura*—Elena Poniatowska, Carlos Fuentes, Octavio Paz, all the literary giants, surrounded by the sounds of *Jarocho, Son huasteco, y música mariachi*.

Twice a year we make the pilgrimage back to Mexico City and the museums, where they make sure I learn to adore the sweep of a Rivera, the colors of Siqueiros, the tragedy and triumph of Frida Kahlo. *"Tesoros, mi'ja,"* they would tell me, *"tesoros de tu gente."*

Treasures are what they want me to remember. I know my rock and hip-hop, and I'm not a stranger to prime-time TV. I'll even admit it: Those big Hollywood action movies are my guilty pleasure. I sneak one in as often as I can, even though my girls tease me all the time about them. Pop culture is great, really, but I know that *mis raíces* make me who I am, and what *mis padres* never want me to forget.

One thing it took me long time to understand is why they insist on speaking English here at home and Spanish only when we go to D.F.—We have books and magazines at home in Spanish, but it's an ironclad rule: "English only, Graciela," they say. "This country requires English; your future requires English." Once, when I was twelve, I asked *Mamá* why it was so important. "If your father and I spoke better, *inglés sin acento*, maybe we would still be teaching." It was the only time I ever saw her embarrassed about how she spoke, how she sounded. It wasn't long after that that I decided I'd become a teacher—it's the least I can do.

✧   ✧   ✧   ✧

Following the stream of people who've just left the blue line subway station, scattering across the six-corner intersection that's the heart of Logan Square, I stop for a second at the corner of Logan Boulevard, Kedzie, and Milwaukee Avenue. Taking a moment, I admire the towering eagle monument soaring up in the middle of the intersection. It reminds me of the Monument of the Independence in D.F. I love the strength of those granite wings, the way they soar from a towering column, slicing against the autumn sky. I'd stay longer, but I'm on my way to El Rinconcito del Sabor. It's about a ten-minute walk; it's where Don Ramiro will make *cafecitos* for me and my girls, my Sister Chicas.

I've been coming to El Rinconcito for almost two years now, with my parents' permission. It started with tutoring Don Ramiro's daughter, Nilsa, in grammar and composition. Then sometime last year, I started coming by myself. Nilsa was getting Bs, and didn't really need me anymore, but I liked having a place where I could spread out and drink coffee and brainstorm ideas for the paper. Over the last four months, Thursday's come to mean something else again. Now it's girls' time to hang out, check in, and be together.

And just who are the Sister Chicas? It's the three of us—me, Graciela Villalobos, Elena O'Malley-Diaz, and Taina Moscoso. We don't look like sisters, and a lot of times we don't act like them either. But somehow we got to be friends. Elena calls herself Leni, for reasons I don't understand, but don't get me started on that. And Taina's the youngest, much quieter and shyer than we are.

It all happened last year, at Whitney Young Magnet School. I was a senior, coeditor of the school newspaper, the *Monitor,* along with a future Pulitzer prize winner, or at least that's what he's always telling me. His name's Jack Jordan, and for an Anglo former jock, he's not too bad. A good friend, really. But that was after I made him get rid of the basketball hoop in the newspaper office, and suggested he get familiar with the Student Committee of La Raza, y *nuestra literatura.* Imagine my surprise when he came a couple of weeks later with *500 Years of Chicano History* and *The Labyrinth of Solitude* under his arm, ready to talk. I never really thought he'd actually read them, let alone come back and pin me down on *historia y cultura.* By the way, when I suggested we research his family tree and I could read up on his ancestors, he said he had a better idea—I had to learn the difference between a power forward and a point guard. As time's gone on, we've just gotten closer and closer. He always finds a way to make me laugh, no matter what. And we talk, really talk—about what we care about, what's important to us, what we dream about. Besides my girls, he's the person I'm closest to, I think.

But I was telling you about Sister Chicas and how we ended up as friends. It all started with my girls joining the newspaper staff. Taina was the only freshman on the paper, and arrived at our first staff meeting fifteen minutes early, straightened hair pulled back in a ponytail, smooth skin the color of chocolate, sharpened pencils and notebook in hand. She quietly took a seat in the back of the room, smoothing her dress, sitting so still. I remember how proud she was in the intro go-around when it came to her turn.

After Celia Chang and Isaiah Marshall pitched story ideas, I looked over to her, and asked what she might want to contribute.

Clearing her throat, she spoke in this tiny voice that kept getting louder as she went along. "I like writing. . . . I write, you know . . . poems, and other things." And then she started grinning, sitting taller in her chair, and that smile of hers was irresistible. That smile, added to the fact that she was so sincere, so serious when she spoke, made me want to take her under my wing right away. And to be honest, I kind of liked the idea of having a little sister, even if it was part-time.

When the meeting was over, everyone else had left, and I was putting on my jacket. Taina hovered by the door, looking like she was trying to make up her mind about something. I started to leave and she came over and tapped me on the shoulder, and without saying a word handed me a sheet of paper torn from her notebook. It was a poem about her mother, watching her mother cook. I was blown away. It was simple, but so clear and strong. You could see the food, smell the aromas, hear the salsa music on the radio in the kitchen. I told her that I thought her poem was great, really wonderful. Her answer? "Yes, I know." Then she caught herself, blushing and sputtering. "I . . . I mean yes, poetry is great, really great. . . . It's really wonderful that you like it." When I asked her if she could handle a regular poetry feature every month, she flashed that thousand-watt smile again and just nodded her head.

As for Leni . . . Leni's another story. We sort of had to grow on each other. She volunteered to work on the paper a month after school started. . . . Well, that's not exactly true. Leni was "encouraged" to join the *Monitor* staff, or spend the remainder of her junior year in detention. As shy as Taina is, Leni is her polar opposite, at least at first glance. She blew into the room a half hour late, creamy, pale skin with a smattering of freckles, purple spiked hair, black vinyl skirt with matching eyeliner. Did I mention attitude for days? That's kind of her basic accessory.

I was ready for her "arrival," since Mr. Federici, our adviser, had called me to his office the day before and explained that Leni's joining the newspaper staff was an "opportunity for growth" for both of us. He felt I could use the "challenge of a diverse staff, different points of view, different personalities," and that "Ms. O'Malley-Diaz has talent that requires structure and support." I'd already heard some gossip that our newest contributor had been expelled from some very expensive private schools, Francis Parker, for one.

Leni skulked into the office almost at the end of our meeting, complaining about "involuntary servitude," ranting about how maybe detention would be better than a year on "Loser Island." Besides noticing she was wearing a belly shirt with WHITE PUNKS ON DOPE blazing across her chest, I checked out the fact she managed to bring a camera, and what looked like a portfolio. The camera was a Leica, and the portfolio was leather, and for the life of me I don't know why, but I cut her off with, "Well, rich girl, let's see if your stuff's as good as the equipment." I usually try to be a little friendlier when I meet someone.

That stopped her midrave. I have to say that I kind of felt like a badass. Leni didn't say anything for what seemed like forever. Out of the corner of my eye I saw Ceca and Isaiah gathering up their stuff, Taina surreptitiously sliding closer to the action, and Jack pretending to dial the phone. It was face-off time.

Finally the diva delinquent spoke. "What the hell did you say?" She gave me a look that could've seared a steak, but to my credit I didn't flinch. I mustered up my best no-expression expression. "I think you heard me. I just asked you to put up or shut up."

Silence again. I thought I could hear the clock ticking. I expected her to storm out, but the unexpected happened instead. She started opening her portfolio, spreading about a dozen black-and-white photos on the nearest desk. Then she motioned me over. "Okay, you want to see photography; here's photography. Oh, by the way, you might want to close your mouth." I hadn't realized my jaw had just dropped open—so much for my girl-from-the-'hood impression. I won the last round, though. Unintentionally.

I walked over and stood beside her. When push came to shove, she wasn't as tough as she wanted everyone to think. Biting a fingernail and rocking back and forth on her heels, she'd tipped her hand. This bad girl was nervous—nervous to show her stuff, nervous about what I thought. She didn't have to worry. They were amazing—candid shots of club kids outside of Neo, a north side club for techno and industrial music. Each picture was a moment frozen in time—excitement, boredom, romance, loneliness—it was all there. And she was clever; the faces were all just hidden enough by shadow that the subjects stayed anonymous. They were technically strong, professional quality. "These are outstanding . . . awesome. We need you." I chewed on my lower lip to keep a straight face, because our new resident genius started rambling, totally flustered.

"Uh, really? Right . . . Okay . . . all right . . . So you like 'em, then?"

"Yeah, I like 'em, and I guess that means you're stuck with us," I said.

"Okay, then I guess I come back next week." Scooping up her pictures and portfolio in one fell swoop, she backed her way out of the office. "Next week, then."

"Uh-huh." I nodded. "Be on time."

"Right, on time. Okay, then."

"Okay, see you."

"Yeah, see you."

About five minutes later she blew back into the room, attitude and swagger back in place. "For the record, photo credits should read Leni D., not O'Malley-Diaz." Without so much as a "Goodbye, see you tomorrow," she was gone.

She's never been late since then, though. At least not for newspaper meetings.

None of this was lost on the previously very quiet Mr. Let-Me-Pretend-I'm-Not-Listening Jack Jordan. Standing up, he shakes himself off and brushes imaginary dust off his clothes. "Well, it looks like we have a human tornado on staff, Graciela." Before I can answer him, he corrects himself. "Make that *another* human tornado, if you know what I mean."

"Your point is what, exactly?" I ask, hands on my hips, tapping my foot, and willing myself not to laugh.

With a grin splitting his face, he walks over and leans down so that we're nose-to-nose.

"I mean . . . there's another force of nature around here . . . besides you."

I feel myself blush, but I manage to get out, "Don't you ever forget it."

Pulling himself to his full height, he salutes me. "Never, my coeditor in chief! Permission to get you a diet Coke?"

"Permission granted," I say, with a mock gruff voice. "What the heck, Jordan, I'll buy."

✧ ✧ ✧ ✧ ✧

Leaves swirl and crackle underneath my feet as I walk a little faster than usual, although my girls constantly tease me that I'm always in a hurry, always busy. Well, there's a lot I have to do, a lot I want to make sure happens. And for the record, even though I'm walking along at a pretty fast clip, I can still appreciate how beautiful this walk is. The boulevard is lined with maple trees, and on days like this leaves dance in the air, fluttering trails of red-brown, orange, and gold. I shiver a little against the crisp wind. I love this too, even though I can feel it through my latest Cheap Rags purchase, a gorgeous black wool sweater, knee length, with belt and pockets. It was a splurge—a thrift-shop splurge, so I don't feel so guilty. I really don't spend money like that; I don't have it to spend. I'm a college student on a budget and I need everything I can save for books, for school, for computer time.

Logan Boulevard is an older neighborhood, a former home to diplomats and wealthy Swedish immigrants. It's broad, at least four times wider than the normal Chicago street. Lined with graystone mansions with tiled roofs and huge lots that used to be the homes of the rich and powerful, later immigrants also added six redbrick apartment buildings with balconies and wraparound porches. Today, this community has Anglo, Mexican, and Puerto Rican families, working people like my family. I really enjoy glancing over at the mothers with strollers rattling past me, cooing to their babies in English, in Spanish, or both. A skateboarder with the Puerto Rican flag on his baseball cap whizzes past me, head bobbing to music from his Walkman.

An idea for a short story for Phaedra's class hits me. "Boarder Boy, Mercury for Modern Times." I could make him the neighborhood messenger, going from store to store, house to house, dropping off shopping delivery lists, telling people when their mothers want them home. I like it; I really like it. It's the first time I'd be telling a story that's so . . . personal, taken really from my own life, from a neighborhood I know like the back of my hand, the people I love to watch.

Writing is . . . wonderful. Writing is addictive. Writing is my secret pleasure. As editor of the *Monitor*, I went over copy and layout, helped with research and editorials. Those are practical skills, useful writing. What I write for myself is different. Stories about this community, about Pilsen, where I live, my parents and their friends. I keep them to myself, but if you asked me I'd say they weren't half-bad. I daydream about seeing them in print, about a magazine or a newspaper with the byline *Graciela Villalobos,* maybe even a book cover, but I know that's not realistic. Writing for a living is too risky. My parents worked too hard to make sure I have a stable job, a secure future. I can't forget that, you know? Besides, there are plans, my plans. I'm going to finish college, start teaching. My parents expect it; I expect it of myself. I'll always keep my notebook, though, I need to. Everybody needs a hobby.

I turn the corner at Fullerton and Logan; I'm close to El Rinconcito now. The wind's picked up, and I adjust my backpack and pull up the collar of my sweater to cover my ears as I turn the corner. My hair's thick, black and cut short, almost like a cap. I like it; there're wisps of curls at my cheeks, and a side part. I kind of surprised everyone when I did it after graduation, but I was ready for a change. Besides, I think it's chic. Although after today I'm making a mental note to hit Cheap Rags soon for a hat and some gloves, and if I'm lucky I can snag a peacoat.

Anyway, back to explaining how my girls and Thursday afternoons became a regular thing. About four months ago I'd just graduated. It was June and everything had fallen into place. I'd be going to college in the fall, my scholarship came through, I got the tutoring and work schedule I wanted. Perfect. Everything was just like it was supposed to be. Except for one small thing.

Guillermo Contreras was breaking up with me. And what bothered me is that it didn't really bother me. It should've; at least, I thought it should've. Everyone in his family thought we were perfect together, and I know *Mamá y Papá* thought the world of him. How could anyone not like him? Let me tell you more about him, about my very first boyfriend.

His family's from Morelia, too, and he adores his parents, just like I do. We have the same interests, we're both only children, and we love writing. Most important, we have commitment—to *familia,* to friends, to *nuestra gente.* It didn't hurt that he was brown-eyed, *bronce,* and editor of the yearbook, either. There was something about the quiet way he spoke, the way his eyes lit up when he smiled. Even with all of that, I still felt like he was more like a brother. I can't explain it. Don't get me wrong; Guillermo was wonderful; he was. But I never felt that spark, that something, the thing people call chemistry. Maybe it was because we were so much alike. I even accidentally called him Enrique, a cousin's name, more than once. But he was sweet and it felt so comfortable to be with him. *Caramelo,* he used to call me, and I thought he was just describing my complexion. Once I asked him, and he shook his head. "Not just that." Leaning in to give me a peck on the cheek, he laughed. "*Caramelo, dulce caramelo,* Graciela. For someone so smart, sometimes you miss the point."

We were together all of senior year—the two of us made straight As, volunteered, and worked part-time jobs. He was busy, I was busy, but Saturday night was always our night. I couldn't help but think maybe we'd get more serious after we graduated. It was perfect. I gave him his first book of poetry for his birthday, and he taught me how to *cumbia* at the Casa Aztlán Cinco de Mayo block party. I still have our prom picture, me in my ice-blue cocktail dress, and Guillermo in a tux with bow tie, his arm around my waist. The two of us had smiles that reached from ear to ear. But sometimes things that look perfect to other people, just aren't.

It ended not because of something bad, not because we didn't really care about each other. On the Monday before graduation, Guillermo met me after my last class to walk me home.

"*Caramelo*, I have some really great news." He was smiling, but the smile never reached his eyes. And that easy, comfortable feeling we always had was missing.

"*Dígame*, Guillermo. You can tell me." I tried to smile too, but I could feel a lump forming in my throat.

"I got a full scholarship to the University of Texas . . . four years, all paid. I'll be leaving right after graduation, first thing Saturday morning."

He did, too. We saw each other a couple of times before that and said our good-byes.

I wasn't angry; how could I be? This opportunity was too important; we both knew that.

I pride myself on doing the mature thing, the responsible thing, and so did he.

A few nights after he left, I felt a sadness I didn't really understand. Maybe it was just missing the closeness, the familiarity of having someone around, the way it all just seemed to fall into place so easily. My parents knew what happened, of course. I didn't talk much at dinner, *Mamá* kept glancing over me at me and then looking at *Papá,* who kept the conversation going. He went over all the new changes at the plant, explained what union's response was, while all I could do was manage to nod politely, finish eating, and do the dishes as always. They never said a word about Guillermo.

I went to my room early that night and slipped into my pajamas, but instead of sleeping, ended up just sitting on the edge of the bed, watching the clock tick. My heart felt like a weight in my chest, and I just wanted to really understand why. This was more than Guillermo leaving, more than breaking up. I reached for my journal on the nightstand next to my bed. Maybe if I wrote about it I'd understand; maybe I'd feel better. But before I could open the book, scribble a single word, there was a knock on my door.

Easing his way over the threshold, my father pointed to a spot next to me on the bed.

"Can your *viejo papá* join you?"

Voice quavering, I smoothed down the quilt right next to me. "*Siempre, Papá.* I was going to write, but I think I could use the company instead."

"That sounds like someone's lonely, *mi'ja.* Missing *tu novio?*"

"Yes . . . No . . . Oh, *Papá!*" Now I was crying, and my journal fell from my hands. Fat, wet tears were rolling down my cheeks, and my father's arms were around me in an instant. I could smell the faint traces of his aftershave mixed with his sweat, spicy, almost like *canela,* and I let myself relax in the warmth of being held. The tears came and I let them flow for what seemed like forever, still enfolded in his arms, feeling the soft rub of his cotton T-shirt. Comfort, that was what I felt. He's always been there to comfort me. I finally finished and started sniffling, slowly sitting back up, and it was *Papá's* strong hands that gently stroked away the tears from my cheeks.

"*Mi'ja,* you know this a good thing for Guillermo, no?"

"Of course! It's everything he's been trying for."

"So, it's saying good-bye to your first love. That's it, isn't it?"

I shook my head and saw the confusion in *Papá's* eyes. I could have said the grass was blue and the sky just turned green and his brow would be less furrowed.

"No! Maybe yes . . . No, that's not exactly it." I shook my head again, trying to get it straight, trying to explain this feeling. "Here's the thing. . . . *Ay, Papá* . . . I don't know!. . . . I do miss Guillermo, but it really bothers me that I don't miss him more. . . . Oh, it's too hard to explain. . . . You must think I'm being silly."

"*Estás bien triste,* because you don't miss him more," he echoed. "How you feel could never be silly to me, *mi amor.* But to say you feel sad because you don't really feel sad? That, I think, could use some explanation."

From the corner of my eye I can see *Mamá* standing in the doorway, nodding her head, her *color-de-café* eyes telling me she understood. To my father, "*Querido,* I think maybe this is something two women need to talk about."

"Ah, *claro que sí.*" Kissing the top of my forehead, he said, "Lucky for me, I have two of the most beautiful women in the world living in my house."

Gently pulling away and standing to leave, he clasped my chin in his hand. "Well, at least you'll be my other best girl for a little while longer." He was trying so hard to make me feel better, so I managed a weak smile and tried to sit up straight. On his way out of my room, he stopped to wrap his arms around my mother's waist, whispered something in her ear, and then went down the hall.

Mamá walked softly across the room and knelt down in front of me, so that we were eye-to-eye. Kissing each cheek and smoothing back my hair, she hummed a song she used to sing when I was little and crying and nothing would comfort me.

"He was a good boy, *mi corazón,*" she finally said, her voice a blurry whisper, "and he was important in your life. But someone else will find you, *mi'ja.* . . . You'll find each other; trust me."

"How can you be sure, *Mamá?* . . . How do you know?" I whispered back.

"I'm your *Mamá.* It's my business to know. I can see a beautiful young woman sitting here, one with a fine mind and a good heart. You have to trust me when I tell you someone wonderful and worthy of you will be there. Believe me, it will happen, *mi amor* . . . perhaps when you least expect it."

"I hope you're right, *Mamá.*"

"*Dígame, preciosa,* when have I ever been wrong?"

I began to feel better then, but it took the Sister Chicas to get my heart to fully cooperate.

I kept my usual schedule the last week before graduation—classes, tutoring, Librería Tzintzuntzán, but everyone at school said I looked tired. Even at the final newspaper meeting that Wednesday, Taina asked if I felt okay, and Leni offered that maybe it was the cafeteria food getting to me at last.

I just focused on our final edition, double-checking that it would be ready on time for distribution on Friday. I made an escape as soon as everything was over. What I missed, I found out later, was Jack calling my girls over and telling them what happened. Apparently he'd heard from some of the other seniors who'd won out-of-state scholarships and put two and two together. I wanted to tell all three of them, but it was just too hard, and I just couldn't let myself fall apart when there were still things to be done before graduation.

Anyway, I made it through Thursday, finished class, and headed out to El Rinconcito as always, even though there was no new edition to brainstorm. I needed something comfortable and familiar, something to make me feel that things would be okay. Imagine my surprise when I opened the door and there were my girls: Leni, wearing platform combat boots, fishnets, a fatigue miniskirt with matching tank top, drinking a *café con leche* and thumbing through a Japanese comic book, and Taina, wearing a matching pink sweater set and brown pleated skirt, studying the menu.

Now it was my turn to sputter and stammer. "Wha . . . uh . . . why . . . uh . . . what are you two doing here?"

Leni raised an eyebrow. "Definitely not your best moment, Villalobos." Then, making a dramatic sweep with her hand: "Why don't you sit down before you keel over? You look like a wreck! We're here because we heard what happened and because—"

It was Taina who cut her off, her voice coming from behind the menu. "Because we're friends, Graciela." Slowly she put down the menu. "Friends take care of one another, right?"

Taking a seat at the table, I let out a breath I hadn't realized I was holding, and held out a hand to each of them. "That's right, *mi amor.*"

Looking over to Leni, I could see her smiling. Trust her to try to get the final word. "Damn straight."

Over *cafecitos,* I explained to my girls what happened. Taina was the first to pipe up, "Grachi, I'm soooo sorry about Guillermo. You two were . . . I don't know . . . so great together. It's got to be so hard to say good-bye to . . . your first . . . you know, your first love."

I took a deep breath, "Taina, *querida* . . . Guillermo was special, very special . . . but it wasn't that way between us." I could see her eyes grow as wide as the saucers our *cafecitos* rested on. "The reason I've been so sad lately is not just that I miss him. It's . . . How can I explain this to you? You can be close to someone, but they're not special in the way everyone thinks they are."

Leave it to Leni to cut to the chase and fill in the blanks. Tapping her spoon against her coffee cup, she said, "So, he wasn't *the* one, right, Grachi? And that's got you down, right, *chica?* I mean, even though I'm not into the whole pair-bonding-boy thing, I get why that would be a big deal for you. Grachi, girl, listen: It just means that now you can shop around!"

"Leni!" Taina and I both chime in, shaking our heads.

"Okay, okay . . . Maybe the shopping part is more me. But Grachi, Tai and I both know that some guy is gonna fall head over heels for you. And until he does, we'll be here to remind you. Right, Tai?"

"Damn straight!" Taina nodded vigorously, trying her best tough-as-Leni expression. I looked at Leni and Leni looked at me. Taina started to say something else, but all three of us dissolved into laughter.

It was right after that we started calling each other Sister Chicas. I could've sworn I said it first over the phone the next day with Leni, but Leni claimed she thought of it on the way home that afternoon, and Taina was sure she scribbled it in her poetry notebook that night before bed. Who gets the credit doesn't matter. The important thing is that we know that's who we are.

✧ ✧ ✧ ✧ ✧

Fast-forward to the present. Now you know the story. And here we are at El Rinconcito, right next door to Bubblelandia, the super high-tech laundromat, complete with vending machines for soap and snacks and TV tuned to *Secretos de Amor* or whatever the latest *telenovela* is this month. Rinconcito del Sabor is a small restaurant, with a tiny lunch counter and six red Formica tables with matching red vinyl chairs. I open the door and walk in to see Don Ramiro scrubbing the counter and singing along to old Cuban love songs. He must be about sixty—average height, but trim, with thick white hair combed back from his forehead, green eyes, and copper-colored skin. He always wears a starched guayabera, and sometimes he'll argue politics with a friend while they both smoke cigars. He serves flan, *bizcochos,* and occasionally, when he can get Doña Isabel, his wife, to make them, *medianoches y croque-*

tas de jamón y queso. But it's the coffee, *estilo Cubano,* that brings people here. Rich, luscious, *sabrosísimo,* Don Ramiro's espresso, cappuccino, *café con leche* are to die for. Forget about Starbucks; Don Ramiro is *"El Rey de Café."*

"Ay, mi maestra, I was looking for you," he says as he comes from behind the counter to pull out my chair. And *maestra* is his nickname for me, ever since I tutored Nilsa.

"I see I got here before my girlfriends," I say, as I settle down at what is now our usual table, near the back of the tiny storefront. I always like to sit facing the door, so I can look out the windows and watch people. Watching people means more writing, and more writing means more stories, and those stories are *mis cuentos,* my love letters, to *los Mexicanos, los Chicanos, los Puertorriqueños, los Cubano. . . . mi gente.*

Don Ramiro brings me my usual, *café con leche,* in the biggest mug he has. I slide my backpack under the table, wrap my hands around the mug, close my eyes, and lean in, inhaling the bitter, sweet, rich aroma. Some minutes pass as I let myself do something that's rare for me . . . absolutely nothing. I sip *café con leche* and stop planning, organizing, and getting ready for what I have to do next. I'm startled out of the moment by two things: first Don Ramiro's hand on my shoulder, and, when I open my eyes, Jack Jordan tapping on the window with one hand and waving what I think is a notebook in the other. I can see his car parked behind him.

Hurriedly, I yank my backpack from under the table, pull open the flap, and see that my writing notebook's gone. Bolting up, I run out of El Rinconcito and almost collide with Jack. Even if I barreled into him, there'd never be any damage. He's about six-two, 195 pounds, looking every bit like the former all-city basketball player he was. He's got a ruddy complexion, blue eyes, and tells everyone he's an "English-Scottish-German" mutt, and has a killer laugh that never fails to get to me once he starts. He's probably my best friend after the Sister Chicas.

"It's a good thing I decided to endure History of Romance Poetry, Graciela. Somebody's got to keep an eye out for you." Jack's also at UIC, and has a double major in English lit and journalism, so it ends up that he's in a lot of my classes. "I believe this is yours," he says, holding out a black composition book, with my yellow Post-it notes still on the cover.

"Jack! My notebook! I could kiss you!" I throw my arms around his waist and hug him close.

He hugs me back, and neither one of us moves. Finally, I start to pull away, and I see him staring at me with a look I don't recognize, something deep at the back of his eyes.

In an instant, it disappears. He's got a grin on his face as he hands over my magnum opus.

"Maybe next time."

I look away. I could try to tell you I was completely embarrassed, but part of me really liked the feel of his arms around me. When I look up again, he's still smiling.

"Well, I guess I should go then. You're meeting the rest of the unholy trio, right?"

"Yeah, I'm sure they'll be here anytime now. See you in class."

"Right," he says, and that look from a minute ago is back.

I turn to go in, but he stops me and brushes his hand through my hair. His palm against my scalp feels so warm, I have to catch my breath.

"Thought I saw a leaf there . . . guess I was wrong. I'll see you tomorrow, Graciela."

"It's a good thing you're keeping an eye on me. See you tomorrow."

I go inside and get settled back down. Jack gets in his car, and it takes him a few minutes before he pulls away. From behind the counter, I hear Don Ramiro whistling. He doesn't say anything right away, but then he asks, "*¿Ay mi'ja, tu novio, no?¿Grandote, también, eh?*"

"No, Don Ramiro, he's just a friend." I hear my tone of voice, and I'm surprised I don't sound more convincing.

"Of course, *maestra. Tus amigos son interesantes, bien interesantes. ¿Más café?*"

About fifteen minutes pass, and I feel more like myself. I don't know what just happened, and I'm not so sure I can figure it out right now. I will say Jack Jordan just surprised the hell out of me. I think I just surprised the hell out of me, too.

Don Ramiro's just set a fresh *café con leche* on the table, but before I can pick it up, the door bursts open and it's Leni with Taina in tow. Today her hair's bright red, and it's motorcycle boots, a plaid mini with safety pins scattered across the front, and a Chicago patrolman's jacket with a British flag sewn on the sleeve. Taina's got on her sensible winter coat, but I can see a mango-colored sweater peeking out from the collar, and a black skirt that comes to her calves. She looks upset, worried. I start to ask what's wrong, but Leni's already talking—ranting, to be more exact.

"Who *are* these people who don't even know about the Sex Pistols and the Ramones?" Flopping into a chair at the table, she's clearly on a roll. "I can't believe it! But it's my own fault; I went into the music store down the street from that throwback granite wannabe monument on Milwaukee. What a mistake! When I tried to ask for something recorded outside of the southern hemisphere, the guy behind the counter looked at me like I was from another planet!"

Meanwhile, Taina's sat down and is fidgeting with the buttons of her coat. When she looks up at me, I can see she's trying hard not to cry.

Our group diva keeps going, "Okay . . . I try writing out the names of the bands I'm looking for on a piece of paper and hand it to the guy—"

"Leni, shut up!" It's Taina in the loudest voice I've ever heard from her.

"I need help! *Mami*'s making me have a *quinceañera!*"

3

LENI

*H*ow the hell do I get myself talked into these things? Look, I love my Sister Chicas, right? But if you had told me that I would be on my way to spending the afternoon at a Puerto Rican old-lady-frilly-lace-and-taffeta dress shop, picking out *quinceañera* dresses, I would have knocked you on your ass. It seems like it's been a year since Taina told us about the freakin' social event of the year, instead of just two weeks. But if poor Taina is going to have to go through with this party, her girls are going to stand by her. Even if they are forced to wear scary *princesa* dresses. I wonder if they make spiked collars in lavender?

The train comes to a stop, and five more people get on. I'm glad it isn't crowded in here. I can't stand being jammed in. I always end up smashed into some sleaze who smells like week old gym socks. Speaking of sleazes, the pockmarked loser with the greasy hair sitting across the way is leering at me. I can feel his shifty eyes going up my black fishnet stockings. I glare at him with my special look that says, *Go ahead and look, a-hole, but if you touch me you will be doing a high dive off of the L tracks!* It works. He's nervously pretending to look somewhere else. I look around at the other people scattered around the car. People-watching is my favorite train-riding pastime. The three women in the middle of the car look boring. Businesswomen with high necklines and way-too-practical shoes. As far as I'm concerned, if they're not made for combat or equipped with really high spiked heels, they're not worth wearing. The man standing over them is a trip, though. He looks like a TV dad, you know the type? Gray suit, collar and tie loosened. And that hair—it reminds me of the yellow paint and creases that passed for the do on the Ken doll I had as a kid. He's carrying a brown worn briefcase that is probably filled with contracts, or other businesslike documents that are not the slightest bit interesting to me. I bet he plays golf on Saturdays and goes to Mass on Sundays. Okay, so that is probably not the most realistic "dad" image, but I gotta tell you I've got little to no experience with the species.

My real dad died when I was eight. Every year I remember less and less about him, and I hate that. He was an architect like my mom. The image I have of him is of a tall, broad-shouldered guy with a mustache, a loud laugh, smiling eyes, and a hell of a temper. And believe me, I got in trouble often. I was a hell-raiser from inside the womb. But I knew how to get by. Men are pretty easy to figure out. He was a man's man most of the time, typically macho, but when we were alone he was kind and gentle, never talking down to me. When he started to get sick (he had Lou Gehrig's Disease), he would go for walks around the neighborhood every night to get some exercise, and he always took me with him. He would hobble along with his cane, getting weaker every day, less and less mobile, and I would follow along on my energetic six-year-old legs. We would talk about anything, really. But whatever I brought up, he always treated it as important. Damn. It really sucks that he had to die.

I was totally destroyed when he died, but with my Mom, it seemed different. I didn't know what she was feeling, but it looked to me like she pretty much forgot I existed. I mean, she fed me, but that was about it. She spent a lot of time in her room, crying with the door closed, alone. It was like I lost both parents. After a year had passed she started to show signs of life again. She spent less time in her room, and began going out with her friends, and even on a couple of dates. She tried to spend more time with me, but it was already too late. I had learned to fend for myself, I even cooked my own meals and did my own laundry, and I wasn't too hot on forgiving and forgetting. I'll never forget the night she came home and told me she was getting remarried. It had been three years since Dad died, and though I knew she and her boyfriend, Mike, were spending a lot of time together, it shocked the hell out of me. We were sitting at either side of the long, white, industrial table, in the dining room, each picking at our lasagna in silence, when she dropped the bomb.

"Elena, honey,"—I should've known right then that something was up: she never called me *honey* unless she needed my cooperation—"I have some exciting news! Mike and I have decided to get married!" It was almost funny the way my fork stopped an inch from my mouth, my jaw on my chest as I stared mutely at my mother.

"I know this might come as a surprise to you, but it's been several years since your *papá* died, and we have to move on as a family. You've always been my daughter, and you will always be your father's daughter no matter whom I marry. You come from a long line of Diazes and a long line of O'Malleys, and no one can take that away from you."

I stared at her for a moment, disbelief freezing me in place. How could she do this to *Papá?* To me? Then something shifted inside me. I threw the fork down, the stainless steel clashing against the classic white china, small drops of tomato sauce spraying across the white surface of the table like red rain. As I shoved my chair away from the table and jerked to my feet, I began to yell at her. "I don't want to be an O'Malley, or a goddamn Diaz! I just want to be me! Elena! Then it doesn't matter who stays or leaves; at least I've still got me!"

I ran off to my room, my cloth napkin falling from my jean-covered thigh like a dying leaf as I ran down the hall. I slammed the door shut and threw my body on the bed, gripping the soft cotton sheets with my fists and screaming into the mattress. I stayed like that for a long time. Later, as I lay there looking around at the walls filled with posters of puppies and glittery pop stars, and the pastel painted letters that spelled out ELENA over my bed, I felt something inside of me snap. I jumped out of bed on impulse and began to tear the posters from the wall, gleefully ripping them to shreds and letting them fall on the wide wooden boards of the floor. I made my way around the room, pulling down all the pieces of the old Elena. When I got to the wooden letters, one by one I knocked them onto the bed, scattering three of them over the pink-sheeted pillows and thick patchwork quilt, while one of the Es and the A hit and skittered across the floor, both coming to a stop beneath the large loft windows. When everything was down, I slumped on the bed and looked around at walls peppered with dirty pieces of tape and pushpins, satisfied. The little helpless girl who decorated that room with her mother two years earlier was gone. I stared at the wooden letters that remained on the bed, L-E-N. If Mom was going to get married, that was just fine. I didn't need her anyway. I didn't need anyone. It was then that I sat on the bed, one leg over the side, the other tucked underneath me, my arms across my chest, my breathing still fast from my outburst, staring at the letters. It was then that Leni was born.

✧　✧　✧　✧　✧

I never felt more alone than I did then. There was no one left whom I could depend on. Except maybe for Carlos.

I remember the trip to Puerto Rico that first summer after Mom and Mike first got married. I was eleven and angrier than hell. Mike didn't come with us—at least Mom knew that that wouldn't be appropriate—but things were so different between me and her. I was furious with her for replacing *Papi*. For moving on without me. Anyway, there was a big bash at *Tío* Esteban's house, and I swore half the island came. There was an army of kids there already when we drove up, and I immediately felt sulky and wanted to hide in the car. I sat there with my arms folded, my lips pouting, and steam coming out of my ears as my mother tried to coax me out of our rental car. I was so pissed off—I knew she was talking but I couldn't even hear her. She eventually gave up and left me there to sweat in the car while the party raged on inside. I could hear laughter and salsa music pouring out of the windows, dishes clanking, and the rich smell of home-cooked Puerto Rican food seeping from the concrete open-air kitchen. I kind of wanted to go in, but I wanted to make my mom suffer more.

The night got darker and darker, and I was getting nervous in that car, but what could I do? All of a sudden I heard two sets of footsteps crunching over the gravel driveway, running. Unable to make out who they were, I started to get nervous and locked the car door. But then my cousin Ana's head appeared in my window and I breathed a sigh of relief.

"Jeez, *prima,* you scared me!" I laughed at her, and then I saw Carlos behind her, smiling. Carlos was the son of my father's best friend, and we were thrown together a lot when we were down in Puerto Rico. He was just two years older than I was, but he was so sweet to me when *Papi* died, always making sure I was included. That I felt welcome. Even in the dark I could see his sparkling chocolate eyes as they smiled at me over Ana's bare shoulder. She looked cute, as usual, dressed in a bright cotton sundress, with strippy-strappy sandals that matched perfectly with her girly dress. I, on the other hand, was wearing a knit short set that I had already spilled Coke all over, scuffed-up sneakers, and mismatched socks. I was suddenly very conscious of my clothes, and pulled my feet under me, trying to hide my shoes.

"Aren't you going to come out and visit with us, *prima?*" Ana asked as she ran her petal-pink-painted fingernails through my messy hair. I wanted to hate her, I really did, but her smile was so warm that I finally gave up and started to say, "No, thanks," when I heard Carlos's voice pipe up from behind my cousin.

"Yeah, Elena, come and play with us! You can be on my team for tag!"

Ana poked his chest with her finger, and said in a flirty voice, "*Ay,* Carlitos, why would she want to—" But I was out of the car before she finished her sentence, and as I slammed the car door behind me I heard Ana's voice say, "Tag! Sheesh! That game is so . . . so . . . messy!" Carlos and I laughed as we ran back behind the house, with Ana skipping behind.

✧ ✧ ✧ ✧ ✧

I'm smiling as I sit here on the train, thinking about my split personality. One day I was a fairly obedient, ponytail-wearing little girl, and the next the spiky-haired, "attitudinal and proud of it" Leni that I am today. I don't even remember Mom and Mike's wedding. I was still pretty teed off about having to go, but I got through it, and they got busy setting up house and pretty much left me alone, which was all I wanted. Mike. You know, he wasn't that bad, as stepfathers go. . . . Or I guess, technically speaking, as of the divorce a couple of years ago he's my ex-stepdad. I don't get a particularly "dadlike" feeling when I think of him.

✧ ✧ ✧ ✧ ✧

Mike was pretty straight, and he came into our family scene at a bad time. But by the time their second anniversary came around, Mom and I had pretty much grown apart, and I was doing my best to be at our New York loft as little as possible. One afternoon when I was shopping at Trash & Vaudeville on St. Mark's place, I met Karen. Her boyfriend, Andy, was the lead singer for a punk band, and she and I hit it off. We talked for hours over bad coffee and greasy eggs at a Greek diner, and we were fast friends. She was like my older sister; I was thirteen and she was nineteen, and she paid way more attention to me than my mother did. I'll never forget the first night she brought me to a club. For the first time in my life I felt like somebody who really mattered.

The band was playing at Continental on St. Mark's Place. I had told Mom I was sleeping over at Karen's house, and she and I took a cab to the club on the Lower East Side. When we stopped in front of the blacked-out storefront I was shocked by what a dive it was, and not a little scared. We walked up to the door and Karen introduced me to the Neanderthal bouncer—who was named, "Razor"—as her little sister. I had to admit I loved the sound of that. We passed right in, no money changed hands, and she brought me up to the front of the stage. I looked around, wide-eyed but trying not to look uncool, the heart-pounding music rebounding off my eardrums, the crowd of black-clad punks pushing against me like a wave.

The piped-in music came to an abrupt stop, the lights went black, and the crowd hushed around us. All of a sudden the spotlight hit Andy's face, and all we could see was a disembodied head floating in darkness. Music started blaring from all around, and lights flooded the stage where the rest of the band was blasting away on their instruments as if they wanted revenge. The songs were short, unbelievably loud, and manic, and I was completely dumbstruck. As I stood there, gawking at the stage, a mosh pit formed behind me, and if Karen hadn't pulled me off to the side I would have been smashed against the stage. During the last song, Andy threw himself into the air over the audience, and the crowd ferried him around the club over their heads, finally returning him to the dirty stage for the last chords.

After the set Karen and I went backstage, and I met the rest of the band. They were really nice to me, and thought it was cool that someone so young got their music. We sat around while they cooled off, drank Rolling Rocks, and told stories about the road and the club scene in the city. I sat and nursed my soda, my eyes wide, taking it all in. They made me feel like I was one of them, not a kid parked at a card table at Thanskgiving dinner, but really one of them. Before we left Andy gave me a kiss on the cheek and handed me passes to their next show. I don't even remember the cab ride back to Karen's. I was high as a kite.

I continued to hang around with the band as kind of a mascot, and the bouncers at the clubs got to know me. Mom didn't want to interfere; she said she knew I needed my "independence," but none of my friends' parents would have let them go to a nightclub. She had given me her old Nikon camera, and I had been fooling around with it a bit, taking pictures of the neighborhood and of my friends. After a year or so I got pretty good, and the band liked my pictures better than their photographer's. Word got out that there was this fourteen-year-old photographer who took great shots, and all of a sudden I was famous in my own New York punk world! It was great. With that band, my camera in my hand, I blended in with all the other punkers. I had more of a feeling of family than I had had since Dad had died. Mike didn't understand. To his credit, I can't say I blame him. I think he expected to be more of a traditional "dad" to me, and in a way I kind of wanted that, but it was too late. I wasn't having any of it. And we were too different.

◇ ◇ ◇ ◇ ◇

You wouldn't see Mike riding the trains, since he never leaves his medical office. I guess that isn't really fair, but I think it had a lot to do with why Mom ditched him. After the divorce, we moved out of our Chelsea loft and away from all my friends and favorite clubs and landed in Chicago and Mom's new job. Sometimes I blame Mike for the move, for putting his career ahead of us, but really, he's been good to me. He sends me all the money I could want, and calls me once a week to "catch up," as he calls it. He tries. When I went to visit him in New York this past summer, he actually asked to come along with me to a club! I guess he had gotten past the issue of my being underage at a nightclub. He knew I didn't do drugs and I was always careful, but he and Mom fought about it all the time. Mom always trusted me and let me go, and Mike never understood that. I guess he finally accepted that there wasn't anything he could do about it.

Anyway, I was shooting photos of some friends and their band, and Mike tagged along. They had a gig at CBGB's, and since I was in town they asked if I would come and take pictures. We took a cab downtown, and when it stopped in front of the club I could tell from his quick movements that Mike was nervous. The usual collection of scary mohawk-wearing, leather-clad punks was congealing outside, leaning against the wall. I knew they were a bunch of posers, but I decided to let Mike worry. It was kind of fun to see the all-powerful internist scared shitless.

I slapped the bouncer, Seth, on the butt in greeting, and Mike and I breezed on in. I don't pay covers. We began to make our way through the crowd at the bar, moving toward the stage. Several of the dope-dealing regulars caught sight of Mike and scrambled for the door. I think they thought he was a narc in his yellow polo, khakis, and loafers. The night was turning out to be way more fun than I had expected. Anyway, we had a really okay time together that night, Mike and I. He couldn't hear anything for a week, since I made him sit in my favorite spot, right in front of the speakers. I like to feel my internal organs vibrate with the bass.

Once my friend's band came on, I had to leave Mike to fend off the slam dancers so I could do the work I was there to do. I decided to start with the bass player, Slasher, so I grabbed my camera from my army-green canvas bag and ducked across the front of the stage, squeezing myself around the speakers. I spent the entire set maneuvering among the crowd and the metallic jungle of equipment and instruments that lined the front of the stage. At one point as I jammed myself between the speakers and lights at the right side of the stage to get an unbelievably cool shot of the lead guitarist hamming it up, I happened to look over and see Mike watching me with a mixture of awe and pride. He had never seen me shoot before—well, only at family gatherings, not professionally anyway—and it rattled me when I found out that the idea made me feel good. Family bonding was not my thing, hadn't been for a long, long time. I hurriedly shrugged off that momentary glow, muttered, "Not today," and continued to shoot the rest of the band. Mike's a good guy, but it's clear he's visiting here from Planet Uptight. But hey, I didn't need his approval.

✧ ✧ ✧ ✧ ✧

But wait, why was I even thinking about Mike? Oh, right, Mr. Dad across the aisle. At the next stop of the L, he gets off with his badly dressed female cronies, and I yell out, "Have a great day, fella!" Guys like that actually use the word *fella*. Scary.

I get off at the next stop, Western Avenue, and make my way to Division Street, where Anita's Dress Shop has been since the dawn of time. Anita's is one of the constants of the universe, never changing. Same 1950s mannequins in the window, with dust-covered, sun-faded dresses, blue eye shadow, and thick black eyeliner. The store has managed to survive, supported by all the tradition-bound generations of Latinas guilted and coerced into succumbing to dated rituals, even with the yuppies and the Starbucks moving in.

I *so* don't want to be here.

I find myself dragging my combat boots and wasting time looking into the bodega's windows on my way to the dress shop. I stare absently at the colorful rows of saint candles and painted plaster religious statues. *Oh, well, might as well just get it over with.* I tear my eyes away from the bodega window and pick up the pace, and soon I see the dress store's faded pink-and-white-striped awning. It seems Taina's mother knows the owner of this place. I guess I should just be grateful that her mom wasn't able to come. That would be way more than I could take. Don't get me wrong: I like her mom, but she just doesn't get me, you know? Like the Pepto-Bismol-pink poodle sweater she forced on me. I smiled politely, thanked her as I backed out of their apartment, and promptly threw it into the Dumpster down the block. As my *abuela* would say, *Ay, Virgen.*

I linger for just a moment outside the door to the dress shop, feeling the October sun on my face. A tricked-out, low-riding cherry-red Chevy crawls by, music so loud the bass makes the windows rattle. As the *vatos* hang out the windows, screaming assorted unintelligible come-ons, I try not to laugh; they might take it as a green light to come sample the goods. I pull my camera out of my jacket pocket and start to shoot them, capturing the leering, kissing faces framed by the shiny metallic red car. Ah, these are my people. Through the lens I follow them as they careen around the corner. I hang the camera around my neck and watch the fallen leaves swirl around the parking meters in front of me, hypnotized by their dance. Sighing, I stop my daydream and shove the door open with a clang of bells and a rush of cool autumn air. That's right, *chicas,* Leni has arrived! The pinched, matronly saleswoman looks me up and down with a sneer on her face like she smelled something bad, and rushes to intercept me. It is probably the first time she's seen a leather jacket on someone who wasn't going to mug her. "Can I help you?" she quips in heavily accented English. Latinos always assume I'm totally *gringa.* "No. I'm here to meet my friends," I snap back at her as I spot Graciela and Taina near the dressing rooms. I walk around her, and make my way toward the *chicas.*

I hug Taina first, and force a smile through my black lipstick. "Hey, Sister Chica! How are you doing?" I ask her, pulling back from the hug to look at her face. But I already know the answer. "I'm okay, Leni; thanks for coming," she says softly. Taina doesn't like shopping for clothes. I think she's beautiful, with her coffee-colored skin, huge eyes, and curvy body, but she doesn't think much of herself. Girl's got some body-image issues. I turn to Graciela and give her a powerful hug. Grachi's like a big sister. Even though we don't always agree, she's gotten me through (and out of) more shit in a year than most people have dealt with in their whole lives. Don't need to ask how she's doing. Graciela wants to be here about as much as I do. I pull away from the hug and ask sarcastically, "So, where are all the black dresses?" as my eyes sweep over the rows and rows of pastel-colored clothing. Taina and Graciela roll their eyes. What do they expect? Look at this stuff; I mean, it's prehistoric! They begin moving toward the closest rack, resuming the conversation they had begun before I made my late entrance.

I just stand there, looking at the rug, my mind traveling to last night's clubbin' frenzy. I met a cute Irish bass player named Billy at Neo whom I can't get off my mind. But I swore off musicians for Lent, so I'd better start trying to make good on it, especially since it is already October and I haven't pulled it off yet. Grachi makes her way back to me with several dresses draped over her left arm, and startles me out of my cute-boy daydream.

"*¿Estás cansada, chica?*" Graciela asks me in Spanish, her fingers lightly grazing the rings under my eyes.

"No, Grachi, I'm not tired. I got two whole hours' sleep!" I reply in English. Girlfriend is always trying to talk to me in our "mother tongue." She's much more into being a Latina than I am. Hey, I don't deny it. It just . . . isn't a big thing for me, you know? Besides, it doesn't really work with my style. A punk rock *Puertor-riqueña?* I don't think so. There's no room for it in my clubbing life. I have my dad's name, Diaz; isn't that enough? Besides, Mom won't let me forget that I'm Latina. Even though Dad is long gone, she wants me to keep in touch with my Puerto Rican side, so she drags me down to PR every year. The first thing that comes to mind when I think of the island is how before we go to visit, my mother, who is usually very cool, tells me that I have to tone it down.

"Your *abuela* wouldn't understand, Elena." Well, I don't like being told what to do. Especially being told to change who I am. When I am dressed in my gear and dancing at a club, I'm not Jorge's daughter, or *abuela's chiquitita,* or the student with an attitude; I am exactly who I want to be. And I'm not changing that for anybody.

"Leni, you still with us?" I hear Taina say through my haze. I look up and see her wearing a full-length, pale pink dress that bells out at the waist and has puffy sleeves. She looks like one of those toilet-paper-roll covers, the dolls with big pink crocheted skirts that the old ladies in my neighborhood make. I realize that she is waiting for my reaction, but for once I don't have anything to say.

"No, *amor,* it's lovely, but it's just not you. How about this one?" Graciela says as she holds up a simple and classic straight silk shift in celery green. Yes, she saves me once again. Grachi is always more diplomatic. An hour passes slowly. Taina tries on dozens of dresses that all look the same to me. I sit in the flowery upholstered chair, keeping my mouth shut and trying not to look too surly, like I wish I were somewhere else. Anywhere else. We (actually, they) finally decide on a simple pale-coral strapless gown that accents Taina's curvy figure, has a few scattered pearls on the bodice, and looks only slightly princessy. Then the moment I have been dreading arrives.

"Okay, Leni, it's our turn!" Graciela says, feigning excitement. I continue to sit on the poufy, flowery chair with my arms crossed and look up at Grachi with an icy glare.

"Taina, I'm just going to take Leni over here and show her some fabric options," Graciela says in a too-perky voice. She grabs my arm roughly and drags me to the back of the store. I am too shocked to even protest. We stand there surrounded by a trio of floor-to-ceiling mirrors that would have been carnivallike and kind of fun if it weren't for Graciela stabbing her tastefully home-French-manicured finger in the air right in front of my face.

"¡Óyeme, Leni! Do you think I want to spend the afternoon trying on these dresses? No! But we are going to smile pretty and get through this without letting Taina down. This is hard enough for her without you pouting the whole time! She's our girl, and this is what we do for one another. Got it?"

"Está bien, está bien, chica. . . . ¡Tranquila, Grachi! You're gonna burst an artery or something. Jeez, all the veins are standing out on your forehead! It's just not attractive, chica!" I throw in the Spanish, knowing that will chill her out. Reluctantly a smile spreads across Graciela's face, and she puts her arm around my neck as she smirks. "¡Sin vergüenza! You are absolutely hopeless!" Arm in arm we head back to Taina, who is staring at her reflection in the new dress, sucking in her stomach and frowning. Graciela leads me to the wall and sits me down in the uncomfortable wooden chair near the mirrors as if I were a child.

"Sit here, Leni; I'll pick out some dresses for us to try." I feel like I'm in the guidance counselor's chair. I spend so much time in his office that I figure he'll put up a brass plaque with my name engraved on it after I graduate. If I ever graduate. "Elena, you're not working up to your full potential!" he tells me, day after day. I think I'll have a T-shirt made that says, NOT WORKING UP TO MY FULL POTENTIAL.

Graciela brings over a simpler version of Taina's dress with thin spaghetti straps in pale peach. Peach! If they buried me in peach I swear I'd sit up in the coffin and strip naked in front of all the mourners!

"Leni," she starts, with her teeth clenched and a *remember what we talked about* look in her eyes, "These go beautifully with Taina's dress." I rip the dress out of her hands, give her a defiant but resigned look, and storm over to a dressing room. I slam the pink door, lock it, and slump down on the little striped, cushioned stool in the corner of the room. I turn my head slightly and glance at myself in the mirror. The image is infested by the peach blob hanging over my arm, which looks exceptionally neon and frightening under the bad fluorescent lights and against my black leather motorcycle jacket. I realize I still have my camera around my neck, and I slowly pull it off, careful not to catch the strap on one of my eleven earrings. I think about throwing the dress on the floor and lighting up a Camel, but I remember what Graciela said, and reluctantly get to my feet. I tear off my jacket and minidress and pull the hideous garment over my spiked burgundy hair. I stab my arms through the straps and pull the hem down over my ripped fishnet stockings. I reach back and pull the zipper all the way to the middle of my back. I drop my arms to my sides and stare at the mirror in horror, but I'm also surprised, grateful that nobody else has a camera to record this moment for posterity.

The bodice fits perfectly, and hugs my small waist and decent breasts, but, oh, my God. What would the other punks at Neo say? I chuckle at the thought, slam open the dressing room door, and stride over to the Sister Chicas. Graciela already has her dress on, and of course she even manages to make the most hideous froufrou dress look elegant. They take one look at me standing there with my hands on my hips, and they start to laugh uncontrollably. Surprised by their reaction, I spin around and look in the mirror. There I stand with the peach satin gown clashing with my burgundy hair, the edge of my red rose tattoo gracing the top of this formal-wear nightmare, spiked black collar around my neck, and black combat boots peeking from under the hem. I burst out laughing, which just makes them laugh harder, until the three of us are falling into one another with tears rolling down our cheeks. The stuck-up spinster salesclerk comes sprinting over in a flurry of squeaking nylon-covered plump thighs, keys jingling, and says, "*¿Señoritas, hay una problema aquí?*" This just makes us laugh even harder, but as the woman huffs away, shaking her coiffed head in disgust, Graciela begins to shush us, trying to control her own laughter. From then on, it's as if we're in church, and we spend the remainder of our time in the store trying not to laugh.

The saleslady measures the hems of the dresses, trying to get them straight even as we shake from giggling. When we are almost finished and I think I am about to be granted freedom from my peach taffeta prison, I feel the tentative and gentle touch of Taina's hand on my shoulder.

"Leni?" I know she is about to ask me to do something I don't want to do, but I also know that I can't resist her little-girl-lost act. Gets me every damn time.

"Leni, can I ask you a really big favor? Would you mind taking a picture of the three of us in the dresses? I . . . just want to remember this." I couldn't have been more taken aback if she had asked me to run naked into the street, waving my arms in the air and singing songs from *Mary Poppins* as I ran. In fact, I would have preferred that.

"Oh, Tai, please! Please don't ask me for that . . . anything but that!" I look over at Grachi who had that *Do the right thing,* hermana look on her face. *Damn!* I glared at the two of them, as I could feel them trying to manipulate me into this hokey stunt with their big, brown eyes. I looked down at the nightmare dress hanging off my body, my beloved tattoos hidden under the tasteful neckline. I could feel my shoulders shore up and the defenses scramble back to the front line.

"No, Tai. I'll take a picture of the two of you, but I am *not* going to give you blackmail material. Do you have any idea how that would completely screw my reputation?" They started in at once, and though I couldn't catch the words—and didn't want to—the tones were the same, pleading, whining, indignant (well, that one was just from Grachi). They sounded like my mother, using the exact tones to make me do the exact opposite of what they were trying to get me to do. I took a photo of the two of them as they posed halfheartedly, a wall of tension as thick as the camera lens growing between us. After a few clicks of the shutter, we all head for the stalls to take our dresses off, and, surprise, surprise, I'm the first one changed and out, tossing the dress at Señora Snotty Seamstress and making a beeline for the counter.

As Grachi carefully counts her change and puts away her receipt, I make my move. I give the woman my credit card amidst protests from Taina. "Let me; this is my gift to you, girlfriend. Well, actually, Mike's gift!" At which the tension eases and we start to laugh all over again. Gotta put stepdad's plastic to good use.

When we're all finished and the order's placed, I'm the first one of us to rush out of the door, gasping for fresh air and freedom.

Taina's next, followed by Graciela. When we reach the sidewalk and fading warm sunlight hits our faces, I ask, "*Café,* Sister Chicas?" I thought we'd hang out after such a nightmare, but Grachi has to go to work. She gives us both a hug, pulls up the collar on her stylish black sweater, and heads toward the L. Taina and I watch her walk for a moment, each of us lost in our own thoughts. Then I turn to Taina and say, "Well, *princesa?* Want to get some *café?*"

Her eyes dart around nervously, and she says she has something to do.

"What do you have to do?" I ask.

"Oh, an errand," Taina answers. Sister Chicas usually tell each other everything, but I let it go.

"Okay, *chica,* see you tomorrow at school." I stand there in front of the dress shop and watch her scurry off. She glances back at me over her shoulder, checking to see if I am still there. What is up with this girl? I start walking in the other direction, but curiosity gets the better of me, and I slip inside a doorway when she isn't looking. I watch her continue to walk for half a block, and begin to make my way to follow her. This is fun! I feel like one of Charlie's Angels.

Taina turns around once more, but luckily a massive woman walking her bigheaded, tiny Chihuahua blocks her view of me. Taina turns a corner and I rush ahead to catch up, careful not to careen around and blow my cover. I hide in the doorway of a store with VICTOR'S FORMAL WEAR painted on the front window, and glance over at a row of five male mannequins wearing really bad wigs and tuxedos, staring down at me. "Hey, boys! How ya doin'?" I smile at their painted wooden faces. I start thinking, *Hey, if I pair one of these tux jackets with a leather miniskirt, it could be hot and I could possibly make it through this* quinceañera! But then I remember why I am there, and I sneak a peek around the corner, looking for Taina, straining to make her out in the dimming light.

I finally see her with her frayed oversize book bag over her arm, and straightened hair blowing wildly in the cooling evening wind. She is talking to someone. A guy. And a cute one at that! He's a tall, black, cool drink of Coca-Cola, probably Taina's age or a little older, with short dreads and a killer body. Hey, it might be getting dark, but I'm not blind! *Who is this guy?* I wonder. Then I notice the garment bag draped over his strong forearm that says, VICTOR'S FORMAL WEAR. Okay, so he was just coming out of this store, and they know each other from . . . where? I still can't make any sense of this, but I know her *mamá* would not be happy to see her *hijita* talking with some guy on some dark street. "You're gonna kill your mother," I whisper, while still checking out Mr. Mysterious over here. Hey, I'll take this one if Taina doesn't want him! Maybe I'll date a younger man for a change.

I'm starting to get cold, but just when I am about to turn tail and leave, Tall, Black, and Handsome leans down, and it looks like he's going to kiss my girl Taina on the lips! Just then the fat lady and her weasely little dog saunter by, blocking my view in the fading light. I furiously try to see around the woman as she pauses to wait for the DO NOT WALK light to change. As she finally moves ahead as slow as a friggin' glacier, I see them moving away from each other, Taina lowering from tiptoe to put her feet flat on the ground. Damn! I missed it! Did they kiss? They start to walk in my direction, and I jerk my body back around the corner, out of sight, trying to get it together. Wait, the tuxedo, the possible kiss . . . this isn't a coincidence. Could it be that Mr. Mysterious is her date for the *quinceañera?* Oh, man, if so, there is going to be a meltdown over this one! I can just see the *Tribune* headlines now: *Riot Breaks out at Puerto Rican Coming-out Party.* Man, my girl has stepped in it this time. But what do I do? Did I really see that? Walking quickly, I start to make my way to the train, my head buzzing.

After a few minutes of walking in the cold, I decide I'm not going to tell Graciela. I'm probably not even going to ask Taina about it. If she wanted us to know she would have told us already, so Sister Chica must have her reasons. I start up the stairs at the el station, and realize, *Hey, this party might not be as dull as I expected after all.* I hear my train pulling in just as I reach the top.

4

TAINA

"Hey, *chica!*" Leni cornered me at my locker, Whitney Young's bustling mural of punks and preppies, b-boys, jocks, and Abercrombies rushing past us to class. It had been over two weeks since Graciela, Leni and I had spent the afternoon in the dress shop and I was already going cuckoo over the whole shebang. Because I was a nervous wreck, I hadn't seen Leni coming, my face behind the metal locker door, rifling through looseleaf poems, lackluster math assignments and frail textbooks. I didn't like walking the halls between classes, unless I was with Leni or Grachi. Usually, as soon as the bell echoed against the walls, I rushed as quickly as I could into the classroom, my face flushed as I slipped into an inconspicuous chair somewhere in the middle of the room. I didn't fit in with any of the other students. In my plain gold hoop earrings and ribbed kneesocks I didn't stand up to their aura of cool. Around here a girl can get looked at wrong if she wears sensible shoes. I was so lucky to have friends like Grachi and Leni, who knew that the clothes didn't make the girl. Except for my coral dress. I couldn't help but smile when I thought how that dress made me feel . . . sexy.

"What's up? Something wrong?" Leni was her usually vibrant self, peppermint hair standing on its hair-gelled end.

"No, nothing. Nothing's wrong. Really. Nothing."

"Right. If nothing's wrong with you, then I'm in love with Arnold Schwarzenegger. Come on, Tai. I can tell. You're doing that thing you do when you're nervous."

"What thing?" I asked Leni, a football player rushing past me, almost knocking me into the wall of lockers. Leni yelled at him as his oversize back rushed away.

"Hey! Watch where you're going, apeman!" She turned back to me and continued what she was saying as if she hadn't been interrupted. "You're twirling your chemically straightened hair, *chica*. You're doing it right now. So? Tell a girl. What's going on?"

"*Mami* wants to see my dress. Tonight. At breakfast, she was like, 'Taina, don't think I forgot about your dress.' She was so sweet about it, I feel like I'm betraying her. I don't know what to do. I'm freaking out!" Grabbing my World Literature text, I shook my head and turned to Leni in desperation. Her face turned red, her mouth cracking into a loud guffaw.

"Why are you laughing?"

"You just said 'freaking out.' You never say 'freaking out.'"

"Leni! I'm serious. I have a big problem here." With that, Leni tried to stop laughing and tune in to my predicament.

"Okay, so you're not amused. I'm sorry. What are you gonna do?"

"Well, I've come up with two options: I can either tell her the store is making adjustments for my chronically big butt or I'm joining the military. I hear they are hiring."

"Stop that. You know you rock in that dress! Why don't you just tell her the truth? This is what you're going to wear for a party you didn't want in the first place."

"You know I can't say that to my mother," I could hear myself whine.

"Man, Taina, you've got to stick up for yourself sometimes. You can't just let it all come down to what she wants. She's pluckin' your feathers. What will you do when it's time to leave the nest, babe?"

Though the whole "plucked-feather" analogy sounded funny to

me, I knew exactly what Leni was talking about. What if I didn't want to stay on the course my mother had planned for me? Though working in the restaurant was fine for now, I didn't want to stay there forever. How many times had I heard *Mami* say to her friends, "It's so wonderful to have a daughter who will stay with me until I'm old and gray." Hearing what a "good girl" I was, her friends would patronizingly grin at me. It made me want to scream out like a child, "No! And you can't make me!" I mean, what if I wanted to go to Africa or South America or Europe? *Papi* had always talked to me about his youth, about those years after he left his father's hillside home in San Germán and took off for Mexico. He was eighteen, the years before *Mami* and I entered his life, many years before he and his wanderlust took off with another woman. But the things he'd say to me nights right before bedtime still clung to my memory. "*Mi India,* always look ahead, even if it's ten thousand feet away from you."

Why didn't I tell my mother the truth about the dress? Forget the dress— why didn't I tell her about Yusef? On top of that, why couldn't I tell Grachi and Leni about Yusef? What was holding me back from opening myself up? The girls would be so hurt if they knew I'd been keeping secrets, I thought, my brow scrunched into a furrow. Watching Leni wave her arms around, exasperated with the whole Moscoso debutante dilemma, I started feeling a memory slowly emerge.

Sometime before leaving Puerto Rico for Chicago, there were two girls I thought had been my friends: Liliana, and Freda. Freda, Liliana and I began playing together at recess in sixth grade. I had shared everything I knew about myself with them. On weekends, they visited my house and we made *dulce de leche* in my mother's kitchen. Freda was tall and skinny, with olive-green eyes and hair so black that in sunlight it reflected blue. Liliana was my height and wore baby pink ribbons in her blond hair. Her eyes were brown, but she liked to call them hazel. Liliana liked to always remind me that my hair was not like Freda's or like hers. In fact, both girls, away from our mothers' ears, fought to remind me that I was not *like* either of them.

Still, I confided in them, telling them about my father and his

"travels." I had spent one Saturday, all of us curled up on my chenille bedspread, bragging about *Papi,* his photograph in my
hands, his ebony face pulling in all the Fajardo sun in a smile.
Mami had taken that photograph on one of our family outings to
Las Croabas, where *pescaderos* sold us their day's catch of red
snapper. While *Papi* cooked the fresh *chillo* right on the beach,
Mami snapped his picture, the only one I had left. Liliana and
Freda didn't say much about him, each rolling their eyes and
passing the photo to me after glancing at it for a very brief moment. Though I noticed how bored they were, I couldn't help
myself and kept blabbing about *Papi.* How he'd taught me to
swim, how he danced in the rain, how he tucked me in at night
with stories of *duendes* and Taino princesses. But all they wanted
to do was argue about which lip gloss was better—cherry or
grape.

"Oh, Taina, is that all you talk about, your father? He doesn't
even live with you, so why bother?" Liliana would sigh with exasperation. Still, whatever I thought didn't matter; Freda and Liliana
were the only friends I had—the only friends I would have for a
very long time.

One day, Freda invited me over to her house, two streets away
from mine. I rode over on my bicycle, the Puerto Rican sun beating down on my head, singeing the part in my hair. I parked my
bike in their *marquesina* and strode happily toward the screen
door. As I moved to pull it open, I could hear Liliana's mother
saying to Freda's mother, "Liliana told me her father's as black as
carbon and just as *feo.*"

"*No me digas. Pues,* at least Taina got some of her mother's light,
right?" Freda's mother's voice sang out like a mynah bird. I stood
perfectly still, but inside my body a hurricane shook bones from
their ligaments.

"Ay, *gracias a Dios,* and good thing—"

I couldn't listen anymore. All I heard was Liliana and Freda giggling in the background, the lilt of their laughter turning my
stomach. I wanted to throw up my pancake breakfast right there
on their beautiful driveway, speckled like a quail's eggs. My heart

threatened to burst; my eyes sizzled. However much I tried to blink them back, tears continued to fall onto my cheeks, down the cliff of my chin, into the pool spreading on my blouse. *That's it for me,* I swore, right there in Freda's carport, *I'll never speak to either of those girls again.*

Mami never understood why I didn't answer the phone when they called for two months straight. *"Qué te pasa, niña?* I like those two girls—why haven't you answered their calls? What am I going to do with you, Taina?" I couldn't bring myself to tell her the truth. I buried that secret too, deep with all the others. I spent the next two painful years a loner, what many classmates called a weirdo. I knew in my bones I'd never be friends with anyone ever again; I'd never trust so much in anyone again.

✧ ✧ ✧ ✧ ✧

"Tai to Earth, Tai to Earth."

Leni broke me from my reverie and I was back in the school hallway. "Huh?"

"Huh? You been dipping into the art class glue?"

"Oh—I don't . . . know. I mean, no!"

"Mmmm, if you say so," she said, smiling, winking at me. I couldn't shake my worry, though, and stumbled; if only I could let all the secrets bubble up, spill right out of my mouth into the air.

"Leni—"

"Uh-ahuh?" Leni said, raising her eyebrows the way soap opera stars do in dramatic scenes that come right before big blows, such as somebody finding out somebody's pregnant or was cheating on them.

"I'm, uh, um . . . I'm beginning to, you know, like the idea of the *quinceañera.* I mean, it's growing on me."

"You'd better get used to it! It's, like, happening in less than a month, right?" The look on Leni's face told me she thought I was one plantain short of a bunch.

"It's just that I . . . excited . . . time . . . well, um, because I am . . . I have . . . kind of . . . a . . . uh . . . a . . ."

"You have a . . . ?" Leni was suddenly intrigued, her body turned to me, both eyes wide like bottle caps.

"Yu—"

"You have a Yu? What's a Yu?"

The obnoxious late bell rang right over our heads. I couldn't tell what Leni had excitedly started blathering out her blue-lipsticked lips. I heard her last word: ". . . kiss!"

"Kiss?" I asked.

The excitement in Leni's eyes kept me from telling her the truth about Yusef in that noisy stretch of hallway. I held my confession in like a hermit crab going back into its shell. Another time, another place.

✧ ✧ ✧ ✧ ✧

Yusef and I began meeting nearly every Saturday afternoon, after the end of my shift at El Yunque. Sometimes we walked; other times we linked hands in galleries, moving from one painting to the next. One time I even coaxed him to go with me to a poetry reading. But usually, Yusef and I strolled through the streets of Bronzeville, a historic neighborhood in the Southside. Yusef pointed out each landmark, my hand warmed by his.

"See that house over there?" he said, pointing to a dilapidated shack leaning on its foundation. "That place was once the Sugar Bones, a thirties juke joint. Talk to the elders around here and they'll swear they jammed with Jelly Roll Morton and Louis Armstrong on those steps. It's sad to see the place dying like that."

Because many of the old families refurbished their row houses, spackling, painting, and repairing front stoops, the neighbors on Bronzeville's Indiana Avenue weren't surprised when Yusef's family, the Clarendons, came in and opened up their dental practice. It was a welcome change from the eyesore the Moot had become.

The Moot was the 1889 brownstone Yusef's parents had moved the family into, a house rumored to have been an underground meeting place for civil rights activists in the thirties and forties. In the sixties it was bought by a Lebanese family who turned it into a liquor store. After two decades it sat empty, boarded up and blinded, nailed against the possibility of squatters. What had once been a manicured lawn metamorphosed into dust. Box hedges starved, azaleas dried up, crabgrass took over.

"When Dad saw it, he wanted to turn around and take the first flight back to Jamaica, but Mom nudged him into falling in love with its architecture. I was only ten, but I remember living out of a small rental apartment for months, visiting the house every day, watching its transformation. Back then, of course, I hadn't started painting, just some scribbling in a notebook, and I couldn't play outside with all the construction, so I rode my bike up and down Martin Luther King Jr. Drive," Yusef told me, pointing down King Drive. I couldn't see where he was leading me to look, but I didn't want to interrupt him as we walked the avenues toward his home. "Man, could Mrs. Baker make a mean peach cobbler!"

When I caught sight of the Moot for the first time, my mouth dropped open. I'd never seen anything like it before; only in art-house movies had I seen a structure like this one. Though it was a lot like the other buildings on Indiana Avenue with their gabled windows, the Moot had three turrets and a bevy of Atlas-like gargoyles, their gazes guarding the Earth below. Though the house might have been brick red a hundred years ago, the house's facade was now peacoat blue, with its door and windowpanes framed in bone white. The house had a short cement fence that was shaped like a wave and encrusted with broken glass and rainbow colored tile, each section leading to the house's cobbled walkway. I fought not to hold my hand out and touch the mosaic. Traffic whirled past us, kicking up the leaves at our feet, but I was not fazed, my mouth open yet wordless. We continued walking toward the house. On its western wall, an ocean scene shone with delicately painted coral, starfish, and anemone, seahorses and butterfly fish. Of the houses on the block, it was the most beautiful.

"What are those cement statues there?" I asked, my lips in a child's crayon circle.

"Oh, those are statues of Yemaja, the Yoruba goddess of the sea. My father's uncle Jeremiah flew in from Jamaica to sculpt them for us. They protect the family and everyone we care about," Yusef murmured, his fingers slightly tightening on mine.

"Awesome," I whispered, snaking up the sidewalk, my neck craned to gather all of the house in my sight. I could see Yusef in every stone and stroke. I should have been nervous, coming to his house to meet his parents. I worried, *What will they think of me? God, okay, forget about it,* I said to myself, gritting my teeth.

"Hi, honey." A gorgeously tall and graceful honey-colored woman looked up from her rose garden, the fat brim of her straw hat casting a lattice shadow over her face. She gave Yusef a kiss on the cheek, after brushing off the potting soil from her hands. "You must be Taina. It's such a pleasure!" A sudden warmth rushed through my veins at the sound of her voice. Mrs. Clarendon extended her bare hand to me. "Yusef described you perfectly. I'm Patricia." She took my nervous hands and put them into both of hers.

My shyness crept up into my bones. I swallowed hard, my palms perspiring. "Nice to meet you, Mrs. Clarendon." *Stop, Taina, stop sweating!* I berated myself. Did she know I'd already kissed her son? I tried to smile, but I could tell she could tell I was sick with worry.

"Please, call me Patricia. Yusef has spoken wonderfully about you," Patricia said, and I breathed a sigh of relief. "I've been wanting to meet you ever since my boy told me you're a poet."

"Mom, I'm not a *boy*," Yusef interjected, rolling his eyes.

Putting her delicate hand to her son's cheek, she said, "You'll always be my boy. Oh, and your father wants you to go to the corner store. Money's on the foyer table. Taina will stay here with me." Yusef looked at us sideways and then bounced inside the house to collect the money for the errand. Patricia, my hands wrapped in hers, faced me. "Sweetheart, why don't you come inside?"

"I don't want to impose—you were gardening. . . ."

"Stop; you're not imposing. Believe me, you're a great excuse to take a break! I've been chopping at that garden for two hours now, getting it ready for winter." Her eyes squinted a bit, as if she were cueing me to relax. "Come inside and we'll chat it up. Do you like sorrel?"

"I'm sorry. What's sorrel?" I imagined drinking something like wet felt in a glass.

"Oh, well, um, let me see if I can remember. Hmmm." Patricia released my hand and looked up at the sky as if the answer were there, staring back at her. "Don't they call it *agua de jamaica* in Puerto Rico?"

An electric shock shot up through me. *Agua de jamaica.* "Wow, yes, I remember my grandmother used to boil the flowers and then keep them in a jar for a day or so. She'd mix the tea with pineapple juice. Abuela would say, 'Taina, drink—it's good for you!'"

"Your people didn't put ginger in it?" she asked, moving to pick up her garden shears and trowel. I bent down to help. "My grandfather swore it was the cure-all for bellyaches. Is your grandmother still in Puerto Rico?"

"Oh, no, unfortunately, she died before we moved here."

"Your dad's mom?" she asked, her hand a visor blocking the sun from her eyes.

"No, my mom's." I didn't add that my grandmother's death was the impetus for *Mami's* and my move to Chicago. It had been too much for *Mami,* and she needed to start over fresh, brand-spanking-new. "Have you ever been to Puerto Rico?" I asked Patricia.

"Oh, years ago, well before Yusef was born. Antonio and I visited close friends who had a house in Cayey. We'd only been married three weeks." Her almond-shaped eyes smiled, filled to the brim with silent memories. Finally she turned to me and grinned. "I'll never forget it. We've always wanted to return. But with a growing clinic, we really only have time to go home, you know?"

"Home?" I looked behind her at the stunning brownstone and gestured.

She chuckled. "No, by home I mean Jamaica. We visit every year. Have you ever been?"

"No, but my father—" I immediately regretted mentioning his

name. What if she asked where he was? Talking about my father's abandonment with the Sister Chicas was hard enough—I couldn't imagine sharing it with anyone else, just yet. Even Yusef didn't know. "My dad visited Jamaica when he was younger."

"Well, maybe you'll get a chance to visit someday. . . ." At this, Patricia squinted her eyes again, the look accompanied by a wide toothy grin framed in plum-colored lipstick.

While we waited for Yusef to return, Patricia offered to give me a tour of the Moot. Apparently the Clarendons had done most of the renovation themselves, returning the home to its original splendor, of course, with its additions and details, such as the statues and the mural. "Can you guess who painted the mural?" she asked me, as we neared the front door.

After a few seconds it dawned on me. "Yusef?" She nodded proudly, putting all her weight against the heavily engraved mahogany door. Once opened, it revealed a gray-veined marble-floored foyer buffered by a grand staircase curling to the second floor. I forgot my manners and looked up and around me, my mouth ready to catch flies.

"Free tour with a tooth cleaning," a strong male voice called out from behind a wall, and I suddenly knew it was Mr. Clarendon, Yusef's father. He, white-coated and pushing a blue paper mask down to his chin, shuttled his last cotton-mouthed patient out the door. I immediately fell in love with the Clarendons. No wonder Yusef was so wonderful, I thought—clearly, the mango had not fallen far from the tree.

Watching Mr. and Mrs. Clarendon as they lovingly ribbed each other and shared their day, I summoned up memories of camping out on the beach with *Mami* and *Papi,* our little insular family, witnessing manatee swim close to shore. In those days, *Mami* had seemed so happy, her face brilliant with laughter, her eyes shimmering. It was so different from the way she was now, always turned inside out. I was not naive. I knew she changed after *Papi* left. Her constant hustle between owning a business and keeping a home together kept her distant. And it didn't help that neither of us ever mentioned my father's name in the house. Secretly, I wished hard (so hard sometimes it hurt my head to think it) that he hadn't disappeared one morning, his toothbrush gone, his dresser drawers empty.

"Hey," a voice whispered behind my ear, and I almost jumped, my heart racing a million miles a second. I was thankful Yusef did not kiss me like he usually did, but half hugged me from behind, his right arm pressed around me. If he had, I would have burned up from the embarrassment. Quickly he moved to plant kisses on his parents' cheeks, each beaming on seeing him.

"Boy, where's my ice cream?" Mr. Clarendon chided, searching his son's hands for the errand's bounty. Yusef pulled the brown paper bag out from behind his back and grinned playfully. So this had been the mystery errand, I laughed to myself.

"Pop can't end his day without his rum-raisin."

Winking at us, Mr. Clarendon replied, "Like my own father used to say, 'All fruits ripe if mi get what mi want.' "

"Honey, you'll have to share that rum-raisin if you want all your fruits to be ripe." Patricia shook a finger at her husband and then turned to me. "Taina, you will stay for dinner, won't you? Or do you youths have other plans?"

Yusef looked at me, his eyes hopeful. Immediately an image of *Mami* blossomed in my mind: *Mami* waiting impatiently for my return, tapping her foot against the tile floor, the sound echoing through the apartment. The message was clear: I couldn't stay for dinner. What could I say to Yusef and his parents?

"I'm sorry—my mother's expecting me home." I looked down at my hands, left and right wringing each other.

"Don't worry. Next time," Patricia offered, leaning in and patting my forearm. "In fact, we'd love it if your mother came along with you." *Fat chance,* I thought, pouting.

Since moving to Chicago, *Mami* had only one good friend—Mirta, who she rarely saw outside El Yunque. Usually *Mami* slaved away at the restaurant, having only "business dinners" with fellow entrepreneurs: butchers, fishmongers, and such. They all ate at the restaurant, their wives or girlfriends on their arms, their suits pressed and ready for shoptalk. I watched my mother in the semblance of a "good time," dressed in her favorite suit, the white lace collar of her blouse peeking over the powder-blue gabardine.

Those nights were the only nights she went out (of course, *going out* meant sitting in El Yunque's dining room). She wore the pearl necklace my father had given her as a wedding present for those "special occasions." From my room, I saw her slowly unwind the silk packet that enveloped the pearls. Then she held them against the light, as if they were prisms casting rainbows. It was a ritual. She did this every time before slipping them around her neck.

Those nights *Mami* sent Fernan the chef home and cooked her award-winning oxtails in tomato stew with steaming rice and pigeon peas, topped off by her apricot bread pudding. Setting the large front table with El Yunque's best dinnerware, she smiled bright and wide for those potential business partners and their wives or part-time girlfriends, noisily but happily eating *Mami*'s good *comida criolla*.

For me, things were very different. Every night *Mami* and I sat across from each other at our stamp-size kitchen table. We ate silently, hearing only the buzz of a new *telenovela* from Mexico blaring from the thirteen-inch TV poised on the edge of the countertop. What would make her leave all that for dinner at Yusef's house? I imagined her sitting across from Yusef and me, cane sugar in her voice, yet all the while piercing me with dragon fire in her eyes.

As if Yusef felt my tension, he pulled me away from the kitchen and began moving me toward the living room.

"Ma, I'll bring her back in a couple of minutes. I just want to show her my work." Yusef interrupted the uncomfortable moment, tugging me by the hand.

Our feet clicked against the dark hardwood floor. Everywhere in the room there was art: from Oaxacan masks to abstract paintings, and one famous piece by the Jamaican artist Milton George. But there was one specific canvas he led me to, his fingers nudging the small of my back.

"Here it is," he whispered into my hair. Right above the sofa stood a mammoth painting of a young girl, her coffee hands clutching a daisy. The daisy missed some of its petals, each lying in the wide skirt of the little girl's robin's-egg-blue lap. But the painted girl wasn't looking at the flower; her attention was focused elsewhere, far beyond the painting's distance.

"Who is she?" I asked, my fingers itching to reach out and touch the museum-quality painting.

"Her name's Gisella—she lives in Ocho Rios, near my parents' house. We go down there every year. It's where I most love to paint." I was close to him, his arm now clutched around my waist, my back pressed against his body. The skin of his arm smelled like linseed oil, but I didn't mind at all.

"Yusef, she's beautiful. I love how the island sun's reflected in her skin. Look how the green is mirrored right under her eye. I really like it." Languidly, I moved away from Yusef and inched toward the painting. This painting was very different from the "bottom-of-the-sea" mural on the side of the house. It seemed to me the little girl was breathing out into the field, like a dandelion about to spread her spores. "I could reach out and touch her, she's so real." The words left me in a sigh, as if they were not meant for Yusef but Giselle herself, her frail body imprisoned in canvas and oil paint.

He stepped closer to me and hugged me fiercely. Though I did not turn around, I wanted him to kiss me again, like that time in his studio his friend Paolo let him borrow.

✧ ✧ ✧ ✧ ✧

In his studio, we usually sat on cold metal folding chairs, the room piled with rolled canvas, cans of turpentine, bottles and bottles of dry pigments, and horsehair brushes. Yusef's workspace was the sardine size of a laundry room, but he adored it for its crank window that opened to a view of the Pilsen neighborhood with its growing arts community. In that room he sketched while I read him poems under the gaze of cobwebs. I loved how he bent into my words, his dreadlocks a net catching the light from the window's lips. A short time ago we were in that studio when Yusef began to ask me questions about the *quinceañera*:

"Babe, why are you so against this thing—this, um kintzanera?"

"It's *quince-añ-era*. You say *añera* like this—as if there were a Y sound after the N, an-yer-ra." I whispered, my lips sounding out each syllable for him to follow. After two failed attempts at rolling the R at the end of the word, Yusef laughed at himself, giving in to the beautiful complexity of a city accent shaped over the music of his Jamaican upbringing. I had to admit to myself that though I wanted Yusef to pronounce the word the way I said it, I loved watching his merlot lips fumble over the tilde in the N.

"It's not that I'm against it, really. It's more about how *Mami*'s made this a commandment rather than an option. She never asked me if I even wanted a debutante party. If she had, I would've said no. But she argues that it's tradition. She had one, and her mother had one, and my great-grandmother wanted one, so . . . I'm stuck. But it's a lot of money, you know? I knew girls back home on the island that never had a coming-out party or whose families could never have one 'cause they couldn't afford it. I'm not so sure *Mami* can either—but she's set on throwing this shindig for me. She'll think I'm being ungrateful, so I'm going along with it."

"Have your friends Grachi and Leni ever had one?"

"No, that's not really their style."

"But they're going, right, Taina?" Though Yusef has returned to his painting, I sensed his eyes were on me. I could guess where this was going.

"Yeah, they'll be there." My voice dropped to a murmur.

"Will I meet them before the *quin-ten-quinzen* . . . the party?"

Though my nerves began to fray, I couldn't help but laugh at his continued but failed attempts at the word. But he was dead serious, his forehead wrinkled, his hand perched on the easel as if holding himself up.

"Of course. I'm just thinking about the right time, you know? Grachi's going crazy trying to get classwork done, and she works at a bookstore and volunteers, so tying her down is hard, and then there's Leni, who's got all sorts of stuff to get done, and—"

"Well, I'd like to meet your friends. Unless you don't want me to . . ." Yusef set his paintbrush down by the easel and peered straight at me, his eyes searching mine for the truth.

"Of course I want you to meet my friends," I said, trying to soothe Yusef. "Just as soon as things calm down, you know? It's crazy right now with all the details and junk." *It isn't enough,* I thought, feeling my stomach sink. Yusef was clearly not convinced, but he settled down and shrugged. We are both quiet for a long moment. I turned to stare out the window at passersby, clutching their shopping bags, coffee cups, or babies. Finally Yusef piped up, breaking the uncomfortable silence.

"Well, it's just a big birthday party, right? I suppose we shouldn't worry about it too much. This should be better than my junior prom."

Breathlessly, I wanted to believe him, to believe that it was nothing more than a birthday party. I looked up into his eyes, the black fur of his lashes shadows on his skin. "Your junior prom? Why?"

"Because I'll be there with you."

Inside my chest, my heart slipped twelve inches down into my belly, and then, as if my stomach were a trampoline, it rushed back up my torso and returned to its normal home behind my ribs. I was flushed. My forehead started to sweat. My knees turned to water. All of a sudden I had to go pee.

"Taina?" He stepped closer and pulled me toward him. Leaning in, he gave me a kiss. Not his usual kiss but the-earth-moved-under-my-feet kind. The kind you read about in books. The kind of kiss my mother would definitely not approve of. My first real kiss!

I opened my lips . . . slow, like an elevator or like a door when a cat slips through it. He tasted like cherry Coke. With his mouth on mine I could feel my body shift, as if I were a swerving car on an icy road, one kiss folding into the next, the Pilsen light slowly dimming. With his left arm wrapped around my waist, I could feel his pulse through the failed barriers of his watchband, my shirttail, and my underwear elastic. I didn't say a word but I didn't need to; the words were there in my response. At that moment, in his arms, I was nothing but the sound of foot traffic creeping in through open window, the *quinceañera* dress on my mind, the taste of cherry Coke on his lips.

✧ ✧ ✧ ✧ ✧

"Read 'Cherry Coke' to me again," Yusef said, bringing me out of my daydream. Eyeing his painting of the little girl holding the daisy, in love with the splash and stroke of color against the canvas, I had slipped into daydreaming. Silly to do that, when my dream was standing right there. I could hear the Clarendons laughing softly in the background. Someone had put on jazz music, and soon trumpet song floated into the living room. "G'won," he said in his Creole.

"Are you crazy? I can't read that poem to you here. Your parents are in the kitchen."

"I don't care. I want to hear it again."

"Absolutely not!" I whistled through my teeth, playfully hitting him on the arm.

"Now, be a good girl and read it or else I'll get my copy and show it to my mother. Didn't she tell you how much she *loves* poetry?" More of that wicked smile. How I loved its shape; how it clutched at every part of me and tugged.

"You wouldn't dare."

"Oh, yeah?" he said, moving backward toward the kitchen, where the sudden sound of something flashing in a hot pan sprouted out into the hallway. The easy scent of curry glided our way.

"Okay, okay. You might be bluffing, but I'm not going to take a chance."

"Now, that's what I like—beautiful and smart, too," he joked, gently taking my face in his hands.

CHERRY COKE
You were Cherry
Coke under a moonlight
Mushroom, a slow swish,
Flickering past my tongue,

down my throat, snaking
its way into my chest,
Around the bend of bloodred
Ribs, and bone bent
to shape around a heart.
You were Cherry
In the afternoon, I was stemless in the night
Of these words trembling the way a branch's
Shadow will write a poem on the walk.
You were a cool drink in the heat
Of what was a long time coming.

I couldn't believe I had memorized it, my mouth full of its
humming words. Yusef and I held each other, the room's air suddenly the texture of a daisy touched by a little girl's fingers.

✧ ✧ ✧ ✧

Later that week, with our cups of espresso coffee still smoking
before us, Leni, Grachi and I got into talking about the quinceañera at our table in El Rinconcito del Sabor. I so wanted to tell
them about Yusef. But something stopped me. I mean, what
would I tell them? Clearly I was being stupid, all nervous about a
boy. A boy! No big whoop, the voice in my head scoffed, what
could they do but . . . laugh at me? Don Ramiro brought us
vanilla flan and we quickly plunged into the dessert. For what
seemed like forever, no one said anything, engrossed in the sticky
and sweet custard. All of a sudden, I felt Leni watching me the
way a weatherman might eye the sky.

"So, Taina," Leni asked, stirring her coffee without stopping to
take a sip, "last night I was surfing the Web, and I'm looking into
this whole *quinceañera* thing, right? And I see something about
damas and *caballeros*. Now, I know what a *dama* is, but a *caballero*?
I had to look it up, being lost in translation and all. But you know
me—I broke the code. Brits call them blokes, but you may know
them as dudes. You get my drift, girls? The male of the species!

You never said anything about dates, Taina!" At this Graciela looked down at her lap, restlessly rolling the edge of the table-cloth into a fine cigarette.

"Oh, right, dates. I forgot."

"Forgot?! Forgot? The Web site said you're supposed to be led out in some Princess Di–sad-fairy-tale-style knife-sword thing by some guy. Now, I could be crazy—"

"No argument here," Graciela looked up to say, a mischievous grin on her face.

Leni stuck her tongue out at Grachi but then returned to grilling me. "Like I was saying, I could be crazy, but isn't the whole deal coming up soon? What I'm trying to ask is, Miss *Quinceañera,* what guy will be escorting you down the aisle?"

That was the perfect time to say something about Yusef. Why didn't I jump in? Why did I feel the need to hold back? I loved the Sister Chicas—they weren't Liliana and Freda. They wouldn't hurt me, would they? Graciela had started to fidget with her plate of flan, slicing each corner of the dessert, her spoon a scalpel dividing it into a million pieces. Why didn't Graciela speak up first? She had Jack. Both Leni and I knew Jack. *Please mention Jack,* I thought, begging. *Come on, Graciela, say something. Save me.* Nothing. Leni jumped on our silence.

"Mmmm. Very interesting. Cat's got Taina's tongue. What about you, Grachi?"

"Me? Aren't we talking about Taina?" Graciela turned to me. "This is all about your special day—who's your *caballero?*"

"I . . . I . . . What about you, Leni?" I tossed the hot potato back to Leni.

"Me? Nice try. Besides, I got nothing. My plan, obviously, was to stag this thing. You?" she said, again turning to Graciela, whose face by now had turned peony pale. She looked about to faint.

"Wow, look at the time," Graciela said, looking at her watch, tapping the face as if it had failed to work long ago. Scraping her chair against the tile floor as she shoved it back, she began to collect her jacket, books, and folders.

"We haven't gotten the bill yet." I stumbled nervously, trying hard to not look at Leni. Shoving through my wallet for bills, I dropped my change on the floor, the sound like glass breaking throughout the restaurant.

"Something stinks in Denmark." Leni looked at Graciela and me suspiciously.

"Leni, it's 'Something is rotten in the state of Denmark,'" Graciela corrected Leni.

"Whatever. All I know is, Taina's got something cooking and it smells like boy."

5

Graciela

The sky is a dull tin roof overhead, the air heavy with the promise of late fall rain. It's Friday, a little before two P.M. Clouds are piling in stacks to the east, and normally this is the kind of afternoon that makes me feel a little sad, wanting a good cry, but not today. On this particular Friday, let the sky fall instead. You can't tell it to look at me, but today I met my destiny. Okay, that just sounds too much like Leni; let me say I got some amazing news today, something that could change my whole life. I should be focusing on what needs to be done, but I can't. The offer I got today is so exciting and wonderful and terrifying, I don't know how I said I'd consider it. But I did. And I haven't even told my parents yet. This is some other Graciela; it's got to be. I'm the girl with the completely planned life, down to the letter. I don't get rattled. But I'm rattled, I'm thrilled, and if I can just get to Librería Tzintzuntzán and start my shift, I'm sure I'll be able to settle down. At least I hope so.

I'm waiting for the light to change at the corner of Blue Island, Loomis and 18th Street. I tell myself to breathe, long, slow breaths, one after another. I am my normal fifteen minutes early for work, never missing a Monday, Wednesday, or Friday for over two years. Waiting at the corner, I let the traffic lights change twice and look around my neighborhood. All the familiar land-marks are where they always are. On one corner, Panadería Nuevo Leon's orange neon sign blinks against the drizzle that's just started. I can see the store window, filled just like always with all kinds of *pan dulces—orejas, marranitos, pasteles,* and *empanadas.* The smell of dough and sugar and *canela* is carried through the wet air. Dori's Moda de Niños, on the opposite cor-ner, has the usual window display of baby clothes the color of Crayola crayons, girls' pristine and shimmery communion dresses, and overstuffed toy animals.

Today, at the end of my fiction writing class, my instructor pulled me aside and told me to follow her to her office. This usu-ally means one of two things: Either you will be told that perhaps another area of study would be more enjoyable for you, or you're given the more direct suggestion of transfer to someone else's class. You see, Phaedra Mondragon is a woman of letters, a diva, a hometown girl who left twenty years ago to wander the globe, writing novels that made her an international celebrity. Tall, her raven black hair worn in a long braid, she's elegant, moving like the former dancer she is. Clad in dark, tailored suits from Italy and France, she's been known to chain-smoke, adorns her full mouth with bright red lipstick, and has also been called *diosa, La Divina,* with good reason.

When I was old enough to appreciate who she was, I loved catching any word on her exploits, either gossip or an article in the *Tribune,* a blurb on the news. Her reputation made her the topic of neighborhood buzz—Where was Phaedra now? Rome? Buenos Aires? Mexico City? Who was she dating? Rumor had it she'd had intense affairs with men and women. Who was the ob-ject of her biting satire? What prize did she win now? Last year she came back home to Chicago to teach after the death of her sister. She's idolized, adored and pretty much acts like she de-serves it. Doña Phaedra teaches what she wants, when she wants, and does not "suffer fools and the talentless or the lazy." She has a reputation for being very, very particular about how she spends her time.

I followed her to the doorway of what looked like standard-issue faculty digs, down the hall from our classroom. I'd assumed I'd completely blown it, that after reading my stories based on what I loved about Logan Square—the Puerto Rican boarder boy, the local shopkeepers, and the *Mexicana* and Polish mothers strolling their *niños* along the Boulevard, she was ready to "encourage" me to spend my time learning computer science, something else, anything else.

That's not what happened. We stopped in front of her office, and the door remained shut for what seemed like a geologic age. Phaedra Mondragon looked me up and down, saying nothing. It seemed like she was trying to make up her mind, and I was sure she was completing her inventory of her soon-to-be-ex-student. Finally I was invited in. La Mondragon leaned back against the door, and I crossed the threshold on cat feet, desperately hoping I wouldn't embarrass myself, praying for the good grace to take my dismissal without bawling *como una nena*.

To say that her office was breathtaking would be an understatement. It was completely organized, but crammed to the gills with art and relics, and books, papers, and pictures. In each corner stood dark wood shelves lined with leather-bound books. With a quick glance I could make out the names Cervantes, Molière, and Chaucer in gold letters beckoning me to come closer. Flush against each bookcase were low, lacquered end tables stacked with files and what I was sure were pile upon pile of student papers.

Along the walls, framed dust jackets of her poetry and fiction competed for wall space with Nicolás DeJesus woodcuts of peasant *ofrendas* and *calaveras* dancing on the cobblestone streets of Pátzcuaro. Keeping them company were several Huichol yarn masks, and handmade tin *retablos* asking *La Virgen* for intercession to heal broken hearts and broken legs.

Directly behind the desk and above her head were photo after photo of La Mondragon with the literary giants, her allies, her enemies. There she was on a dais, debating Octavio Paz, dancing under a palm tree with Carlos Fuentes, drinking champagne on a sailboat with Isabel Allende. At the very center of this gallery was a wooden frame, gilded and ornately carved. It held a black-and-white photo of Phaedra blowing out the candles of a huge birthday cake, with a short-haired brunette woman whispering in her ear.

With a wave of her hand she gestured for me to take a seat in a red leather armchair. I eased myself into my chair and carefully set my backpack on the floor in front of her desk, mahogany with brass fittings. Almost big enough to be a landmass, it sat dead center in the room, like a burnished red-gold island. Settling into a wing chair covered in the same leather, she pulled off the multicolored embroidered flamenco shawl that had been resting on its back and draped it over her shoulders. There still hadn't been a single word exchanged, and it was all I could do to keep from fidgeting in my seat.

Tapping her fingers on the mirror-bright surface of the desktop, she said, "Get out your notebook, Ms. Villalobos."

I hesitated for a minute, wondering why she wanted to hear more poor writing before she sent me on my way.

"Is there a problem?" she huffed.

"No, Doña Phaedra! Just give me a moment."

As I dug out my notebook, I could see out of the corner of my eye La Mondragon picking up a box labeled *Gauloises* and a gold cigarette lighter from a blue handblown glass ashtray. Pausing momentarily, she grimaced and put them back.

Clutching the black pressboard tome labeled COMPOSITION, I tried to sound relaxed and confident. "I have it here."

Leaning back in her chair and looking up at the ceiling, she announced, "Good. Now read the last story you submitted to me . . . and read it clearly, as if you actually have some confidence in your work. You were unable to do that in the front of the room in class today."

Breathe, I tell myself. *Breathe, and don't panic.* I open my notebook and find the story. I pull myself up, sitting as tall and straight as I can. Clearing my throat, I begin, my voice clear and strong.

" 'This year's been rough, but Danny Mercurio thinks he's finally got this job nailed. Who knew it'd become a five-day-a-week-after-school-and-half-a-day-on-Saturday thing? Talk about being careful what you wish for. But who could blame 'im? He's smart, he's handsome (ask his girlfriend, Selena Luna; she'll tell you), and most important, he' s fast, very fast. That's why his one-man door-to-door message delivery service has taken off.

" 'Olympia Boulevard will never be the same.

" 'It all started when Dionisio Quesada, the liquor store owner, grabbed him by the shoulder and told him he was tired of seeing Danny whizzing back and forth in front of his store on that blasted board of his, doing nothing. He shoved an envelope into his hand and told him to get it to Juno Delgadillo, manager of the bridal shop, up the street and around the corner. It was Juno's daughter, Minerva herself, the neighborhood librarian, who was finally getting married, and Dionisio needed her to check the list of what the guests would drink at the wedding.

" 'Danny zoomed there faster than chain lightning, swifter than the wind that slices down the boulevard when winter comes.

" 'The return trip was a blip, a blink, a shudder of a second. Dionisio and Juno told the rest of the shopkeepers of this marvel, this amazing business asset, and store owners on the boulevard soon realized what a find they had in this boy, this winged wonder on wheels. . . .' "

La Mondragon turns her attention away from the plaster ceiling overhead, cutting me off. "That's it! *That* is how you should read, always. Ms. Villalobos, could you please explain why you were shuffling and mumbling in class?"

"Doña Phaedra, I . . . I just thought you might not like it."

"Please allow me the courtesy of expressing my own opinion, and I would suggest you avoid trying to read my mind."

"Absolutely, I . . . I understand . . . I'm glad you liked what I have."

"It needs work, but there's a core of . . . well, a core of something worth reading. Clever references to mythology, too. Apparently you're somewhat well-read."

"Can you help me make the story stronger?" I ask, feeling flushed and suddenly bold. *La Divina*, La Mondragon, likes my work! *Bendito sea!* I have a core!

"Yes . . . in class. Come prepared to read like this, and pay attention next week when I review the importance of editing."

"Of course . . . Is there anything else, Doña Phaedra?"

"Actually, now that you mention it . . ."

There was no boom lowered, no talk of transfer. Instead, La Mondragon announced she submitted my name to Tilbrook Colony, known all over the country, as her personal recommendation for a young writer's residency she'll be leading next summer. I'd get a full scholarship, room and board for the entire month of July. It would mean traveling to the upper peninsula of Michigan alone, being away from my family and friends for the first time. No studying, no working that month, no tutoring, just talking about writing with other writers, time to myself, and writing, writing, writing.

At first I was stunned and silent, until Phaedra waved her hand to get my attention.

"Ms. Villalobos, this is where you accept gratefully—unless, of course, I'm horribly mistaken and you're not really a writer."

"Oh, no," I managed to stammer out finally, after a pause so long it seemed like time turned in on itself.

" 'Oh, no,' as in, you're not a writer, or 'Oh, no,' as in, I'm not mistaken?"

"No, Doña Phaedra, I'm honored, of course, and you're not mistaken. This is an amazing opportunity."

"Well, yes, I know that." She chuffed, looking both impatient and amused at my embarrassment. "The question is, are you ready to seize it?"

Again, time stretched and stilled as I flashed on telling my parents, the owner of Librería Tzintzuntzán, the staff and kids at Casa Aztlán, that reliable, always-there Graciela, was leaving town to chase some dream of hers. I couldn't accept, could I?

"People count on me." I tried to look away. Somehow gray, institutional floor tile was becoming especially fascinating. I couldn't, though; La Mondragon knew how to capture an audience, even if it's an audience of one.

"Look at me, Graciela." Her voice was suddenly kind. It wasn't lost on me that now she called me by my first name. "I come from a family of immigrants, a family that struggled and sacrificed. What you've shared in class about your family and your life tells me you do, too. I can guarantee you will always have responsibilities." She leaned toward me, emphasizing each word as she spoke. "This is an opportunity. . . . Trust me; you may not always have those. Sacrifices mean nothing if you don't have the courage to seize the opportunities those sacrifices paid for. That's the point, isn't it? So are you going to consider this offer?"

"I have to talk to my parents . . . to a lot of people."

"That goes without saying." Her usual, commanding attitude was firmly in place. "Your answer, please."

"Yes," I said. "Yes, I'll have an answer for you on Monday."

After being dismissed with a wave of her hand, I'd made it about halfway to the door when I turned to look back. Phaedra was watching me. I think there might have been a wisp of a smile on her face, but don't hold me to that.

In a blur of panic and excitement, I managed to get to the train, get off at my stop, and make it in one piece to this corner. I can't turn down a chance like this, but it's complicated. I like feeling clear, knowing what to do without hesitation. This is different, foreign territory for me. Part of me wants things to stay the same, wants the satisfaction of being the daughter my parents deserve, carrying my own weight, working hard, giving something back to *mi gente*. But there's the writing, the feeling I have when the words come, when I see them on the page. It's something that pulls at me more and more; sometimes I have a hard time sleeping because of some idea I need to write down. I didn't plan for this to happen; it's like the writing found me and won't let go. And now I have a chance to pursue it, see how good I really am. You know what it is? It's hard to say I want this for myself, but I do. That scares me. I'm afraid I'll make the wrong choice, do the wrong thing, forget who I am, where I came from.

I can feel my heart start to race again, so I scan the rest of the corners, looking for those outposts of everyday comfort. Kitty-corner to where I am Mi Lindo Michoacan's windows are filled with trays brimming with red-brown, glistening piles of *carnitas*.

Taped to the door of the squat redbrick flat is a hand-lettered sign, RIQUESÍSIMOS TAMALES, TORTILLAS HECHOSA MANO.

There are the other familiar landmarks scattered on the remaining corners. *Billares* Cholula, a hangout for pool-shooting boys, some in gangs, some just wannabes. There are no windows in the front, just a small sign on the one-story cinder-block building with its tar-paper roof. And as always, there are one or two surly, scowling older boys, wearing dark blue denim and white T-shirts, who apparently spend their whole day scoping the traffic, then periodically turning back to yell at the players and make bets.

Last but not least on the corner to my right, my destination for today, Librería Tzintzuntzán. It's located on the ground floor of a stately and beautiful old granite flatiron building, complete with cornices carved to look like tree boughs. The wooden door has a brass knocker shaped like the sun, and even in the rain it catches the light, glowing against the dark wood. The front windows are small, so Pilar is always changing the display, tempting customers with an array of book displays on beautiful fabrics, vintage shawls, hand-woven *tapetes* from Oaxaca—rugs shot through with color and Zapotec symbols. She lovingly places stacks of poetry from around the world, novels from Mexico and Latin America, and children's stories from many cultures. It's a family business, an old one, and neighborhood people, students, professors, and, more recently, yuppie artists from the north side come to buy books they can't get at Borders.

I scurry across the street and push open the door and the sound of music rushes toward me. Pilar Teruel, the store's owner, is adjusting the sound on a ministereo next to the cash register. Pulling off Cheap Rags peacoat and beret, I recognize the voice of Mercedes Sosa, singing about justice, about Chile, about roots and the land. The check counter, register, and the gift-wrapping station are situated near the door. The front of the store is so narrow there's room for only that, two small bookshelves, and a small table where there's perched a small electric teapot, cups, cream, and sugar. Keep looking, though, and the store opens up into a giant vee, with floor-to-ceiling bookshelves running horizontally all the way to the back wall. I labeled all the sections—fiction to the right, poetry to the left, organized by country of origin, then author, then theme. That was a special project, one I loved doing, since it got me familiar with the titles, gave me ideas for gifts, for my own wish list. And then there's the back wall, my favorite section. The shelves are crammed with children's books, stories from all over the world—funny ones, sad ones, stories that teach, stories that make you laugh. Books for babies, for toddlers, for children of all ages, for every kind of family you can imagine.

Pilar, a small, round woman, is about the age of my mother. She insists that I call her by her first name, and so I do. Today she's her usual cheery self, humming away as she fiddles with the volume. As soon as she realizes that someone's there, she turns and exclaims, "Ah, my most reliable employee!" Glancing at her wristwatch, she adds, "And early for your shift, as usual. What would I do without you?" Normally a compliment like that would make me grin from ear to ear, but instead I feel myself freeze and say nothing, a second later fussing with my things as I walk over to the coatrack next to the wrapping station. I can feel Pilar watching me, looking curious and concerned at my silence.

"Graciela, are you all right?"

"I'm fine, really good." I manage to dredge up a wan smile from God knows where. What should I do? That's the question of the day, and I'm still struggling for an answer.

"Well, I know it's really tedious, but I think I want you to set out a new display . . . one for Mi Mamá, la Cartera. I think a pyramid on the card table in the front of the children's section will really catch people's eye. We just received all the new orders today, and everything's downstairs in the office. Could you take care of that?"

"Sure, no problem." I don't tell her, but I'm thrilled to have a chance to do something repetitive, something I can place all my attention on, something other than the most wonderful, upsetting news I've ever gotten. I head for the downstairs office for boxes of books with a sense of relief.

Two hours later, I'm smoothing and tucking in the last of the volumes. Success. Easy. Everything should be so easy. I look with pride at an impressive, geometrically precise pyramid of books worthy of a spot in Gaza. Pilar has been busy at the front, reconciling the register tapes and ringing up today's customers' purchases. I stand back to admire my handiwork and I hear someone walking up behind me.

"Graciela, are you sure you're okay?" The voice of Pilar, sounding concerned and more than just a little worried.

I turn to face her, puzzled at where that came from. "I'm okay . . . why would you ask?"

"Take a look at the books, *mi'ja*. I think the content is a little mature for the children, don't you?"

I look, and my mouth falls open when I see that instead of *Mi Mamá, la Cartera*, I've stacked the table with copies of *Aphrodite* by Isabel Allende, a book filled with references to food, love, and lovemaking. "I don't know what to say . . ." I murmur, my voice trailing off as I redden again, feeling totally humiliated. What's going on with me? So much for distraction and focusing on the little things.

Pilar laughs warmly and puts her arm around my shoulder. "Everyone's entitled to a bad day, Graciela, even you. Why don't you go downstairs and take a break?"

Maybe that's not such a bad idea. Let me ask Pilar if I can call my girls. Maybe if I just tell them, I can get a grip on myself. I'd say something about troubles shared becoming troubles halved, but *trouble* doesn't exactly fit my situation. "Pilar," I ask hesitantly, "would you mind if I use the phone?"

"It's fine, go ahead, *corazón*. I'll be downstairs in a little while. My son will be here soon, and I think I have a little moving project for him."

I take the winding staircase to the basement office, piled with boxes of books that ring her file cabinets and an old oak desk. The walls are covered with photos, some black-and-white, some in color, of her family in the store, the five generations of them as well as some of the authors who've read there. I carefully maneuver the narrow aisle that leads from the door and scoot to the side of the desk. As I pick up the phone I ask myself, *Who first? Leni or Taina?* Either one will be surprised that I am asking for the shoulder this time. Not that it's never happened before; it's just that the times are few and far between. Older-sister complex on my part, I guess. And the truth is, I usually handle things on my own; I'm usually the one who checks in with everyone, sees if everyone else is okay. I decide to call Leni first and get her teasing out of the way.

I catch her just as she's running out the door; apparently there's a huge sale at the Dungeon and she's a woman on a mission: Stud collars and Russ Meyer Super Vixen T-shirts are half-price. I almost hang up, but she can hear the strain in my voice. I'm trying really, really hard to sound like my usual self, but it's not working.

"Hey, *mujer,* what's up? I thought we dished all the dirt yesterday at El Rinconcito."

I'm tongue-tied, hemming and hawing. "It's just . . . oh, nothing, really."

"*Chica,* whatever it is, you'd better tell me."

"It can wait. . . . I'll try you later." I try for perkiness here, but crash and burn miserably. I get the Leni-on-a-roll voice, and I know I'll have to spill.

"Grachi, you're gonna tell me, and you're gonna tell me now. God, I love bossing you around."

I knew that one was coming. I also knew that I couldn't keep the news to myself, so I unloaded on Leni, breathless and in a hurry, telling her my amazingly scary good news.

"Wow," is the first thing she says. "I thought those things were held someplace cool . . . you know, London, Paris, at least San Francisco."

"Leni, this is one of the few times I'm asking you for help. . . ." I can feel the exasperation growing. Maybe this wasn't such a good idea after all.

She shifts gears, and the teasing in her voice is gone.

"Grachi, I'm only kidding. Bad joke on my part. Listen, *corazón,* even though you think Black Flag, John Doe, and the Gits are the only things I pick up on my radar, I know who Phaedra Mondragon is. I'd have to have lived in a cave not to. In my opinion, it's just proof of what a genius she is that she picked you. You are one amazing writer, you are. . . . Really." Her voice goes soft with that last statement. But being Leni, she wants to make sure we get to the point. "Tell me you said yes."

"I said I'd consider it . . . that I'd talk to people and tell her on Monday. *Dios mío*, I haven't even told my parents yet."

"What is there to discuss?" Now it's her turn to sound exasperated—I believe pissed off is actually more like it.

"I have things planned, Leni, you know that. Pilar expects me at the bookstore, Casa Aztlán needs me for summer tutoring, and I'm sure my parents want me close to home. . . . These are all important things, meaningful things."

All I hear at the other end of the line is the sound of a chicken clucking. Funny. Very funny. But the twinge I feel in my heart tells me that my girl is on to something. "Are you finished?" I ask.

"Yeah, I am." There's a warmth in her voice I can feel coming through the phone. "Grachi, just answer me one thing. Do you want to go?"

I try to deflect. "It's not that simple. . . ."

"Answer the question."

"Yes." And it feels like a confession. "But it doesn't mean I will. . . ."

"Grachi!"

"It's doesn't mean I won't either."

"Damn, girl! Did you call just to work my last nerve?"

We both start laughing. I tell her I'm on break at work and I should go. I do want to try a quick call to Taina before I go back upstairs. My girl manages to get in the last salvo.

"Villalobos, listen up. Four words. Chance. Of. A. Lifetime. Promise me one thing, okay?"

"What's that?"

"If you actually make it up there, you've gotta tell me if there are any hot guys."

I'm chuckling as I tell her good-bye.

My call with Taina was a lot shorter. I was a little nervous since the blowup about the dresses a few days ago. The phone rang several times, and she was out of breath when she answered. "Whew . . . I had to . . . run upstairs. The restaurant phone's not working."

I feel a little shored up after talking with Leni, and I don't want Taina to think her big sister is a mess, so I try to break the news with this approach. "What would you say if I told you I might attend a young writers' retreat next summer, led by Phaedra Mondragon?"

"*Válgame a Dios!*" Taina's voice rises several octaves, "Grachi! Grachi! Oh, my God, that's tremendous! Wait! You said might. You mean you might not go? Why? Is it money? Maybe we could have a fund-raiser. . . . Oh, Grachi, you *have* to go!"

"No, no *mi'ja*. Everything would be covered. I have *responsibilidades, me entiendes?*"

We're interrupted by Taina's mother yelling in the background, "Taina Sol! Get yourself down here! We're in the middle of making *alcapurrias* for a party of fifty!" Turning away to answer her mother, Taina's still a little out of breath.

"*Mami!* I'm coming! I'm on the phone with Grachi; it's important!" I hear heavy steps in the background, like someone climbing stairs, and the voice of Taina's mother's coming closer. "Taina Sol Moscoso, tell Miss Graciela Villalobos that your mother needs you. *Now.*" I can hear Taina sighing deeply, "Yes, *Mami,* I'll be right there."

She turns back to me. "This is so special. . . ."

"So, you think I should go then?"

"Of course! But whatever you do, you know I love you, right, *mi hermana?*"

"I know, *querida;* I love you, too."

Taina's mother again: "This is the last time I am going to tell you. Taina, you are going to give me *un ataque de corazón!*"

"Grachi, I've gotta go. Love you."

"Love you, too. 'Bye."

I hang up the phone and turn to go back upstairs, and it's Pilar, standing in the doorway. "Graciela, I've been thinking—why don't you take the rest of the afternoon off? Gabriel is here, and he can help me with things today."

My worst fears are coming true. Just the offer of something like Tilbrook, and already I'm such a mess that I can't even do what's right in front of me. "Pilar . . . please. It's okay. I'm sorry, really I am. Let me go upstairs. . . ."

"Graciela, you're entitled to have a bad day. It's human, *mi'ja,* after all. I'm giving you the afternoon off, no arguments. I'll be fine, the store will be fine, and you're still my best employee. Take care of yourself. Go and feel better; that's an order from the boss." An order given with a grin and an understanding nod of her head.

Pilar seems firm in her decision. I surrender. "Maybe that'll help. I'll be here for my regular shifts next week, though."

"Yes, I do know. Can I make a suggestion? I'll tell you what works for me: Do something outside of your usual routine."

If you only knew, I say to myself. *That's the problem.*

I start the walk to Cermak and Hoyne and my house, when I realize that it's still at least a couple of hours before my parents' shift at the factory is over. I don't really want to be alone, still feeling unsure. I should go home, tell my parents about the offer, but I can't. Not yet. Maybe a *café con leche* and Don Ramiro are what I need. El Rinconcito del Sabor two days in a row? Well, at least it's following Pilar's advice, something outside my normal routine. It's still drizzling, and a little colder, so I walk quickly to the Eighteenth street el stop and run up the stairs just in time to catch the train going away from my home, my neighborhood. As I settle down in an empty seat, I let myself stare out the window, looking at everything and nothing, but not before I catch a glimpse of my reflection. Tilbrook is an amazing chance that other people would give their eyeteeth for; I know that. I have commitments that I can't take lightly, things that have an effect on others, make a contribution. Spend a month just writing, just doing something for myself? Leni's clucking rings in my ears. I'm not afraid; I'm not.

"Rebel," I murmur to that other Graciela, but she just blinks and says nothing.

About a half an hour later, thanks to my blue line train running express past five stops, I'm walking through the doors of El Rinconcito del Sabor, and am immediately comforted by the sight of the red Formica tables, the red vinyl-covered chairs, the smell the aroma of *café cubano,* and Don Ramiro. He's behind the counter, carefully setting out little blue dishes with *bizcochos* dusted with sugar; Doña Isabel must've been here earlier. He's wearing a tan guayabera the color of tobacco—crisp, spotless, pressed with so much starch it almost shines. Looking up from his task, he declares

"*Preciosa!* Twice in one week you grace my little café. *Siéntate, por fa-vor,* and tell me what brings you here."

I slide into my usual seat facing the door and shrug off my coat, not bothering to take off my beret. "Oh, Don Ramiro, it must be your *cafecitos sabrosos.* They're addictive, you know."

Although I'm trying for bravado, I look over to find him shaking his head. He says nothing, and after turning on the radio to the music of Machito, busies himself with making coffee and heating the milk for *café con leche.* Soon a steaming cup and a plate with two *bizcochos* are set before me. I turn to look up at him, appreciating how laugh lines have sketched his handsome, elegant face. As he smiles down at me, there's a knowing tone in his voice. "You know, *joyacita,* be careful. Sometimes my *café con leche* acts like a truth serum. Who knows what you might tell me?" Ambling back behind the counter, he sets up *la máquina* for more *café,* tamping finely ground coffee into the tiny brewing cup, slipping it into the holder for the hissing brass steamer.

And after a sip of *ambrosia estilo cubano,* I tell him everything, the whole story from start to finish, barely stopping to take a breath. As I watch him closely for a reaction, he nods sympathetically.

"*¿Un día increíble, no?*"

"It's not just incredible, Don Ramiro; it's confusing. Part of me wants to go. . . ."

"Then what's holding you back, *joyacita*? Chances like these don't come along every day."

"I know, I know. . . . What do I say to my parents? They know I love to write." But not how much, I admit to myself. I didn't know until this chance got dropped in my lap, wrecking my neatly ordered life. The other Graciela knows how to handle this, not me.

The other Graciela doesn't bat an eye when the game plan changes, when she has a chance to do something just for herself. The other Graciela said yes to Phaedra Mondragon. The least she could've done was stick around long enough to help with this. I guess she must've stayed on the train and kept going. There's only me left, and this me is having a hard time with all of this.

"Pues, está planchado. Certainly they'd know what an honor it is to have been chosen by La Mondragon."

"Of course . . . but what about my job at the bookstore, my tutoring? Summer is one of the busiest times for Pilar, and Casa Aztlán has the summer tutoring program. I can't just run off, Don Ramiro." I halfheartedly drink of my *café con leche* and leave the *bizcochos* untouched.

"Mi'ja," he says kindly. "You have a few months before this thing, no? Forgive me, but I think perhaps everyone could spare you for a month with that much notice." Pouring himself an espresso, he takes tiny sips and gives me a quizzical look, waiting for my response.

"Well, I . . . I guess so." He's right, too. And I would work really hard before and after I left, maybe even put in extra time. There's still a gnawing feeling in the pit of my stomach, something I can't quite put into words. Wonderful. Now I'm inarticulate. Confused and inarticulate. Perfect.

"Dígame, preciosa, there's something else, no?"

"It's just . . . it seems selfish to go. What I do at Casa Aztlán, my work at the bookstore, those things give something to *nuestra gente,* something tangible, something practical. I can see there's a positive effect, that I make a difference."

"And the writing . . . *es un divertido?"*

"Exactly!" That must've been it. That's what I couldn't express. "When you compare it to concrete hard work, writing is an amusement, it's entertainment, not something that changes people's lives. Don Ramiro, what would I do without you?"

"Ah, me entiendo," he says, then takes one final sip of his *cafecito,* and sets the empty cup in the sink behind him. He starts puttering around, fussing with something under the counter. Leaving me alone for moment, he goes through the swinging door into the kitchen, and returns with two cardboard boxes under him arm.

"Preciosa, por favor, would you mind helping an old man?"

I'm up in a flash and behind the counter before he can even tell me what needs to be done.

A full, rich belly laugh erupts from him. "I have an eager

helper. Could you pack up what's underneath the counter, *mi'ja?* I
need to take care of some things in the kitchen."

"Of course I can."

"*Muy bien.* Now let me attend to a pressing matter. Once you're
finished, would you mind bringing the boxes back to me?"

"Absolutely not."

Disappearing behind the swinging door, I stoop down to find
the shelves underneath the counter are crammed with books.
Mostly paperbacks, books by Gabriel García Márquez, Chinua
Achebe, Italo Calvino, Carlos Fuentes. Books that challenge and
inspire, books that stir hearts and minds. Novel after novel, pas-
sionate, powerful stories. They're all well-worn, with creased
spines and thumbed pages, many still have little bookmarks in
place. Even though they've obviously been read, someone wanted
to go back and find something that moved him, something that
had caught his imagination. *Divertido*—I don't think so. Point
made, Don Ramiro.

It takes me fifteen or twenty minutes, but I clear the shelves.
Gathering up the last book, a hardcover, I accidentally let it slip
and it tumbles to the floor before I can catch it. As I pick it up, I
can't help but notice a photo on the back cover. I know that face
even though it's no longer young like in the photograph, even
though the picture is at least thirty years old, maybe forty. It's a
handsome man, dressed impeccably in a black double-breasted
suit, white shirt, red tie, and pocket square. It's the smile that
does me in. To be precise, it's the face of the man on the other side
of the door. I carefully turn over the book and see emblazoned on
the cover, *Sombras y Sol—Memorias de Cuba,* followed by the author's name. I open it and the flyleaf declares it is ". . . part memoir, part fiction about a young man's odyssey from his homeland,
leaving the new Cuba, despite having been a freedom fighter with
Fidel." The blurb goes on: "It's a story about dreams of democracy
failing, and one man's journey away from what he loves to a
strange new world in America."

I'm stunned, I'm impressed, and more important, I'm curious.
I leave my newly discovered treasure on the top of the counter
while I carry the filled boxes into the kitchen. I find Don Ramiro

sitting at a table across from the stove, eating *croquetas* with a satisfied look on his face. I suspect it's not just Doña Isabel's cooking that has him so pleased "Finished already, *mi amor?*"

"Why, yes, all done." I place the boxes in front of him. "All except for one last thing."

"What's that, *querida?*"

Backing toward the door, "*Un divertido,*" I say. Another belly laugh from him.

Seconds later I'm back with the book in my hand, presenting it to him like an offering.

He takes the volume and sets it gingerly on the table, to the side of the boxes and away from his plate. Rising slowly, he bows from the waist, clasps me by the fingertips, and kisses the back of my hand. Then, straightening up to his full height, eyes twinkling, he declares, "*Ay,* you've found me out, then. Luis Ramiro Rendón, *a sus ordenes.*"

"Don Ramiro, why is there only one book?" I at least manage to get out that question. There are a hundred swimming in my head right now.

"Because, *preciosa,* some of us only have one story to tell. But you . . . I know you have many inside you. This is where you need to trust an old man's wisdom."

"I didn't mean what I said before about writing. My family taught me how important it is. I know it's not something trivial."

It is Don Ramiro who appears to be curious now. "Then why act as if you believe such a thing?"

"Because"—my voice is quavering as I realize my secret fear—"because I'm not sure I'm good enough, good enough to change people's lives, good enough to make a difference." I look down at the floor, not wanting to cry.

"Ah, *preciosa,* there's no guarantee anyone can give you. The only answer lies in the writing." He steps close and takes my face in his hands, tilting up my chin. "Tell me the truth: Do you love it?"

"I do."

"Then go home. Tell your *mamá y papá* about *la oportunidad de la vida.*"

By the time I get off the train at the Hoyne stop, it's raining heavily, and I practically sprint all the way home. It's only four blocks, but by the time I make it to the front door I can feel the damp coming through the heavy wool of the coat. Home. I'm finally back in the place where I started the day. It's a small, two-bedroom yellow-brick bungalow, with a brown-shingled roof and a postage-stamp-size backyard where every year *Papá* grows tomatillos, and *Mamá* has a bed of peonies, and where I try to find the constellations in the night sky, despite the city lights.

Home. I breathe a sigh of relief as I open the door, quickly pulling off my hat and coat, hanging it on the coatrack just to the right, in a tiny alcove. Past our little entry nook is a hallway that branches off to the left, leading to the kitchen. The bedrooms are a little farther down on the same side. To the right is the living room, which is also the music room, the library, and the study. Everything is there for comfort, the furniture, all overstuffed re-sale bargains, the color scheme, shades of brown, beige, and blue. *Tío* Ruben and *Papá* built the cabinets, and found stereo equipment and the television and VCR at a flea market. The shelves are packed with my parents' books, my books, CDs. The walls are hung with prints, good prints, a splurge my parents insisted upon. There's the Rivera with the man and woman picking cotton, solemn dignified, beautiful. Frida graces the opposite wall, alone in the forest; she's both a wounded deer and a wounded woman. Over the sofa is a Rufino Tamayo of a full-bodied woman, back turned, beckoning you to come closer. *Papá* usually makes a point of waiting until my mother's sitting there, then whispers something in her ear that makes her giggle like the schoolgirl she was when she met him.

Sitting in the living room on the edge of the sofa is Jack. My parents call him *el Grandote*. He's been coming over a lot, and having dinner with us twice a week ever since I asked him to come with me to the *quinceañera*.

Jack and I seemed to be falling toward each other ever since graduation, slowly getting closer and closer. But I never thought things could turn out this way, not until that brush of his fingers in my hair, not until I saw that look in his eyes. Ever since it happened, I couldn't shake the feel of him, traces of him lingering like a current in a wire. I kept thinking about that single, frozen moment outside of El Rinconcito and how it made me feel. I wasn't sure what to do, what to say. I didn't even tell my girls until I knew for sure.

The Monday after Taina broke the news to the Sister Chicas was when I got my proof. It was Chinese takeout and a fortune cookie that did it. Here's how it happened.

Normally Jack and I eat lunch together every day, usually in the campus cafeteria, sometimes at the hot-dog stand at the far end of the quad. That morning I waited for him in front of the Alumni Center as I usually did. In front of the towering glass windows and rows of cement columns, I tried to center myself.

Everything looked the same; everything seemed normal. Everything except that my heart was a rattle in my chest. I was hopelessly excited, and a little more than anxious. Maybe I was wrong; maybe I was reading something into a friendly gesture when he dropped off my notebook. I mean, it was just brushing a leaf out of my hair! I just couldn't ruin everything between us by taking some crazy leap. But I couldn't be wrong; I just couldn't. That was real. It was . . . *chemistry.*

Taking a look at myself in the mirrored glass of the center's entrance, I tried to steady my nerves. Pulling off my beret, I ran my fingers through my hair, reshouldered my backpack, closed my eyes, and took a deep, deep breath. Before I knew what hit me, someone's warm hand clasped my shoulder and spun me around.

"You don't need to check; you're the fairest of them all."

"But you know I'm not Snow White."

"Doesn't matter; the title's yours."

Taking my beret, he slipped it tenderly onto my head, and there was that feeling again. Then we were completely still while people walked around us, book bags and briefcases in hand. We barely noticed the traffic. Jack was smiling and so was I, and I don't know how much time passed, but finally he leaned down and whispered, "C'mon, I've got a surprise for lunch." It was then I noticed there was a large white paper bag on the ground next to us.

Grabbing the bag in one hand and my arm with the other, Jack led us to the center of the quad. We stopped to sit on one of the wooden benches clustered next to a half dozen maple trees busy shedding the last of their red-gold leaves. Jack made a production of opening the bag, dispensing lunch like it was a blessing; handing me a soda, plastic cutlery, and napkins. I plopped my backpack next me and gingerly opened my containers. There was a rush of aromas, and I was treated to the scent of chilies and garlic, briny shrimp and earthy black-bean sauce. It's kung-pao chicken and woo sen noodles with seafood, my favorites. I glanced up at Jack, who'd already chowed down on a forkful of what looked and smelled like Szechuan beef.

"So tell me, Jack, what's the occasion? Not that I'm complaining." I put a heaping forkful to my lips, and it was just as delicious as I thought it would be.

"Happy birthday, Graciela," Jack managed to get out, despite a full mouth.

I swallowed and dabbed a napkin to my lips. "My birthday's in March, and I know you know that. Why the special treat?"

"Maybe I just couldn't resist doing something for you. How's that for a reason?" His eyes twinkled, and he had that cat-that-swallowed-the-*canario* look.

"Works for me, but why do I get the feeling you're hiding something, Mr. Jordan?" I took a sip of diet Coke and cut him a look from the corner of my eye.

"You wound me, Ms. Villalobos. Besides, it wouldn't be a surprise if I told you."

"I knew it! You have to tell me."

"Nope."

"Nope?"

"Is there an echo?" Leaning over, he speared a shrimp from the cardboard container of woo sen. He made a move to scoot closer to me and I met him halfway. "Graciela?"

"Yes, Jack?"

"Eat your food before it gets cold."

We finished the rest of the meal basking in the late-autumn sun and watching the sparse shower of leaves blanketing the cobblestones underneath our feet. Jack did most of the talking, and I let him, as we commiserated about assignments and pop quizzes. As the conversation wended its way through our meal, he was in rare form, giving me the full-court press on the latest chopsaki movie he wanted to get me to see.

It was a huge effort, but I stifled my growing curiosity, and told myself he'd show me his surprise whenever he was ready. We finished eating and I started stuffing the empty containers with used napkins and plasticware.

I got up to toss it into the trash, but he grabbed my hand, stopping me.

"Don't go. I've got something for you." Fishing into his jacket pocket, he pulled out a single fortune cookie, one Scotch-taped together from end to end.

Holding it in my outstretched hand for a moment, I felt that excitement and nervousness rush back. My heart wasn't a rattle anymore; it was timbál. I carefully peeled away the tape and broke open the brittle cookie. In unmistakably familiar handwriting, there was the message, *Someone close to you will become more important.*

Looking over to him at last, I locked my gaze with his. I smiled so hard, I was convinced my cheeks would hurt the next day.

"You sure about this fortune?" I asked.

"Absolutely. The cookie doesn't lie."

I shook my head but made sure there was plenty of teasing in my voice: "Well, I'm pretty sure this is wrong."

"And why is that?"

And I leaned in and crooked my finger, stage-whispering like I was telling him a secret.

"Because it's already true."

The next thing I knew he was kissing me, and the satin scrape of his lips on mine made me forget where I was. I was flying, that was what I was doing, flying with him, and counting in my head—*one thousand one, one thousand two, one thousand three. How long will this feeling last? One thousand four* . . . Physics with Dr. Rajahnanpoor.

Breaking away I checked my watch, then scrambled to my feet. "Oh, my God! I've got class!"

Jack laughed so hard, I thought I could see tears in the corners of his eyes. But he still managed to grab the bag of trash from where I left it on the bench and waved me on. "Go . . . I'll see you later."

I snatched my bag and start sprinting toward the science building. But something derailed me, and I turned and ran back to him. Panting and out of breath, I hurried to kiss him on the cheek.

"Lunch . . . everything . . . was wonderful."

"I know you are," was what he said.

✧　✧　✧　✧

Back to the present, here he is, waving at me in my living room, wearing an olive-green button-down shirt, khaki pants, and high-tops, my not-so-secret *novio, el Grandote.*

I start to walk toward him when my mother comes out of the kitchen, the conversation following her. It's voices I recognize, friends of my parents from work. I can make out that they're talking about higher wages and better benefits. Not bad, since there must be about five different people talking, my father included, with the volume cranked pretty high.

"*Mi'ja,*" my mother yells, "*Papá* and I are just finishing some discussions about work." I knew their old contract would expire soon and their union would have to start working on a new one. "The negotiating committee wants your father to join them this time. This shouldn't be much longer, then we can all have dinner. Jack too, of course."

"Maria Isabel! *Ven acá,* I need you here; we're talking about the pension plan!"

Mamá turns away to yell back to my father that she'll be there in a minute, that he needs to practice patience if he's the new member of Local 185's negotiating committee.

I mouth to Jack, *I've got amazing news.*

He mouths back, *What?* There's a smile and a question in his eyes.

I swallow hard and silently mouth that all-important one word: *Tilbrook.*

My mother turns back to me. "As you can see, these men can't do a thing without me. I'll let you go see what *tu novio* is up to. Dinner in a half hour." Then she slips back into the kitchen, where the heat is already turned up high.

When I get to the sofa, Jack gently grabs my arm and pulls me down next to him. There's just a seam of light between us.

"Tilbrook? Are you serious?" Jack knows how important this is. After our Composition 101 class, we'd daydream out loud about where we could go to become better writers. And now that daydream was coming true for me. "Next you'll be getting a Pulitzer and we'll be seeing your name on the *New York Times* bestseller list."

"I think I have to write the book first," I laugh.

"That's a minor detail." After a second in which there's nothing but Jack looking at me, nothing but pride in his eyes, nothing but him stroking the back of my neck with his fingertips, he says, "This is great, Graciela. You deserve this." He blinks, and there's a long, long strand of time during which it seems like he's deciding something. "There's just one thing."

"What's that?" I murmur. That charge, familiar as breathing now, is there again, ribboning between us.

"I'm really going to miss you." As he speaks, his eyes darken with something I recognize, something I feel.

"I know what you mean."

"I don't think you do." Cradling my face in his hands, he leans in and there's his warm, soft lips on mine, and my mouth slides against his, and I do understand; we both do.

Luckily, we break the kiss just as *Papá* comes out of the kitchen, union people in tow, the aroma of *Mamá's guisado de res* following them. We made a batch last Sunday, and today we'll have leftovers *muy sabrosísimo.* I tell Jack I should go in the kitchen to help, and he offers to set the table. Gotta love a guy who knows enough to do that. As we're getting up, *Papá* stops to introduce me to the crowd, announcing that I'm an honor student, a community volunteer, in other words, his pride and joy. He makes a point of introducing Jack as my young man. Jack surreptitiously pokes me in the back after hearing that, but I manage to keep a straight face.

Twenty minutes later, it's a wonderful scene. We're eating at the kitchen table, talking, laughing. *Papá* is detailing the plans for the new contract, describing all the players, poking fun at the company lawyers. Jack asks specifically about the new demands, not out of obligation, but because he's really interested, I can tell. *Mamá*'s watching it all, watching the two of us sitting side by side. I catch her eye and we share a private smile. For the first time today I feel comfortable. After dinner, after Jack leaves, I'll tell them about Tilbrook, and how much it means to me. For the first time today I think everything will all work out.

"I almost forgot my special announcement," *Papá* goes on, looking at me. "I've been chosen to head the negotiating committee. *¿Tu Papá es muy impressivo, no?*"

Before I can say anything, before I can stop him, Jack makes an announcement of his own: "You must be really proud, Mr. Villalobos; there's your news and Graciela's residency."

"Residency? What residency?" Turning to my mother, he says, "Maria Isabel, do you know about this?"

"No, Alejandro, but I'm sure Graciela was just about to tell us."

I don't look at Jack; I can't. I never said I hadn't told my parents yet; he just went ahead as if it were no big deal. Wrong assumption. Big mistake. My father is silent and stony; my mother looks pained, worried. I take a deep breath and explain all about Tilbrook, the doors it could open, the honor it is, the fact that I said I would have a decision for Phaedra Mondragón by Monday. When I sneak a look at Jack from the corner of my eye, he's picking at his food, head bowed. There a warp of time, a pause, and then my father's voice: "*Mi'ja*, are you finished?"

"Yes, *Papá*."

"I'm glad you finally decided to include your family in this. Who else have you graced with this wonderful news?"

"Leni and Taina," I say, voice flat. I put down my fork. I'm not hungry anymore.

"Sir—" Jack starts, only to be cut off curtly and politely by my father.

"I think you've said enough, don't you, son?"

"*Papá,* please." I try to salvage the situation. The ease of just a few minutes ago seems far, far away.

"Graciela, we will talk about this later." Seeing that everyone has stopped eating, he says, "Please, everyone, let's finish this delicious meal." But he's not smiling and neither is anyone else. We pretend to eat; now everyone's picking at their food, moving it around their plates, saying nothing. Finally I ask to be excused. I can hear Jack's sigh of relief. We start to get up from the table, but *Papá* stops us.

"You know, *mi'ja,* your cousin Raoul will be in Chicago the same weekend as Taina's *quinceañera.* I think he would enjoy going with you. As your escort, of course." Looking over to Jack, he says, "I'm sure you won't mind. After all, family comes first."

Jack and I look at each other, and I see the mirror of my own sadness in his eyes. "Not at all, sir," he says without looking over to *Papá.* "I think I should go now." My parents say nothing, and before I can get a word out he's already walked out of the kitchen. I get up and run to catch him before he can leave, stopping him at the front door, grabbing him by the arm.

"Don't go like this," I plead.

Confusion and hurt swirl across his face, like storm clouds darkening the sun.

"Graciela, what the hell happened?" His voice is a low rumble, but it's clear how upset he is.

"I shouldn't have told anyone about Tilbrook until I talked with my parents."

"That's it? You've got to be kidding!"

We whisper, but it's clear we're both far from calm.

"No, Jack, I'm not. This is a huge thing, and I should've brought it home first."

"That's ridiculous. . . . You're telling me that's why your father's nose is bent out of shape?"

I can feel myself getting frustrated, but I keep my voice low, trying to keep a lid on this, trying not to make things worse.

"Listen to me; that's how things are with us."

"Who's *us,* Graciela?"

"People like us, people like my family, people in this neighbor-hood."

There a long silence where all we do is stare at each other; then Jack closes his eyes, draws a long, hard breath, and shudders it out. Swallowing down the lump in my throat that I'm sure has got to be my heart, I start to say something, but he cuts me off. "I don't understand, Graciela, I don't. . . ."

"Jack—"

"But I want to." There is a tenderness written on his face that almost takes my breath away, but there's still hurt there, hurt that has taken residence deep in his eyes.

"Oh, Jack . . ."

A split second later, his hands loosely clasp mine. "I'm an idiot. I'm sorry I blurted everything out. I'm sorry about everything." Now he's angry at himself for not keeping my secret.

I'm upset, but with myself for not handling this the right way. I don't know even what to think about my father. It's not like *Papá,* but then, my not telling my parents first isn't like me, either. And I'm crying now, and I don't want to cry. "It's not your fault; it's mine." My chest feels tight. I swallow back the rest of my tears and manage to say, "You don't mean you're sorry about us, do you?"

Jack takes my hand and presses a kiss in my palm. "No, how could I? Nothing about how I feel about you is a mistake, Graciela. Listen, I need to go; you need to talk to your parents." He makes himself smile. "Try to remind your dad that I'm a great guy, okay?"

And then he's out the door and gone.

Later, much later, the last of the dishwater is gurgling down the drain, and I'm wringing out the sponge, staring down at the water swirling away, trying not to think, just do. One foot in front of the other, one thing at a time. I'm on autopilot, trying to make every-thing seem normal, trying to still my head, my heart, and failing miserably. I won't let myself cry; I can't. If I do I won't stop, and I know there's still *Papá* to talk to. *Mamá* has already come in to try to comfort me, telling me that things will work out, that everyone just needs some time. I ask her how she can be sure, and all she does is kiss me and hold me close.

I can hear *Papá* come into the kitchen, pull out a chair, and sit down at the kitchen table, waiting for me to turn around. *Please God, let me say the right thing, do the right thing.* Moving slowly, I slide into the chair across from where he sits. We look at each other, his brown eyes mirroring how I feel—sad, confused, hurt.

"Graciela, I'm disappointed in you. I hadn't realized that *tus amigas y tu novio* have become more important to you than your family."

"*Papá,* that's not true! It's just that after I found out I was so excited. I didn't know what to do, what to think. I knew you and *Mamá* were still at work. I couldn't call you there, so I called my girls." I decide not to even mention Don Ramiro; it would only make things worse. "I'm sorry I told Jack before you," I went on. "I wanted to tell you both as soon as I got home, but you were both busy, and Jack was here."

"Yes, Graciela, we had some business to take care of. But the daughter I know would've told her boyfriend that she had something to talk about with her parents. She would've apologized and explained that she needed some family time alone. That daughter would have waited to call her friends."

I didn't have an answer to that. It's true; I would have before. But things are different. I felt that today was about me, and decisions I have to learn how to make. Somehow, I've turned a huge corner in my life. I'm different now, too. I hesitate before I speak. "*Papá,* I'm not a little girl anymore."

"I know, *mi'ja.* I told your mother I just wasn't prepared for what this was going to look like. Your mother told me that we have to trust you, that we raised you to do the right thing."

"You can, *Papá,* you can." My voice quavers, and a second later I'm crying, hot tears streaming down my face, and I can't stop; I don't want to stop; I think I've earned a good cry. Somehow I find the strength to keep talking. "Trust me, *Papá,* trust my decisions."

"And this Tilbrook, you want to do this? What about your job, your tutoring?"

"I'll give them enough notice, and I'll work extra hours before I go, and when I come back. I'm not quitting, *Papá.* Just leaving for a while. Nothing else changes, nothing."

"*Ay, mi'ja.*" He sighs. "That is *una promesa* you must never make. Everything changes, except *familia. Familia* is what makes everything else possible."

"I know, *Papá,* I do."

"Will I know you when you come back, *mi'ja?*" Getting up from the table, he comes over to me and dries my face with the back of his hand, like he always did when I scraped my knee or fell off my bicycle. "Will I?" His beautiful brown eyes well up, but he's my *papá* and he will not cry.

"¡*Papá!* You mean . . . ?"

"Yes, you can go. Your mother and I have discussed it. It's an honor to have been chosen, by La Mondragon, no less. But you must keep up your responsibilities otherwise. You've given people your word, Graciela. That's not something to be taken lightly."

I leap from my chair, and he captures me in his strong arms and holds me against his chest. I feel like I'm about five; I feel all grown-up; I feel like we've both opened a door that we can't close, only walk through together.

Easing away, I gather my thoughts, steady myself, and ask the next big question: "What about Jack, the *quinceañera?*"

"He's a good boy. If I didn't think so I wouldn't have invited him into my home, allowed him to spend time with my only daughter. Be with him; that's fine. But I've asked you to do something for your family, *entiendes?* Something for me."

"*Sí, Papá,*" I say, making every effort to hide my disappointment. "I won't let you down."

He kisses my cheek. "I know, *mi'ja.* Now let me go see what your mother is up to. Believe me, two women in the house is enough—more than enough."

As I watch him head for the bedroom, I realize this is the first time he's ever referred to me as a woman. It was always "girl."

Always, until today.

By ten o'clock I'm ready for the end of this day, pajamas on. *Mamá* and *Papá* have gone to bed an hour ago; they'll have to be up by five A.M. I try to sleep, but I can't. Reaching over, I turn on the lamp on the nightstand next to my bed. Warm yellow light cascades over my quilt, dances on the surface of the wrought-iron bed frame. I think about what my father said tonight, about Tilbrook, about Jack. If I want to be treated like an adult, then I have to do the mature thing, the responsible thing. I get up and creep softly into the living room and pick up the phone. Standing in the dark, I dial the number and wait while it rings once, twice, three times. Then it's him; it's Jack.

"It's me," I whisper, loud enough for him to hear, soft enough not to wake up my parents.

"Graciela," his voice softening as he speaks. "Are you okay?"

"Yeah, I am. My father and I talked about Tilbrook, and I've got my parents' approval. I'll still have to make sure I take care of everything at the bookstore and Casa Aztlán, but I can go."

"That's great. . . . Listen, I'm sorry I left like I did, but it seemed like the best thing."

"No, I think you were right; it was a good idea. It gave me a chance to talk to my family. Actually, I should've asked you not to stay for dinner."

"Ouch. You're bruising my delicate ego, here."

I don't answer right away, but finally I respond, "Listen, Jack—"

"I know," he cuts me off. "You didn't get a chance to tell your dad what a terrific guy I am."

"Jack, I want you to listen to me. A lot has happened to me today, a lot that I have to get comfortable with. I just think that it would be better if we don't . . ."

"Don't what? Get serious?" I can hear him take a breath and let it out. "Too late, Graciela. I'm in love with you, and it's about as serious as it can get."

"Jack, I can't do this." Still whispering, holding the phone in one hand and clenching my fist with the other to keep from sobbing. I will not let myself fall apart; I won't. "Be my friend; just be my friend."

"Is that what you want?" His voice is rough with feeling. "Just tell me you don't feel the same way."

Silence. I can't say a word; I can't tell that lie.

"I knew it," he whispers. "Let's just take things slow for now. We've got all the time in the world. . . . Graciela, please."

Finally: "Okay, we'll take things slow . . . but I don't know how long—"

"It doesn't matter. I love you."

Silence looms large, and I want to say I love him too, but I don't. It just seems like too much right now.

"If at any point you want to jump in on that and save my sorry ass, that'd be terrific."

Now I'm laughing, he's laughing, but I manage to say, "I know. You're crazy, though."

"We're good, then."

"Yeah, we're good. See you Monday at school."

"Count on it. Night, Graciela."

"Night, Jack." Before he has a chance to hang up, I stammer, "I . . . I . . . just . . . you know how I feel, right?"

"It's okay, Graciela. Get some sleep and I'll call you tomorrow." His voice is so warm over the phone.

" 'Bye," I say. "Talk to you tomorrow." I hope he hears the feeling that lies behind those four words.

I'm exhausted; now I can sleep like the dead. I drag myself back to my room, careful not to wake up my parents. Crawling into bed, I feel my eyes slip shut before I can even thank God for getting me through this day. Soon I'm dreaming about my family, my girls, about Jack. All through the dream I'm flying, soaring in and around everyone, and everyone claps as I soar higher and higher.

6

LENI

For once, I'm the first to arrive at El Rinconcito del Sabor for our weekly coffee date. I'm even early. I can't wait to show the girls my "surprise." The look on Grachi's face is going to be worth ruining my rep for being fashionably late. I sit down at our usual table. Don Ramiro is busy attending to and charming the support hose off of a crowd of middle-aged Cuban ladies. And judging from their blushing and nervous schoolgirl giggling, he must be doing a hell of a job. I watch him for a moment as he bends at the waist like a waiter in an ultrachic restaurant, the ladies hanging on every word of his perfect Spanish. He must have been quite the hottie when he was my age. That kind of old-world charm is like nothing else. My dad had it in spades. When we used to go to weddings, christenings, or O'Malley family gatherings, he would go from table to table, working the room like a fine, dark rum warms the body limb by limb. I wouldn't mind having a little of that myself, although "in your face" with a dog collar seems to work better when you're hangin' at the club.

Don Ramiro sees me, gives a short wave in my direction, and gallantly exits from the gaggle of bouffants. Walking toward me, he flashes me that famous smile, bows at the waist again, and says, *"Buenas tardes, Señorita Elena ¿Quiere un café con leche, como siempre?"*

"Sure, Don Ramiro, sounds good."

"A sus ordenes, joven."

I have to admit, like the *abuelas* at the next table, I find him a tough one to resist. It feels good to be treated so well. But back to Taina's surprise . . . I've been hatching this plot for two weeks, ever since Carlos first brought me to hear his new band, and I can't wait to spring it on them. I'm just so glad that the guys went along with my plan.

Don Ramiro returns with a steaming hot cup of *café con leche,* my favorite coffee drink. No one makes them like he does. *"Gracias,* Don Ramiro," I smile, and as he walks away I take a long, warm sip and close my eyes, feeling the sweet milk and sharp coffee flavor coat my throat. My fingers run back and forth over the fifties abstract pattern on the rim of the white *caribe* china. I'm jolted out of my caffeine reverie by the clamor of the bell on Rinconcito's front door, and I hear the sounds of my girls bustling in. They stop short when they see me. Okay, so I'm not usually so prompt, so sue me!

" 'Bout time, *chicas!* I was wondering when you were going to get here!"

Taina and Grachi break out of their trance and head for the table, smart-ass smiles spreading on their faces. "Hey, it's not like I've never been on time before!" I exclaim, my hands still wrapped around the coffee.

"Actually, it *is* like that, Leni. Usually, anyway." Boy, Taina's starting to sound like Grachi! Great, now I have two moms, instead of my Sister Chicas. Well, since my own mother doesn't play that maternal role I suppose somebody's got to.

"Okay, okay. Enough with 'picking on the punk chick' time. Listen up, *chicas,* I have a surprise."

Grachi and Leni raise their eyebrows, and I can see they aren't sure what to expect. This is going to be good. Don Ramiro comes over to the table with Grachi's and Taina's regular coffees and sets them down. He smiles at Taina and then puts his hand on Grachi's shoulder as she smiles back at him. What's going on there? Seems to be a connection between the two of them that wasn't there last week. Oh, well, I think I'm pretty sure it's not an affair. The thought makes me chuckle out loud, and all three of them look at me. Don Ramiro walks away, and Grachi launches in.

"So what's the big surprise, Lenita?"

"If I told you, it wouldn't be a surprise, now, would it?" I snap my fingers, then give them the once-over. "Both of you need to finish up your *cafés, chicas;* I'm takin' you on a short trip." While I wait, I change the subject and ask Grachi how her parents took the news about the writer's retreat. She fills us in on everything, their support, her dad's forcing cousin Raoul on her, and Jack's big time confession of love.

"Oh, my God! This is all . . . so incredible! What a week you had!" Taina manages to spit out after barely swallowing her coffee. I think we were both holding our breath trying to take in all the news.

"Week? That was one day, *amiga!* My head is still spinning."

"Well, *chica,* it's about time you start doing your own thing. You have to check out this writer's deal, and please don't tell me I have to spell it out about Jack. They don't get much hunkier than him, Grachi!" When she glances away and starts fiddling with her coffee cup, I can tell she's still holding back, and I realize this has got to be a toughie for her. Time to change the subject.

I take one last slurping sip of the dregs of my *café con leche,* stand up, slap ten dollars on the table, and announce, "Come along, *amiguitas;* we have places to meet and people to do!" Grachi and Taina finish their drinks and follow me as I march out the door, all of us calling out good-byes to a smiling Don Ramiro as we pull on our coats and push out the glass door to the rush-hour filled street. I hook an arm through Grachi's and the other through Taina's and turn them around, urging them briskly along toward the factory district.

We chat excitedly as we head toward the old abandoned watch factory that has become a band rehearsal space.

"*Por favor,* where are you taking us, *chica?*" I can tell that Grachi is a little concerned and probably protective of Taina. The factory district isn't the best neighborhood in Chicago, but it's cheap, and musicians are notorious for being broke, broke, broke. Did I mention broke? And I should know—I date them! We arrive at the front of the Hole, and I practically drag the girls inside. The room is massive, industrial-looking, with old machinery arranged around the edge of the walls in between chairs and tables. The windows are huge and streaked with dirt, but some muted afternoon sun seems able to push its way through the grime. The smell of dusty machinery, stale cigarettes, and sour, cheap beer hangs in the air. Carlos and his guys are setting up on the makeshift stage, talking loudly in Spanglish. Taina and Grachi are whispering to each other, and I decide to put an end to that right away, so I put my arms through theirs again and lead them over to a single row of gunmetal-colored, beat-up folding chairs.

"This way, *chicas,* this way." As Grachi closely inspects the seat, I pull her down, teasing, "Don't worry, Graciela; it won't bite! Might collapse, or leave some really interesting stain on your pants, but it won't bite!" She smacks my arm, brushes the dust off the seat, and gingerly sits on the edge. Taina follows suit, staring up at the stage, having just noticed the band setting up.

"Oh, this is a band for the *quinceañera.* . . ." She's got that deer-in-the-headlights look, and I can see my plan is working. Step one of my plan is in effect.

Grachi begins to fire questions at me: "Where are they from? What kind of music do they play? Have you known them for long?"

"Chill, *chica!* Why don't you hear them first and then you can ask all the questions you want!"

"Well, Leni, at least they're Latino. Are you sure there isn't someone joining them with a green mohawk?" quips Grachi.

I can't help but smile smugly at her. At that moment, as if on cue, Carlos and the boys rip into an English/Spanish cover of the Clash's "London Calling." While the loud strains of the *rockera* band ricochet around the cavernous ceiling, I look over at the girls. Taina has her hand slapped over her mouth and her eyes are the size of LP records; Grachi's jaw is clenched as she stares at the band in disbelief. I can almost see them straining to not put their fingers in their ears. I let them suffer for five long, awkward, and very loud minutes, until the song comes to a dramatic finish of drumrolls and guitar solos. I smile at the Sister Chicas, watching them squirm, and I'm loving every minute. Grachi's straining to find something diplomatic to say, while Taina's studying the concrete floor. I take mercy on my girls and I yell toward the stage, "Okay, Carlos, they've suffered enough." The guys erupt into goodhearted laughter, which spills over to my two *chicas*. The band begins to play a lovely *cumbia,* and I can hear Taina breathing a huge sigh of relief. I explain that Carlos's band is known as both Los Dead and, with the addition of horns and more percussion, Sonido Tropical. I smile and add, "At least if we are going to have old-school music, we can have a band that's younger than our parents, *¿verdad?*"

After the Latin song is finished, the band begins to pack up, and Grachi and Taina start to talk about a possible music list. I head up to the stage to thank Carlos and the guys and let them know they got the gig. I watch Carlos direct the careful packing of the instruments, and I smile to myself. It's so weird that he and I have known each other since we were in diapers. Our fathers were friends since the Stone Age, or at least high school. Whenever we went down to PR we would spend a day with their family; it was a ritual. I remember always being nervous when we first arrived at their house; the kids were always thrown together, like at that party after Dad died. Since I couldn't speak much Spanish, I felt weird, different. But Carlos always stood by me protectively, and it wouldn't take long for him to make me feel like part of the gang.

He was the first boy I ever kissed. Right after he saved my life.

Carlos's father was a Puerto Rican supreme court judge, and they lived in a house perched on a hill in Guaynabo in the middle of ten acres of land, a massive amount of space on an island the size of Long Island. The property was filled with gorgeous tropical plants that Carlos's father had cultivated himself. Their bright colors lit up the white concrete walls with riots of vivid orange, pulsating fuchsia, and brilliant yellow, and their sugared scent hung all around the house like a curtain. The inground swimming pool wasn't bad, either. But what really impressed me were the horses. The family had a stable out behind the house, and I was fascinated by the small size of these Puerto Rican ponies. Until then I had seen only the full-size ones that pull the carriages in Central Park. I imagined that I would need an escalator to ever be able to get on them. But these . . . these I was sure I could manage.

On this particular trip when I was five, I finally convinced my mother that I was old enough to ride them. Carlos, who was already seven, was totally comfortable riding, so Mom agreed to let me try if I went with him. My father gently lifted me onto the back of Hidalgo, the smallest of the bunch, and while I ran my hand along the soft but bristly chestnut coat, the adults continued to talk and laugh as if we weren't there. They always seemed to do that when we were down there. Like us kids became invisible or something. But it was okay; I was totally absorbed in the horse. I just lay there with my chest on his neck, feeling his muscles twitch under my bare, skinny legs, and breathing in his warm, musky smell. I swore that he was talking just to me as I listened to the clacking sounds his teeth made on the metal bit.

All of a sudden Hidalgo lurched, whinnied, and took off down the hill at full gallop. I was scared shitless! I didn't have a clue what to do except to clutch at his mane. I managed to look back over my shoulder, my head jerking up and down as the horse kept up his clip. My parents and the other adults just stood there, waving their arms frantically and yelling instructions I couldn't hear. Adults were supposed to take care of things. Yeah, right. I looked back ahead and realized with terror that Hidalgo was heading for the front gate and the main road. Then I heard an echo of a horse's hooves, just slightly off from Hidalgo's, but going faster and faster. I saw that Carlos had closed in fast on my right, drawing his horse up alongside of mine, totally in charge. He reached over and grabbed Hidalgo's reins, bringing him to a jerking stop right before the gates and the buzzing traffic. Hidalgo whinnied and threw his head back like he was pissed off. Guess he was sorry he didn't get to mangle the irritating little *gringa* on his back. Carlos turned us around and slowly led my horse back up the hill, smiling at me the whole time. All I could do was look back into his black velvet–trimmed eyes. I was fiercely independent, even then, and I rarely let anyone take over: But I let him.

That was it. I was in love. It was like one of those heinous chick flicks and this boy had saved me. I stared at him all the way back up the hill, and later, behind the barn, I kissed him on his cheek. Nothing major; I was only five after all. It was a sweet, simple kiss, and I spent the next year thinking about it . . . and him. I announced to my mother one day that I was going to marry Carlos. "That's wonderful, honey!" she said, placating me. But she didn't understand.

With each visit I saw less and less of Carlos. By the time we were teenagers he was rarely around when I was in PR. He was always off on a trip to Europe, or at a party in Ponce. I grew angry at him too. Once again someone I really cared about wasn't there. But it didn't really matter; with time I thought less and less about him. He went off to boarding school and wasn't home much, and I started getting into bad boys and rock 'n' roll. We didn't get in touch again until he moved to Chicago last year. His mother called my mother to hint around about how nice it would be if I were to show him the city. I'll never forget that first day when he showed up at our loft.

The last time I'd actually laid eyes on Carlos I was almost fourteen, so imagine my surprise when I opened the door and saw this tall, lanky, spiky-haired guy wearing a massively cool floor-length trench and hoop earrings. But the eyes . . . in the eyes I saw my kind childhood friend.

"Carlos? Is that you?"

"Leni, *amiga mía,* you look great!" He stepped forward through the doorway and hugged me warmly. I've never been good with hugs, so I gently eased back and held him at arm's length.

"Whoa, boy! What the hell happened to you? You look like a tall Robi Draco Rosa!" I said, genuine surprise and affection in my voice.

"Well, what about you, Leni." As he looked me up and down with his dark eyes, it was clear I was getting sized up—but not in a sleazy way. Suddenly I felt my face flush, and I wondered if pale punk makeup, kohl-rimmed eyes, and purple lipstick would help hide me. What the hell was that about? "*Bella* and cool, the best combination! I bet you're breaking hearts all over Chicago, *amiga!*"

After Carlos said hello to my mother in a totally gallant and old-style way (he actually made both of us blush when he told her how I obviously got my beauty from her—the boy always could charm the paint off the walls), we headed off to a tour of the downtown music scene, bypassing all the hinky tourist traps that our parents expected us to visit. Turned out we liked the same music, fashions, and movies. It was like no time had passed since we were kids and hung out in the yard at his father's house. I could talk to him about anything. Since then we get together a couple of times a month to hang out and listen to vinyl, and remixes of the Ramones, Dead Kennedys or Black Flag on CD. We start by raiding the refrigerator, eating my mother out of house and home, grab a couple of sodas, and then head to my room. There we lie, side by side on the floor, shoulder-to-shoulder, rolling back and forth to the music, singing along with the songs, laughing at each other's mistakes with the lyrics, smiling into each other's eyes. It is so easy to hang with Carlos. He knows where all the skeletons are buried, and he gets my story, you know?

I stop walking halfway between the girls and the stage and take a long look at this guy I've known practically my whole life, and I suddenly see him as the Sister Chicas must see him. He's lean, but built through the shoulders, shorter than Jack and more wiry, but strong-looking nonetheless. Tight black jeans draw my eye to his runner's thighs and flat stomach. And ya gotta love the black Timberland boots. He's wearing a Che Guevara T-shirt with the sleeves ripped off, showing off his muscled, bronze arms. His thick, black, wavy hair is longish, and it occasionally falls across those brown eyes fringed with long lashes. The whole look is completed with silver hoop earrings that occasionally glint from beneath his hair.

Whoa.

Guess I haven't really noticed what a babe he's become. When did that happen? I feel like I am five again, and I have the sudden urge to kiss him, and this time not on the cheek. I look at his lips, full and deep red, like an apple. I wonder what it would be like to taste the edge of his lips; would they be salty or sweet? Would he close his eyes or look straight into my mine? I shiver and shake my head to clear it, start walking again, and greet the band. "Thanks hugely for the set; that was incredible! We totally yanked their chains!"

"No problem, Leni. We haven't had that much fun since we sneaked in the Sex Pistols' 'God Save the Queen' at Pedro's *abuela*'s seventy-fifth birthday party!" Carlos chuckled.

"Yeah, bro, I thought *Abuela* was going to flatline for a minute there!" Pedro added. We all laugh and I tell them that they got the gig. Carlos puts his arm around my shoulder and we start to talk about the details with the rest of the band. I can feel the warmth and hardness of his body through my leopard-print sweater. I can't really listen with his body touching mine, and I try really hard not to blush. In my nervous excitement I look over at my girls, only to find that Grachi and Taina are staring at us. And smiling. What are they up to? The conversation winds down, and I reluctantly pull away from Carlos. I give him a kiss on the cheek and the rest of the guys a high five, and walk over to the Sister Chicas.

"What? What is up with you two, anyway? Geez, haven't you ever said hello to anybody?" I sit down next to Grachi, reach over, and teasingly slap Taina's thigh. Grachi slaps me right back.

"Oh, come on, *chica*! Didn't you see the way Carlos looks at you? It's really too bad you have that ridiculous 'No Latino dating' policy. The poor guy doesn't stand a chance!" Grachi says smugly with her arms across her chest.

Suddenly I'm embarrassed that I noticed his looks earlier and got off on having his arm around my shoulder. I scoff, "Carlos? He's just a friend. His parents were friends with my parents for, like, ever. You know."

Taina pipes in with, "Leni, he is un *papi chulo! ¡Míralo, chica!*"

"Listen, *chicas,* it's not that kind of vibe, okay? We're just friends!" But Grachi was not about to let me off that easy.

"But *mi'ja,* a friend is the best person to date. Especially after the string of Goths and punkers you've gone through! Besides, it would be so nice to go out with someone who understands where you come from. Where your family comes from."

Something snaps. I hate this speech, and I can't stop myself from barking, "What, you mean a man like *Papi?* Or maybe Guillermo? Oh wait, I forgot . . . he wasn't exactly the love of your life, either!" The minute the words leave my mouth, I regret them. My mouth seems to have a mind of its own lately.

"How could you say that?" Graciela's eyes begin to fill with tears, and I know I've gone too far.

"I'm sorry . . . really I am. You and I . . . we're just two different people, okay?" I furiously try to backpedal, to make everything allright. "Look, Grachi, I'm not like you. I just want to have some fun . . . you know, fun with some fringe benefits. And that's just easier with Anglo club boys. Maybe you could use a little fun yourself, *corazón.* All work and no play . . . you know." I smile weakly, hoping Grachi isn't too pissed.

I can see her recovering her usual cool. She lifts her chin and straightens her shoulders and sighs. "It's okay. . . . Don't worry about me. I'm fine, really. But listen to me, Leni; all I'm saying is someday you might get tired of the 'boyfriend-of-the-week.' Maybe someday *nuestra gente* won't look so bad to you."

At that moment, again as if on cue, Carlos walks over to meet the girls. He flashes a warm smile, turns to Taina, and says, "You must be Taina! I've heard so much about you too. We can't wait to play your party!"

Taina shakes his hand and smiles back, distractedly saying something about how much she enjoyed their music. "Well, the second song, anyway," she specifies. They chuckle and turn to Grachi and me. Embarrassed, we have abruptly stopped our disagreement, but the tension is still there.

Carlos turns to Grachi. "You have got be Graciela. You're a writer, right? Leni's told me all about you. I need to tighten up some lyrics. Maybe we can get together sometime and talk shop."

Grachi's shoulders lower; she smiles and lets out a big breath. Carlos is good. Grachi replies, "That would be great. Maybe you, Leni, and I can talk music sometime. . . ." At this last statement she shoots me a look. I can see I should have told them about Carlos a while ago. But we all fall into easy conversation about the *quinceañera,* and I am happy to see that Taina is actually excited. Mission accomplished.

Grachi carefully excuses herself from the conversation and explains that she has to leave to meet her parents for dessert. She gives Taina an easy hug, hesitates for a second, then gives me one, too. Before she grabs her sweater, she whispers in my ear, "Think about what I said, *chica*," and we all watch her walk toward the exit.

We hear the factory door clank shut, and after a few minutes of getting time, money, and dates together, Taina adds, "I have to go too, Carlos. Thank you so much!"

In her excitement she gives Carlos a quick shy hug, and I call out, "Wait, Tai, I'll head out with you." I give Carlos a quick peck on the cheek, and the two of us grab our coats from the metal chairs. Taina and I walk out of the warehouse together in silence. Now that I have Taina alone, I figure it's the perfect time to fish around about the boy I saw her with on the street. I'm worried about her inexperience and the whole secretiveness about this. As we reach the sidewalk, I blurt out, "Taina, speaking of *papis chulos,* if you were to meet a guy whom you were really into, and you wanted to, you know, do it for the first time, you know that you could talk to me about it, right, *chica?* I mean, I could take you to see my friend Colleen at Planned Parenthood so you're sure to be protected."

Taina's hand goes up to cover her mouth again. Maybe the spring on her arm is broken or something.

"Oh, no, Leni! Not the birth-control lecture! I've heard you give that speech a hundred times to half the girls at school! What is up with you?"

At this I get serious. I can't help it. Something about this girl makes me protective. "Look, Tai, us sisters have to stick together, and I don't want you to become a statistic! Talk about a stereotype! How many *chicas* get knocked up at fifteen and spend their lives tied to some wannabe player who just wanted to get in their pants?"

Taina starts to squirm. "Okay, okay, *Leni!* ¡*Basta!* Enough! ¡*Ay, Dios mío!* You're starting to sound like Graciela! I know you feel strongly about this, but what brought this on? You know how I feel about waiting until I'm married."

At this point I realize that I'm about to tip my hand that I know about the mystery man, so I figure I better drop it. I don't want to put my Doc Marten–booted foot in my mouth a second time tonight. "It's cool. I just want you to know that I got your back . . . just in case. Okay?" I put my hand on her shoulder.

Taina stiffens and starts to say something and then stops herself, her eyes nervous and a little bit sad. It almost looks like she shakes something off.

"Okay, Leni. Look, I have to go. I have to . . . go somewhere. Thanks for hooking me up with the band." She starts to walk away, but at the last minute turns around, rushes back to me, and gives me a big *abrazo,* then scurries off toward the bus stop. I feel better, but once again I'm left standing on the sidewalk, wondering what is up with my Sister Chica. What was she about to tell me, but decided not to? Was it the boy? I worry about that girl, I really do. I want to talk to her about this guy, if that's what's going on, but I also understand not wanting to let people in on your stuff . . . I especially understand that! As I watch her disappear around the corner, hustling off with her coat collar pulled up around her neck, that beat-up old messenger bag banging on her thigh, I shrug and decide that I'd better just leave it alone. She'll come to me or Grachi if something big comes up.

I hope. . . .

7

TAINA

I have been sitting on my bed for what seems like an hour, my mind sifting through layers and layers of memory. But the dreaded moment has arrived: *Mami* wants me to model my dress for her. *"Taina? ¿Qué haces?* Put on your new dress and come down, please. I want to see you." God, what will she think? I pull open the closet, slipping the hanger off the rod as if I were a disrespectful child choosing her own switch off a tree for punishment. Unzipping the plastic, I watch the pale coral silk peek through a bit. I remember how much trouble it took to sneak the dress up to my room.

After Leni bought me the dress and we all separated, I had sneaked home. I was still buzzing from Yusef's kiss as I slipped through the restaurant's rear exit. I passed my mother, who was in the middle of an argument with Fernan the chef, both of their voices rising above the restaurant's busy din. I climbed the stairs to our apartment two or three steps at a time, avoiding their notice, and rushed into my room, shutting the door behind me with a click. I'll hide it, I thought and then quickly slid the dress inside the arms of my fat winter coat, the houndstooth print hiding the coral in its teeth, a tiger chomping on a flamingo. Every day since that afternoon, I've peeked at the dress behind its cover, my

fingers grazing its saffron softness. Last night, while I was brushing my teeth, steam from the hot water fogging up the bathroom
mirror, a poem started to happen in my head. My brain swam
with metaphors and images, the poem forming itself like a forest,
thick and green.

> A *plena* dancer is born
> dancing barefoot,
> circling island
> *plazoletas,* swerving her simple ruffle
> against *el Caribe*'s pearl ear. On a night
> the sea meets her moon, the *plena* dancer's
> dress is the lip of a conch whispering
> against sand and skin, a bit of coral
> caressing the earth's shoulders, a swirl of fabric
> a kiss telling the world its love stories.

"*Taina!*" *Mami* calls again.

"Okay, I'm coming!" I shout back. I unzip more and more of
the dress's plastic sheath, hearing the shell of the dress whisper
against the cover's skin, as if it had already been filled with a body.
I imagine two dancers moving together, the swish of the dancer's
skirt the movement of the sea against the curve of a boat. I begin
to slip the dress over my head. *Mami* will hate it, I think. She'd absolutely hate it. And she'll hate me for not listening to her.

"Taiiiinaaa!" my mother called, lengthening out the last A, as if
I had somehow forgotten my name. "Hurry up. The restaurant
will open soon and I still haven't cut the *tostones*. What are you
doing? Come down, please. And put on your new dress. I want to
see you."

As I pull up the side zipper to the strapless shift, I couldn't help
but begin to admire the girl in the mirror, the soft S of her shape
filling the silk against the cocoa of her skin. I suddenly didn't feel
fourteen nor fifteen but almost ageless, the dress stirring me toward new beginnings. I push back my hair, which was slowly beginning to get some kink back into it. Soon my mother would
traipse me back to Rosa's, where the scent of cheap drugstore per-

fume collided with no-lye relaxer and alcohol. I pin my hair into a loosely knit chignon, drawing out a few strands to frame my face. With one hand on my hip, I promise myself that I will do all I can to wear this dress to my *quinceañera,* no matter what.

I sigh as I make my way down the stairs. My imagination starts to run away with itself. What will happen when *Mami* sees me? Something in me dreams.

"*Ay, Dios mío! Que vergüenza! Qué has hecho, nina! Mi hija! No! Qué tipo de color!* Oh, my God! You look like a—I can't say it. I can't say it. A *puta! This* is the dress that Leni bought for you, that you let her buy for you! Blessed *virgen en the cielo.* What have I done to deserve this? I've been a good *mamá.* I bring you all the way from Puerto Rico so you can dress like a woman without shame? Oh, no. Oh. *Ay!* I'm going to have a heart attack. I feel my heart breaking. Right. Now." I picture my mother collapsing, dragging me down with her to the floor, where she would gasp one final request for my shaky salvation. "Ask God to forgive you, my little *nena,* and don't you dare wear that dress to my funeral."

Okay, last step. I see *Mami* around the corner of fleur-de-lis-wallpapered wall, her hands wrapped around a mug of *café con leche,* the white froth rising over its edge. It is the first time this week she is actually sitting down in a chair, resting. With her legs crossed, she knocks the tip of her bloodred pump against the steel table leg anxiously. *Clink-clink-clink.* The sound echoes in my chest, as if my own heart were mimicking the beat. Her hair is wrapped up in a small French bun, shiny with Luster's Pink Oil, the last vestige of what had once been a complicated daily beautification ritual. Seeing her at that table reminded me of a time when I was little and my mother was happy.

✧ ✧ ✧ ✧ ✧

Back when he was still around, *Papi* and I watched *Mami* from within her bedroom's door frame. I was seven then and I loved memorizing her every movement, the ways she primped her face and curled her hair before an outing. She looked like a painter, carefully lining her eyes, the kohl reaching the corner of her eyelids like an Egyptian princess. Afterwards, she'd swoop her hair up into a tight bun, even though *Papi* and I loved it loose. We loved the way her hair fell around her shoulders like a black shawl but she always complained about how hot the hair made her in the Puerto Rican sun. "One day, I'll cut it, just you see," she'd warn. *Papi* and I turned it into a game: who could stand in the doorway of my mom's room and watch her the longest. We could never out-last each other—*Mami* would never give us the chance. Though we could tell she was faking her annoyance, she'd send us out of the room, her manicured hands waving us away like gnats. But *Papi* and I would sneak back to her door anyway, the chunk of my young body playfully knocking back against my father's legs, the knobs of his knees poking my back.

"*Váyanse, mis cariños,* leave me be. With all your gawking, I'll never finish getting ready!" *Papi* and I would then noisily wrap our bodies around hers, my arms around her hose-covered calves, my face in the crepe de chine bathrobe *Papi* had brought back for her from Osaka as her engagement present. Back then I had always loved visiting her room, proudly eyeing the vanity table she kept meticulously dust-and fingerprint-free, perfume bottles standing like sentries amid the foundations and puffs, eyebrow liners and blush. Back then, before the move and the restaurant and *Mami*'s crazy rush, during those rituals, *Mami* lightly spritzed the curve of her neck with orange-blossom water, the *Mayaguezana* sun falling through the louvered windows, dousing all of us with warmth, *Mami*'s shadow silhouetted against the peach tile floor. *Papi* would lean down to me, whisper, "I wish your mother knew that all that stuff doesn't make her any prettier than she already is." But secretly, even at seven, I knew she wasn't doing all this for herself; she was doing it for him, for all those times *Papi* up and took off for weeks, even months on end, leaving *Mami*, me, and countless bills behind. *Mami* called the early days of his absence "boy vacations." On those days, she'd paint my toenails a brilliant red that made me feel as if I were a shorter version of my mother. Seemingly honoring some goddess of girlhood, *Mami* and I would play dolls on her queen size bed with the satin spread and take long, luxurious baths that smelled like mango. One day, on a surprise return from what he called his "secret venture," *Papi* found us nestled on the cool kitchen tile playing Crazy Eights.

"*Papi*'s home!" I squealed and dropped all the cards out of my hands, my curls bouncing up and down on my face as he bent, with a slight grunt, to scoop me up into his muscular arms. *My Papi's so strong,* I'd think, cozying up to his face with new stubble, the scent of sandalwood rising up to my nose.

"*Cariño,*" he'd whisper to my mother, but she didn't rise to kiss him. Instead she stood at the stove and turned her back to us, like I've seen all the soap opera wives do when they are really peeved with their husbands for whatever soap opera reasons. Usually, they never fought in front of me, their arguments drawn-out and muffled behind closed doors, outside the boundaries of my reach. But that day they didn't hold back.

My parents burst with emotion, first *Mami,* flailing her arms and punctuating her anger with sobs, then *Papi* raising his voice louder than I'd ever heard it, even louder than when we went to the baseball games at El Colegio Mayaguez to watch the San Ger-man Atléticos get smashed by the Mayaguez Indios. For the first time in my life, I saw *Papi* cry. His voice cracked the way a co-conut cracks when *Tío Dario* smacks it with machete for its juice.

"I know what this is all about. You're ashamed of me. You were ashamed then and you are now. You think I'm just another failure, another *negro,* like your father thought. Remember what he called me that day at your house when I asked him for your hand? I said, 'Don Gustavo, *amo a tu hija.* I'll take care of her.' And what did he say?"

My mother couldn't respond; her own voice seemed locked be-hind a weird grimace. They didn't see me standing behind them; they couldn't hear me sobbing. A day later, *Papi* was on the road again. With his suitcase in hand, he planted a nervous dry kiss on my cheek and one on my forehead, his face contorted like a twist tie around a bag of bread. I didn't know that would be the last time I ever saw him again.

"*Papi,* where are you going?"

"Taina Sol. Promise you'll be a good girl."

"Where are you going?"

"To find our fortune. To make us rich so you and your *mami* can have everything your hearts desire and love me even more."

"I don't want anything." Though that wasn't all the way true. I cherished the dolls he brought back from his excursions, figurines in their national dress: a plump Polish girl with braids and blinking blue eyes, a girl with a kente-cloth head wrap, a rag-doll girl from Haiti, and other girls from all the other places *Papi* said he'd traveled to "find our fortune."

So many times before he finally disappeared, Papi would call me to him and whisper, "*Chiquita*, here is some treasure I found for you." Then, he'd crack open his beat-up old suitcase and pull out from under his crisp shirts and neatly folded underwear dolls swathed in bathroom tissue; no box or special ribbon, just pink, white or blue Charmin. I'd clap excitedly and *Mami* would "humfph" at this father-daughter performance, as if she'd seen enough of the show and knew what came at the end: another long trip away and heady return, bearing gifts for his two girls, gifts to please, gifts to placate. It wasn't until later that I realized that was all my father could give me.

During the early part of their marriage, *Papi* had joined the U.S. Army. After two years in service, he fell off what he called an M-60 battle tank and slipped three disks in his back. After months of painful rehab and, later on, surgery, they retired him. I guess he didn't get enough money once he retired—he and *Mami* fought about not having enough all the time. It was then that he started to roam what he called the world. But *Mami* and I never really knew where he went: He never sent letters or called, unless he needed *Mami* to wire him money for a night's stay at a hotel. I'd always thought it silly to argue on the phone—but *Mami* and *Papi* made it look easy, *Mami* with her hands on her hips, as if the motion could will her husband's return; *Papi,* his voice on the other end of the line reaching loud and hard through the holes in the receiver toward her ear or her sympathy.

"*Mami,* let's call *Abuela* Moscoso. Maybe *Abuela* knows where he is," I'd offer, my hands trying to pull Barbie's pants down without yanking off her leg. The year before *Papi* left us, *Abuela* Moscoso had kindly hammered the leg back in place with a large black carpenter's nail. The hardware had made the leg difficult to manipulate, but at least I didn't have a legless Barbie for the other girls on Uvas Street to mock. We called *Abuela* Moscoso, but even she didn't know where her son took off to every few months or so, and when he finally left and didn't return, *Mami* never called *Abuela* again.

"*Papi*, stay here with me and *Mami*, please?" I couldn't let go of him, my fingers numb under the strength of my grasp, clutching to his pant legs so tightly I could feel the grooves in the denim skin.

"*Nena*, stop. You're acting like a baby. You have to be a big girl till I get back. Okay? Just till I get back." And that was that. Out the door he went, spare toothbrush, boar-bristle brush, and every last bit of clothing, everything he owned but me, stuffed into his ratty army duffel bag, slung over his shoulder like a body. Though he hadn't said it, I knew that was the last night I'd see him.

Later that night, after having been closed up in her room for hours, *Mami* called me to her, a sad cantina song from Carmen Delia playing on the turntable, her face stiff like a bed with military corners, her puffy eyes and small smile holding her heart away, her voice turned down to an unusual stillness. "*Hijita*, come here. Let me look at you." I would step closer, tears pushing through the blink-back barrier I had erected against crying. "*Ay, nena, no llores*, please. We can't both cry. Here." Then, in a gesture of kindness that pushed a toothy grin through my tears, she dotted behind my ears her prized Coco Chanel. It was the Coco Chanel used only on special dinner-and-dancing nights *Papi* would drive the old Toyota Camry down the long, swirling, potholed highway to the capital's San Juan Hotel and Casino. *Mami* always looked joyful when she wore it. Like *Mami* and me, Coco was one more thing that would fail to bring *Papi* back.

✧　✧　✧　✧

Knocked back to the present, I straighten my body out as if my spine were a piece of pipe. *Mami* hasn't heard me come down the stairs, the hem of my dress brushing against my ankles. Turn around, I think, turn around and look at me. I shuffle back and forth on my bare feet.

"*Mami,*" I whisper, my voice stumbling on the letters as if they were stuck to the ridges of my esophagus. I imagine the M and I clinging for dear life. She swivels quickly, her face a bright circle of expectation. But that look doesn't linger. Her face falls in disappointment, the way a hungry person will stare at a nearby empty vending machine. Finally what little hope she had collapses like a deck of soapy dinner plates in El Yunque's busy kitchen.

"*¿Qué es eso?*" Her face contorts with confusion, possibly disgust. I start to feel as if my magical, beautiful moire dress is tightening all around me. Instead of fitting me like a glove, it's too tight—-I can't breathe—-I can barely think. *Please,* Mami, *can't you see what I saw when I put it on the very first time?* Her eyebrows rise painfully, and as soon as I see that look I know *Mami* hates the dress and everything about the dress. Her Spanish bubbles, erupts out of her mouth, floods my ears with frustration. "*¿Qué has hecho, niña? ¿Yo no te mande a comprar un traje? ¡Yo no visto una cosa mas fea!*" She hasn't seen anything uglier, she says. Nothing uglier? Uglier than what?

"*Mami,* please. Why don't you like it? I really love this dress. I think I look pretty."

"Pretty! You look loose. All the stray dogs around this street are going to chase you if you wear that thing. Red? For a *quinceañera?*"

"No, it's not red; it's coral—just a little darker than pink . . ."

"Taina Sol, don't take me for a fool. That thing is red. Forgive me, but it's *puta* red. What would our family think about me if they saw you with that . . . monstrosity on? Your friends put you up to this, right?"

"I . . ." My words stick in my teeth. I want to cross my arms in front of my chest, but that would be disrespectful. Instead I shift back and forth on my feet.

"I know it must have been that Leni girl. *¿Dónde está su madre?* How could her mother let her walk around like that, *tatuajes* and all that green hair. But I can't do anything about her. And I have only one daughter. I've raised you better than this, *nena.* Do you realize how much I've worked to make up for all the damage your father did to this family? You want to ruin that? Become like your *prima* Linda? *Ay,* no—you will not wear that dress. You will stand in front of this community like a proud Guzman—"

"*Mami,* I'm a Moscoso, too," I say low, under my breath.

"Whatever you think you are, until you turn twenty-one you are my responsibility. I decide who you are! You will not make the mistakes I made. *Papá* was right, so right," she whistles between her teeth, shaking her head, a strand of her hair coming loose.

My blood boils. I hate it when she mentions *Abuelo*'s hatred of my father. Everyone in the family knew *Abuelo* hated *Papi* for being black. *Negro bembón,* he called him. How could *Mami* side with her father now, after so many years? I swallow hard.

"*Mamá,* it's only a dress. I haven't done anything wrong." As soon as these innocent words fly out of my mouth, I think of Yusef and what she would fail to see in him, his kindness, his sense of humor, his talent. Not to mention the warmed chocolate halo of his twisted locks, his thick biceps he wrapped around me in hello, the way his kiss left me smiling like I never had before.

"I'm not saying you've done anything wrong. But wearing this dress says you have. I won't allow it. Tomorrow it goes back. I'll have another dress shop take care of it. How much money did your so-called friend pay for this?" she asks, flicking the softly pleated band that wove like a series of ocean waves around the bottom.

"I'm not sure, *Mami.* She gave it to me as a gift." I am depleted of energy, as if a team of vampires had swept in and sucked out all of my blood.

"Well, then, tomorrow you will take the dress back and make sure your rich friend gets all her money back. *Punto ¿Me entiendes?*"

"*Mami,* please. Don't do this. I really want to keep it." It's no use. Begging never works with my mother. It's something I learned long ago, after countless disappointments—no Girl Scouts, no sleepovers with girls from school. In truth, the whole sweet fifteen seemed to be a farce. The guest list is a long line of names I don't recognize, mostly *Mami*'s business arrangements, acquaintances, and their bratty rich daughters. I had no long list of friends to invite, other than the Sister Chicas and Yusef.

Having moved to Chicago from Puerto Rico not too long ago, I was still nervous in class whenever called on, as if, at the mention of my name, every girl in the room were sizing me up, measuring me against what a "real" girl looks like. My knee-length pleated skirts, pink tailored shirts with scalloped edging, embroidered cardigans, and sensible loafers couldn't possibly stand up against high-heeled kiltie pumps and belly-baring half shirts with CUTIE sprinkled in glitter across the front. My dress—my *quinceañera* dress—this coral flirtation was the only item in my closet that said I was something different—different from the popular crowd of girls with their MTV fantasies. I love that Leni and Grachi were the ones to make this happen for me, help me blossom. And here was my mother ready and willing to pull the grass skirt right out from under me.

"*Ay, no,* I didn't come all this way from my island to see all my hard work thrown away in shame," *Mami* continues to fuss. She presses her hand against the table, as if trying to push its legs through the floor. "I want to be able to hold my head up when I walk with all the *Americanos* on this street. You will do as I say if you want this *quinceañera* to happen. I can still cancel it. It'll break my heart, but I promise you I will cancel the whole thing, the church, the priest, the ballroom at *La Reina Borinqueña*. I'll do it if I have to."

I can't believe she's saying this. *Mami* had already bought her own outfit, a baby-pink pantsuit dotted with a miscellany of sequins, a dress made by Mirta, her designer friend. She had already ordered the pink-and-white lily centerpieces, and arranged for the food out of El Yunque's staples, typical Puerto Rican fare, of course. Crab stew in its *mofongo* bottom, *yuca* and plantain crisps with romaine and avocado salad, and roasted pork tenderloins with a side of *arroz con gandules*. All to be topped off with a tier of *tres leches* cakes, each layer crowned with a sugar ganache of lilies in different stages of their bloom. *Mami* had not asked me to help her design the menu. What I want doesn't matter.

And let's not forget all Leni and Grachi had done: Leni had already talked to a band and Graciela had asked for time off from work. And what about Yusef? How ironic—the people I love don't know each other! *Mami* would never accept my having a boyfriend, especially a boyfriend like Yusef. What if he reminds her of my father? That was definitely not a good thing. And the Sister Chicas . . . they'll never understand my lying to them in the first place. God! What am I going to do? I've really messed things up. We couldn't cancel it now—there's no way I would let her cancel now. I won't cry. I can't cry. To stop the crowd of tears pushing for spill space, I bite my bottom lip and look down at my bare feet. The dress skirt swooshes at my calves, and I swear I see my skin turn the same coral shade, as if I were a mermaid at the end of my shore leave, called back to the sea. There is no turning back. Sometimes you have to pick and choose your battles. I give in.

"I'll take the dress back tomorrow, *Mami*. I'm sorry I upset you."

"Thank you, *hija;* you know I want the best for you. Only the best."

I nod, the tears finally welling over the bridge of my face, my mind caught on one slowly fading image: Yusef, his arm wrapped around me, the dress's jewel skin hugging both of us as we swirl and swirl and swirl.

✧ ✧ ✧ ✧ ✧

"What? Return the dress?! You have *got* to be kidding me!" Leni throws her arms up in the air, then smacks them back down onto her hips. In her exasperation, her bright green Ramones T-shirt held together by safety pins slips off her shoulder. I struggle to not pull it back up into place, so instead I slip my hands onto my lap, my fingers fidgeting nervously.

Don Ramiro shuttled our dishes back to the kitchen. I had spent the entire night worrying over the dress. If the world made worrying an Olympic sport, I'd surely get the gold. After *Mami* laid down her law, I dragged my weary body upstairs and threw myself on my bed, facedown. Fearing all of Chicago would hear me, I clutched my grandmother's afghan of pink crocheted rosettes to my mouth, bit down on the acrylic-wool blend, and screamed. *I hate her, I hate her!* Of course, I don't really. At least, not enough to tell her the truth or change the course of things. I just want *Mami* to be okay with the things I want, not to fight me at every turn. It isn't fair!

"I'm serious; *Mami* insists . . . I . . . can't wear the dress."

"Man, your mom's got a stick up her ass," Leni huffs. Grachi throws her an exasperated look.

"Okay, I'll get a grip. I'm just wondering why she has to screw with Taina so much?" Turning away from Grachi, and back to me, there is one wicked look on her face. She points her finger at me and says, "Oh, wait a minute. You just have to wear that dress now."

"*Cálmate*, Leni. Let her tell us what happened." Graciela put her arm around my shoulders and squeezes a little. I look at both of them, one sitting with her hands on her hips, the other looking motherly at me, her no-nonsense cropped hair shining in the Rinconcito light. I need them. I really do.

I start from the beginning, unearthing truths about my life they might have already known or assumed: my father's slow desertion, my mother's crazy need for perfection, her fight to control everything, even down to what kind of underwear I wore. But I don't stop there. No, I keep going, down to my shyness, even talking about our first meeting, the poem sweating in my palms, the wish to bubble up and speak to them in that square classroom, with the painted crank windows making the room stiff and hot. I even tell Leni and Grachi about Liliana and Freda, those ghosts that haunt me. Graciela and Leni sit quietly, letting me talk, letting all the words wash over me. Part of me feels like the room opened up a hole I could dump all of my anger into. I rattle on and on until I hit on Yusef, the fifty-six bus encounter, the tuxedo, the kisses, the fact that I'd secreted him from *Mami*, who knew nothing about my first and new love.

"So this is the boy I saw you kiss that afternoon near the dress shop," Leni blurts out.

"Kiss near the dress shop? Leni, you were spying on me?"

"Well, not really spying. That word is soooo, you know . . . uh, you know, negative. . . . I just happened to catch the two of you. Hey, I wasn't making out in a public place, okay? Grachi, come on—help me out here."

"I'd plead the Fifth if I were you." Graciela lets out a rich bottom of a belly laugh, and it makes me laugh too, much of the stress starting to slip out of my bones and into the air.

"All right, all right, chill, *chicas*," Leni says, shrugging her shoulders as if she were giving up. "You got me. But I will not apologize for making sure my little sis is okay. It's not like we ever met him before. . . . By the way, why didn't you share this scrumptious tidbit with us before?"

"I don't know, Leni. I guess I wanted to know if it was real. Half the time I'm with him, I feel as if I were dreaming."

"Besides Cute Boy being just that—a boy—and your Mom being a complete pain, why would she be so pissed?" Leni asks.

"She's not a pain, really," I say, suddenly feeling a sense of protectiveness, though I knew Leni didn't dislike my mother. "There's some weird family thing on my mom's side about how my dad was black and poor. They thought he couldn't hold a job and be a good husband and father."

"How do they treat you?" Grachi puts her hand on mine.

"Oh, fine. I mean, besides the whole kinky hair issue, they want to make sure I marry someone who is not like my dad. They're so full of . . . crap!" Both girls stare at me in disbelief. I am not sure if they're shocked because of what I'd just told them or because I said 'crap' but I continue anyway. "They were really mean to my Dad. They didn't hide how much they hated him, even in front of my mom and me. I think he just got fed up. I don't know. I'm not sure if that's what's going to be the problem with Yusef, you know? I'm really scared to find out what my mom thinks."

"So will we meet this Yusef before the party?" Graciela interrupts the difficult moment, changing the subject. She nudges me with her elbow, a mischievous grin on her face.

"I don't know. I'm not sure seeing him is the right thing to do anymore. If *Mami* didn't have a massive coronary about the dress, meeting Yusef will surely kill her."

"So you're gonna kill her a little. She'll get over it. I mean, your mom's a bit intense. Okay, understatement of the century, but she's not going to hate Yusef. I mean, unless he's a serial murderer or a rodeo clown, I think she'll like him," Leni quips.

"I think Leni's right," Grachi agreed. "It might help to talk to her about it, *mi amor*."

I couldn't do it, not just yet. My mom had been through too much the past few years. Though everything in me fights against her control, part of me realizes that she didn't need me pushing her buttons. I muster a grin for my two best friends. The tension begins to wash away, down from my shoulders toward my hands, still cradling the large white dressmaker's box that houses the sweet coral temptation of my fleeting freedom.

"Taina, the night's coming soon. Think about how Yusef will feel—you'll break his heart," Graciela offers. And she's right—Yusef doesn't deserve being someone's secret.

"God, no, I . . . don't want to do that. I . . . I really like him so much. I just . . . don't know what to do."

"Well." Grachi's hand shifts through the flurry of croissant crumbs flaking the white El Rinconcito tablecloth. "Keep the dress . . . there has to be a way to make this work out."

"Right! Somebody's gotta wear it, and it won't be me!" Leni pipes in, and we all roar with laughter, remembering that day in the dress shop, standing in the racks and rows of pastel and candy-colored taffeta, the entire store looking like a box of saltwater taffy. I am suddenly relieved, sitting there in El Rinconcito with the sisters I'd never had, blinking streetlights reflected against the restaurant's windows, the end of twilight fading into blue night.

✧ ✧ ✧ ✧

"Where are they?" I can tell from the way *Mami* is crimping her purse strap that she is at her wits' end. La Reina had been reserved for the *quinceañera*'s rehearsal on a Tuesday two weeks before the big day. *Mami* had excused me from school so we could visit Father Canton at Sacred Heart and make sure all the details for the morning ceremony were set. While we waited for Father Canton to return to his office, *Mami* turned to me and asked, "So, *nena*, your friends are meeting us tonight at La Reina, is that right?"

"*Sí, Mami*. Graciela's leaving right from work and Leni'll be at home, so they should be there on time."

My girls would never let me down, I had thought then, sitting there in the priest's wood-lined office, an orange wave of affection for the Sister Chicas cresting in my chest.

But here I am now, biting my nails down to the quick, that same orange wave now crashing against my heart, beating it back into fear. Both Leni and Grachi are moving into dangerous territory. It's almost eight and both are late. The salon attendants are already starting to lift and stack the pristinely white French café chairs back against the walls. I miss Leni and Graciela horribly. I miss Yusef, that caramel smile of his beaming down on me. Right before the rehearsal is to start, *Mami* introduces me to Mario, the son of Mr. Rosti, an Italian barber in their neighborhood.

"Taina, Mario going to be your *caballero* for tonight."

"*Mami*—"

"Well, you don't expect to dance your *valsa* with me, do you?" She laughs, straightening my shirt collar.

So Mario had been enlisted—more likely kidnapped. I am going to have my first waltz with Mario, who looks as if his father had cut his hair, comb-straight black, perfectly parted down the middle. New-car shiny. He smiles and braces glimmer back at me. His blue eyes do too. Yeah, well, he's nice but he's no Yusef. No one is like Yusef.

At eight o'clock everyone is there, except for the girls (and Yusef, of course). At this point I am thinking, *How ridiculous this whole party idea is! I'm no different. I'm just going from fourteen to fifteen. Who gives a holy crap! I'm still* Mami's *little girl and Papi's . . . whatever.* I feel my chest rise and fall like a racehorse leaning toward the finish. I'm growing angry but can say nothing, nothing to *Mami*, to Mirta, to Ramon and Lupe, who have gone off to sit on fold-out chairs outside of everyone's view. *Nobody takes me seriously,* I think, *and the three people who do aren't even here!*

Smile big, really big, that's what they teach you. Smile and wait for Graciela and Leni to arrive. Smile and wait. When they still don't come through the door, *Mami* whispers through clenched teeth, "Your girlfriends are very irresponsible, Taina."

Ramon and Lupe are dressed in their El Yunque red velvet vests and black slacks, acting as stand-in *caballeros,* lords for the evening at $6.50 an hour. Sr. Milagros the photographer and Mirta are there to soothe Mrs. Teresa Moscoso's nerves and see to her every wish, forgetting I am the *quinceañera's dama*. Except for Leni and Graciela (and Yusef, of course), everyone who needs to be there is there; even the butcher, the baker, and the candlestick maker are at attention, following all of my mother's instructions. What about me? Where am I in all this? It's my friggin' party!

Mami and I have not been friendly to each other since our fight. Yesterday I found a new dress on my bed after returning from school. Ugly with a big U. It was a poufy chiffon Cinderella-style dress in torpedo-stiff Spanish lace, the skirt and bodice pocked with tiny pearl buttons. It reminded me of those poor little confirmation dresses. I hate it! I was surprised she didn't choose white patent-leather flats to complete the whole picture. I hadn't even been scheduled for a fitting, so unfortunately (or, in my mind, fortunately) the dress felt awkward, pinching in some places, too loose in others, rubbing against my skin. This thing didn't perfectly hug me the way that the coral *plena*-like dress caressed my figure. I should have taken a pair of scissors to this ugly lace explosion.

Okay, that's it! The Sister Chicas are thirty minutes late. My mother can't take much more and I've finally gone crazy. The way her coiffed hair is slowly curling around her right ear, I can tell *Mami* is just about to explode.

"*¡Ahí tienes!* How many times have I warned you to be careful about who you pick to be your friends! *¿Muchísimas veces, no?* Do you realize how embarrassing this is? Taina?"

"*Mami,* I'm sure Leni and Grachi can explain. Maybe Graciela couldn't get out of work on time, or Leni, uh, Leni . . . I don't know. Something must have happened. They'll explain when they get here."

"Explain? Explain what? That I have wasted my time and money? I closed the restaurant tonight to do this!" At this point everyone is looking as my mother and I exchange words, especially the banquet coordinators, who have finished stacking the chairs and pushing the many round particleboard tables toward the wall.

"That's not fair, *Mami.* This whole thing was your . . ." I can't get a breath to continue; the words clog up in my throat like hair in a bathroom sink.

"Say it; you want to blame me for this. Go ahead. You're not the first to lay blame, *hijita. Ay, no, a mi no me vengas con eso.* Your friends are your friends. They aren't mine. You chose them." She is right. You can choose your friends but you cannot choose your mother. I keep these words in my mouth, angry words boiling under my tongue, hot and hurtful words scalding my heart. I feel them turn over and over, looking for a way to escape.

"*Tere, ya, déjala.* She's nervous. This is supposed to be a happy time—for both of you." Mirta coos, resting her hand on my mother's shoulder. I can almost hear my mother's thoughts: Neither of us is sure what happy is at this point.

I hear the rustling of plastic and turn to see Graciela sheepishly looking at us, her hand rolling in that self-conscious way she has of getting a thought out of her head and into the air.

"Taina, Mrs. Moscoso, I'm so sorry. I was at work and then I was at the train and then . . . I'm never late like this—"

My mother raises her hand. "Graciela, please. Don't explain anything. The night is over. This . . . rehearsal . . . is . . . done." Then *Mami,* in an uncharacteristic move, turns her back to Graciela. I couldn't believe it. My mother can be a lot to deal with sometimes, and annoying in her rush to make everything perfect, but she is never rude. She's all about manners. *Ética,* she says, is what people will always remember about a woman. Graciela, Mirta, and I stare at her, dumbstruck.

"*Mirta, ve voy.* Home. I'll talk to you later, *cariño,* is that okay?" Though *Mami* plants a kiss on her cheek, Mirta can't say a word; she stands tree-stiff, shock in her eyes. There is a delay of five horribly long seconds before Mirta acknowledges *Mami's* statement with a nod. Then *Mami* turns to me. "Taina, get your things."

So things were going to be like this, were they? Order, order, order. I can't take this anymore. Silently I grab my bag, the white Disney horror that is to be my sweet-fifteen dress, and suddenly rush out of the parquet-floored room, past an openmouthed Leni, a blur in black lipstick, studded choker, rubber bracelets, and this

week's dyed hair. I rush out alone, not really sure where I am going, down what street, in what direction, but I don't care. I don't
care. I keep going, down the long stretch of red carpet and mirrored hallway to the glass revolving doors and into the cool air
outside. Tears careen down my face and collect on my jacket like
a pile of lemmings falling off a cliff. Where am I going? Where at
this time of night? Not home. With Leni and Graciela inside La
Reina Borinqueña, I know only one place I can go. I walk briskly
toward a phone booth, jiggling my pockets for change. I hope he's
home. I really hope Yusef is home.

I know what I've done and this time there is no *Tía* Monse to
save me from straying. Though I couldn't see what was going on
in *Mami's* head, I imagine it isn't pretty. She probably thinks I've
gone off to take drugs in some dank corner of the city, huddled
around derelicts and budding criminals. I've got to get to Yusef's
house. I turn around and realize I'm lost. Nothing looks familiar
in the dark. Fourteen and in the big city. I don't even know how
to get around the Loop. Leaving the La Reina in such a flurry of
tears and fat Spanish lace, I blindly fall into the neon night with
nothing but my ballet-flat feet. The dress is getting heavier and
heavier in my arms and I have no sense of direction whatsoever. I
look at my watch—it's close to nine. I've been aimlessly walking
for about forty-five minutes. "Where am I? This looks like I'm in
the *jurutungo!*" I worry. How far have I run? Which direction
should I go? If only I can get to a payphone. Ah, there! I spot a
payphone nestled on a brick wall close to a man huddled against
the cold. I move toward it and nervously press Yusef's digits. My
fingers stiffen up. Five rings and no answer. I hang up and peer
around me. A group of boys in baggy jeans with their plaid box-
ers showing skulk past me. They look me up and down, their eyes
lingering on the white lace ballgown I practically drag along the
pavement. This should make *Mami* furious, I think. Disobedient
fourteen-year-old girl mugged in a lost corner of the city, I imagine tomorrow's headlines will read. The boys turn to look at me
wearily. I know they think I look like a freak—birthday cake
dress and all. "Hey, can you guys tell me how to get from the blue
line to the green line?" I ask, my voice perched on its last chord of

calm. I am not going home—I don't care what my mother thinks. One of the boys, sporting a blue-black baseball cap with the letters NY intersecting at the limbs, steps up to me, real close, his face near mine.

"Yeah, you got a ways to go, baby. Howz 'bout I show you the way?"

"Hey, Rigo, step off," said another, his eyes hidden behind sunglasses. If I had had an older brother, he would've been him, minus the baggy jeans and untied sneaks. His curly black hair peeks out from under his baseball cap and a fine nose flares at the nostrils as if he were breathing heavy. He has a long neck around which five long glass beaded necklaces shine in their alternating colors: green and white, blue and white, black and red, red and white, green and orange, yellow and orange. He smiles big and says, "Listen, walk five blocks down that way, past the bakery. There you'll see the blue line. Just transfer to the green line at Clark and Lake. That's the Loop. It'll take you where you're going."

"Thanks, really." I whisper with relief. He nods and they all continue on their way down the broken boulevard of liquor stores and check-cashing places. Looking around me, I gather my dress again in my arms and begin stepping towards the dimming light of the *Panaderia* El Trevino, it's night shift crew stepping silently through its glass doors.

"Hey!" the boy I thought could be my older brother breathlessly calls out to me. "Hey, how old are you? The truth, right?"

"I turn fifteen soon."

"You can't walk alone. I'll walk with you. By the way, I'm Jake."

"What about your friends?" I ask, distractedly.

"What about them? They can find their way. You can't." Though shielded behind his shades, I can tell he's grinning with his eyes. I thank him gratefully and we walk towards the metro. It's a pleasantly brisk walk, though Jake doesn't talk very much; still, every so often he looks up and beams at me, as if I'd said something witty or ingenious.

"I'm Taina. Hey, I like your necklaces. Why do you wear so many?" I ask Jake.

"You've never seen these before? Come on. Where are you

from? Each eleke represents a God that protects me. The blue and white one is for Yemaja, green and orange for Oshun, red and black for Eleggua, the god of the crossroads. You needed that one tonight," he laughed. At the end of the journey, Jake holds out his hand. I take it and thank him with a hug. Even though the lace monstrosity fills my arms, I step up the stairs to the platform feeling a million pounds lighter. Now if I could only get a hold of Yusef.

✧ ✧ ✧ ✧ ✧

Patricia meets me at the door and peers at me quizzically, noticing my tear-streaked face. But I expertly play it off, saying something about how the cold autumn air made me tear up. "It's my allergies," I lie. But I know she knows better but graciously does not pry further. Instead, she shows me to the large foyer, holding my hand affectionately (something my mother hadn't done in a very long time) and leads me to the living room. Patricia leaves me, climbing the stairs to the second floor, most likely to Yusef's room to let him know I am downstairs. Sitting there, in the plush chenille of the sectional sofa, I suddenly feel weird . . . ashamed. What am I doing in his living room so late at night, my wrinkled dress bag in hand making my forearms sweat? All I can think is how Yusef was going to come in the room and think, "God, what a flake! What a nut-job. Forget her!"

"Hey, did you try to call? We just got home from dinner at a friend of my dad's. I saw two missed calls but there weren't any messages." A brilliant smile stretches across Yusef's face. It doesn't hurt that he has dentists for parents, I think. Suddenly all my worries fly off, like a fly when you slap it away from a plate of food. For a brief moment, a blip of time, I forget about my mother, my father, and the *quinceañera* that had sparked the various *fracasos*.

"Something's wrong," he asks, sitting next to me. I so want to grab him in that moment, huddle against the wide-angle of his chest, let the stupid Sweet Fifteen dress crumple on the floor like a dead white satin animal. But I hold back shyly.

"Oh, nothing. Just drama at the rehearsal. Graciela and Leni were really late and *Mamí* pitched a fit. I think she was right to be upset but not angry. Sometimes, she just doesn't let up. She's not like your mom."

"My mom? Ha. My mom's no piece of cake." He laughs as he says this, throwing his head back against the sectional sofa's creamy fabric. I look at him quizzically. "Taina, she's a mom. I mean, she's cool on some things but I have to stay within certain dotted lines, too." I secretly wonder which "dotted lines" Yusef had strayed away from in the past. There is so much I want to know about him, so much I want to learn.

"Yeah, but still, she gives you a lot of room to do the things you want."

"So she's not making me have a *quinceañera*," he says, his mouth methodically spelling out each syllable to get it right. Pleased with his attempt, he again grins. "It's not like either of them let me go crazy. Listen, two years ago, I had a chance to go to Tangiers with Chris, a friend of mine. Mom was like 'no.' So, I pitched a fit for a good couple of days, arguing that in many countries all over the world, I would be considered an adult. I mean, I was paying for everything. Still, no-go. You would have sung the theme to *Law and Order*, I did such a good job defending my case. Even Dad backed down. But it didn't take with Mom. Uh-uh."

"So what did you do?" I ask, looking up into his cocoa eyes. By now, he is holding my hand in his, his thumb unconsciously rubbing my palm's supple patch of skin.

"What could I do? Nothing but suck it up. Not that I spoke to either of them for a couple of days. Spent a lot of time slapping paint on canvas, painting my frustration out. Might have been some of my best work that year." At this I nod, thinking about all the times I'd spent with the Sister Chicas at El Rinconcito, spending those magical Thursday afternoons away from my mother's prodding, sipping tamarind juice and chatting away with the girls, reading them poems from Lucille Clifton and Judith Ortiz Cofer. I tell Yusef about those Thursdays at Don Ramiro's place and he nods softly, his dreadlocks catching the light from the Tiffany-style floor lamp leaning above his head.

"Do they know about me yet?" he whispers, eyes glowing with a hope he can't keep secreted. In his eyes, I see all the pain I am causing him, how much in danger I am of losing him.

"Oh, yes, I told them all about you!" The words rush out of me like a dog after a soup bone. "They're really excited to meet you the night of the *quinceañera*. Actually, um, Leni already sort of knows you."

"Huh? How?"

"She spied us kissing one afternoon near your tuxedo shop."

His eyes open up wide in surprise. "No way! You serious? And she never said anything?"

"Well, I hadn't said anything so she figured we were keeping it hush for the time being."

"Oh." He pauses, eyes suddenly falling to his lap. He keeps holding my hand, only this time the grip tightens slightly and he stops caressing my palm. "What about your mother?"

"My mother? She doesn't even know where I am right now." I swallow hard. He clenches his teeth, hearing the answer in my silence.

"Taina . . . Running away from home isn't exactly the way to get her to know me."

"I'm sorry—I just. . . . there's so much. . . ."

"Think about how I'm feeling for a minute, would ya? What am I supposed to do the night of your birthday party? Just show up?" Sarcasm rings throughout each word. His sardonic tone is unfamiliar; it clings to the air between us like bad breath.

"No, of course not. I mean, I'm going to talk to her. I'm just waiting for the right time. Please, Yusef. Don't be angry at me." He lets out a long breath between his teeth and shakes his head, as if shaking away his irritation. We both sit silently for a time, each half-expecting the other to say something that would crack the ice. I still want to kiss him, maybe even more so. But it seems the moment has come and gone.

"Yusef, I think it's time you take Taina home. Her mother must be concerned," Patricia calls from the stairs. He and I stand up and walk out of the warm living room towards his mother's lilting voice. Though a muscle in our relationship had strained itself close to tearing, I am relieved Yusef has not let go of my hand.

"Okay, Ma."

"Take my car, please, and be careful. It's late." Patricia blows us a kiss good night and then traipses up the wide chestnut brown stairs towards her bedroom. I can see the light of a flickering television as Mr. Clarendon laughs at Jay Leno's jokes, each laugh calling his wife into their room, her "okay, okays" lacing her slight Jamaican accent.

Yusef maneuvers the damp streets towards home in silence, weaving down Milwaukee Avenue towards the corner restaurant with its neon Closed sign. I can't tell if the blinking neon welcomes me home or sends me a warning in its hard red light, so I close my eyes and do a quick prayer to *La Virgen del Cobre*: Please let my *Mamí* have gone to bed. Please let her not be waiting up for me. Gracias, *Virgencita*. Amen. Opening my eyes, I notice we have stopped on the side street. Yusef eyes me quizzically. "Are you okay?"

"Yeah, I'm just tired," I lie, again, though I was slightly worn out from the day's chaos. I am not sure how to handle all of this, how I can summon up the nerve to talk to my mother or to the Sister Chicas. Even talking to Yusef seems painful, though I still really yearn to be held by him, to kiss him under the bluish lamplight, giving Ashland Avenue a painterly quality.

"Well, you should get inside. Come on," he mumbles, turning off the car's ignition and stepping out into the night. He comes around to my side and opens the door, wide. It creaks like an old hinge and I am shocked how the sound seems to swallow the cool gulf streaming between us. I grow sadder and sadder every minute, feel it sink into my marrow. We move towards the building's side entrance, a small motion light illuminating our faces in the doorway that would lead to the restaurant's mudroom and the staircase to the upstairs flat. I fiddle with the key, all the while looking at him, turning the cold metal over in my hands, feeling the teeth against my fingers like the teeth of a dull paring knife. Though Yusef stands in front of me, he doesn't say a word, his hands deep in his jacket's pockets, eyes floating somewhere above my head. I don't want to talk. I just want him to hold me. But I can tell Yusef is frustrated, he has every reason to be. I have to make things right and soon.

Very soon. I fizz inside like a shaken plastic bottle of Coke. I can't help myself anymore. I reach out and pull down his windbreaker's polar fleece collar, bringing his face down towards mine. The skin of his lips is cold but I don't care and press closer to him, feeling his body suddenly warm to my touch, my shyness slinking away out of my body down the long edges of the avenue. I love the length of him, the way my arms outline his arms, his shoulders, the lines of neck. "I've never kissed him there," I think and the image suddenly flashes through my mind like a camera flash. I tenderly press my fingers against his neck, feel his pulse underneath my fingertips. In his surprise, Yusef stops breathing, but now, further into the kiss, he breathes hotly against my face, our lips opening, weaving together. Tonight, he doesn't taste like cherry Coke but I don't care. There's garlic somewhere there. I tangle my fingers in his hair. I forget we're outside. I forget we're outside my mother's house. I forget everything not involved in this generous kiss, this moment. We kiss so hard our teeth chink; we laugh softly at our eagerness, our clumsiness. As Yusef embraces me, his arms wrapped around my body tight like a new sweater, mine wrapped under his arms and around his back like a brace, I know I'll never revisit that kiss, that embrace, never feel that way again if I don't confront my mother and tell her the truth about my first love. My first real love.

8

Graciela

I can't even look at anyone else in the court; I'm beyond
mortified; I have to escape. Rushing as fast as I can
through the foyer of La Reina Borinqueña, the heels of my
boots click against the blue-and-gold tile floor. Leni's right behind
me, muttering something under her breath. I can hear her foot-
falls, the crackle of the garment bag, but I ignore all of it. I can't
say anything right now. I need to get some air; I need to calm
down and think of a way to make things right.

It's completely unacceptable—I know that; believe me, I do. I
was late, a half hour late! I should have been here on time, especially tonight of all nights. It's the final step before the big event,
time to see that everything's in its place, and I let my girl down.
Late! I can hardly believe myself.

I fell asleep on the train and missed my stop. It's the extra
hours at the bookstore and Casa Aztlán. Starting last month, ever
since accepting the Tilbrook residency, I've worked more hours,
volunteered more, trying to make up in advance for my absence
this summer. It's been hectic, but I've managed, keeping up with
everything—work, volunteering, school.

Now would not be the time to fall behind in my studies. *Mamá*
and *Papá* keep checking to see if it's too much, but I reassure

them, reminding them that I'm their daughter, after all, and it's only a little extra work for just a little while.

Even Jack's concerned. I nodded off at the movies last Saturday, but I told him I was fine, really. It feels like things are starting to unravel. But today after tutoring, I was . . . I was just . . . tired. It was so warm in the train, I closed my eyes for a second, just a second, resting my head against the window, drifting while the train swayed back and forth, back and forth. The last thing I remember was the blue line train entering the tunnel in the Loop. When I woke up I was three stop past Division. I jumped out and I hurried back as fast as I could, even running from the train stop to the hall, juggling my dress and my bag, hoping things weren't as bad as I thought.

I was wrong. So very wrong.

Everyone's head turned as I made my way to the bandstand, to Mrs. Moscoso and Taina. I heard the way she talked to my girl, the judgment in her voice ringing in my ears. Taina frantically tried to explain to her mother that this wasn't typical for me, that I was very responsible, while I was frantically trying to explain to Taina. I thought there was a chance we could smooth everything over once I explained what happened. But when my girl got an eyeful of Ms. Orange-Hair-Rubber-Bracelets, it was only a minute before she left in tears.

Heart pounding in my chest, I take a deep breath and push open the polished glass door, careful not to crush my dress, still carefully sheathed in plastic. For a split second Leni and I are a pair of shimmering faces, a gilded reflection. She starts to say something, but I look away. I need to get outside, into this cold Tuesday November night, and try to get a grip on what happened.

Division Street is awash with the yellowish glow of sodium streetlights overhead, and the wavering blue and red neon of the stores and restaurants that are strung together from Ashland Avenue to Humboldt Park. Block after block is lined by tire and clothing stores, right next door to restaurants, bars, grocery stores, all with names of towns in Puerto Rico. Names like Restaurant Jayuya, Utuado Auto Repair, Moda Feminina San Juan. Right now the street is fairly empty. Later on, there will be late-night bar-hoppers and couples out to dance, cars swarming up and down the street like a hive of bees.

The wind has whipped up and the sky above is inky blue. Ahead of me to the east, strands of low-hanging clouds wreath the tops of buildings in the Loop. I must look ridiculous, like some fugitive, practically running down the street, garment bag flapping in the wind. With a glance at my watch, I see it's eight thirty. *Dios mío*, we should've been halfway through rehearsal, reviewing dance moves with our dates or, in my case, a stand-in for Raoul. Right now I should be taking mental notes to tell my cousin, so we could practice when he got into town Friday. Instead I'm running like a bad dog with its tail between its legs to the wrought-iron doorway of Farmacía San Juan. *Gracias a la Virgen*, it's closed for the night, and I take some deep breaths to clear my head.

I'm praying that Leni will just clomp off to grab a taxi at the cabstand in front of La Concha, the nightclub across the street. *Just go home, Leni,* I silently plead, *go home and when I calm down, I'll call you and we'll work out an apology to Taina and her mother. Just run across the street and let the doorman flirt with you while you slide into a cab.*

No such luck. She follows me into the doorway instead, and the two of us stand not looking at each other, not speaking until she breaks the silence.

"Wow . . . they totally overreacted, didn't they? I swear, it's gotta be Valium time for the Moscoso family. Medication would really help them."

I pivot toward her, and she's fiddling with the button of her army jacket, shaking her head, looking world-weary, like she's seen it all before.

"Leni, *basta!*" I snap. "Look at how you're dressed! The hair . . . spiked and neon orange, bracelets up the arm, the miniskirt, the fishnets, the Doc Martens . . . What in the hell were you thinking? You didn't even bring the right shoes!" I adjust my backpack, where my *tacones* and jewelry are neatly stowed, and throw my shoulders back. Elena O'Malley-Diaz doesn't have a clue, clearly doesn't care about Taina, about how this was supposed to be something special for her, for the Sister Chicas, and I can't take it anymore. "How could you be so selfish, so completely self-centered!" I hear myself, over the edge, angry, and I don't make any effort to calm down. I don't care that I'm getting louder and louder the longer I speak. "Would it kill you for once to show up looking like a regular person instead of a background singer for . . . who is it? . . . Exene Cervenka, Joan Jett . . . any of the punkers who are so much more important to you than Taina? More important than *algo con sus Sister Chicas, su gente y nuestra tradiciones?*"

Swallowing back a lump in my throat, I will myself to stay strong to deal with this. She is not going to make me start crying.

"Don't go there, Villalobos." Leni waves me off, flicking her hand toward me the way you would try to brush off an annoying fly. I can see there's a whirlpool of emotions in her eyes, including pain and regret, but she doesn't hold back. Taunting me in a voice sugary and laced with sarcasm, she's revved up for a fight. "Why don't you just worry about the fact that you were late, *chica?* Late, late, L-A-T-E, late. What happened? Santa Graciela fall from grace? Could it be she's just an ordinary, flawed human being? Maybe not. I'm sure it'd kill you to be in the same category as me."

She keeps goading me, and it's working. It's taking all my effort to answer as calmly as possible, but I have to comment on what I think her problem is, what I know it is. I can't help it.

"That's where we're different, Leni. I have respect for people, for the things that hold us together."

"Oh, and that's why you were late. . . . It was a gesture of respect for Taina, for our fabulous culture."

"No, I screwed up! Don't you think I know that? Don't you think I'm sick over that? I fell asleep on the train tonight. . . . I've been working too many hours, but that's my problem; you wouldn't understand." I shift the dress to my other arm and pull up the collar of my peacoat.

"No, *Santa* Graciela, I wouldn't understand that you took on too many hours at the bookstore and Casa Aztlán. I'm way too selfish to notice that you're working too much, that you look tired all the time lately. And I'm way too self-centered to figure out that you feel guilty about going to goddamn Tilbrook this summer and you're trying to make it all right. And I'm certainly too selfish to figure out that maybe you're stuck on martyrdom. I'm sure it's more acceptable than being who you are without apologizing. Isn't it? I mean, what if you just yelled from the rooftops that you were thrilled to be chosen to go, that you deserve it, for Crissakes, and that you're gonna love having time for yourself? Oh, wait, that would be selfish, and we just can't have that!"

I feel like the wind's been knocked out of me; I can hardly breathe. My ears are ringing; my head's throbbing. How could she say that to me? Tears spill down my cheeks, and I can't stop myself. I quickly turn away, hoping I can hide from her. Hide. Why do I feel caught? Why do I feel like my secret's been found out? I take several long breaths, trying to calm down, trying to think.

"What the matter, *mi'ja*," she keeps on, that saccharine voice taunting me. "Can't come up with just the right thing to say?"

That's it. My face flushes white-hot, and before I can think I pivot around, poking her in the chest with my finger. "You just can't stand the thought that you *are* like us, that we have something in common. . . . Being a rebel, some punk misfit, keeps you from owning up, from having to belong somewhere to people who care for you, who share something with you!" My voice keeps getting louder and louder, but I don't stop. If there were any passersby, I'd draw a crowd. "Goddammit! You can run all you want, Leni, boredom and attitude plastered all over your face, but you can't run away from who you are, your family, your people! How do you think it makes me feel to see you push us away, me and Taina and everything that's important to us, everything we love? What would your father think?"

Slapping away my hand, it's Leni who's now poking me in the chest. For a second she hesitates, taking in my tear-streaked face, but it doesn't stop her. Instead of that earlier pseudo-sweet voice, instead of yelling, her voice is a harsh whisper, a hiss in the night air. There's a world of pain in her eyes—so much, so deep, it stuns me. I try to speak, desperately try to get a handle on myself, try to stop what's going on, but it clear that's not going to happen.

All of a sudden a rush of understanding hits me. I'm not help-ing Taina; I'm just tearing everything down.

"Leni," I plead.

"Shut up, *Santa* Graciela! Don't even think of bringing my fa-ther into this. You don't know how we were, how I felt about him . . . how I feel about him!"

I feel panicky now, my heart pounding a tattoo against my chest. *Dios mío,* what's happening? What are we doing? I soften my voice, try to let her hear I'm sorry, so very sorry.

"Leni, we can fix this!"

"Maybe I don't want to fix it. Let's just get it all on the table, *Santa* Graciela. What were we talking about? Running . . . yeah. Speaking of running, how long do you think you can run away from Jack? Have you told him how you really feel? Have you even admitted it to yourself?"

"Jack? Jack knows how I feel."

"Oh, really? So you're telling me you've told him you love him, is that what you're saying? I mean, I've never heard it, not when we're together, not when he drops you off at Rinconcito or when he picks you up. I don't buy it, and I bet Jack's patiently waiting to hear those three little words. So don't you dare say a word to me about dealing with emotions! If you don't know by now how I feel about Taina, or you, you can just go to hell!"

"I . . . I don't know what to say." Stammering, I feel my throat closing, my head spinning. *Please,* I pray, *please make this stop, or give me the words to make it all right.* Nothing comes. I'm silent, and the only thing that's between us now is the shushing of the wind.

Leni laughs, but it's a hollow, bitter one. "Well, that says a lot, Grachi. Enough for me to know it's time I got my selfish, insensi-tive ass out of here."

And before I can say a thing, she runs out of the doorway and across Division. I follow her, not even looking for traffic. I can feel a car whizzing behind me, but I don't care. I can't catch her, though; she's too fast, hopping into a waiting taxi outside La Con-cha. I wave my arms frantically, yelling at the top of my voice. She glances back at me, but I can't make out her expression.

"Don't go like this, Leni! Please! You're my sister!"

✧ ✧ ✧ ✧

Almost in a trance, I haltingly make my way to the train to go home. I'm so far past crying, the tears choking my heart instead. Staring blankly out the window, stop after stop, I don't see any of the city, any of the stations. All I can see are tears slipping down Taina's smooth, brown cheeks, and Leni's darkened, wounded eyes. My sisters. My only sisters, and look what I've done. Leni is right about me, about feeling guilty, about trying to do too much, about not being able to seize my good fortune. Instead I push myself too hard, stretch myself too thin, trying desperately to make up for *el pecado* of getting something I really want.

It's a miracle I recognized my stop at Hoyne. On top of everything else, there were two train delays, and it took me forever to get back to Pilsen. I lumber off the train, garment bag in hand. My legs match my heart, heavy as lead. I stumble down the street and into my house, not even bothering to turn on the lights, not even noticing until I'm in my room that *Papá* and *Mamá* aren't here. Then I remember they're at a local union meeting and won't be home until eleven. Hanging my dress in the closet, I open the garment bag and run my hands along the length of the skirt, smoothing down the fabric and wishing I could erase the whole day, erase the heartache I feel, the pain I know I share with my girls.

Slipping off my coat, I just sit on my bed in the dark, alone, for how long I don't even know, working out in my head an apology to Taina . . . to Leni. Nothing sounds right; nothing seems like it will help. I should go tomorrow and see them both. I'll cancel Casa Aztlán tomorrow; this is too important. If I can talk to them and look them in the eye, I'll make them see how much I love them, something I've taken way too long to put into words. I'm hanging up my peacoat when I hear the phone trilling in the living room. I run as fast as I can and pick up by the third ring.

"Did you mean it?" It's Leni, her voice hoarse and raspy, like someone who's cried so much they can hardly speak.

"Leni, *chica!* Oh, my God! Leni, I'm so glad you called. . . ." Tears, more tears. I'm so very sorry, and I'm praying for all I'm worth that this will all work out. But I'm cut off before I can recite the litany of how wrong I was, how she and Taina mean the world to me.

"Stop, Graciela. Just answer me. Did you mean it?"

"Mean what? Which thing?" I'm scared all of a sudden that this is just going to be a rehash of what happened tonight, one last nail in the coffin before Leni writes me off for good.

"That I'm your sister. Did you mean it?' Brash, boisterous Leni is nowhere to be found. On the other end of the line there's just a girl sounding wrung out, lonely, and afraid she won't hear the right answer. *Mi* Elena.

"Yes!" I insist. "*Tu eres mi hermana,* Leni. If you never believe anything else I say, please believe me now. You and Taina are more than friends . . . *somos familia.* I want to apologize for everything I said. I don't know what . . ." All I hear is soft sobs coming from Leni. "*Mi amor . . . no te lloras, por favor. Lo siento por todo.* Please Leni, don't cry."

The tears keep streaming down my face, and it all comes out half stutter, half plea, but that doesn't matter. I can't stand to see my girl hurting so badly.

"*Por favor, no llores más.*"

I hear several sharp intakes of breath, and after a couple of false starts, Leni finally speaks. "Grachi, you were right. Your method really sucks, but you're right. I totally blew off Taina tonight."

She's talking to me. *Thank God,* I think. I can hardly believe it; Leni and I are going to be okay. Part of me wants to laugh with glee that *mi* Leni is back. My "method" was a complete disaster, no argument there. "Sucks" seems like a charitable description. I wipe my face and nose on the sleeve of my sweater, and try to feel like less of a complete mess.

Leni voice is soft. "Grachi?"

I have to own up. "Just call me *Santa* Graciela, the martyr of Pilsen."

"Oh, my God, it's gotta be the apocalypse!"

I hear laughter at the other end, tired laughter, but laughter nonetheless, and that's good enough for me. I starting giggling, too, partly from the sheer relief I feel, partly from realizing that maybe the truth wasn't going to be such a bitter pill to swallow after all.

"So I wasn't off base then, huh?"

" 'Fraid not, *mi'ja*. How does it feel?"

"Pretty weird . . . but in a good way, I think. But what are we gonna do about it?"

I'm silent for a minute or so, and I can tell Leni's lost in thought with me, the weight of all this still settling in. This has been one horrible, revealing night. Leni and I have found out some hard, true things that we have to deal with. Things that are causing us heartache and pain for ourselves and each other. And the worst thing is, we hurt someone dear to us, someone who only wanted us to celebrate with her, *como familia*.

"For starters, we straighten out the mess we made tonight." I sigh. Instead of drinking *cafecitos* tomorrow like we do every Thursday, going over last minute details, we'll be lucky to mend the serious damage we did.

"Do you even think we can fix this, Grachi?"

I hear the worry creeping into her voice, that same worry echoed in mine. "We have to try. Tomorrow I'm calling the bookstore and Casa Aztlán and going back to my regular schedule. That's a start." I can already feel the embarrassment tightening my chest at the thought of having to go and tell everyone I need to cut back. "*Santa* Graciela is crashing and burning at this pace. Maybe everyone will settle for plain old Graciela."

"Grachi," Leni insists, "you don't need to kill yourself. Everyone who knows you . . . knows the kind of person you are. And 'lazy' is not a word that applies, believe me. You care about what you do and how you do it. What I said before . . . I . . . I just meant that you don't ever have to be sorry that someone recognizes your blood, sweat, and tears . . . or your talent." There is a fierceness in her voice, too, a pride.

"I needed to hear that right now. It's going to be hard for me to talk to people tomorrow."

"I know, Grachi . . . but don't ever doubt it. And people will understand; you'll see."

I feel shored up. "Then let's just go to her mother's restaurant right after we're done with classes. Taina will already be home from school, and we'll apologize, to both her and Mrs. Moscoso. . . . We'll just have to see what happens after that."

"Okay, tomorrow at the restaurant . . . So when should we meet?"

"If we leave right after our last classes, we should be there by three, since Mrs. Moscoso's restuarant is closer to campus and to Whitney Young than Rinconcito."

Leni tries to speak, then stops, the sharp intake of breath tells me she's struggling to say something. "Grachi, I'll tone it down, too. Hat covering the hair and just pants and a sweater."

"I think Taina will appreciate that," I say simply, knowing how hard this was for her to offer up.

And it's quiet again. It's a long stretch this time, the silence almost palpable. It's clear something else needs to be said.

"*Mi cultura* . . . what does that really mean? Grachi, I don't even know where to start. You and Taina . . . it's different for the two of you. It *is* who you are."

"It's who you are too, *mi'ja*," I reassure her.

"You mean there's more to me than sex, drugs, and rock and roll?"

I can hear the tremble on the other end of the line despite the wisecrack. "Yes, *mi hermana*. So much more. More than what's in any book . . . Although I have tons of them if you're ready to crack the books, Leni D." I try to tease her too, try to let her know it'll all be okay.

"Let's not get crazy, Villalobos," she teases back, still the *chica* I know, and something more.

I don't want this to end this without her knowing she's not some stranger in a strange land. "Leni, it's all around you. . . . It's inside you. All you have to do is open your mind, open your heart."

"But I need to find my own way, different from you and Taina."

"I know. We're here for you, for whatever you need. Count on it."

"I will; I do. . . . Speaking of open hearts, Grachi . . ."

"I know—Jack."

"Maybe there's something you should tell him."

"I know there is. You're enjoying the hell out of being right about this, aren't you, Leni?"

"You have no idea. . . ." A long sigh. "Hey, are you as tired as I am?"

I start to tell her that I could probably sleep standing up at this point, but I'm cut off as she puts me on hold. Waiting for several minutes, I wonder who's calling her this late at night. I make myself squelch the thought that it's some club boy trying to pry her out of the house to cruise Neo, and that soon she'll be out clubbing all night. Most important, I squelch trying to scramble back into the driver's seat again, trying to fix everything and everyone but myself.

When Leni gets back on the line there's stunned surprise in her voice.

"Grachi, that was just Taina."

"Oh, my God! How is she? What did she say? Was she still crying?"

"No . . . she sounded . . . I don't know . . . grown-up."

"What? What are you talking about? Just tell me what she said!"

"I tried to apologize for both of us, but she wouldn't let me. She said to meet her at Rinconcito tomorrow right after school, that she had some serious things to discuss with us. What do you think, Grachi?"

"I think we'd better be on time, and—"

"No fishnets or spiked collars, right?"

"Right."

A huge yawn coming from Leni fills my ears. "Hey, I gotta crash. . . . G'night, big sister."

I can't help but join her, exhaustion in every part of my body, but still feeling my heart swell in my chest, despite it all. "Night, *mi hermana*."

Face washed, pajamas on, I don't even bother to put my clothes in the hamper. I slip under the covers, and the warmth of my blankets soon lulls me into sleep, blessed sleep.

Somewhere deep into dreamworld, Taina, Leni, and I are in a sunlit room, sitting around a large wooden table. Scattered everywhere are pieces of colored fabric, brilliant colors, the colors of the rainbow. We're sewing a quilt, and with each stitch I feel closer and closer to *mi hermanas,* my Sister Chicas.

✧ ✧ ✧ ✧ ✧

Thursday morning and afternoon pass by in a blur. Extra coffee from the cafeteria vending machines keeps me on my toes; I can't be sluggish today. Running out of my last class like a woman on a mission, I catch the blue line train as it's pulling into the station. I do not fall asleep on the train ride over, something for which I thank the Virgin as I sprint up the stairs at the Logan Square stop. I'm in such a hurry, I don't even do my usual check of the street life, the passersby, not today.

It's ten to three when I get to Rinconcito del Sabor, but as I push open the door, I can see that Taina's already there, a tall glass of *jugo de papaya* in front of her and Don Ramiro sitting at her side. It's clear the two of them are in the middle of a conversation as I make my way to our table. They stop and Don Ramiro looks up and smiles. Taina, for once, doesn't welcome me with that fresh-faced, eager grin. Sitting tall in her chair, she has her hair swept up in a French braid, and instead of a pink or lavender sweater, she's wearing gray, looking older, and maybe wiser somehow. She finally acknowledges me. Her eyes tell me she's pleased to see me, tempered with a certain restraint. A look I've seen in my mother's eyes, and sometimes in my own.

Don Ramiro leans in and whispers something into Taina's ear and rises from the table, Patting her shoulder, he turns to me. *"¡Ay, princesa! Es un placer a verte, como siempre."* A second later he's bustling behind the counter, making *café con leche.* The *máquina* hisses as I slip out of my coat and take a seat across from my girl. No one says anything, but I notice Taina fiddling with a napkin, despite the calm look on her face. Don Ramiro places a steaming cup in front of me, just as Leni walks through the door.

A quick glance at my watch tells me it's three o'clock on the dot. Wearing some plain black pants and a thick cable sweater, her makeup simple by Leni standards, she tucks an errant strand of orange hair under a woolly cap. Taina gives my girl a look, the same subtle look that speaks volumes of how our little world has literally changed overnight.

Don Ramiro starts to whip a *cafecito* for Leni, but she stops him, "Nothing for me right now, *gracias*." She grabs a chair between Taina and me, scooting it back so that both of us are on one side of the table, facing our girl.

Taina's calm, clear voice rises above the din. The napkin is firmly set aside and there's not a sign of nervousness. "*Chicas,* listen to me. I have some things I need to say. I don't want either of you to interrupt; *¿me entienden?*"

I swallow back my apology, perching at the edge of my chair. Underneath the table, Leni's hand reaches for mine. We don't look at each other; we just wait for what's coming next.

"What happened yesterday hurt me . . . really hurt me. You are *familia,* and I expect you to treat me *con el respeto de una hermana.*" Taina speaks *con calma,* the pace measured, almost as if she's giving a speech. "Now, I've talked with my mother, and after this we're going to the restaurant, where you're both going to apologize. This *quinceañera* is going to happen; you two are going to be part of my court. . . . *Mami* was able to get another rehearsal set up for next Wednesday night at seven. Be on time and be dressed appropriately." She leans over toward the two of us. "I don't ever want to feel like I'm not important to you, because . . ." Her voice starts quavering, and a single tear slips down her cheek. We try to move toward her, but she holds up her hand. "Because both of you mean the world to me."

Warning not heeded, in a blink of an eye we leap from our chairs. Leni and I scoop Taina into a giant hug, sobbing and laughing and kissing the top of her head. We're so loud, I'm sure people on the street can hear us, but it doesn't stop us.

Bustling over to our ragtag party, Don Ramiro inspects our tear-streaked, happy faces. "*¡Dios mío!* I thought someone let loose some *gallinas* in here. But instead, I see *mis reinas* are just celebrating something. Ah, this calls for some *antojitos!* Let me bring you some of Doña Isabel's *yuca sabrosa!*" His baritone laugh trails behind him as he disappears behind the swinging door. As soon as he's gone from sight, we all start talking at once.

Conjuntos. Together. We're together, and that's all that matters.

9

LENI

See what Grachi's done to me? I don't know. It must have been all that talk about "facing up" and "responsibility," but here I sit. At home. Alone. Reading. A memoir about Puerto Rico by Esmeralda Santiago, no less! My mother gave it to me for my last birthday and I never touched it until now. I swear on the soul of Johnny Ramone, my life is getting bizarre, even by my standards.

After the scene at Rinconcito with Taina, and surviving our apologies to Mrs. Moscoso, I was ratcheted up. I was on overload, like after an O'Malley family gathering. I felt the love, but my head was swimming. After we said good-bye outside of her mother's restaurant, each of us not wanting to let the other two leave, I realized I couldn't go home. I wandered around the West Town neighborhood for hours. I found myself listening to the bustle around me, the musical sounds of Spanish, playing a game to see how many words I could catch, what I could understand. I walked along the wide streets, and for the first time really looked at the faces of the guys on the stoops, their rides parked in front of the buildings, radios blaring salsa, talking rapid-fire with cigarettes dangling from their mouths. Occasionally their raspy voices would erupt in rowdy laughter. Farther down the steps the old men slid dominoes into place on the edge of the concrete stairs, concentrating despite all the noise of the city around them and the cold autumn wind biting through their worn jackets. Older women in wool coats and sensible shoes strolled along the street in no particular hurry, arm in arm. People are just too uptight here in the States. Some homophobic crap, I figure. My family in PR is always all over one another. Not that I go for that kind of lovefest, you understand, but it's kind of nice that they can do what they feel.

As I walk along, the aromas of dishes from my childhood weave their way around me, the heady smell of *sofrito,* the rich scent of plantain deep-frying in a hot iron pan. Looking into the windows of the shops, I spied products I hadn't seen since my *abuela*'s house in Bayamón. Goya guava paste, *Café* Yauco Selecto, those nasty lollipops—I think they're called *pilones*—red with sesame seeds on them that my *tío* is always trying to get me to try. Sesame seeds on lollipops? Ugh! I caught a glimpse of a huge pyramid-shaped display of Malta just inside the Bodega Vieques window. My father used to love Malta. I just have one word for that sickly sweet and heavy malt beverage: ewww! In the window of the bakery next door, I spotted a fresh batch of *torta de guayaba.* I went in and bought a pastry to go, conducting my business entirely in Spanish. The matronly woman behind the counter smiled at me as she handed me my change, and I thanked her. I wondered if she was smiling because I massacred her beautiful language or just because she was nice. What the hell; I assumed it was the latter. I stopped for a moment on the sidewalk in front of the store, ignoring the stinging cold autumn wind, and took a bite of the crusty pastry, letting the bright red, sweet guava filling sit on my tongue as I closed my eyes. I licked the crumbs from my lips and thought, *Oh, man, it doesn't get better than this.* As I continued to walk along the streets, absorbing the life that was flowing around me, I realized that if you ignore the bitter November weather, it could have been any street in Puerto Rico. And with my undercover look, no one was even noticing me. I could almost pass. Almost.

My mind swam with all the things Grachi and I said. Maybe it was true; maybe I fit in with these warm and friendly people passing by me like water rushing over a stone. Like water, with time they've made their mark, even on a boulder like me. But what about the other parts of me? Where does it all fit in? Exhausted, I headed home well after dark and crashed into bed, fully dressed from my boots to my knitted wool cap. And that's the way I woke up on this way-too-bright Saturday morning.

✧ ✧ ✧ ✧ ✧

Well, at least I have time to do some reading and go through my portfolio and add some of the new shots I took for that school project last month. Actually, this hanging-out-at-home thing is kind of okay. No one's gonna see me, so I lose my "conservative" getup, wash off what makeup was not left on my pillowcase, and put on Dad's old flannel shirt and my ripped sweatpants and socks. I can blast my music earsplittingly loud, and eat as much junk food as I want. I'm sitting at the butcher-block island in our large, steel kitchen on the vintage Herman Miller stools Mom was so excited about finding at the antique show in Nantucket last summer. They might be stylish and ultra-Bauhaus-revival, but they're not very comfortable. I have to adjust my position every ten minutes or so as the hard stainless steel seat makes my ass fall asleep.

I shove another half of a Twinkie in my mouth and turn the page of my portfolio, opening to a shot of my mother I took a few years ago on one of our annual trips to Puerto Rico. This particular shot is in color, a shock since I'm a black-and-white kind of girl. You can almost feel the warmth of the Caribbean sun rising from the print. Her head is tilted, a tender smile playing across her berry-colored lips, the tropical breeze blowing her long, thick blond hair to the side while the sun caught the highlights, making a golden halo around her face. For a blond *gringa,* Mom always loved being down in PR. Sigh. She sure is a complicated chick . . . for that matter, so am I. The day I took this picture was a pretty cool day. Probably the best we had together since Dad died.

Mike and Mom were just divorced, and I think she dragged me

down to PR that year not for me to "get in touch with my roots," as usual, but because she wanted to escape. The divorce wasn't nasty—it was actually nice and friendly, at least as much as those things can be—but she was fried. Even I could see that. I was already heavy into my punk lifestyle, and with my black clothes, spiky hair, and heavy makeup I was pretty sure I was going to get flak from *la familia,* but I didn't give her a hard time. I figured she'd been through enough crap for the year.

We usually didn't do touristy things when we were down there, lots of sitting on porches with old ladies, drinking Coca-Colas, and rocking back and forth, back and forth in the gaggle of cane rocking chairs that seemed to be permanent fixtures on every self-respecting Puerto Rican's veranda. I think I could count on one hand how many times I'd actually been to the beach. And those times it was my uncle Esteban who saved me from old-lady land. He would bring me to the beach in Isla Verde with Ana and Maria, my cousins. We had a blast, building sand castles and eating snow cones, but he couldn't rescue me every year, and I had learned not to expect it.

That particular visit didn't start out any different from our earlier ones, except that we stayed at a hotel for the first time instead of at *Abuela*'s. We spent the first few days visiting relatives—all of them ancient, and I swore that we must be related to everyone in a fifty-mile radius. I bit my lip and tried to be polite while they all asked (thinking I didn't understand) if I had a boyfriend ("*¿Ella tiene un novio?*") and talked about how I looked like *mi papá.* When I finally threw myself on the large, freshly made hotel bed on the fifth night I couldn't believe I had lived through so much. The next day there was a painful lunch we were to attend—in honor of some distant aunt's eightieth birthday—and I imagined another afternoon of having my cheek pinched and forcing a smile over clenched teeth, but I was in for a surprise.

After breakfast in the hotel restaurant, Mom was staring out the window at the sun-baked streets of Old San Juan, thinking about something, or someone, far away.

"You all right, Ma?" I asked after a long sip of my *café con leche.* She sighed and looked at me, coming back from wherever she had been, a mischievous smile starting to sneak from the edge of her mouth, rolling across the middle of her full, coral-painted lips.

"So, Leni, would you be crushed if we blew off today's plans? I feel like playing hooky."

For a moment I just gaped at her. I wasn't sure if I even understood the individual words. *Blew off . . . Hooky?* They just weren't words I'd ever heard out of Mom's mouth.

"Well, don't just stare at me. I like to have a little fun every once in a while, too, ya know!" She laughed, finishing off the last of her Earl Grey tea.

After about five minutes the shock wore off, and I sputtered, "You mean, like, not go to the lunch? Really?" Then I started to worry, "Wait a minute . . . and do what instead?" I interrogated her, certain we were trading one tedious old-lady event for another.

"Actually, I want to surprise you! Take you somewhere fun!"

I still couldn't grasp this concept. It was like calculus. "Well . . . okay . . ."

"Oh, come on, Elenita." She knew I hated when they called me that down there, and she played the word up for effect. "What's the matter? Don't trust your *mamá?*" She smiled a kid-who-stole-the-cookie-from-the-jar-and-got-away-with-it smile, grabbed her bag and my arm, and dragged us both out of the restaurant.

We went back to the hotel, and Mom had me put my bathing suit on under my clothes and pack a day bag of towels from the hotel bathroom. I couldn't imagine that we'd do something that was actually fun; after all, that was never the deal with these annual trips. Mom made the compulsory call to *Abuela,* making up some story about how it was "my time of the month" (I almost died) and that we were staying in today and resting.

We drove east from San Juan, taking the scenic route along the water, toward Loíza. The weather was perfect, and we chatted excitedly as I watched the wooden hut *quioscos* go by, each one overflowing with the same cheap souvenirs with PUERTO RICO painted on them to lure the tourists. I started to think we were heading for El Yunque, one of the few places I actually *had* been that was even slightly touristy. Visiting there usually involved lots o' hiking, stifling humidity, thousands of mosquito bites, and blisters. I sure as hell didn't want to go there again. But as we drove by the road leading to the rain forest, I breathed a sigh of relief, but then began to really wonder where we were going. I had never been east of the rain forest before. A few miles later I saw a stone sign on the side of the road that was painted aqua blue, faded from the sun so it was mottled like the surface of a pool: WELCOME TO LUQUILLO. We turned left and drove down side streets that were lined with rows of low concrete houses painted in a range of bright Caribbean colors, like a roll of tropical Life Savers. The street was a dead end, a thick procession of palm trees bordering the far end of the road. We parked the car, gathered our stuff, and started walking along the curb, toward the end of the row of palms. We walked in silence for a few minutes with the sun streaming down on our shoulders and the tops of our heads.

"Where are you taking me, Ma?" I said after a while, looking at her out of the corner of my eye.

"Oh, to a place that was very special to your *papá* and me. You'll see."

We reached the end of the row of trees and low flowering bushes, and turned to our left. I was looking at my feet, careful, since the road had been more pothole than asphalt, and I noticed the terrain had turned to bright white sand. I looked up and saw an expanse of pristine beach, the kind I had seen only in travel brochures and irritating TV commercials with plastic couples sauntering along, holding hands. The expanse of sky was an electric blue, and the ocean below was divided into stripes of cobalt, growing lighter as they neared the beach. The sand was very fine under my feet, and there couldn't have been more than five people on the entire beach.

I stood there with my mouth gaping, bags hanging at my side, forgotten. "Whoa." It was all I could get out. Mom laughed, clearly pleased.

"I know. I was speechless when Juan first took me here, too. The large public beach is up a ways, but we always preferred this one."

"I can see why!" I shook myself out of my beach-induced coma, dropped my bag on the sand, kicked off my sandals, and ran for the water. I stopped when I got to the water's edge. I'd swum in the northern Atlantic, so I expected it to be cold. But as I gingerly placed my toes into the water, the warmth spread throughout my entire body, and I started to wade in. I stood there for some time, looking around at the receding coasts in either direction, while gentle waves splashed against my knees. I looked down at my pale calves, the length and shape distorted by the clear swirling water, watching the small white fish dart around my legs. Eventually Mom joined me, and without a word we swam in farther side by side. It was incredible. As we bobbed up and down in the clear turquoise water, Mom floated on her back, her eyes squinting in the bright Caribbean sun, and she began to talk about Dad.

"We used to come here alone, whenever we visited the island. We would find a way to sneak away from family obligations. It was our secret place, ever since we started dating. Dad said he felt closest to God here in Luquillo, where the water meets the horizon." Mom's eyes seemed to fill with more than seawater, and I didn't want to say anything. She didn't talk about him often, and I didn't want to break the spell and take the chance she would stop. After a few minutes of silence, we both started walking out of the water and toward the beach. We sat down on the industrial white hotel towels, letting the sun dry our puckered skin, powdery salt residue slowly covering our bodies. I loved that feeling of taut skin as the last drops of the ocean water disappeared.

"We took you here, you know. When you were just a baby." She looked at me then, her hair still stringy and wet, but shining a darker gold in the midday sun. "He wanted to share our space with you. He spent hours swinging you above the water, making you giggle as the warm water tickled your chubby feet. He wasn't so sick then, and I thought he could have held you like that forever. I'd never seen him so happy." She stared off at the ocean, her eyes soft with memory. Turning to me suddenly, she pivoted her entire body around to face mine, and I instinctively pulled back a little, surprised by the movement. She wouldn't let me pull too far away, though. She took my hand and stared into my eyes and spoke more directly to me than she had in years.

"Leni, I know I pulled away after your father died, but I never stopped loving you. I know you need your independence, but I brought you to this place so I could tell you that I'll be there when you need me." She stared into my eyes for a second longer. It didn't seem she expected an answer from me; she squeezed my hand as she held my gaze, then sat back on her towel, stretching her long legs out in front of her and crossing them at the ankles. I took a deep breath, grateful that she didn't push me to respond. I think she was giving me time to make sense of all of this. But I stared at her as she closed her eyes, lifted her chin, and let the sun wash over her face. I watched her for a long time, her hair drying, a gentle smile surfacing from her thoughts and playing across her lips. It was then I slowly took out my camera and started to shoot photographs of her.

❖ ❖ ❖ ❖ ❖

As I stare down at the picture I realize that though I felt like Mom and I weren't always tight, we did have one very important thing in common: our feelings for my father. I'm certain that that was one of the things she was trying to tell me that day. She had never stopped loving him.

The phone rings and I jolt, like, a foot in the air. Hadn't noticed how quiet it was in here until now. I jump up, knock over the uncomfortable German designer stool, and run for the kitchen extension. Mom's spending her Saturday at work, finishing up the plans for an office building in the South Loop. I grab the phone off the hook just before the machine picks up and breathlessly bark, "Hello?" into the receiver. I can tell even before I hear a voice on the other end that the call is from Puerto Rico. The calls always crackle, like in some 1940s movie or something. For God's sake, it is the twenty-first century; you would think they could get some decent phone lines installed on the damn island.

"Elena? Is that you?" I hear a voice say, bubbling up through the static from the other end of the line. I don't recognize the voice, but it is somehow familiar. I don't often talk to people who are so damn cheery.

"Yep, that's me. Who's this?"

"Elena, it's Ana! *Tu prima en Puerto Rico.*" Aha. Ana. I immediately feel my shoulders slump and I am suddenly conscious of my sloppy clothes and lack of makeup. Even over the phone she has that effect on me. Ana and her sister, Maria, are the only children of my favorite uncle, Esteban. At eighteen, Ana is one year older than I am, and Maria is twenty. It's no surprise they've both grown into ultrastylish, petite creatures with long, shiny sable hair, huge, dark eyes, and flawless *café con leche*–colored skin. They basically look liked they walked off of a page of *Latina* magazine. And to top it all off, they're nice! It is enough to make you sick. I can't help liking them, and I hate that.

I recover myself and unconsciously put my free hand up to my head and smooth my lopsided, bed-head, Day-Glo orange hairdo. "Hey, *prima*! How ya doin'?" I respond after a few moments of uncharacteristic silence.

"Wonderful, Elena, thanks for asking! *Óyeme,* I have a surprise! I'm flying into Chicago tomorrow and will be in town for twenty-four hours, and I was hoping to see you! Are you free?"

My jaw drops and nothing comes out of my mouth. What was I going to say? I see Ana once a year, and I actually enjoy spending time with her . . . other than being left with that boy-do-I-suck-I'm-fat-I-need-new-clothes-and-I-really-should-have-learned-to-speak-Spanish-years-ago kind of feeling. "Sure! I'd like that," I respond, at least partially meaning it. "Where will you be staying?"

We work out the details, and I get the sense from her excitement and this highly unusual visit to the Windy City that Ana has news. Well, at least I know she is past the *quinceañera* age. I don't think I could take another one of those anytime soon. As we're about to hang up, Ana says, "Hey, Elena, is Carlos around these days? I would love to see him too, if possible. I mean, if that's okay with you." Underneath her sweet voice there's a low, rich tone that I've always been jealous of in my Latina cousins. They seem to be born with it, and generally it drives men wild. So Ana has a thing for Carlos. Don't blame her, but I'm surprised to discover that I don't like it either.

"Sure, I'll give Carlos a call," I offer halfheartedly. "He doesn't have rehearsal on Sundays, so he should be around."

"Great!" she says, *way* too excited for my taste. "Maybe after spending some time together, just you and me, we can hook up with him for *café* or something." Yeah, or something. My head is buzzing, and suddenly I want this conversation to end. After another pause I reply, "Okay, *prima*, I'll see you tomorrow at four o'clock." I hang up the phone and take a deep breath. Well, at least I have twenty-four hours to get it together. I head to my room to try to pick out some clothes that will make me feel less like a Teletubby and more like the punk diva I am with everyone but Ana.

❖   ❖   ❖   ❖   ❖

Four o'clock Sunday afternoon comes along way too quickly, and I find myself sitting at a table in the excessively overpriced coffee shop in Ana's hotel. This showing-up-on-time thing is a drag: all this staring at your fingernails. The waiter is eyeing me from his station, whispering to his female coworker, who seems to have a matching piece of oak stuffed up her ass. I guess they don't often get punks in this establishment. For just a moment I think about putting my patent-leather, skull-heeled boots up on the table, but decide against it. Given my luck Ana would walk in at that moment. Instead I look back at them, shove my fist up in the air, and contort my lips in classic Billy Idol fashion. They pretend not to see me and concentrate on the check they're entering into the register. That took care of them.

I feel a rush of cold air from the lace-curtained door, and in walks Ana, looking as if she just stepped off the catwalk and not off a crowded four-hour flight. The snooty waiter rushes over to greet her, a simpering smile on his face. Ana sizes him up with a look, then waves him off with a "Thank you, but I see my party over there." His face drops as she strides over to my table with a big smile on her face and hugs me warmly as I stand up. Points for Ana.

We sit down after the flurry of high-pitched endearments and greetings that always seem to accompany a reunion with my Puerto Rican family. It does have a way of making you feel welcome. I look over at my cousin, warmly smile, and say, "Well, *prima*, you look fabulous, as usual. Can't you, you know, get fat or something? It would make me feel *so* much better."

"*Ay, chica*, you are so beautiful. If you would only let me take you shopping, or at least maybe I can do your makeup. Your gorgeous eyes are hidden under all that liner!" She reaches for my face, and though I don't pull away like I would with practically anyone else, I shoot her a disgusted look. Her laugh, warm and smooth like a shot of Barrilito rum, is a comforting and familiar sound. For me it carries with it the sound of the surf, the taste of a mango *piragua* shared at the beach, and joyous company. She touches my cheek gently, pulls her manicured hand back, and says, "*Yo lo sé*, I know. Back off. See? You can't say that to *Abuela*, but you've said it to me enough times, *¿ay, prima?*"

I smile at this. She knows me too well. And, unlike the older generation of my Puerto Rican family, she accepts me. Orange spiky hair and all. She doesn't get me, but she takes me as I am. That's all I ask, people.

I can't wait any longer, and I ask her the question that has been on the tip of my tongue since she called. "So, *prima*, what brings you to the mainland?"

Ana goes on to tell me about the visits to colleges scheduled over the next few days. She spent the last year traveling around Europe—I have a pile of colorful postcards from spectacularly glamorous places—and now it is time for her to continue her education. Of course she's hitting all the Ivy League joints, and you can bet they are fighting to get her in. Did I mention she is a straight-A student? It just never ends. I ask all the appropriate questions, and we order coffee and low-fat blueberry muffins. I make a mental note to myself: Low-fat or no, I'm eating *way* too much pastry these days. Oh, well, maybe I was wrong about there being other news. I'm actually enjoying myself. Then the other *zapato* drops.

"Elena, the real reason I wanted to see you in person, other than wanting to spend time with you, *mi prima favorita*, is to tell you the big news *en la familia*. Maria is getting married!"

I sit there, my jaw slack, no idea what to say. Honestly, I can't imagine getting married at twenty, and I never really cared for her uptight lawyer boyfriend, but hey, she's family, you know? I pull my jaw off my chest, smile, and say, "That's wonderful, Ana! I'm so happy for her." I go back to eating my muffin in an attempt to cover up my shock—and fear of what might be coming next.

"But here is the best part, *mi'ja*. We want you to come down and be in the wedding party!"

I damn near choke on a piece of my muffin, and cough so violently that the snooty waiter scuttles over with a glass of water, certain that this freakish punk is going to die on his shift, simply ruining his afternoon. When I can breathe again, I take another sip of water and look over at Ana. Again, what can I say? Damn. I can see it now. Another sea of silk moire, kissing old ladies' powdered cheeks and dancing with strange male relatives. This is just not my year.

"Oh! that's so . . . great . . . !" I just sit there. Staring at her I can just imagine what the expression on my face must look like from where she sits. Kind of like a deer in the headlights. But a deer who's carrying an Uzi.

"Are you okay, Elena? Aren't you happy about being part of the wedding?" She looks kind of hurt, but concerned. Damn. I rush to make up for my weird—although pretty damn accurate—reaction. Reassuring her that yes, I am gosh-darned excited at the prospect of flying down for the wedding in the middle of the scorching summer, smothering in yet another nightmarish *princesa* dress, and being part of the wedding party. Not in those exact words, of course; even *I'm* more diplomatic than that. I can see my act is working as Ana starts to relax and tell me about the plans for the elaborate event to take place next August in Old San Juan. I listen and nod my head every once in a while, a smile frozen on my face like some kind of demented flight attendant. I wish the best for Maria—really I do—but *¡ay, Dios mío!* Why me?

Ana goes on to update me on the family news. This doesn't take long, as nothing much ever changes. I think they like it that way, actually. I would lose my mind. I try to forget about the impending nuptial nightmare and ask about all the cousins, aunts, and uncles I care about down on *la isla bonita*. Then I ask for the nonpostcard version of her European excursions. I am rapt as Ana describes a steamy romance with a gorgeous Italian guy in Florence, when the door to the coffee shop swings open. We both look up and there is Carlos, looking absolutely delicious in a black leather motorcycle jacket, black jeans, and Timberland boots. He glances around the restaurant, and his face lights up when he sees us. Was that smile that reached his eyes for me, or for Ana? Jeez, I'm losing it.

Following Carlos through the door is Luis, the band's rhythm guitarist and his best friend. I sigh with relief at the sight of Luis and watch him politely and gently close the door on the cold November wind. Not only is he cute, but he is a business major and an appropriate upper-class distraction for Ana. The guys come over to the table, and Ana stands up to give Carlos a warm hug. Even in her spiked, high-heeled Manolo Blahnik pumps, she is quite a lot shorter than Carlos, and has to stand on her tiptoes to really hug him. I give Luis a quick but friendly hug, never taking my eyes off of Carlos and Ana. They separate after what seems like an eternity; Ana seems reluctant to let go of Carlos's buff chest. Carlos introduces Luis, who bows his head in polite fashion, his eyes only briefly resting on her face, his usually boisterous manner short-circuited by Ana's beauty. I've seen that look on hundreds of men's faces over the years I've hung out with Ana. Hell, she had that effect on boys when we were eight!

We all sit down, boy-girl, boy-girl. Carlos puts his hand on mine and softly asks how things are going with Taina and Grachi. I had told him about our disagreement last night on the phone. "Everything's cool, thank God." I smile back, looking into his dark eyes.

"Great," he says, just to me. Then he turns to talk to Ana. Well, she is our guest and he hasn't seen her in over a year. They start chattering away in rapid-fire Spanish, and I feel left in their dust. I can follow what's being said when someone's speaking slowly, but in conversation the language comes fast and furious, and I have trouble keeping up. Luis and I start to talk about the band's next gig, and his upcoming midterm, but I'm distracted. I look over to see Ana throwing her head back and laughing, and I don't even know why, but I begin to feel anger creep up from my belly. Without thinking my hand goes up to my face; my cheek is already warm. Carlos turns to me and says, "I'm so sorry, Leni; it's just so nice to hear Puerto Rican Spanish that I got carried away." He goes on to give me the Cliff's Notes version of what they were talking about, how this friend from Ponce quit his job at his father's advertising firm to go grow fair-trade coffee in the mountains, much to the fury of his family. And how this other one is sneaking around with a married government official . . . and so on. I wasn't listening. Oh, I looked like I was listening, and acted like I was listening, but I wasn't following the rundown even though they had switched to English. Was Carlos into her? Look at her! How could he not be? Suddenly I feel sick to my stomach, and it must have shown, as Carlos stops talking, puts his hand back on mine, and asks, "Leni, are you okay?" I see the concern on his face and I look over at my cousin. I can see worry on her face, as well, and once again I realize that I can't hate her. And why would I? What's going on with me? "I'm fine, really. Thanks."

Ana starts to talk with Luis about his studies, and Carlos joins in, but leaves his hand on mine. I can feel the heat from his strong hand, and I notice how soft his skin is, how long and elegant his fingers are, and I imagine them picking at his guitar, or pulling my face closer to his. . . . At that moment I realize that someone must have asked me a question, as all three of them are looking at me expectantly, but I don't have a clue what is going on. Carlos saves me with, "Luis was just telling Ana about the fantastic photos you have been taking of musicians around the city."

"Oh, great!" I'm not sure what to say.

"I'd love to see them sometime, *prima*! I'm afraid it can't be tonight, as I am meeting a friend for dinner. We went to high school together in San Juan and now she's in her first year at Northwestern." She looks at her platinum Rolex and sighs. "I really have to get going, *con tu permiso, mi prima*." As she stands, both guys jump up from their seats. So well mannered. Such jerks.

Ana says her good-byes, lingering again in Carlos's arms. When she moves to hug me, I want to pull away, to not hug back, but I look in her face and she is just Ana. We hug tightly with promises of seeing each other at the wedding next summer. She kisses my cheek as she pulls away, and whispers, "*Te quiero, prima.*"

Suddenly I feel like an idiot for being irritated with her. "I love you too, *prima.*" She starts to walk out of the restaurant in a flurry of flipping silky hair, clicking heels, and waves of her red-tipped fingers.

The door closes behind her, and I just stand there for a moment as the guys sit back down, finishing their coffees and launching into a conversation about some French documentary on underground music they're going to see that night. I'm so damn confused. I slowly sit down, nearly missing my chair entirely, when Luis's cell phone rings. He looks at the incoming number and says, "I've got to take this, bro. Be back in a minute." As he nears the door, we hear him saying, "*Dígame, Chino, ¡qué pasó?*" into his phone as he goes onto the street. Carlos and I are left alone at the table. All of a sudden I wish Luis were still there. I awkwardly turn back to my coffee, trying to avoid his eyes.

"Well, it was nice to see Ana, wasn't it?" he offers in a voice too friendly for my taste.

"Yeah, nice." I reply, my mind swirling like water in a drain leading nowhere.

"I know you two have always been close." Silence. I don't know what to say, how to cover my tracks. I think Carlos knows me too well.

"Is something wrong, Leni? You've been so quiet all night. Not like the usual ninety-miles-an-hour Diaz I know and love." Then he touches my face gently, his long musician's fingers warming my cheek like the heat from a campfire. I get this feeling, like a low-level current coursing through my body, beginning at my belly and spreading down to my toes. For just a second I close my eyes and tune out everything but the feeling of his hand on my face.

I'm jolted out of my trance by the sound of the café door and the rush of cold air that accompanies Luis like a clingy date.

I pull my head upright, out of its comfortable resting space against Carlos's palm, look into his face, and see him smiling at me, a soft look in his liquid brown eyes that I've never seen before, and I can feel the blood rushing to my face again. It's times like these when I wish I didn't have my mother's pale Irish skin. I try to cover by taking a sip of my already cold coffee, but it sticks halfway down my throat. I sputter, trying to come up with something snappy to say, something Leni-like. Anything, really, would be better than having him smile into my beet red face.

"Damn, body malfunction again."

"It looks fine from where I'm sitting, Leni," Carlos replies, still smiling. As Luis returns to the table, I try to look busy with my napkin and spoon, but I just end up feeling awkward. Suddenly I think of a diversion, and call out to the waiter, "Can I get the check here?" *That's it, Leni, retake charge.* I think I have it back, the attitude, when Carlos lays his hand on my arm. I can feel that warmth again on my skin.

"Ah, Leni, Ana charged it to her room, remember?"

Damn. The red is coming back. I look up and see the waiter smirking at me. Oh, great, Mr. Charm caught that one too. Carlos leaves his hand on me—why does he do that? Doesn't he know it scrambles my brain?—and says, "So, Leni, do you want to check out this movie with us?"

I look at the person I've known since I was a kid, his chiseled face framed by a crown of black curls, and I can't breathe. I've gone to the movies with him dozens of times; why is the idea making my heart race now?

"No, thanks, Carlos, I . . . I have to take a rain cheek . . . I mean check . . . I . . . I really have to go . . . to meet . . . to do . . . something." I stand up, knocking over the dregs of the coffee onto the white linen tablecloth. The nasty waiter comes over and gives me a look, but I'm almost relieved to see him. I attempt to bolster myself up and out of my confusion. "I've gotta go," I say again, this time more assuredly, backing up toward the café door. As I feel my back hit the brass doorknob, I wave casually at Carlos, trying to regain my cool. "Catch you later, Carlos, Luis. . . ." I turn around to open the door and slam directly into a suit-clad middle-aged man who is coming into the restaurant.

"Where are you rushing to, honey?" The man says to me with a grin as I brush past him in a flurry of black leather. I slam the door behind me, catching the lace curtain in the door as it shuts, and I take a deep breath of the cold evening air.

I cringe as I think about the scene I just left. Why am I losing my grip? Shit! I'm usually so calm around Carlos. Ever since that rehearsal for the Sister Chicas, I've been nervous around him. I start to walk off, and I look back into the large, lace-covered front window of the café. I see Carlos smiling at me through the frost-trimmed glass. The electric current is back, this time tingling at the spot on my cheek where he touched me. I absently put my hand to my face and stare back at him. It's official: I'm losing it. Really losing it. Trying to get a grip, I wave again feebly, and start running, trying to look like I'm in some kind of hurry, on my way to meet someone important, get somewhere special. *Just get away, Leni,* I tell myself over and over again, like some kind of mantra. *Get away and figure out what the hell is going on.* I need to get Carlos's face out of my mind. His voice out of my ears. I need to forget the feeling of his hand on my skin. As I run I hear the train approaching on the elevated tracks, and as it rumbles by above me I'm grateful for the earsplitting roar and screech of its progress, jostling me into the here and now.

10

TAINA

ami is quiet, thumbing through the receipts and the RSVPs for the *quinceañera.* Neither of us has yet recovered fully from the brouhaha at La Reina Borinqueña. Since the night of the rehearsal fiasco, I can't read her. I mean, I know she's livid for my running out of the ballroom without her Mother Superior permission, but I just couldn't stay there, glued to the parquet floor like a dumb ass—yes, I said dumb ass—stuck between Graciela and Leni and my mother and our collective anger, so I took off. I don't really remember deciding to do it. It just happened. I'd never done that before. Oh, well, I mean, I hadn't done that sort of thing since I was seven.

❖ ❖ ❖ ❖

Mami had been sleeping for two days straight, sluggishly getting out of bed only to make me oatmeal for breakfast and a pot of rice and beans for dinner every day, all meals she burned. "Don't worry, nena. Just scrape the black parts off. Okay?" And with that okay, she turned on her bare feet and again slipped silently down the hall towards the haven of her room. She hadn't been her usual self since *Papi* had left. Her hair was mussed, sticking out at the sides like a lopsided crown. She'd stopped wearing her oriental silk robe with the peonies splashed down the front. It was sweatpants and tshirts for days. That is, until someone called *Tia* Monse, *Mami*'s older sister, to the rescue. One afternoon, *Mami*'s fifth day in bed, *Tia* Monse rolled her black bat of a Mercedes into the marquesina of our little blue cement two-bedroom, oil stains pocking the driveway's cement. *Tia* Monse, an angel in her feather-white summer dress, showed up and I didn't have to eat burned oatmeal anymore.

I stood outside the house wearing my favorite worn Keds and baby-pink jumper, eyeing the three girls down at the end of the block as they played a rowdy game of hopscotch.

One afternoon, I stood outside the house wearing my favorite worn Keds and a baby-pink jumper, eyeing the three girls down at the end of the block who were playing a rowdy game of hopscotch, their twisted hair flying at each jump, their giddy shrieks and shouts resounding down the street toward me. I looked back toward the silent house, thought of *Mami* practically comatose in her bed, her eyes swollen from crying, lashes brushing her pillow. I didn't know the girls except for the passing hellos our mothers shared every Saturday morning as they dragged us to the *plazoleta*'s market. Though we had been living on Uva Street for a few years, *Papi* and *Mami* weren't sociable. They never had people over, and we were never invited to anyone's house. My parents seemed content with only our nuclear family.

Mami had closed all the louvered windows, the cedar slats looking like eyelids shut to the sun. I took one step away from the front door. I took another, passing the motionless porch swing. Another and another, till I was suddenly skipping down the cracked sidewalk, my Keds stomping on the mimosa weeding itself out of the cement. I admit I could hear *Mami*'s voice inside my head: "*Nena*, you are not allowed in anyone's house without my permission; do you understand?" But the closer I came to the girls (who were, by now, climbing up a *flamboyán* to their tree house) the smaller my mother's voice got, till finally it altogether disappeared.

Later, well after what was supposed to have been my suppertime,

I skipped back home, nonchalantly opening the door to the house. As soon as my foot crossed the tiled threshold, I saw my mother sitting on the couch, face contorted, hands balled in her lap. Her voice flew out of her mouth, tinny and uncontrolled.

"Where the hell have you been? *¡Carajo!*" At the time I didn't know what the word meant, but I knew that it was bad, and *Mami* never said bad words. "I've been worried sick, looking up and down this street for hours, knocking on strangers' doors to see if anyone had seen you. What were you thinking?"

What did I answer? What every seven-year-old answers: "I don't know." *Tia* Monse and *Mami* frowned at me, the house suddenly reverberating with *Mami*'s exasperation, the long end of her shouting overshadowing my rebellion about my *Papi*'s leaving. Monse consoled her, softly cooing into her hair, holding her shoulders up as if my mother were about to fall. I was slightly scared to see my mother crumble this way—my mother, the strong one, the one who held everything together. I was relieved when it was *Tía* Monse who punished me, a dose of smacks on my butt accompanied by a serious scolding. I followed it all with a bout of tears and hiccups, apologizing to my mother and to *Tía* Monse. I was then sent to my room to "think about what I'd done."

Even with the spanking, I loved *Tía* Monse. She was a party on high heels, always bringing by goodies from her store in Old San Juan. She owned a bakery on Calle Luna called La Deliciosa, near Pigeon Park. Whenever we visited, I'd crane my head way back to admire the building's wide second-floor balconies with their curlicue wrought-iron balustrades. But *Mami, Papi,* and I only went as far as the shop's interior, a wide tile courtyard of sweet delights nestled behind glass. Gold and silver paper stars hung from the domed ceiling, with its celestial mural of clouds and cherubs. Our eyes gleamed in the sugary lights reflected off of *almojabanas* (rice-meal buns), *quesitos* (cream cheese–filled croissants) with their glittering crusts, heart-shaped *tembleque* (coconut custard) dusted with cinnamon and cooled in little tinfoil cups, brilliant *brazos gitanos* (pink-and-white pinwheels of cake and strawberry jam), guava cakes so sweet they were almost bitter. I stood in that sweetshop and imagined each morsel melting on the tip of my tongue.

"Taina Sol, *¡despégate de ahí!* You're getting your fingerprints all over the *vitrine!*" *Mami* would say, pulling me back from the glass by my dress collar. She would wipe her lacy handkerchief along the étagère's surface till all of my breath and touch were erased, the glass made shiny again. *Papi,* though a tad uncomfortable, shifting in his leather loafers, would chuckle and lovingly pat my shoulder.

We never went up the long, winding marble staircase to the second floor, where *Abuelo* lived. I would stretch my neck, feel the cool air circulating in that stone hallway. The air there was so different from the bakery's air, which felt more like the hot breath in a dog's panting mouth. Sunlight spilled through La Deliciosa's arched windows, right onto the bakery's clientele, mostly women in high heels and bulky handbags, their lips whispering about how they were "just looking," their eyes betraying the truth of their awe, lips quietly pursed in an O at the sight of dewy papaya compotes and espresso truffles.

Though *Mami* loved her sister, she didn't like going to Monse's shop; she knew it made *Papi* uncomfortable. He tried his best, though, his eyes always darting up that secret staircase, his eyes telling me *El Cuco,* the bogeyman, lived there. I'd heard of *El Cuco* before. All the kids at school were scared of *El Cuco. El Cuco* came only when parents were angry, when they were at the end of their rope. Nobody I knew had ever seen him, but we'd all agreed one day in the schoolyard that we never wanted to. At the mere mention of his name, *El Cuco,* we'd straighten up. Whatever or whomever you were angry at or with, whatever was wrong in your world that deserved your complaint or tantrum or pout would suddenly disappear, because you were warned . . . *El Cuco* was coming.

One of those muggy Sundays when it felt like the air was being squeezed right out of my chest, and it seemed a union of mosquitoes had voted to swarm all over La Deliciosa, and *Mami* was ignoring all my heated requests for coconut squares and *mantecaditos,* I decided to climb that long, winding marble set of stairs to the second floor to see for myself if *Papi* was right about my grandfather, how *El Cuco* lived there. As quietly as I could I made my way up, right hand against the curved peach stucco wall, all the while holding my breath, trying my best to silence my shoes against their incessant *click-clack*ing on the marble. The farther up I went, the faster people's voices in the bakery downstairs mingled into one soft murmur, the way I could always hear the muffled voice of the dryer turning clothes on the other side of my house. Finally I reached the summit; perched at the end was a long hallway darkened only by the shadows of closed doors. I thought how strange it was that all the doors were shut against my curiosity, since back at our house in Mayaguez, closed doors were not allowed, but kept wide open, letting in the sun from all corners of the yard.

I kept walking on tiptoe, fingers now against my sides, nervously fisting the fabric of my dress. What would I see? What would *El Cuco* look like? I'd never seen pictures of my *abuelo*. Would he have hair? Would he be asleep on the floor, like a dragon? Like a rabid dog, would he bare his teeth? Suddenly there was a cough so loud I could hear it through the first thick door to my right. I leaned in, fingers flat on the cool varnished surface, the scent of lemon oil whisking itself up my nostrils, reminding me of *Mami*'s lemon tree at home. I turned the tin knob slowly, cracking the door open. Fitting the side of my face between the door and its frame, with one wide eye, I scanned the room, and there, sitting in a wide red recliner, black robed and reading a newspaper was . . . *El Cuco.*

"Come here so I can see you," his voice said from behind the crisp pages of the *San Juan Star.* For a moment I felt frozen, unable to place one foot in front of the other. I again scanned the room, this time with both eyes, drinking in every inanimate object standing in the room: tall mahogany wardrobe, thin rocking chair, fat four-poster bed, Spanish lace curtains heaving with the force of the breeze coming from outside. I could see the ocean from this vantage point, blue and waving to me from the distance. He folded one corner of the newspaper, revealing the left side of his face. "I said come here." I moved slowly closer, stopping three paces from him, feeling goose bumps rise on my forearms. The silence divided us.

"I guess your mother and father forgot to teach you manners." I knew what I was supposed to do. Tradition instructed children always to give their elders a kiss on the cheek, asking them for a blessing. How would I do this? I turned my ankle back and forth, twisting a triangle of my dress's hem with my fingers. *Abuelo* unhurriedly creased the paper and held it in his lap. There was no smile on his face, only a tight, thin-lipped line that crossed from cheek to cheek, as if he were trying to keep his teeth inside his mouth. He hawk-eyed me, top to bottom. I nervously looked away, my eyes falling on the pictures on the wall, one of my mother in her twenties, tanning in her two-piece in the Crash Boat Beach sun, posing on a rock like a mermaid, her long brown hair curling around her angled arm. He coughed again, breaking my reverie. I stepped closer to him. One pace. Two paces. Three. Moving closer to his face, I could smell Vicks VapoRub on his pale skin, his chest gurgling in each labored breath. I kissed his cheek quickly, whispering, *"Bendición, Abuelo,"* against his face.

He did not respond with the requisite, *"Dios te bendiga,"* but coughed again, a rough, bristling cackle in his chest, spittle flying out between his lips as he searched his chair for his handkerchief. I searched too and found it, handing it to him at arm's length. He snatched it out of my hands, his eyes never leaving me. With the silk napkin folded against his mouth, *Abuelo* looked me up and down, his flecked-green eyes ungracious, cold, and hard. A chill filled my bones.

"Taina! Taina Sol!" My name wound up the staircase, dashed down the hall and into *Abuelo*'s room. Without looking at my grandfather I rushed toward the door, seeing my mother in its frame, her body stiff and annoyed. She grabbed me by the arm and pulled me to her. I felt the pot of her belly against me, what *Mami* and *Papi* called "Taina's house," the place I lived for the nine months before I entered their world.

"Papá . . ." It was the only word she spoke, moving away from me toward *Abuelo*. She bent down to give him the same kiss in

bendición, but he turned his face from her, looking down at the floor where he'd let his paper fall from off his lap.

"You should teach your daughter to knock."

"Sí, Papá. Perdóname," Mami whispered, the stiffness suddenly going out of her shoulders, slinking down her legs to the Persian carpet on the floor. She slowly stepped back. I could not see her face, but I knew then that she was hurt and that I was in some sort of big trouble. She took my hand and we both slipped out the door, closing it behind us till it clicked.

Mami's grip tightened as we made our way back down the spiral to the bakery, where I knew I could forget getting mantecaditos, churros, or paletas de chocolate or any such sweet till the next time we visited Tia Monse's La Deliciosa in the district of Old San Juan. I never saw my abuelo again and though *Papi* stopped calling him names, I never stopped thinking of him as the true El Cuco.

✧ ✧ ✧ ✧ ✧

I remember El Cuco as I sit down across from my mother to help sort out the past month's catering orders. Though I too am silent, inside my brain is screaming out. I am going to stand my ground, I tell myself. Nothing's going to hold me back. Fortunately the Sister Chicas are back to normal—insert a sigh of relief here. After my five-minute diatribe at Don Ramiro's, the three of us were back again together, the Sister Chicas. All would be well, at least in this department.

But there's Yusef. I haven't heard from him in a couple of days, and I admit I am growing worried. Usually we speak to each other every day. What if he's still angry about not meeting my mom? What if he's turned off? What if he never wants to speak to me again? Graciela thinks I should tell my mother as soon as possible. Only a couple of days left and I'll be fifteen. This would be the moment. *Mami* does not look up at me. I put the orders down and drag my feet toward my room. A poem starts to unfold in my brain; it feels like sparks going off in my head, each word a charge that explodes into image upon image, like a chain of fireworks at

a *fiesta patronal*. I throw myself onto my bed and pull the notebook out from under my pillow.

Last year I started writing poems after a teacher introduced me
to an anthology of Japanese women poets from the early nineteenth century. I loved how the poems were short but seemed
packed with lots of information about where and how they lived,
how they loved and lost. I want to do the same in my own poems,
so I keep them close, for whenever the sparks start to fly in my
head and a poem rises out of the fire.

A GIRL BECOMING
A woman whose heart pounds, brain cranks,
lungs breathe in and out. Two arms and legs move.
Wind-up hips, body an ancient sundial.
Fourteen years now work against you. But there is no doubt
You are a girl. Hairs poke out of many places, secret
and warm. Three years ago your first blood rushed down,
a faucet some forgetful person leaves dripping at the end of
     every month.

I am a girl, no longer a baby waiting for her *Papi* to come
     home.
From a girl on an island to a mainland city, from shygirl
to Sister Chica and first kisses shared with a Jamaican boy.
From loafers to froufrou Cinderella pumps,
dresses the color of angel cake
exchanged for coral from the bottom of the sea. Snap. Girl,
     speak up.
Stop your turning like a top, open your mouth, still
your silent dancing,
under your skin, in your veins. Let your words turn fifteen,
let your words turn you into a woman.

I put the pen down. Wipe fresh tears away. That's it. I have to confront *Mami*. I can't keep this secrecy up, I think, hurrying back
downstairs.

Mami tears open another RSVP with the thin blade of a table knife. There are a scant number of patrons left in El Yunque, each quietly gathering their things as the restaurant's closing time nears. Ramon and Lupe bus the last tables, their eyes every so often falling on mother and daughter, the sound of *Mami* ripping open envelopes echoing through the salon. I see them shake their heads softly. They pass us as if passing two hungry lions and slip into the kitchen to finish cleaning up. I swallow hard and open my mouth. Whole words, full sentences come out; I watch them float up beyond my lips into the air, dive toward *Mami's* ears. Though she says nothing, she stops opening the beaded ecru-colored card stock and closes her eyes.

"*Mami*, listen to me, please. I know you're angry with me. I know I haven't made this *quinceañera* very easy for you. And I know I didn't like the idea of having one at the beginning, but now I do. I really want the party. I'm happy to continue the tradition in the Moscoso family. But I also need you to know that I am not a little girl. I want certain things—"

"Yes, you want to wear that dress your friend Leni bought you," *Mami* interrupts me. It is the first time she looks at me directly in the eyes.

"I do. I really love that dress."

"What's wrong with the one Myrta designed for you?"

"It's too froufrou on me. It's like a wedding cake."

"*Ay, hija, por favor*. Don't be silly." *Mami* sighs, then throws the invitations back on the table.

"That's the thing. Any opinion I have you consider silly. I'm not silly, *Mami*. I've given everything a lot of thought, serious thought." *Mami* turns her body, looks at me, her face less tense. Though she does not smile, I sense a certain release in her, as if a dam has been broken.

"*Nena*, I know you are not silly. I just want you to be careful. There are too many bad things that can happen in life. Too many." Her eyes move away from me to the corner of the room, as if not only fighting back tears but also beating back a painful memory.

"*Mami*, not every guy is like *Papi*."

"Oh, you know all men now?" She turns to me, her face twisted with sarcasm.

"No . . . but I know . . . one." I lose all my saliva at the end of my confession. My mouth goes dry like a stale bit of bread. Afraid of looking at her, I look down at my hands, fingers clutching one another as if they were castaways on a lifeboat in the middle of the ocean, holding one another for dear life. *Oh, God, let this go smoothly.*

"Oh, you do? And do I know who this boy is?" The air between us collapses to the floor, leaving a vacuum I imagine will suck the tablecloth, table, even the sconces and paint off the walls. I really know how to talk to my mother, I think.

"Well, his name is"—another gulp—"Yusef. His parents are dentists from Jamaica—"

"Wait a minute! How do you know his parents already and I haven't even met this boy?" Her surprise heats the room. I scootch my chair back away a bit. "Where did you meet him—and don't tell me any more lies."

"The fifty-six bus a few months ago when you sent me on errands," I mumble.

"¡Ah, pues, claro! You can forget about running errands from now on. I'll send one of the boys." Only the beginning and things were already going badly. *Remember the poem*, I think, *remember the poem.*

"I really like him, *Mami*. Yusef's a good person. He's an artist. He wants to go to art school."

"An artist, huh? That's going to pay the bills? Don't you learn, *nena?*" She closes her eyes and leans heavily into her hands. Something in me tells me to stop, but I have to continue. There's no going back.

"I've asked Yusef to be my *caballero* for the *quinceañera*. He's already gotten his tux and he's excited to meet you—"

At that she shoves her chair back, scraping the varnished floor she had refurbished herself one afternoon two weeks before El Yunque's opening. Before she can escape toward the kitchen, the front door chimes. Apparently Ramon had not locked the door at closing time. There, in black jeans and a thick cable-knit sweater, stands Yusef, in his right hand a small sunshine-colored bouquet of yellow roses. *Peace offering,* I think. Ramon sprints from the back of the restaurant toward him. "I'm sorry, we're closed," he says, pointing the way out. Yusef cranes his neck over Ramon's shoulder, looks at me, and smiles. I notice *Mami* look up suspiciously. Oh, God, I think I have to pee. Suddenly my skin itches; my head hurts. But I stay perfectly still, waiting for the ceiling to collapse. What's he doing here? I don't know if I should be angry at Yusef or bless him with hugs and kisses.

"I'm not here to eat. I'm here to see Mrs. Moscoso." Ramon, sensing trouble in the air, lets Yusef pass. The plate-glass vitrine behind him reveals the rushing street through a reversed view of the island's treasure, the hand-painted cursive script of El Yunque dotted with ten thumbnail-sized tree frogs. He looks strained and pulls the turtleneck of his sweater nervously. Feigning ignorance, I grab a menu and walk over to Yusef (slowly, though inside I itch to run into his arms).

"Hi."

"Hi. You look surprised," Yusef says, stuffing a hand into the pocket of his jeans.

"Wasn't that the point?" I answer, my own hands sweating against the plastic menu. "What are you doing here?"

"You're not happy to see me?" Yusef laughs. Though I know he's uncomfortable with the whole scenario, he helps me relax. Surely meeting him will make my mother thaw a bit. Unfortunately I have to fight back the urge to hug him. I feel Ramon and Lupe look on from the kitchen's rear.

"Well, I'm here. What do we do now?"

"If only you knew—your timing is incredible. I just told her about you."

"And?" His face twists with worry.

"And I don't know. She's not really said anything yet," I lie. I've really botched things up.

"Look, Taina, I've liked you since that first day on the bus when you fell flat on your cute ass. But I can't deal with this much longer. I understand that your mother is old-fashioned and deal-

ing with her own stuff, but there's no real reason I should be anyone's secret."

"I know. . . . Believe me, I don't want you to be." With that, I
gather Yusef's hands in mine and pull him toward my mother. Ramon's mouth has pulled itself into a smile. He winks at me approvingly.

"*Mami,* I'd like you to meet Yusef." Uncharacteristically, Yusef
stumbles toward her, one hand in mine, the other clutching the
slowly wilting flowers. For a second I am disappointed that my
presence in Yusef's life has caused him worry and pain. I hurriedly toss away those thoughts, and smile as much as I can. *Mami*
does not immediately take the flowers. She stares at them and
then at him. Her face looks strained and suddenly tired.

"Both of you, please sit down." Yusef and I look at each other,
as if we'd just been told to slip our own necks into nooses and
kick the chairs out from under our legs. But we follow her order,
pulling out chairs, both of us careful to not make a sound, as if
doing so could endanger any chances at her warming to the idea
of Yusef being my *caballero,* Yusef being my boyfriend. Yusef puts
the roses at the edge of the table, carefully avoiding the flurry of
RSVPs and receipts. *Mami* watches him as he does this, and I am
slowly afraid of what's coming next.

Mami sits down in the same chair where I'd found her, her
hands now folded into her lap, her legs crossed delicately. "First,
I'd like to know how old you are."

"I'm seventeen, ma'am. I'm in my senior year at the University
of Chicago Laboratory School."

"What are your plans for after you finish school?"

"I've applied to several university art programs—I'm waiting to
hear from them. I'd like to stay in Chicago, though. My family and
I are very close." He's very nervous, rubbing the front of his jeans
legs. It is the first time I've seen Yusef in this light, and I feel so
sorry for having put him under my mother's wheels. Her back is
tree-trunk straight, and she's not letting her guard down, I can
tell. I am between the two of them, like a minor chess pawn ready
to fall off the board.

"Well, you realize that I am not pleased with all this. Taina's kept you a secret. Why would she do that? Why she wouldn't tell me the truth?" At those words, Yusef winces. I feel his grip tighten. Inside I rail against *Mami* for her cruelty.

"*Mami*, I didn't lie," I interject, but she shoots me a look that brings me down like a duck rifle-shot out of the sky.

"You've been seeing someone behind my back. You don't call that lying? *¡No me digas!*"

Oh, God, please don't let this deteriorate. I bite my lip, feel the salt collect in my mouth.

"Mrs. Moscoso, I know you're worried, but I'm not going hurt Taina. I want to prove it to you."

"How?"

"I don't know. Maybe with time, now that you know about me. My mother and father want to invite you and Taina over for dinner. And I'd love to help out here in the restaurant. I'm a painter—I can fix your window—"

"My window? There's nothing wrong with my window. What's wrong with my window?"

"If you don't mind my saying . . . the lettering is crooked. And the colors are off."

"*Mami*, Yusef paints island scenes all the time," I offer, hope ringing in each word. She's quiet, looking away from us, as if the sight were too painful for her to swallow. She bites her lip the same way I do, and I suddenly wish I had told her the truth from the start.

"Mrs. Moscoso, please let me escort Taina to the *quinceañera*."

✧ ✧ ✧ ✧ ✧

Mami does not answer Yusef but rushes up and runs upstairs, almost knocking her chair to the floor. With a knee-jerk, Yusef stands up, pale and shocked. "Taina," he whispers, confused. But what can he do? I tell him to sit back down and wait for me. As I slip upstairs to my mother's room, I suddenly see her so very clearly, as if I'd been looking at my mother through a dirty lens for years. I imagine my mother's whole married life rushing back in, memories she'd fought so hard and long to push away, now dropped at her feet: *Papi*'s abandonment, her father's spite, her loneliness. Now all the hurt was back, the way a healed bone will ache when it rains.

I knock on her bedroom door. Though she doesn't answer, I hear her sobbing, a soft mewing that means my mother is trying hard to hold everything in. Slowly, I crack open the door. She is at her vanity, the same one she's had for years, now scratched and pocked and marred from the journey from island to windy northern city.

"*Mami?*" I ask carefully.

"*Ay*, Taina. Go back downstairs."

"No, I want to make sure you're allright."

"I'm fine. I'm fine, really. Go back to your friend." Her back faces me, so I step gingerly toward her, worried for real now. What have I done? What if I've burned her with the news? What if she and I never make up?

"Do you hate me?" I haven't seen my mother cry in such a long time. What else can I do? I want to lay a hand on her shoulder, but I can't touch her just yet, afraid she'll break apart into a thousand crystal pieces and sink into the pile rug.

She turns to me, mascara streaking down her cheeks, lipstick smudged against her sleeve like a bloodstain. "No, *clara que no*. How could I hate my little girl? I just . . . started to remember."

"But . . . you're crying. I don't want you to cry, *Mami*."

"Your friend just reminded me of the past. *Nena*, I don't want you to get hurt."

"I know he's black like *Papi*, but he won't do what *Papi* did."

"What? What do you mean when you say 'he's black like *Papi*'?"

"I thought you'd be angry because he's black."

"Nina! Where did you get that idea? Have I ever shown you I'm ashamed of . . . of . . . *¡ni lo puedo decir!* What kind of *madre* would I be? And you . . . how I adore your beautiful skin. . . . How could you think that about me?" She sits up quick as lightning and caresses my face, her sobs heavier now than before.

I felt something tighten up in me. "You said *Abuelo* was right."

"Yes, I said my father was right about the mistake I made

marrying your father, because your father had no backbone. He ended up caring only for himself. No father should abandon his children. But that, *cariño*, had nothing to do with his color!" *Mami* whispers, her eyes beginning to swell as if stung.

"*Perdoname, Mamá.*"

"*Hija,* I know I'm always rushing around with the restaurant. I know I'm not always understanding or patient. I know we don't talk. I want to change that."

"I do too. I promise I won't lie to you again."

"*Ay.*" She pauses, looking at her hands as if finalizing some invisible tally of thought. "Yusef seems like a nice boy. I'd like to meet his parents. Maybe they can come visit here for dinner. It's such a long time since I cooked for guests or friends. Do you think he likes Puerto Rican food? Oh, that's silly. He's Caribbean. He should love it." She stops and plays with the last button of her blouse. "*Ya, todo esta bien.* Yusef can be your *caballero.*"

Oh, my God! I shriek and hug her, thanking her again and again, almost pulling her off her chair toward me. She chuckles and grips me tighter. "Just promise you'll be good and not get into trouble."

"*¡Ay, Mami!* Yes, yes, yes! I promise you." And this time I meant it.

Suddenly *Mami* stood up, as if she'd forgotten something very important.

"*Ven conmigo;* I have something to give you," she says, slipping her hair back into a knot. "You think Yusef will be okay downstairs for just a minute more?" she asks me as I follow her into her closet, almost tripping on the boxes of shoes scattered on the floor. I nod, and she bends down into the forest of dresses and slacks and pulls out a velvet box the color of the sea. "*Toma.* The jeweler delivered it this morning."

In my trembling hand, the box is heavy, my fingers gently rubbing its exterior. I look up at *Mami,* her face streaked with fresh tears, but beaming in her grin. "Open it, *nena!*" she hurries me. The lid squeaks as I crack it open to reveal a shimmering tiara. If you had asked me two months ago if I wanted a tiara, I would have run away in fear. Now, seeing the beautiful crown in its velvet casing, I am thrilled, my excitement growing by the second. Each gem is trained to another in a long braid of curlicues, glowing like firelight. My mother, feigning impatience, picks the tiara out of its home and carefully sets it on my head. I can feel its weight, the miniature combs at each side pressing into my hair. Gently, *Mami* turns me around to see myself in her full-length mirror.

"Ay, *Mami* . . ." I am speechless, words crowding in my mouth. For the first time I see the beauty the Sister Chicas, Yusef, and my mother see in me.

✧ ✧ ✧ ✧ ✧

"You did what?!" I can tell that Graciela is clutching the phone tightly in her hand.

"I introduced Yusef to my mom." The phone crackles again. It's clear Graciela is struggling with the news. After Yusef drove home and *Mami* went to bed, I called Leni and Graciela, our usual three-way whenever life-changing events came up. Tonight definitely fell into the life-altering category.

"Weelll? What happened? I'm about to bust!" Leni croaks into my ear.

"Yeah, Tai, tell us. Did it go well?"

I start to tell them what happened and they listen intently, the line filled only with my voice and a few intermittent guffaws and oohs and aahs weaving in from the girls on the other side of town.

11

Graciela

It's about three o'clock Sunday afternoon. Usually, after Mass I write in my journal before I help make dinner. Instead I'm just lying on my bed, careful not to wrinkle my maroon skirt and sweater. Letting myself sink into my quilts, I lazily watch the cumulus clouds stack up against the steel-blue horizon. Winter's coming soon, and I daydream about the possibility of snow, shut my eyes, and picture the drift of snowflakes. In my mind's eye everything's covered; everything seems hidden. But I know winter's just a temporary ending; the world always drifts toward spring and new beginnings.

Ever since our big blowup this week, I haven't been myself. It's felt like . . . like I let go of a breath I didn't know I was holding. I feel lighter somehow. Taking off *Santa* Graciela's halo has helped, you know? Usually I'm always working on something, or getting ready, or planning to start, or finishing up. "Just being" is new to me. . . . Strange and new . . . I think I like it.

Jack noticed it too. I felt freer with him. When we had lunch after English lit on Friday, I took the lead in joking about the amount of assignments that Professor Reynolds dishes out; usually it's the other way around. He told me I seemed frisky. Frisky? Who'd believe it?

After I got home from El Rinconcito, I called Librería Tzin-tzuntzán and broke the news to Pilar that I needed to go back to my regular schedule. Lo and behold, the Earth did not stop spinning on its axis. Lalo at Casa Aztlán seemed just fine with my decision, too. *Santa* Graciela was really disappointed, but Graciela Villalobos did just fine. What was amazing to me is that I didn't apologize, I didn't feel guilty. There was just this deep, calm feeling all the time I was talking.

When I called Leni to tell her, she was reading. *Reading.* Can you believe it? I could've sworn I had the wrong number. And it was *un libro Puertorriqueño*, no less! When I asked her about it, she laughed. "Maybe we swapped bodies overnight, Grachi. Let me know if you have an uncontrollable urge to buy a leather bustier and spike your hair."

As I got ready for bed that night I thought about Taina, how when she finally told us the about Yusef, her usual shyness dissolved *como azucar en café*. She was no longer my little sister who hovered at the edge of things. With every word she was clear and strong and alive, so alive. I remember thinking, *Love must make you more yourself,* just before I fell asleep.

I lazily pull myself out of bed. I'll need to be helping *Mamá* soon. I stand on my tiptoes, stretch and yawn, and slowly walk over to the mirror over my dresser. I inspect my reflection. I look the same, but I don't feel like me, at least the old me. Instead of more thoughts of snow and wintry blasts, one word comes to mind: love. How love changes things without anyone trying. Things like brushing a leaf from your hair becomes someone's mark on you, and yours on them. Love takes a phone call in the dark and turns it into a promise. It turns a wisecracking ex-jock, my best friend beside my girls, into *mi novio, mi corazón.*

It should be the two of us celebrating at the *quinceañera*. I want him to stand with me in Taina's court. I want him to spin me around the floor of La Reina Borinqueña. I want to feel his lips over mine, brush imaginary snowflakes from his hair, taste real snowflakes on his skin. I check my reflection for embarrassment. Who I see looking back at me is clear-eyed and unafraid.

Now all I have to do is tell him and my parents.

My parents . . . *mi Papá.* For the first time in my life I'm going back on a promise to him, something that meant a lot, something he asked me to do. I wait for my heart to sink, for that feeling of guilt so strong that I immediately change my mind, but it doesn't come. All I feel is that quiet calmness, that same stillness and strength as when I talked to Pilar and Lalo. Taking this stand is right for me, and I have Leni to thank for waking me up to the truth. I love Jack. I've made my decision; I just have to find the words.

Everything I want to say is swirling around in my head. I scramble off the bed and grab my journal and a pen from my desk. I want to hold on to this feeling, these things I know are true, not have them fade away. Once I put pen to paper, it's all so clear, the words just rush free, almost as if they're writing themselves.

> *I love you, Leni, and you, too, Taina.*
> *You're my girls, the other part of me. . . .*
> *My Sister Chicas,* mis hermanitas.
> *You, Jack . . . What I feel for you seems so much bigger than just four letters. I want you to know what's in my heart. I don't want you to be sorry you waited for me.*
> *Te quiero, Mamá. Te quiero, Papá. Por siempre. I never hesitate when it comes to you. That's why I want to get this right . . . that's why, Papá, you have to listen to me.*
> *Papá . . . Ay, mi papá . . . I learned something today. Love changes you and changes people in ways you never expect. Look at you and Mamá; such different lives from what you planned when you were young. I know all the things you gave up because you loved me. This is hard for me to tell you. . . . I made a decision today that I want you to understand. I could make it only because of you, because of everything you've done. I know that hearing it may hurt you, but you taught me to be honest with you.*
> *And once I tell you, if I seem less like your* hijita, *believe me when I say I will always be your Graciela.*

I hear *Mamá* calling from the kitchen, "*¡Querida!* I'm ready for you! Come and help me!"

"I'm coming," I yell, as I hurriedly put my things away. "I'll be right there." I stop in the bathroom to wash my hands and I take one last look at myself. Same brown eyes, same cap of black hair. Funny how I still look like I always do when I feel so different inside.

As I dry my hands, I whisper to the empty room, "I hope you're ready for me, *Mamá,* I really do."

La cocina is *Mamá*'s sanctuary. Cooking is usually a solitary thing for her, but Sunday afternoon is our time to share this place, share time with each other. She told me she looks forward to being alone—dicing and stirring, sampling and seasoning. When I was about fifteen I asked her why she loved it so much.

"*Mi'ja mía,* it's where I get to be alone with my thoughts. It's my time for myself."

"But *Mamá,*" I said, "you're always so busy. And you work all day long with your hands."

"Graciela, *mi amor,* you don't understand. Work is work, *está bien.* But here, in my room, my thoughts soar *como una paloma;* my spirit flies. This isn't work," she proclaimed as she proudly gestured to the little dishes of flan she had just pulled from the oven. Golden yellow, glistening, streaked with perfect caramel crust, orange brown, a burnt-sugar offering in the hands of my mother. "This, *mi amor,* is art. Lucky for you and *Papá,*"—she laughs—"I share *mis obras con mi familia!*"

The kitchen's also her *ofrenda,* the walls covered with pictures of family. We have photos scattered all over the house, and albums filled to bursting, but the ones she chose for this room are special. They show family celebrations, four generations—us, her parents and their parents before them. Even though my father teased her, for her "extravagant taste", she had him paint it butter yellow, the color of sunlight. It makes the old wooden shelves and the Formica table and vinyl-covered chair seem inviting.

This time of year, vases and jars are crammed onto the sills and counters, brimming with marigolds, *zempasuchitl. La cocina* is the place where she takes the hiss of oil in the pan and creates a masterpiece, where she meditates to the sound of her cleaver against a wooden cutting board. My mother's a woman whose prayers waft to heaven in the aroma of her *comidas exquisitas*. My mother's kitchen is where she celebrates life and honors the dead.

"*¡Finalmente!* I was starting to think you'd disappeared." My mother's wearing a chef's apron over her Sunday dress, her long hair swept up into a chignon. Even though the dress is resale, it fits perfectly, made from good wool. She is still beautiful, still the one who stole *Papá*'s heart so long ago. Her eyes sparkle as if she's enjoying a private joke as I enter the room.

"Important personal business, *mi'ja?*" Handing me a bowl of masa, she shoos me to the table, where the *tortilla* press is waiting, lined with the little oiled circles of plastic wrap.

"*Lo siento, Mamá,*" I tease back, "I was trying to make myself beautiful like you."

"Graciela, *corazón*, you're already beautiful. Beautiful in your own way, as it should be. Now help me make the tortillas; the *caldo Tlalpeño* is almost ready."

I roll the masa between my hands into a ball, then set it in the press, which reminds me of two tennis rackets with a handle, fastened with a hinge. It's easy work, and I'm happy to do it. The press sits on the table. You open the lid and place the oiled plastic over the top and bottom on the inside. Center the masa in the bottom, pull the handle, and a tortilla is ready for the grill. We usually have our own assembly line, our little ritual. I make the tortillas; she cooks them on the griddle, careful to wrap them in a dish towel when they're done, so they stay *calientito*.

Before I finish pressing the masa, I'm distracted by the scent of *caldo*. I leave my post and slip over to the stove, where *Mamá* is stirring the pot and humming to herself.

"You can't resist your *Mamá*'s cooking, can you?"

I shrug my shoulders. "It's not my fault it's so delicious."

"I see, so this is my fault. *Pues,* I guess this means I'd better let you have a taste, or else we'll never get any tortillas made today."

I nod my head eagerly, grinning while she dips her ladle into the bubbling liquid. A second later she's grazing my lips with the edge of the big spoon. Amazing soup, perfumed with *cebolla y* earthy *ajo*, the sharp green scent of cilantro, the warmth of chipotle. Chunks of *pollo, zanahoria, calabaza*. Definitely not Campbell's.

I close my eyes and savor every drop. *Mamá*'s chuckling the whole time, and when I'm finished, she pinches my cheek.

"Now get to work, *chiflada*."

Soon I'm lost in the syncopation of roll, press, remove, the spark of *grasa* sizzling on the griddle. It's seamless; it's almost a dance. I make the tortillas, handing them off to *Mamá*. Toasting one side, she flips it and toasts the other, then one-handedly undrapes the growing stack and covers it again. By the time she's done I have another ready.

The rhythm is soothing; neither one of us says a word for a while. Part of me doesn't want this to end, *la intimidad entre nosotros*, this simple bond of shared work and silence. But I breathe, and set my feet firmly on the floor and start the conversation.

"*Mamá*, when did you know *Papá* was the one?"

"Why *mi'ja*, I think I always knew . . . but it took a while for me to realize it."

"What do you mean? *Papá* always said it was love at first sight."

"That's true . . . for him," she laughs. "I had to come to my own conclusions. He was my friend for a long, long time. It was almost four years before I felt something change."

"But something happened and you knew, ¿*verdad*?"

"Something happened, *mi amor*. Something as silly as him standing in the rain outside *la casa de tus abuelitos* the morning of my twenty-first birthday. It was pouring, and he was drenched and *las flores* were completely ruined. And as soon as I opened the door, and saw *mi* Alejandro miserably wet, cradling an armful of drooping *rosas y margaritas,* I knew *adentro de mis huesos* he was the one. . . . *Este fue un momento importante*. A person has only a handful of them in a lifetime, *mi corazón*. When they happen, you have to pay attention."

"*Mamá* . . ." I try to say it, I do, but I'm overwhelmed. I feel so much right now. Love for her, for *Papá,* for Jack, for my girls, for my life as it is, for where it seems to be taking me.

"*Dígame, preciosa;* you can tell me anything."

"Jack, *Mamá* . . . it's Jack . . . I love him. I love him, *Mamá.*"

Throwing a towel over the tortillas, she hurriedly turns off the stove and comes over. "Ah . . . *mi'ja,* I wondered when you would tell me."

"You knew?"

"Of course, I'm supposed to notice these things." Gathering me into her arms, she strokes my hair just like she did when I was little.

"Oh, *Mamá,*" I cry, "I love you too! And *Papá!* And Leni and Taina!"

"*Claro que sí.* There's room in your heart for all of us, *¿verdad?*"

I nod, and pull away just enough to see the tenderness soft as velvet, the world of feeling in her eyes. Eyes just like mine.

"*Mamá.* I want him to come with me to Taina's *quinceañera.*"

"Well, then I guess we'd better make a really good meal for your *papá.*"

"*Mamá,* be serious, what do I do?"

"*Mi'ja, estoy en serio.* First we feed your *papá;* then we'll tell him."

I take the dishes out of the cupboard and start setting the table. My mother stops me with an arm on my shoulder.

"Go call Jack while your *papá* is still on his walk and ask him to come by after dinner. Say you have *una sorpresa* for him."

I make sure the call is brief, although Jack did his best to keep me on the line, trying to get me to give up my secret.

Papá comes home just as I hang up the phone, hugging me and laughing as I shiver from the cold that clings to him. While he hangs up his coat, I hurry back to the kitchen and help *Mamá* get our meal on the table.

My father holds court while we eat, extravagantly praising *Mamá's obra del día,* proclaiming her *caldo* worthy of a Neruda poem, and her tortillas deserving of an essay by Fuentes. Making sure he asks me about school, he's especially interested in what I'm writing for La Mondragon's class. He charms *Mamá,* one minute flirting with her, the next asking about the latest neighborhood news. He's particularly happy, since contract negotiations are almost over. I can see the pride in his face, how it adds its strength, how it makes him sit taller in his chair as he recounts each important detail. The major victory is that the company wasn't able to cut benefits, partially due to *Papá* working hard behind the scenes, making sure the committee and the members stayed strong, visiting people at home, making phone calls from the union office, making sure the members knew what was at stake. It meant a lot of late hours over the last few weeks, less time with us, but it's clear it was worth it.

Mamá teases him. "Alejandro, I was just getting used to the peace and quiet!"

"You can forget about that, *mi amor*. I'll be home again every night to chase my beautiful wife around the house." Announcing he wants more *agua de jamaica,* he gets get up from the table. But instead of going to the refrigerator, he throws his arms around *Mamá,* nuzzling her neck until she's almost breathless with laughter.

"*¡No más! . . . ¡Por favor!*" she shrieks, reaching around to pull him toward her.

"Can't get enough of me, *¿verdad?*"

Cupping his face in her hands, she bestows a kiss on his smiling mouth, then pushes him away. *"Tenemos sed también, mi amor."*

Papá pushes himself free and turns to wink at me. "You see what I have to put up with?" When he turns away to fetch the pitcher from the refrigerator, I look at *Mamá,* who's already read my mind. Nodding in unison, we get ready to break the news.

The glass pitcher makes its rounds at dinner, the *agua de jamaica* sparkling like rubies underneath the kitchen lights as *Papá* pours us all more to drink. I clear my throat and sit straight in my chair.

Mamá, smoothing her hair into place, announces, "Alejandro, there's something we need to discuss. Graciela has already spoken to me about it."

"*Pues,*" my father teases, "do I need to sit down for this?"

"*Sí, Papá,* I think you do."

All the amusement ebbs from his voice, and his eyes darken with concern, shifting in seconds from *color de café* to *obsidiana* as he takes his seat.

"*Mi'ja*, is there something wrong? A problem with school?"

"No, *Papá*, school is fine . . . nothing's wrong. It's . . . I've made a decision."

Somehow my father guesses this is news he won't be happy to hear. Pushing his chair back from the table, he folds his arms across his chest. "I see. . . . And exactly what is this decision?" This is the voice I've heard all my life, the voice of the man who was always the center of the universe. Full of strength, full of conviction.

I shift a little in my seat. I can feel my heart race. I plunge ahead; I need to; I have to. "Taina's *quinceañera, Papá*. I want to bring Jack. *Él es mi novio*, I should be going with him." This is the hardest thing I've ever said, but I don't crumble, don't shirk from his gaze.

"Ah, I see . . . so promises to your father should be broken, then."

"*¡Papá!* It's not like that—"

He cuts me off before I can finish. "*No, es exactamente así.* You tell me you're going to do something; now you go back on your word." His words are laden with disappointment and a growing anger that we both can see he's trying to tamp down. He swallows hard, the lines in his face seeming to etch themselves deeper the longer he speaks.

"Graciela, *dígame*, is this how I've raised you to behave?"

As I falter for an answer, my head swims. He's right: For the first time in my life I'm breaking a promise to him. I am going back on my word; I know it. I still don't back down. I don't say a thing, struggling to find a way to make him understand. *Please*, Papá, I silently beg, *can't you see I'm choosing my own life, not turning my back on anyone?*

Mamá comes to my rescue, her voice as calm as still water. "Alejandro, *no te enojes.* Listen to me: I agree with our Chela. She should be going with Jack."

He turns, unable to hide his surprise. "*Qué dices a mí?* Am I no longer the head of this household? I asked our daughter to do something for me *y por familia.* Is my judgment being questioned?"

"*No, mi amor,*" *Mamá* answers, her voice soothing like balm on a wound. "But a wise father trusts that all his hard work has given him a daughter to be proud of. One whose judgment he can trust. A wise father would do anything to give that daughter her heart's desire. A wise husband knows his wife wants only what's best for their child."

My father says nothing, the quiet looming large as he looks first at me, then at *Mamá*. Por favor, I pray, *let this silence become a bridge between us and not a door closing*. There are so many questions in his eyes, and something else I don't completely recognize, something that seems like a kind of grief.

Finally he clears his throat. "*Pues,* never let it be said that this family lacks a wise father and husband. . . . Chela, you have my permission—"

Before he can say another word, I jump out of my chair and run over to him. Flinging my arms around his neck, I cry, "*¡Ay, Papá!* Thank you . . . thank you so much!" I'm surprised to feel him holding himself stiffly, as if he's gotten bad news.

He eases out of my embrace, and those dark eyes still glint with something tragic.

Pressing a kiss to my forehead, he pushes away from the table, even though there's still *caldo* in front of him.

Turning to *Mamá*, he says, "I'm going to get some air, *mi amor*. I'll finish your wonderful meal *mas tarde*."

I try to follow after him, but *Mamá* stops me with a hand on my shoulder, "*Mi'ja*," she whispers. "*Tu Papá* needs some time to himself. Help me clean up and then you can see how your father is doing."

Stillness descends again as we clear the table, put away the supper, and do the dishes. As I finish drying the silverware, my mother pulls me into a loose hug. Resting my head over her heart, I can smell her perfume, feel the rasp of the wool against my cheek. We don't speak, but I know I am still her daughter, no matter what. I will never be too old for her to hold me like this, for her to show me she understands everything about me with a simple gesture.

Smoothing back my hair, *Mamá* ends the quiet, her voice

husky. "Why don't you go out on the porch and talk to your *Papá*."

I look up to make sure she's not crying, "*¿Mamá, todo está bien?*"

"I'm fine, *mi'ja*. . . ." She smiles, radiant like the sun. Her eyes glitter, mirror bright with feeling, with tears unshed. "Everything is as it should be. Go on . . . It will give your *mamá* some time for herself."

I hesitate, and she spins me around and pretends to spank me. "I told you to do something, Graciela." She laughs. "*Ándale:* your father needs some looking after."

I scurry away toward the front door, hoping that *Papá* will be glad to see me.

When I step outside, I'm hit with a wave of cold, crisp air. I smell traces of the last of the dying leaves underneath the sharp tang of burning wood from the few homes that still have old fireplaces. *Papá*'s leaning against the mailbox, hands cupped around his mouth, huffing away the chill. His breath spirals upward, up and away.

"*Papá*," I say. "Are you all right?" The wind kicks up and I can't help but shiver, hunching my shoulders against the cold.

Gathering me close, he cradles my hands in his, rubbing them together to keep them from freezing. For a split second I'm not the newly independent Graciela with her big news. I'm five years old again. I'm his *princesa*, grateful for his protection.

"You still need me for some things, *¿eh, mi'ja?*" He seems thoughtful, a little amused, maybe a little wistful.

"Oh, *Papá* . . ." I sigh. Glancing up at him, I'm relieved the sadness from before is gone.

"Graciela, remember when you asked me about Tilbrook?"

"Of course I do."

"This is what I meant when I said no one can promise to stay the same. . . . Everything changes, *mi'ja*. You. Me. *Mamá*. You grow up, we grow older, and hopefully we have *la gracia* to see that we will always be *familia*, whatever comes our way."

"Papá, I'm still your *hijita*." The words are puffs of breath, punctuating the space between us like little markers.

He smiles, and the corner of his eyes crinkle, his handsome face holding both *alegría* and longing. Shaking his head, he says, "You're my daughter, Graciela . . . but not a little girl, not anymore."

I burrow into his shirt, sighing into his chest as his arms enfold me. My eyes drift shut as I memorize this perfect, important moment. We stand together, breathe together. I am his daughter, now and always, and I am myself more than ever.

"Graciela . . ." *Papá* drawls my name, his voice laden with teasing.

"*Sí, Papá,*" I answer into his shirt, not moving away, not breaking his embrace.

"*¿Novio?*"

I nod, and feel him begin to laugh, a deep, rich laugh that jostles me loose.

"Jack is very lucky, *mi'ja*. Make sure you tell him I said that."

"I will, *Papá,*" I assure him, laughing now too, ignoring the sting in my cheek from the cold. "Or you could tell him yourself. . . . He'll be here in a little while."

Clutching his heart, *Papá* pretends to stumble. "The *novio* coming already? *Ay,* you're giving me *un ataque de corazón. . . .*" When all I do is laugh at his "distress," he announces, "*Vamos, hace mucho frío.* Let's go in so your poor old *papá* can warm his bones."

As I open the front door, my father can't resist adding, "And you, Señorita Villalobos, better hurry and get ready for your date."

I spend the next hour in my room writing down what happened. And yes, changing my clothes. Three times to be exact. After I put away my journal, I have a rush of nervousness that if Leni or Taina ever saw it, I would be the subject of *las bromas* for the rest of my life. I think I'm entitled, it's not every day I tell someone I'm in love with him. After thinking my church clothes seem too serious, as in, *Jack, I have an announcement to make,* I change into sweats, thinking that casual might be the way to go. You know, *Hi, Jack, love you lots.* Then I remember this is someone who knows me, who loves me as I am. Finally, I settle on black slacks and a cream sweater, not cashmere but really soft, my latest Cheap Rags bargain. The first time I wore it was weeks ago at school. We were in the library, supposedly researching a paper on Elizabethan poets. At least I was. When I looked up from the stacks to ask Jack a question, I caught him staring at me. How he managed to look miles away and completely focused on me at the same time, I'll never know. When I asked him what he was thinking, he leaned down and whispered in my ear, "One word. Wow."

Lightly stroking his way down my sleeve, he trailed his way from my shoulder to my wrist. "Soft," he murmured, "so soft."

I forgot what I wanted to ask him. My head buzzed; my skin tingled in each place he touched me. Jack had a faint smile on his lips, and his eyes held a dreamy cast. We just stood there, suspended, ignoring everything else, blocking the aisle between English literature and anthropology.

"Wow, huh?" I asked him.

"Most definitely wow," he replied.

Wow seems like a good idea today.

Clothes on, boots on, teeth brushed, hair combed, I'm ready at last. I add the final touch of putting on a little lip gloss, when I hear *Mamá* call me.

"Graciela! Someone's here for you." I grab my peacoat and my beret and hurry to meet him.

It's about four thirty in the afternoon and I'm not surprised that it's already starting to get dark. *Mamá* winks at me as she goes back in the kitchen, where she has my father finishing his dinner. Our front door's partially open and there he is, half inside, half outside, the porch light casting a halo around him. Tall and lanky, brown hair tousled from the wind, wearing a black leather jacket and a red muffler draped loosely around his neck. Sporting a smile that threatens to split his face in two. It's at least a month early, but you'd think it was Christmas morning. My Jack.

"Hey," I say.

"Hey right back atcha. . . . Looks like you're going somewhere."

"I am . . . with you."

Linking his arm in mine, I pull him outside, and don't let go as I use my free hand to shut the door behind us. Sneaking a peek at him from the corner of my eye, I can tell he's surprised and pleased. Clattering down my front stairs, he yells, "You gonna tell me what we're doing?"

"We're taking a walk," I yell back.

As we make our way down my street, the windows of brick bungalows and two flats glow golden with the lights silhouetting families having Sunday dinner, spending time together. The wind kicks up, and Jack halts our procession to pull up the collar of my peacoat. I return the favor by making sure his scarf is firmly in place.

"This isn't the big surprise, is it?"

"No," I dryly reply, "I think we've both walked before."

"Ouch . . . Since when have you been a woman of mystery?"

"Keep it up and you have to force it out of me."

"Oooh . . . Sassy, Graciela. Okay, I'll play along. Just drag me wherever you want."

I keep my secrets awhile longer, as we walk past houses and corner *taquerías*, finally arriving at the corner of Damen and Nineteenth. Mayor Dailey calls this place Harrison Park, but everyone in the neighborhood knows it as Parque Zapata. We zig and zag across the broad open space, passing the Mexican Fine Arts building, the scattering of concrete park benches, the stands of naked trees and clumps of old grass that shimmer pale yellow under the overhead lights.

We walk around the batter's cage and keep moving until we're smack dab in the middle of the baseball field. Turning to the east, we see a break in the line of neighborhood buildings and we're able to see the city skyline glittering like a necklace on the throat of night. There are no stars visible, no moon, only a billowing frame of low-hanging clouds that starts crawling toward us.

"I wanted you to see this." I feel him slip behind me and I lean back, resting all my weight on him. I could fall if he moves away, but I know he won't. He never has.

"It's beautiful, Graciela," he whispers, draping his arms over my shoulders, resting his chin on the crown of my head.

"Should I tell you my surprise?"

"Only if you feel like it. Tonight's been pretty surprising already. . . . I'm not complaining, though."

"I . . . I want to ask you to Taina's *quinceañera*. I know it's late, and you don't have—"

"Ssssh. . . . You're not giving me a chance to say yes, and I want to say yes, Graciela."

"There's something else I have to say." I don't turn around; I think if do I'll lose my nerve.

"I know; you don't have to tell me." He laughs. "We're gonna have to make time to practice the dancing, and I have to hurry and get a tux, and I'd better not be late, and your father probably wants to buy me a one-way ticket to Nome."

"I love you," I answer.

Then he goes still, still, still. I don't feel him move; I don't think I move either. Then slowly he turns me around so that we're face-to-face. I can't make out the exact color of his eyes underneath the sodium lights, but they're some kind of blue I've never seen before. His gaze pins me where I stand, and I feel hot and cold, and so alive I can't help trembling.

"Yes?"

I can barely make out what he's saying because my heart's drumbeating has almost drowned him out. He's asking me, making sure.

"Yes," I say.

Jack takes a long, slow, careful breath; then he's anything but careful, pulling me to him in a joyful, urgent, clumsy mess. My eyes flutter closed and he brushes his lips against mine, presses his open mouth to mine; and then all I know is he's warm, so warm. And he's kissing me hard and pressing his fingertips against my spine, and something in us has been set loose, and we don't stop, won't stop, not for a long time.

Something does bring an end to this, something falling, falling, falling. Falling softly on my face, his back, slowly blanketing us with pinpoints of white. I break away and make him gaze up at the sky with me. Snow. Snow in his hair, snow on my lashes, snow on the collar of his coat. I remember my daydream from this afternoon and grab his scarf, pulling him down to my level. Without hesitating, I press my lips to his neck right where a snowflake just fell. It's as delicious as I thought it would be.

"Graciela," he groans. "Pinch me or slap me . . . I must be dreaming."

I kiss him instead, covering his satiny mouth with mine. When I'm done, I take my thumb and slowly wipe away the last remnants of my kiss from his lower lip.

"Not what I asked for," he quips, "but I can live with that."

"You'd better plan on it, then."

"Bossy, aren't you?"

"Hey, you're the one in love with me."

"That I am," he answers. "That I am."

He walks me home, and we can see *Papá* standing in the window, trying to look nonchalant, waving as he see the two of us approaching. Jack waves at *Papa,* then winks at me before he gives me a brief, sweet kiss and whispers, "Better behave myself." As he walks to his car I stay on the porch, watching him drive away until his car turns the corner and disappears.

Later that night, it's dream after dream of loose-leaf notes that turn into love letters, love letters that turn into kisses, kisses that turn into snowflakes, snowflakes that blanket Jack and me.

12

LENI

I just can't get the image of Carlos's smile out of my head. I can still feel the warmth of his palm on my face even though I stumbled out of the coffee shop over an hour ago. What was that all about, anyway? Was I actually jealous of Ana's interest in Carlos? I don't get jealous! I make other people jealous! Besides, Carlos is just a friend. Right? But he is hot. Really hot. *What the hell is going on with me? Leni, get it together.* Oh, well, maybe this walk in the fresh air will clear my head. I stop and zip up my worn black leather motorcycle jacket. It might technically still be fall, but winter is skulking in fast, creeping around the buildings, low along the sidewalk and up my black-jeans-painted legs. I continue walking, not sure yet where I'm heading. I stare down at the round, shiny, black tips of my boots going in and out of view as I walk briskly, and I feel kind of hypnotized by their rhythm. That scene with Carlos really shook me. I can't seem to stop buzzing. What happened when he touched me? He felt it too. At least I think he did. So I think he's hot, so what? I've thought that about lots of guys. But Carlos is different, and I know it. He's the only guy who gets me. Who straddles both of my worlds, and is comfortable in either.

I stop at the corner, consider hailing a cab home, but change my mind. I can't go home. Not yet. I stand on the deserted corner and stare at the traffic lights changing from red, to green, to yellow, back to red. *¡Ay, Dios!* I'm never out of it like this. I'm not a stare-at-the-wall-and-space-out kind of girl, you know? I need to go somewhere where I can let my hair down. I run my fingers through my short, spiked orange hair and smile. Okay, bad metaphor. I want to have a drink, do some meaningless flirting, and dance. Yup, that's just what the doctor ordered. The plan of action snaps me out of my haze, and I cross the street against the light.

I decide to keep on walking rather than take a cab, as the cold air does seem to be bringing me back to life after a wild and woolly day. I turn west, leaving the Gold Coast, and start heading toward Lincoln Park. It's a long walk, it's cold out, and I don't care. I need to clear my head. I turn the corner of Clark Street, and smile as the familiar and comforting neon glow of the sign for Neo comes into view. Ahh, my favorite club. My home away from home. I stop, take a deep breath, and realize it was really my first of the night. I unzip my jacket pocket and pull out my cell to call home.

"Mom, I'm going dancing at Neo. Just for a while."

"No problem, honey, be careful. And take a cab home."

I press "end" and zip the phone away, shaking my head. Mom and I used to be more like roommates than mother and daughter. I don't know what is up with her lately, some middle-age crisis or something, but she has been acting almost maternal.

I stride into the club, attitude overpowering my scrambled brains, and I give Norman the bouncer a high five. Head held high, my eyes sweep over the club. Man, this place is dead! The piped-in punk music is blaring, and the band is nowhere in sight. I look at my watch and realize that it's not even eight o'clock. It's still early. I look over at the empty rows of bar stools, and just as I am about to give up and resign myself to home and a hot bath, a familiar face pops up from behind the bar. My buddy, bartender, and makeout artist, Kevin O'Donnell. Thank God! Things are looking up already. At least there will be one cute guy to flirt with. A guy who doesn't confuse the hell out of me. I head toward the bar, my hips remembering their flirty swagger atop my knee-high, shiny-slick boots.

"Hey, Kevin, what's up?" I shout over the strains of Iggy Pop. I pick out my regular seat from the row of torn red leather stools, and before I even settle in Kevin has set my usual drink in front of me. "This is just what I needed." I sigh, mainly to myself. I look up and smile into my boy's light blue, crinkled eyes. I've always been a sucker for boys who smile with their eyes. And I can pretty much guarantee that the only feeling I've ever had for Kevin was lust. Yep, he's a straightforward, fun-to-grope-but-forget-about-the-next-day type of guy. I take a long and refreshing sip, feeling the warmth of the vodka and the coolness of the citrus and tonic travel down my chest. I close my eyes for a second, enjoying the taste. When I open them I find Kevin staring at me, an amused look on his face. His intense gaze makes me feel a little uncomfortable, but I'm not sure why. I should be feeling relieved. Kevin is one of my "club buddies." He's one of those friends who know me only when I come out at night. Under throbbing strobes, we sweat on the dance floor against the beat of industrial or old-school punk, a wall of noise. I like the wall; I need it. Most of my "friends" don't even know my last name, and they certainly don't know I'm still only in high school. That works for me. I'm looking for escape. A Neo escape. "So Kevin, who's playing tonight?" I ask, putting my drink down on the shiny black bar in front of me and looking at him with a flirtatious grin.

"Terror X. Totally raw, hard-core, you know? Their manager keeps trying to get them to cover Dead Kennedys, but he's an ass-hole. You've heard 'em before, right?"

"No, what are they like?" I ask, not really caring, trying to zone out.

Kevin goes on to rave about their original stuff, their arrest record for drunk and disorderly conduct, and the amount of "world-class" groupies they attract. Half listening, half decompressing, I take another long sip of my cocktail and feel my shoulders relax. Yes, this is much better. I don't drink much, and no, I'm not interested in a lecture right now. I can start to feel myself loosen up when I'm distracted by a commotion to the right of the bar. Out of the corner of my eye I see a new busboy struggling with an overloaded bin, trying to push his way through the swinging door that leads to the kitchen next to the bar. The container is almost larger than he is, and he is trying to carry it while pushing the door open with his narrow hips. I smile sympathetically. Must be his first day. My attention returns to Kevin, but he is droning on about how the lead singer is a communist from London, and I start to zone out. Maybe I am too tired for this. All of a sudden I hear an outcry in Spanish, and I look over to see the busboy stumble, and the three of us watch the bus bin filled with glasses crash in slow motion to the floor, splashing stale beer and ice cubes on Kevin. For a second no one moves. The busboy's eyes are wide and his jaw hangs open. Kevin is looking down at his soaking wet Sex Pistols T-shirt and black jeans. His eyes slowly rise, and I can tell Kevin is pissed off as he glares at the frightened busboy, his blue eyes not looking so cute or crinkled anymore. Poor kid looks like he couldn't be more than fifteen years old.

"Why don't you just clean that up and get back into the kitchen, okay, Enrique?" Kevin says in a syrupy, condescending way, like he is talking to a naughty child, his arms held straight out at his sides, his hands curling in and out of fists. I am surprised to see this side of Kevin. He's acting like a jerk. Enrique looks panicked and embarrassed, and after he puts the glasses back in the bin and cleans up, he backs into the kitchen, the bin tightly grasped to his chest, his eyes on the floor. The door swings closed, and Kevin curses in my direction. "Fucking wetbacks!" he spits as he wipes off his creased black jeans.

For a second I can't believe what I've heard. I feel the blood start to rise to my face. "Wh-what did you say?" I ask Kevin.

"You just can't trust those people to do a goddamn simple job, you know, Leni?" Kevin gripes as he grabs a clean bar rag and begins blotting his shirt with finicky and surly motions. *I can't deal with a man who is overly fussy with his clothes,* I think absently.

Suddenly Kevin's last comment sinks in. I'm surprised to feel a white heat burning in my chest, replacing the gentle warmth of the vodka. "Those people? Those people?" For the tenth time in a week, I have no words. I sputter at Kevin, a feeling of rage foaming up behind my eyes. "Kevin, what is your problem? I had no idea you were such an asshole! Give the guy a break." But it's not just about Enrique anymore. It's much bigger, and I am confused by the intensity of my anger.

"Jeez, Leni! Give *me* a break!" Kevin starts to try to make nice with me again. "You understand, don't you? They're just not like you and me," he says with a smile that doesn't quite reach his eyes.

For a few seconds I just stare at him, my eyes wide and my mouth open. I am floored that this dickwad is actually including me in his bigoted little club. My anger exceeds the boiling point and hits that scary calm. I lean over the bar as an ice-cold smile spreads across my face and I stare into Kevin's pale eyes, sarcasm dripping off my lips, "Well, what makes you think I'm anything like you, you fool!"

"Leni, I don't know what you are so pissed off about! All I mean is just that we're not like him! He's just a little spic!"

At that point I can no longer control my rage. I continue staring at him, my arms holding me up on the bar as I stand on the rungs of the bar stool, white fire burning behind my eyes just inches from his. Before I even know my hand has moved, I push off from the bar, grab my almost-full vodka tonic with a twist, and hurl the contents of the glass at Kevin's face. I stand and stare at him as the piece of lemon slides down his eyebrow, and I am amazed that the flames coming from my eyes don't ignite the alcohol that's streaming down his hair and face. Staring at this drowned, spineless rat, I get the sudden urge to laugh. But we both just stand there, shocked by what I've done. Just then, out of the corner of my eye I see Norman's bulk coming my way—he's quick to spot trouble—and it breaks my trance. Before he reaches me, I jump off the stool and turn on my heel. I put up my hand in the "stop" motion to Norman, and he obeys. This bruiser of a guy who benches 350 and doesn't take shit from anyone is standing there speechless and not sure what to do with little ol' me. I feel new-found power in this wrath, and it doesn't feel all bad somehow. I wonder if this is how Grachi feels all the time. Norman starts to stammer my name, and I cut him off with, "Don't bother, Norman; I'm leaving. The company here sucks!" I jerk my head toward a muttering Kevin. I swagger toward the door, anger and disgust controlled by certainty and righteousness, and I hear one

last word echo from behind me as I step into the cool evening air:
"Bitch!"

✧ ✧ ✧ ✧ ✧

For the second time this weekend, I'm glad to be home. Mom
turned in early, so I have the whole place to myself. The hot bath
did me a lot of good. I'm not sure what got into me, but as the
oversize, Italian-marble tub filled, I grabbed a box of Mom's old
L'Oréal hair color—when she flirted with the idea of being a
brunette—and before I had time to think too much about it,
slathered the Medium Honey Brown goo all over my head. Of
course, I ignored the clear plastic disposable gloves that were
pasted to the instructions, so my palms now match my hair color.
I shrug. Maybe I can start a new trend. But when I slid into the
Jacuzzi's jet-streamed water, I could feel the weight of the day
slide off of my skin. I closed my eyes and breathed deeply, feeling
the lavender scent of Mom's bath oil spread throughout my tired
skull like rain on a forest fire. My mind emptied and I concen-
trated on the warmth caressing my body and the relaxing sound
of the gurgling water.

I only climbed out of the tub when my skin was so wrinkled
you couldn't tell what my tattoos looked like any longer. I
grabbed Dad's worn flannel pajamas that I wear on cool nights off
of the hook on the back of the door, and wrapped myself in them.
I opened the door, steam rushing out from behind me, padded off
to my room, and sat on my zebra-skin patterned rug to towel-dry
my hair. I've been sitting here, just staring at the wall for a while
now. Seems to be a new pastime for me, this staring gig. I catch a
glimpse of myself in the full-length mirror on the antique armoire
in the corner of the room, and I'm startled by the normal-looking
teenager staring back at me. Whoa. It's almost my natural hair
color. Well, at least what I remember my natural hair color to be.
I haven't seen it since I was ten. Oh, well, I can still spike it. I take
my fingers and pull the damp brown hair upward until I'm satisfied with my reflection. Can't have it looking too suburban now,
can we? A smile spreads across my face when I imagine Taina's

and Grachi's reactions when they see this hair color. I must bring my camera for that one.

I glance over at the careless pile of clothes that still lie where I dropped them when I came in just over an hour ago. My black jeans still hold the shape of my body as they lie on the floor like a shed skin. The sight of them reminds me of the scene at the club, and I shudder. I start to feel a little sick to my stomach, and I'm glad I forgot to eat dinner tonight. Less to throw up. I can feel the few sips of alcohol burning in my empty gut. Kevin. What an asshole. I can't believe I actually made out with him last month! My stomach lurches, and I rub my hand over my flat belly like my mother did when I was little (only then I didn't have a pierced belly button), trying to calm it down. I can see Enrique's scared eyes, and I feel bad all over again. I'm afraid my mother's liberal tendencies didn't prepare me for blind hatred like I saw tonight. I just don't get it. I don't get Kevin. And the intensity of my anger sure took me by surprise. I mean, I have a temper, but that was something else. I look up at the picture of my father on my ornate carved dresser and stare into his swarthy, intelligent dark eyes. My mother snapped the photo on the steps of the Columbia University campus, where they had met while in architecture school. They had just started dating, and he is smiling playfully at the camera, his dark, wavy hair falling into his eyes, just reaching the collar of his 1970s wide-lapeled blue suit. He's leaning on the arm of the *Alma Mater* statue that sits in the middle of the marble steps in front of the Low Library.

He took me to visit the Columbia campus the year before he died when I was seven years old. We walked along the cobblestones, and I held on tightly to his increasingly withered but still strong hand. I spent much of the time running up and down the hundreds of steps as he patiently stood, watched, and smiled. I ran up to the bare feet of *Alma Mater,* and her lap looked so inviting as she sat there stoically in her robes, grasping her scepter, that I imagined her laurel-ringed head was looking kindly down at me. I turned to Dad, and without saying a word he knew what I wanted. We both knew you weren't supposed to climb over the revered *Alma Mater,* but *Papi* was like me, all about rule breaking.

He grabbed me by the waist and hoisted me up on her waiting knees. I sat there on her cold, stone lap and surveyed the campus that spread below as if we were a queen and princess and Dad were our king. I saw him smile charmingly at the frowning security guard who stood at the top of the steps, and I knew my time on the throne was limited. "*Vámonos, mi cielito,*" I heard *Papi* say, and I ran my fingers along the statue's face, whispered good-bye, and jumped into my father's outstretched arms.

I can't seem to tear my eyes from the photograph. The summer after Dad died I used to spend hours staring into the picture, because if I stared long and hard enough, his image seemed to come alive and I would pretend we were talking the way we used to. For several years after it was the only way I could fall asleep.

"Well, *Papi,* it's been too long since we've talked, *¿ay?*" I say to his image in the large gilded frame. I suddenly have an urge to touch things that belonged to my father, another ritual from childhood. I throw the towel aside, push myself up to my feet, and walk over to my closet. I throw open the large double doors, crouch down, and dig behind the sea of black clothing. I pull a large, worn, and familiar cardboard box from behind the army of punk footwear. I drag it out and over the rug, set it in the middle of the room, and sit down cross-legged next to the box. I run my hands over the purple child's handwriting on the side. ELENA'S BOX. HANDS OFF!!!! Hmm, I guess my attitude hasn't changed much over the years. I open the flaps on the top and as I reach in, the first thing I encounter is one of my grandfather Sebastian's record albums. "Ah, Gilberto Monroig. I remember this one well, *Papi.* This was one of *Abuelo*'s favorites. You used to play it all the time when we lived on Ninety-sixth Street." I carefully take the album out of its worn sleeve, walk over to my stereo system, and place it on the turntable I bought at a flea market last year. "To hell with CDs. Give me a good disk of black shiny vinyl and I'm happy." I drop the needle down on the record and smile as the horns come to scratchy life. I close my eyes. The rhythmic sound of the table's turning and the needle's sparking the music always reminds me of my father.

As Gilberto begins to sing, I sit back down on the rug and reach into the box.

"Well, *Papi,* I think you would have been proud of me tonight."
I go on to tell Dad all about the confrontation with Kevin, his mis-
treatment of Enrique, and my anger. "I can't believe he dared to
talk that way to me! I mean, what does that pale, narrow-minded
Irish boy think, anyway? He doesn't even kiss well! He should
wish that he had anything in common with me . . . and my people. . . . My people." At first my voice sounds odd and a little hollow in the empty room, but the accompanying melodies of the
Puerto Rican ballads make it feel less lonely. Almost as if *Papi* is
there.

I reach back into the box and pull out the *güiro* we bought at
the outdoor market in Old San Juan during our last trip to PR as a
family.

We had been walking through the Plaza de Armas, Mom, Dad,
Abuelo, and I, eating guava-flavored *piraguas,* laughing at each
other as the deep red snow cones melted in rivers down our arms
in the heat of the afternoon. We passed under the tents that
housed a dozen handicraft vendors and their wares. We walked
among the tables, admiring the folk art and enjoying the brightly
colored paintings. I came to a woodcarver whose table was covered with dozens of eggplant shaped wooden instruments. I had
never seen a *güiro* before, and I stood there staring at them, running my fingers over the carved tops. Dad smiled at my interest,
greeted the proprietor in Spanish, and picked one of them up.
The man behind the table handed him what looked like a crude
wooden-handled fork, and *Papi* began to run it across the grooves
carved into the hollowed-out gourd's side.

"*Mira, cielito,* this is the instrument of the *jíbaro,* the country
folk." He placed the fork in my small hand and guided it up and
down the length of the instrument, producing a rhythmic percus-
sive scratching sound that made it impossible to not move your
hips. My *abuelo* grabbed my mother, and they danced around the
square laughing and singing as my father and I played, the pi-
geons scattering in confused flight as the pair took each dance
step. I watched my mother twirl in her long cotton summer dress,
her head thrown back in laughter in the warm Caribbean sun. I

hadn't seen her smile in a long time. Not since Dad had found out he was sick.

All of a sudden I realize it's ironic that after all these years the *güiro* survived, but *Papi* didn't.

As Gilberto sings on, I turn the gourd over in my hands and run my fingers over *Puerto Rico* carved on the side. I dig back into the box and produce the fork. I relax into a comfortable position on the floor, and begin to play the *güiro* along with the music. It sounds the same after all these years. I smile, and am surprised at how easily I get into the rhythm of the crude instrument. When the song ends, I gently put the gourd and the fork back in the box and pull out the next thing my hand falls upon. It is a small, white leather Spanish Bible. It has gold scrolling details, a metal clasp holding it closed, and elaborate hinges like a castle door. I pull open the clasp, open the elegant book to its first page, and see my *abuela*'s name, the name we share, written in beautiful Catholic-school script, and underneath the same name written in a child's scrawl. My name. My scrawl. For a moment I am confused. Then I remember.

We had just arrived in Puerto Rico, my mother holding my white-gloved hand as she rushed me along the linoleum-floored airport hallway. She stopped for a moment to wipe her eyes with a handkerchief—she had been crying every day for a week—and reapply her lipstick. When she was done she resumed her deter-mined pace, pulling me along after her. We passed through secu-rity and baggage claim, hauling our briskly packed carry-on luggage, and as we walked through the glass doors to the parking lot and waiting crowd I felt the heat hit me like a wall.

I heard them before I saw them, my father's family standing to the side. They were also wearing a lot of black dress-up clothes. Usually Mom let me wear shorts when we went down there. I pulled at my white cotton tights, irritated at how hot they made my legs.

As soon as she saw my mother, *Abuela* began to sob. They hugged and cried and hugged and cried. I didn't understand all the crying. I was hot, and I wanted to sit down and have a drink.

No one was paying attention to me. My uncle Esteban seemed to sense my discomfort, and he picked me up, gave me a tender *beso* hello on the cheek, and brought me over to the soda machine to buy me a Coca-Cola. My short legs dangled from under his thick arms, and I noticed how my patent leather Mary Janes looked very shiny in the bright sun.

"How are you doing, *mi sobrina favorita*? Okay?" he asked as he put me down next to him on a nearby bench. I nodded to him and took a grateful sip of the cold soda. We sat for a few minutes in comfortable silence with *Tío's* arm protectively around my narrow shoulders. After a while we managed to corral my mother and grandmother to the waiting cars, drove out of San Juan, and headed toward Bayamón, where my father was from. Where was my father? I was confused, and my mother wasn't really talking to me. Oh, she hugged me a lot, but she was acting weird.

We went straight to the old cathedral in Bayamón's Parque Central. I'd been there many times before. We went there every Sunday when we were in Puerto Rico. But *Papi* was always with us. As we walked through the doors, I swung the flat black rubber strips that hung down in a curtain over the huge open doorway. *Papi* told me they were there so they could keep the big doors open but keep birds from flying into the church. But to me they really looked like the curtain that comes toward you in a car wash. I liked to run back and forth through them, pretending I was a bird immune to their boundary, seeing how high I could make them swing in the air. But this time *Abuela* grabbed my arm roughly and dragged me along. I was angry. *Papi* always let me do it.

We walked to the front of the church slowly, as *Abuela* introduced Mom to people along the way. She didn't usually know so many people there. I stood behind her, occasionally stamping my now somewhat scuffed patent leather shoes in impatience. Every once in a while I had to smile politely at some ancient old woman who would pinch my cheek and murmur, "*Ay, que linda. Pobrecita.*" We sat down in the front pew, and I was excited. We didn't usually get to sit this close to the show. I fidgeted around in my seat under the disapproving eye of *Abuela* and the sad smiles of *Abuelo*. Mom just sat and stared toward the front of the church, an occasional tear rolling down her cheek. The church filled with people, many of whom came by to hug *Abuela* and Mom. I kept scanning the faces of the people filing into the church, looking for *Papi*. I expected to see him walking down the aisle, his crinkly eyes smiling at me from under his shock of dark, wavy hair.

The music started, everyone stood up, and I saw the priest walking toward us down the aisle wearing a shiny white dress and a serious face. I liked the bright red flame on the front of his dress. I looked down at the lace bodice of my party dress and imagined I had a red flame there too. Behind the priest I saw *Tío* Esteban and my dad's cousin Carlos walking. They were carrying a big wooden box on their shoulders. There were a bunch of other cousins and friends of *Papi's* walking behind them, all helping to carry the box. I turned to Mom and, forgetting to lower my voice, I said, "Must be a really heavy box to need all that help!" My mother started to cry again, and put her hand on the top of my head. *Abuela*, annoyed at my comment, hissed at me, "*¡Cállate, niña!* That's your father, and you should be more respectful!" What? *Papi* was in the box? What was she talking about? I sat down hard on the seat, hitting my shin on the kneeler, but I didn't care. I was mad. I sat there with my arms folded, watching them bring the box up to the front of the church and place it on a stand. Then my uncle and cousins sat down in the row behind us.

The priest began to talk in Spanish and raise his hands to the crowd. Now I was bored *and* angry. Then I remembered what Mom just told me when we were back in New York, packing for the trip. She told me that she had sent Dad to Puerto Rico earlier that day.

"Is he going to come back with us?" I asked, not understanding why he hadn't said good-bye like he always did when he went on a trip.

"*Papi* isn't coming back, honey. He's gone to heaven."

I glared at the box at the front of the church. That was the first time I felt the white heat burning behind my eyes. All of a sudden I began to understand, and I didn't like it. *Papi* was in the box and he wasn't coming out. He wasn't coming back to New York with us. He wouldn't be going on a walk with me tonight. Or ever. I stood up, my arms tight at my sides with white-gloved little fists, and pushed my way out of the aisle, stepping on my family's toes with the heels of my dress shoes. I took off down the aisle and ran toward the door, the sound of my shoes clicking on the stone floor echoing loudly from the high ceiling. When I got there I stopped and held up the strips, urging the birds to fly in and stop the whole stupid thing. I couldn't breathe. I wanted *Papi*.

I expected Mom to follow me, and was surprised to see *Abuela* shuffle down the aisle, carrying a small white book in her hands. She didn't seem mad at me anymore. I thought she would be even madder, since I was holding the strips up for the birds, but she smiled and said, "*Mi'ja*, come sit over here; I want to talk to you." She led me under the strips, outside, and over to a bench. She sat down slowly next to me. It seemed hard for her to sit down. She looked tired. "Elena, I know it is hard and you miss your *Papi*, but you have to be strong for your mother. She needs you now, and you are like your *tía* Ana and me. We are the strong ones in the family, and we have to take care of everyone. *¿Comprendes?*" I nodded, but I was tired of this speech. Of how I was like her. A Diaz. A strong one. What did this have to do with *Papi*? She handed me the shiny white book she was holding. It had looked so small in her hands, but it was the perfect size in mine.

"Here, this is for you. It was my Bible from when I was a young girl. It is yours now, and when you get older you can use it to pray to your father when you miss him. But no crying, *mi'ja*. Be strong."

I had never seen such a fancy book, and I turned it over and over again in my hands. It had a latch like my jewelry box, and I opened it and turned to the first page. I saw my grandmother's name written there, similar to mine: *Elena Luisa Diaz*.

On the plane on the way back to New York, I used my mother's pen and wrote my name below *Abuela*'s in the fancy white book. I closed the latch and hugged the book to my chest, wishing for *Papi*. But I never cried. I had promised *Abuela*. I gazed out the window of the 747 jet and looked at the floor of clouds beneath the plane, wondering if *Papi* were out there somewhere.

Here I was, ten years later, grasping the same book to my chest, wishing for *Papi*. "*Abuela* can't tell me what to do anymore, *Papi*," I said as the tears began to spill on his pajamas. I sat there and cried and rocked. And cried and rocked. I thought of *Papi*, and of Enrique's pained look earlier that night, and of the angry little girl in the square in Bayamón. I sat there with the images running through my head like one of Mom's slide shows, all the while never letting go of *Abuela*'s Bible. I also started to think of the warm breezes and turquoise-blue water of my father's island. Of how kind his family has been to Mom and me. I'd been down to Puerto Rico every year since Dad's funeral, but I'm starting to realize that I was so angry at them for taking him away that I couldn't let down my guard enough to enjoy the very things he loved about *la isla*.

"Maybe Grachi is right, *Papi*. Maybe I avoid getting close to guys, like Carlos, because I don't want him to leave me like you did. And maybe I do deny my Latina side because I'm still angry about losing you. You were Puerto Rico to me. But this year it's going to be different. When I go down I promise I will have my eyes and heart open. But I'm still not letting *Abuela* take me to her beauty parlor. I love you, *Papi*, but I draw the line at teased hair."

The record comes to the last song and as I hear the strains of *"Así Era Mi Padre"* hanging in the air, I say to my father, "You made me independent just like you, *Papi*, so maybe I can stand on that bridge and be the punk Leni and the *Puertorriqueña* Elena." I stand up, walk over to the closet, and take out the garment bag that reads, ANITA'S DRESS SHOP in bright, cotton-candy-pink, curly script. I slowly unzip the bag, and the peach silk moiré bursts through the open zipper as if grateful to be released from its white plastic prison. I stand there for just a moment, sigh, and start to gently remove the dress from the bag. I drop my pajamas to the floor and slip on the dress. As I pull the zipper up, I walk over to the full-length mirror, my bare feet making indentations on the plush black-and-white rug.

Wow. So maybe this isn't so bad. Honestly, the brown hair does look better with peach than the burgundy. I stand there looking at myself, almost twirling like some crazed post-punk Cinderella, imagining what Carlos might think to see me dressed like this.

I'm jolted out of my fashion epiphany by a soft knock on my door.

"Leni? Are you okay?" I see the top of Mom's head tentatively peek out from the edge of my door. "I saw your light on and just wanted to make sure everything was okay."

She pauses at the threshold of my door, careful not to look around. Mom is hyperaware of giving me my privacy. And believe me, there have been times when I was particularly grateful for this.

"It's okay, Mom. Come on in."

She steps softly into the room with her bare feet, wearing her rosy pink, kitschy pajamas with pictures of cosmopolitans all over them (her signature drink) that *Papi* gave her one Christmas. I notice for the first time how well that shade complements her warm, blond, tousled new bob. *Papi* was good at things like that. His architect's eye found just the right color, just the right pattern to suit Mom's funky style. She looks tired, though, without makeup, and for the first time it dawns on me she's getting older. I am surprised by the thought that Mom, my trendy, ex-SoHo, loft-dwelling artist Mom could ever grow old.

"I had a rough night. That's all," I reply, and I notice that she is staring at me, almost in awe. For a moment I forgot I was wearing the dress, and I quickly add, "I figured I would try this on. You know, to get use to the torture of wearing something so super-femme." I'm trying to deflect the wonder and surprise on my mother's face, and she puts her hands to her mouth and begins to walk toward me.

"Oh, Leni! You look so . . . so . . . ."

"Ridiculous, I know, Mom. I know."

"*No!* Beautiful . . . you look beautiful! Oh, my God." She cuts herself short and tries to recover. "I mean, I love the other looks, the vinyl, the PVC. . . . It's just . . . your father would love this. . . . Not that he wouldn't love everything about you . . ." Who is this woman, and what has she done with my hip mother? She touches her hands to my upper arms as she admires the dress.

"Mom, it's just a dress! It's not like you've never seen me in one before!"

"I know, I know! Seriously, though, you girls did a great job picking these out."

"Mother, I promise you, it was not *my* idea!"

"Yes, it does have Grachi's touch written all over it. Well, anyway, you look great." She starts to get a strange look in her eye as she remembers something.

"It's just missing one thing. Wait here."

I watch her scurry out of the door toward her room. I'm scared. Am I trapped in an episode of *The Brady Bunch? Please, God, do not let her bring back a matching lace hair bow.* Just the thought makes me shudder. But she's too cool for that . . . right? Although, after this old-school mother-daughter vignette, nothing would surprise me. As she rushes back in the room, her eyes are bright and excited. Judging from her expression, whatever it is, I can tell I'd better like it. I see a flash of silver as she begins to fasten something to my right wrist.

"The bracelet was your grandmother's. Your dad began collecting charms to add to it whenever he traveled for work. He had hoped to fill it up, but before he died he told me I should give it to you when the time was right. Now is that time." When she is satisfied it is on snug and secure, Mom steps back and looks at me.

I look down at the thick silver chain with dangling little figures encircling my wrist and don't move. Mom continues to watch me quietly. After a moment I pick up my left hand and turn the bracelet around on my wrist to get a better look at the charms. There is a miniversion of the Parthenon from Greece, the Leaning Tower of Pisa, the Eiffel Tower, a map of Puerto Rico. I don't know what to say. I remember Dad taking trips and coming back with dolls and puppets and snow globes, but I never thought about all the places he had been. And here were pieces of his travels. Pieces he had bought for me. I well up, but I fight the urge to hide from Mom. To run away like I have done so many times. But I stay. I'm not sure my legs would be able to move if the room were on fire.

"I know, Mom; I've been talking to *Papi.*" I realize how weird that sounds, and quickly add, "I mean, I've been thinking a lot about *Papi.*"

"It's okay, honey; I talk to your father all the time. I think of the things we did, the places we went together. It makes me feel better when I'm blue. I know that your father would have wanted you to have this now. I think he would want you to feel proud of your Diaz roots. It's hard to get away from the O'Malleys, with our annual family fun fest. Lord knows, I've tried! I know you've gotten plenty of exposure to Celtic culture at its best. But there is so much of *Tía* and *Abuela* in you that I would hate for you to not celebrate that."

For once I don't dismiss her as "interfering." For once I think about what she's really saying.

Mom sees I want to talk, but I don't know how. She tries to keep things light, to make it easier. "Hey, I'm hungry. Do you want to split a pint of Ben & Jerry's Cherry Garcia while we talk?"

I let go of a breath I didn't know I was hoarding. "Sure, Mom. Sounds good."

She puts her arm around me, and as we start to walk out of the room she touches my hair. "Brown, huh? Pretty radical for you, babe. I figured you'd be going peach to match the dress!"

I smile. "Don't tempt me, Ma . . ." I say as we head toward the kitchen. "Don't tempt me."

EPILOGUE

TAINA

"Take a deep breath, Taina—you'll be fine," Graciela tells me, her hands clutching my bouquet of dewy lilies, their pink-and-purple-dotted petals pouting around her fingers. I take a deep breath; the gulp fills up my chest and fills in the dress. Leni crosses her eyes and sticks out her tongue at me. A brilliant flash of laughter spills out of my mouth and I breathe again, suddenly calm and collected. My Sister Chica consorts and I are nestled in a reserved dressing room in the west wing of La Reina Borinqueña, a room of pink pin-striped wallpaper with overstuffed armchairs and Hollywood vanity mirrors.

To further relax me, the girls begin to chat about our handsome *caballeros*, but I barely hear them. A song my *Mami* used to sing to me while tucking me in to sleep, her hands fluffing the mosquito netting over my bed, infiltrates my thoughts: *"Arroz con leche se quiere casar con una niñita de la capital. Qué sepa cocer, qué sepa bordar, qué ponga la aguja en su campanal. Tilín, tilín, ayá viene Juan, comiéndose el pan."* I sang it back to myself silently, thinking about what the words would be in English: "Rice with milk wants to marry a girl in the capital. She should know how to sew, she should know how to embroider, she should put a needle in her bell. (What?!) Ring, ring, here comes Juan, eating his bread." Ugh. The meaning gets lost in the translation. Still, I smile warmly as I imagine singing it for Yusef, how he would tongue-tie each sylla-ble of Spanish. Waking me out of my reverie, Leni pulls anxiously at her own peach moire that has begun to ride up her side a bit. As I help her straighten it out, I chuckle, appreciating the amount of sacrifice my girls have made this day . . . for me. I realize that for the first time in my life I am part of a circle of women, each of us from different ribbons of lives but each interwoven by our love for one another. This moment with my Sister Chicas feels no dif-ferent from sitting in El Rinconcito, sipping cups of *café con leche* or tamarind juice, sharing photographs and stories and poems. It feels no different from standing in the chaos of Whitney's science wing or in the *charro*-music-doused comfort of Graciela's bed-room, *bochinchiando*, as Mrs. Villalobos teasingly called it.

Okay, this is it, I think, as I slide my feet into a pristine pair of raw-silk pumps. A few inches higher, the heels digging into the dressing room's plush carpet, I suddenly feel majestic. "Okay, what do you think?" I ask, turning to my girls, the answer in their faces, mouths stretched out in boat-wide smiles. Graciela grabs me by the hand and twirls me around.

"Bellísima." Graciela beams, her hand clutching mine.

To think how just this morning my Sister Chicas had looked at me as if I were a lunatic, standing in El Yunque's doorway, their hands on their hips. Right about that time, all three of us had our mouths down around our ankles. I had to push a loud *ahh* back down my throat as soon as I saw Leni and her hair! No, not her usual experiment in Kool-Aid-red, nor her Halloween-candy-corn orange, not even her patented-patent-leather black. This time her hair was an exercise in subtlety—the color of rain-drenched hay. Tortoiseshell waves of honey brown, hair tinged with sunlight coming through the *café* window. Standing next to her was Gra-ciela, eyes wide, her usual swan self; she was perfection in the gown, the shade accentuating the pearl in her skin tone, the pink in her lips. *I love them,* I thought, something grabbing in my chest, clutching to my ribs. Still wrapped up in my own awe, I failed to

". . . Jamaica?" A delicate touch on my shoulder wakes me from
y reverie. Without turning to look, I recognize those two fingers
ainst my shoulder blade, index and middle held together like a
y Scout sign, those two fingers always that held my chin in a
ss as if searching for a pulse. Surely, at this moment, it raced
ster than a cat's. I turn to Yusef and he peers quizzically at me.
as he said something? What? "Ocho Rios—Jamaica—you, me,
om," he repeats, and I hear him but I don't hear him, my head
oozy from all the excitement, his mouth a beautifully rendered
um pout against the ensuing ruckus of voices rising over the
arlor stairs. "Are you all right?" his face asks. He reaches down,
hispers past the curlicues of my hair into my ear, "What do you
ink?"

I look out at the room. All the guests are standing around the
bles, their faces gazing at me as if I were the only one in the
om, their hands slapping together in two-beat rhythm. *Ta-i-na,*
a-i-na, Ta-i-na. I nod happily, up-down, up-down like a bobble
ead, my smile an equator reaching around my face. I hold my
heeks with my hands and laugh. I lean back against Yusef, my
ody sensitive to everything about him, his dogwood scent, his
on's grace, his brilliance. I love how he seems to hold me up
ow, now his body leaning into mine, concrete with a heartbeat.
"I'm here." I sigh. "Really here." My skin starts to hum.

Yusef nudges me slightly toward the top of the stairs. I am still
nodding dreamily, the room miraculously melting under me, the
mirrored walls, the waxed parquet, the wide, toothy steps that
ead to my feet. With a soft smile, I make my first step toward the
ccordion of red carpet. I am canary-in-the-mouth happy, a birth-
lay señorita, ready to start my day as Taina Sol Moscoso, fifteen
nd loving the newness of it, with all my family, my boyfriend, my
riends. My chicas. Chicas. Sisters.

GRACIELA

Carefully easing myself down on the edge of my bed, I'm
swathed in glorious shades of peach. I don't want to wrinkle my

notice how visibly astonished they were by my transformation.
Both girls looked at each other, puzzled. The restaurant was
closed for the day, though passersby peeked in through the windows, staring at the three girls in formal wear, especially at the
brown girl in the white wedding lace. Their faces seemed to wonder whether they were missing some magnificent private party.
There and then, with the Sister Chicas staring at me as if I'd
walked right out of a *Twilight Zone* episode, I started to unroll the
story of my white *quinceañera* dress and the Iglesia del Sagrado
Corazón compromise.

The morning of the *quinceañera*, Leni and Grachi watched me
twirl and pose in the *puntilla* dress, with its slight bell skirt scraping my ankles. I still didn't like my mother's choice, with its tight
bodice and long lace sleeves, but I loved the idea of surprising her
at Church of the Sacred Heart. Would she fall to her knees, clasp
the shiny pew with one shaking hand, and thank God and every
last one of his saints and angels for my suddenly seeing the light?
Or would *Mami* simply beam, her face glowing like an aluminum
Christmas tree? Luckily for me (and all guests present) it was the
latter. *Mami* was so surprised she kept turning around to her
friends and pointing at me, as if to remind them, "She's my
daughter!" Suffering through the ceremony in the tight, scratchy
lace was almost worth seeing her so proud, so lit up, so very . . .
happy. Of course, the past couple of days had been weird ones.
Our last brutal argument in El Yunque registered 6.1 on the
Richter scale, so one would think that making up was hard to do,
but it wasn't . . . really. Though earthquakes are followed by after-
shocks, ours had been a relatively smooth one. I guess *Mami* and
I had already broken some glass and cracked some cement.

Okay, enough with the extended metaphor. Anyway, yesterday
while I buttered my daily ritual of toast, *Mami* pulled me to her
from behind, her arms clasped around my chest tightly. She practically lifted me up, right off the floor. I dropped my toast. Knife in
hand, I stood very still. Honestly, other than the lottery of holi-
day/birthday/honor roll hugs and kisses, *Mami* hadn't held me like
that in years. *Mami's* hug felt good, warm like *pan de agua* just out
of a baker's clay oven. Soon I melted into her warmth, snuggled up

close like an infant, huddled into her quilted blue housecoat, her reading glasses tucked into her cleavage. I admit, with all this *madre-hija* stuff happening like a magic rabbit pulled out of a hat, it wasn't hard to compromise on the dress. In fact, right there, in that moment, I decided it: I'd wear the cake-topper dress for the *misa* at Church of the Sacred Heart, and the coral silk moire for the party at La Reina Borinqueña. I'd follow at least one part of some unwritten tradition, like *Mami*, like my grandmother, and just like her mother, back in the old country—Ponce.

That night I sprang back up the stairs toward *Mami*'s room, where for the first time since I was eight, I slipped into the powder-scented niche of her body and fell fast asleep, the moonlight brilliance of El Yunque's lights illuminating the street below.

◇   ◇   ◇   ◇   ◇

"It's almost time, Taina Sol; everyone's seated and waiting," my mother warns, peeking her head into the room for a moment and then shutting the door quickly. Graciela tugs gently on the corner of my dress's coral hem, the edge falling like a river over the smooth curve of my ankles. She smiles at me, one tear blinking dangerously off the corner of her right eye. Grachi flicks it away, the grin never leaving her face.

Leni holds out a crooked arm, *"¡Lista?"* I sling my arm through it and then through Graciela's, the three of us laughing. To passersby, we might look like a scene from *The Wizard of Oz,* all of us having opened our hearts, each braver, making our way down the Yellow Brick Road. Leni opens the door, and there, to our surprise, stand Yusef and my mother, her hands busily pinning a boutonniere to Yusef's satin lapel. I gulp with surprise and worry and exhilaration all at once. I don't hear what they say to each other, but I can see my boyfriend towering over my mother's head, grinning like a schoolboy at all the special attention. Successfully positioning the young lily on his lapel and brushing off an unnoticed bit of lint, *Mami* approvingly pats Yusef's upper arm and grins back at him. A million clichés for love bounce on the trampoline of my heart. *That's what she used to do for* Papi, I think,

and something pounces in my stomach, climbs into my throat. For a minute, he's standing there: *F* cherry peppers and rice. *Papi,* who loved singing in *Papi* slicing plantains in the morning. God, don't let him today. Any day but today. But I am powerless— tion takes over, straightens up, shoves Yusef over, m of room for my absentee father. He's wearing a skyl his trim belly ribboned in a satin cummerbund. I ther is uncomfortable in his tux because he keep sleeves down with his fingers. Still, he looks over N me, nods like he's proud. *Mami* sticks a pearly pin heart. *Uh-oh.* My bubble pops. I shake my head again under *Mami*'s careful hands. They grin at ea friends and suddenly there's a flutter in my veins. A in my lips. *Dios mío,* don't let me cry yet. I am too cl over. Speechless, I grab Leni and Graciela closer.

"La familia Moscoso-Guzman tiene el gusto de p quinceañera, nuestra preciosa señorita Taina Sol!" A Spanish-impaired people: "The Moscoso-Guzman lighted to present to you the sweet-fifteen Taina Monse announces from a microphone at the bottom room's stairs, after *Mami* and my Sister Chicas have way down the long red carpet. Applause rings out salon-slash-ballroom and whirls up the steps toward fill up, witnessing Jack gently nudge Graciela at the back. The way he touches her makes me think of love been together a long time. Graciela returns the gestur ing nudge of her shoulder against his upper arm. Sr schoolgirl, Leni reluctantly pulls herself away from he versation with Carlos and smiles as she takes Mari arm. I watch Carlos as he returns to his spot on the l like him, I think warmly, having seen another, softer, diamond that is Leni. *Tía* Monse and *Mami* are in th embrace, *Tía* Monse's head resting on her sister's sho *cas. Chi-cas. Chi-cas. Sis-ter Chi-cas.* I whisper the word caught on each of them, remembering all they mean *cas. Chi-cas.*

gown as I look over La Mondragon's notes one more time. *There's a voice of truth here, Ms. Villalobos, one that you should continue to cultivate. It pleases me that my confidence in you is not wasted.*

The words are carefully wedged in the margin of my latest assignment, her handwriting clean and spare. I wrote a story about a young woman, one of three sisters. She's given two gifts, both she was in danger of losing. The first gift she openly accepted, but couldn't allow herself to enjoy, always busy, always working. The second she thought she should keep a secret, never holding it to the light, for fear it would weaken her resolve, distract her from all her responsibilities. A huge fight with her middle sister finally wakes her up to what she'd been missing. And the youngest, seeing the rift between the other two, brings then all together, smoothing the hurts, and reminding them how family behaves.

"Chela." My mother pokes her head through my bedroom doorway. "Are you ready? Jack will be here any minute!"

"I am, *Mamá.*" Not just meaning today.

"Let me get my coat and your *papá.* Don't believe it when anyone tells you it's women who are the last ones to get ready!" We both laugh, knowing *Papá*'s habits all too well. I hear her heels click on our linoleum floor, then a pause, and seconds later she's back in my doorway.

"*Mi'ja,* you look lovely, *mi amor.*"

Her words buzz in my ears as I rise from my perch, put away the story, and grab my coat from the closet. Soon I'll be standing with Taina, celebrating her happiness, celebrating my own with Jack at my side.

✧ ✧ ✧ ✧

Once Taina is announced to the crowd, she and Yusef proudly stride to the center of La Reina Borinqueña's glistening inlaid wooden dance floor. After both bowing to Mrs. Moscoso, they begin a slow, languid waltz. At the end of the night there will still be the traditional *festejada*, just she and Yusef alone, but this first dance takes the place of the one Taina would have with her father. My girl won another victory, one that places her with her friends at the beginning of this chapter of her life, one that makes sense for who she's become.

I can't get over how solemn and lovely she is, floating across the floor—my Sister Chica, my girl, yet someone new to me, someone new to us all. Her gown frames her perfectly, rustling softly as she moves across the room with such pride. Wreathing her head, her tiara's a scattering of stars circling a heavenly body. This Taina is sure of who she is, sure of the importance of this moment. Turning and swirling around and around, Yusef beams at her, and she matches him smile for smile.

And Leni! My girl went the extra mile and more, simple and subdued, her own hair color, I think, and looking gorgeous in her moire dress. Taina's mother and her *comadres* murmured appreciatively, voices breathy and honey sweet, when she made her entrance. And my girl's running with it, holding herself regally, making small talk with all the right people. She's clearly comfortable in her skin, in showing to the world the side of herself I had a hunch was there all along. Rising to the expectation the day requires, she was on time, dressed to a tee, a charming partner to her chamberlain. She and Mario moved confidently to our table, Leni looking as if she's been doing this all her life.

✧ ✧ ✧ ✧ ✧

While the band's setting up, I can't help but notice her looking over at Carlos, and what passes between them when she unexpectedly catches his eye. The electricity sparks across the room; I can feel it all the way on the other side of the hall. I wonder . . . *Cálmate, Santa Graciela; do* not *try to play matchmaker. One: Leni knows where you live. Two: Just remember how long it took for you to wake up and let Jack know how you felt. Three: If the two of them get to spend any time together, they're not going to need anyone's help.*

As the music swells, signaling the court's entry, we're a little hesitant, but I don't think anyone notices. Jack and I move together without a hitch, with careful, measured steps. Thank God our last-minute rehearsals in the living room paid off. The *damas* are a whirl of peach, flower petals drifting around Taina, coral-blossom perfect. Our chamberlains dance us around in a circle, and I imagine us looking like blooms heralding the coming of spring. More snow will cover the ground soon, and the darkening days tell the story of how things end, but not for us. November's chill wind is blowing outside, but on the dance floor of La Reina Borinqueña, *es la primavera.* New beginnings for my Sister Chicas, for me.

Jack's holding me the old-fashioned way, one arm clasped loosely around my waist, the other holding my arm aloft, clasping my hand, fingers entwined, and as we skim over the polished parquet floor, he starts stroking my wrist softly in time to the languid rhythm of the old-style *canción.*

As we glide in a slow waltz, I follow his lead, and with subtle, almost imperceptible touches, I try to let him know how I feel. Time seems slowed down now, each moment flowing seamlessly, like syrup spilling over the edge of a spoon. Blue eyes meet mine. Eyes that smile, eyes that show me all his secrets.

As we circle around and around, we find ourselves in front of a full-length mirror flanking one of the walls near the entrance. Catching a glimpse of ourselves in the shimmering reflection, we are elegant, fitted to each other, Jack standing tall, his light brown hair smoothed back from his forehead, looking older in his tuxedo; me, moire sheathed, jeweled pin in my hair, the two of us sharing one smile. Part of me wonders if that image can somehow be etched into the glass.

It must have held some magic, because after one last trip around the room, we find ourselves dancing in front of it again. The glimmering from the chandelier streaks across the mirror, making us shine, making us shimmer in the light.

I won't forget how I shimmered tonight, how this feels. I won't let Jack forget, either.

"You're beautiful . . ." he whispers.

The music keeps floating around us, as the formal part of the procession ends. Now couples rise from other tables to join us in the *danza.* We slow down until we're almost completely still, leaving us swaying in front of the mirror, not really aware of who's dancing past us. I fit myself snugly to his chest. Jack's arms tighten around me, and he dips his head to whisper in my ear, "Happy?"

"Very . . . and you?" I smile against his chest, the silky, soft feel of his jacket.

"I am. Really happy. I should show you how much. . . ." Tipping my head back with his hand cupping my chin, he brushes his lips against mine, a satiny feather sweep.

"I love you," I whisper when he's through.

"That works out then, since I'm head over heels, Ms. Villalobos."

"Ms. Villalobos? That's a little formal, given what you just did."

Trying to paste a serious expression on his face, he wears a grin that just won't go away. "Well, I guess it's all this attention from the crowd."

I take a look around, and dancing couples are smiling and pointing at us, and Mrs. Moscoso and her *comadres* are watching, chuckling, and waving to us.

"Oh, my God, people are staring at us!" With the blush creeping across my face, once again I'm reminded the mirror doesn't lie. "Oh, Jack . . . I . . ." Stammering seems to be the only thing I'm capable of.

Leaning down, Jack whispers in my ear, his breath warm, not helping my blushing at all: "I told you you were beautiful. People have been looking at you all night."

Just when I'm about to tell him that the crowd is not just responding to how I look, a warm hand clasps my shoulder, and someone clears his throat. A voice I know.

"Can a father get a dance with his beautiful daughter?"

Papá's wearing a charcoal suit, his good one, and a starched white shirt and burgundy silk tie. He looks polished, his salt-and-pepper hair tamed for the occasion. *Mamá* is breathtaking in her long-sleeved burgundy sheath. It's shantung, her one good dress, worn for only the most important events. Garnet earrings from her wedding adorn her ears, and her hair is swept up in a chignon. It takes my breath away; all the years of sacrifice and hard work, the late hours and too little money all fade away.

For a split second they're just two young lovers at the crest of their lives together. In the blink of an eye we change partners, and *Papá* and I glide away and Jack and my mother swirl past us. She says something to him that makes him blush now, and, laughing, she turns and looks over her shoulder to me and winks.

The music washes over *Papá* and me as we move together easily. I close my eyes, remembering when I first danced with him, five years old, standing on his feet. *You carried me,* Papá, I think, *carried me my whole life. You and* Mamá *carried me right up to this minute.* I don't mean for it to happen, but a tear slips down my face. Before I can do a thing, his strong hand wipes it away with a tenderness I feel deep in my soul.

"*Preciosa,*" he whispers, "what's wrong? Don't tell me you're too grown-up for this." Brown eyes capture mine and I see love and worry and pride. I try to reassure him nothing's wrong. It's that so many things are right.

"Nothing, *Papá,*" I say, "It just . . . it's just . . . I'm not sad; really I'm not."

"More happiness than you can hold, is that it, *mi'ja?*"

"Yes!" I exclaim. "That's it, *Papá.* How did you know?"

"I knew because I felt the same way the day you were born," he answers.

LENI

Okay, so maybe it's not so bad at the Planet *Princesa* party. I hate to admit it: I'm actually enjoying myself. It's so cool to see my Sister Chicas in such a different setting. We all look so damned grown-up! Sure, the traditional stuff is kind of hokey (when *Tía* Monse announced me and Mario and we shuffled awkwardly into the hall, all eyes on us, I felt like I was on some bad reality show: Survivor *Quinceañera! Three girls, three pairs of dyed-to-match high-heeled shoes, and eight dozen gawking relatives . . . at the end, who will be left standing?*), but I've always liked being in the spotlight. Speaking of the spotlight, look what it's doing for Taina! Who knew my girl was a debutante? Sashaying from well-wisher to well-wisher, she's dancing like a total *salsera* with her gorgeous

Yusef, and working the room like she was born to royalty. It's hard to even imagine the shy, too-quiet girl of a few months ago.

Watching Graciela and her dad dance was wonderful; I mean it. It's just that after a few minutes, it was almost hard to breathe. I just stood there staring, fingering the charm bracelet around my wrist. Times like that make me feel the absence of *Papi* like a weight on my chest, like the air's been taken out of the room. I think Grachi knew, because when they finished she whispered to her dad, and Mr. Villalobos came over and asked me to dance. I felt shy at first, but he is a true *caballero,* a real gentleman. As we danced he held me as if I were a piece of fine china he was show-ing off to the crowd. When we finished, he smiled at me and said, "I'm certain your father would be proud of the *hermosa* young lady you have become, Elena." I wanted to tell him how grateful I was for his kindness and his daughter's thoughtfulness, but I couldn't say anything. I just stammered and smiled, but I could tell by his eyes that he knew. He bowed to me, and as he walked away I smiled at Grachi. Thank God my Sister Chicas are always there to keep me from falling into poor-l'il-ol'-me mode.

I made it through the round of obligatory dances with my arranged *caballero* date, Mario, who, by the way, is not a bad dancer. Could have fooled me! Underneath that slicked-back 1950s hair and railroad track of braces beats the rhythm of Tito Puente! We swung around the floor with Taina and the rest of her court looking, I might add, *tremendo cache.* Once the promenades were done I started to make the rounds of the tables. I figured it was part of my duty as a member of Taina's court (and besides, the only guy I really wanted to flirt with was busy playing music, so there was nothing else to do). I started out feeling uncomfort-able and out of place, but Taina's family and Ms. Moscoso's friends were so warm and welcoming it didn't take me long to re-lax and enjoy the mingling. What always kills me about elderly Latinas is that they get done up, honey! I mean, there ain't no blue-haired, no-makeup, dowdy-housedressed mamas here. No, sister! These ladies are perfectly coiffed, tastefully made up, man-icured, and perfumed. They hugged me, talked about how lovely I was, and bantered away with me in Spanish. It reminded me so much of my family in Puerto Rico that I caught myself thinking about the island longingly. Hey, if I can make it through this event unscathed I can certainly handle Maria's wedding!

I spent the last hour flitting from table to table with the Diaz charm set on stun. I am particularly proud of my conversion of Taina's crotchety old great-aunt Marisol. You know the type? The cantankerous kind that you are certain would keel over of a stroke if they even attempted a smile. Well, by the time I was done, she was as warm and sweet as a Toll House cookie fresh from the oven. She was laughing and holding my hand, hesitant to let me go, complimenting me on my stilted yet respectful Spanish. God, I'm good.

I may have inherited *Papi*'s charm, but let me tell you, it is hard work. Right now I have to just sit and let the air out. I fall into a chair at an empty table at the edge of the dance floor, kick off my peach satin pumps, and wriggle my toes on the thick burgundy carpet. I just want to sit and watch the dancers. Graciela hasn't gotten off the floor all night! Who would have thought Miss Button-down could party so hard? Carlos instructs the band to switch from merengues to a slow *danza*. I watch Grachi gracefully and subtly lead Jack through the unfamiliar rhythm of the formal dance. They look gorgeous in their dress-up clothes and faces that shine from the inside. They stare into each other's eyes (well, Grachi looks up into Jack's eyes; even with heels he still towers over her) with the assurance of a romance that blossomed between friends rather than strangers. Yep, Grachi's a goner. I couldn't be happier for her. And Yusef and Taina—that energy could light a bonfire the size of the Sears Tower!

Being the belle of the ball, Taina's been pulled in a hundred different directions all night, but she always comes back to Yusef. That boy does just fine on his own anyway. I even watched him make *Tía* Marisol's eyelashes flutter like she was sixteen again. (Hey, I warmed her up for him.) They join the rhythm of the small crowd of couples swirling around the dance floor, and I watch them settle into their own swaying pulse. You can almost see the arc of current between them. Once again I am struck by how confident Taina looks, so sexy and comfortable in her body. And

Yusef . . . well, don't get me started on him. Boy's got *male model* written all over his fine self.

I feel eyes on me and I glance up toward the bandstand. Carlos is looking right at me. Suddenly the room feels really warm. Why am I slouching? I sit up straight and shove my tired feet back into the *tacones*, trying to regain my diva-ness as Carlos whispers to Luis and steps off the band platform, striding toward me in his elegant black tuxedo. When we first arrived at the hall and I saw him dressed like that, I thought I had died and gone to heaven. But he's just Carlos. The same guy whom I've been friends with since I was six, right? Whoa. Myrta's *coquitos* are making the room spin. Or is it the proximity of Carlos?

Carlos comes over and extends his hand to me, pulling me out of my chair and toward the dancers. He takes my arm and carefully guides me over the edge between the carpet and the wooden dance floor. Luis leads the band in a slow, sexy rhumba, and I feel Carlos's strong hand on my back pulling me in close. Friend . . . he's a friend. My heart is beating faster than the band's drums as we shift from foot to foot, the steps slow and sensual, and I am vaguely aware of the other couples, all moving in perfect syncopated rhythm. I can almost feel a tropical warmth coming from the movement of the dancers as they move back and forth like the tides to the Cuban-African beat. Carlos's hands are strong but never pushy as they guide me around the floor. I must say, having his body tight against mine, gliding around the floor, I realize I could get to like this a lot more than the group grope of the mosh pit at Exit.

I can hear the strains of the song coming to a close, and I don't want it to end. I look down and for the first time stumble over my own feet. Carlos lifts my chin, locks my gaze with his huge brown eyes, and smiles. I feel the edges of my mouth lift, and he leans down to me, his face millimeters away from mine. The song ends, and I hear Luis calling Carlos's name from what seems miles away. Carlos keeps his face close to mine for just a second; then he shrugs, lifts my right hand to his lips for a gentle kiss, bows quickly, and is gone, sprinting up to the bandstand, his tuxedo jacket billowing behind him. The band breaks into my favorite

Robi Draco Rosa song, and I just stand there, gaping at him. If I try to walk, I swear I will tumble to the floor in a pile of peach moire. For a friend he certainly makes my knees weak. Okay, so maybe we could be more than friends.

I am suddenly aware that Grachi and Taina are watching me from across the dance floor, whispering and smiling conspiratorially, and I smile back and shrug. They come running over and throw their arms around me and we all fall to the floor, a pile of peach and coral moire, giggling like five-year-olds, not caring what anyone thinks. We hug and cry and laugh and then it hits me, really hits me, that I'm not an only child anymore, that I'm surrounded by my sisters.

"I have a genius idea!" I shout as I grab a hand of each of my Sister Chicas and pull them to their feet. I drag them across the reception hall, halfhearted complaints of "Where *are* you taking us, *chica?*" trailing behind me like the tail on a kite. I pull them into the coatroom and hunt for my jacket amidst a sea of wool and fur coats. I find it, pull out my camera, and thrust it at Taina. "Hold this a second, Tai." I yank the jacket off the wooden hanger, shove my arms into the sleeves, pulling the worn black leather over the smooth, shiny dress as the girls smile at me, confused. I grab the camera back from Taina and throw my arms around my girls, holding the camera at arm's length above us over Taina's shoulder. "Now smile pretty, *chicas!*" I feel their arms pull me in tight and we all smile at the lens and yell, "Sister Chicas rule!"

¡ES FINITO, CHICA!

SISTER CHICAS HELP YOU
FIGURE IT OUT!

Glossary

abrazo: hug, embrace

abuela: grandmother

agua de jamaica: a nonalcoholic iced-tea drink made from *Jamaica* (hibiscus) flowers, popular in Mexico and the West Indies Mexico, especially Jamaica.

ahí tienes: there you have it; there you go.

ají: red pepper

ajo: garlic

alcapurrias: beef or seafood filled plantain fritters

alegría: happiness

americanos: Americans

amiga: a female friend

amiguitas: little friends (female), term of affection

amo a tu hija: I love your daughter

a mí no me vengas con eso: don't try that with me

ándale: hurry it up

ándale, pues: Get going, already.

antojitos: appetizers, small snacks; cravings

arandela: frills, flounce

arroz con gandules: rice with pigeon peas

a sus ordenes: at your orders; at your service

ay, Dios: Oh, God

ay, no, a mí no me vengas con eso: Oh no, don't give me that!

ay que linda: oh, how pretty

¡*Ay, Virgen!*: Oh, Virgin Mary!

Barrilito: a rich dark rum made only in Puerto Rico, aged in oak barrels.

basta: enough

Bayamón: part of the metropolitan area of San Juan and the second largest populous city.

bella: beautiful

bellísima: very beautiful

bendición: blessing

bendito sea: Blessed be, or, more colloquially, Bless me! or God bless me!

beso: a kiss

billares: billiards

bizcochos: cakes

bochinche: gossip

bodega: small grocery

bronce: bronze

buenas tardes: good afternoon

buen provecho: Have a good appetite! (*literally*) Enjoy your meal

caballero: a gentleman; in the *quinceañera, aballeros* are the male escorts to the *damas*

café con leche: A coffee drink made with espresso and steamed milk

cafecito: a small cup of dark, rich coffee, like espresso

cafetín: a small café

calabaza: pumpkin

calaveras: the skull or skeleton—it is the number one symbol for the Days of the Dead. But it is not presented to terrorize. Instead, the *calavera* represents the playfulness of the dead, as they mimic the living and frolic among us.

caldo: broth or soup

caldo Tlalpeño: soup popular throughout northern and central Mexico, especially DF, with origins in the state of Jalisco, made with chicken, chipotle chiles, garbanzo beans, and garlic

calientito: a little warm

calle: street

¡Cállate niña!: Be quiet, girl!

cálmate: Calm down

canciones del amor: songs of love

cantina: tavern or bar, primarily a male domain

¡cara!: short for *caramba*; damn it!

carajo: an obsenity

caramelo: caramel

caribe china: China dishware made in Puerto Rico in the 1950s and 1960s

cariño: dear, my love

carnitas: roasted pork meat

Casa Aztlán: House of Aztlán (*literally*). Aztlán is the southwest portion of what is now the United States, the land base that served as the roots for the Chicano movement in the seventies and eighties. In Chicago, a community center serving local youth and adults.

casera: home-style; homemade

cebolla: onion

chamberlain: in the *quinceañera*, escort for the damas in the court

Che Guevara: Revolutionary leader, born in Argentina. He trained as a doctor, but went on to play an important part in the Cuban revolution. He held various government posts under Castro, and became worldwide ambassador for Cuba in 1961, but left in 1965 to become a guerrilla leader in South America. He was captured and executed in Bolivia in 1967 at the age of thirty-nine. He has become a symbol for rebellion among the youth of the twenty-first century.

Chela: short for Graciela

chica: girl

chicano/a: *chicano* was at one time considered a derogatory term, used to identify migrant farm workers in the United States in the early 1900s. Today, the term has been embraced by Mexican-Americans who are of Mexican descent but who were born in America.

chiflada: crazy one, silly. Used in playing with children, especially.

chillo: fish—red snapper

chinita: little Chinese one: used as a term of endearment for a girl with long, straight black hair. Referring to the Chinese influence in Mexico, i.e., immigrant influences—La China Poblana, the folk heroine who played a role in Mexican independence.

chipotle: fully ripened and smoked jalapeño pepper

chiquita: little one

cielito: my heaven—term of endearment

Cinco de Mayo: The holiday of Cinco de Mayo, the Fifth of May, commemorates the victory of the Mexicans over the French army at the Battle of Puebla in 1862.

claro que no: of course not

claro que sí: of course

color de café: coffee colored

comadres: godmothers

comida criolla: traditional foods of Latin culture

comidas: food; culinary dishes

como azúcar en café: like sugar in coffee

como siempre: like always; as always

como una nena: like a baby

como una paloma: like a dove

¿Comprendes?: do you understand?

comunidad: community

con calma: calmly

conjuntos: together

con tu permiso: with your permission

coquitos: Caribbean eggnog

corazón: heart; term of endearment

croquetas de jamón: ham croquettes

cubanos: Cubans

cuentos: stories

cumbia: a Latin-American dance with African roots that originated in the Atlantic coast of Colombia

dama: a lady; a term of respect to refer to a woman. In the *quinceañera* party tradition, the *damas* are your "ladies in waiting"

danza: dance; in Puerto Rico the *danza* is the musical genre of the New World that most resembles European classical music. The style of the *danza* can be romantic or festive, but it is an integral part of Puerto Rican culture.

despégate de ahí; get away from that/there

dígame: tell me

Dios: God

diosa: goddess

Dios mío: My God

Dios te bendiga: God bless you

divertido: amusement, diversion

La Divina: the Divine One

Don: sir—a title of respect

Doña: ma'am—a title of respect

dónde está su madre: Where is her mother?

duende: imps; in some countries, *duendes* are legendary for stealing young girls away from their fathers and making them their brides.

dulce: sweet

dulce de leche:

El Colegio Mayaguez: the school of Mayaquez (a town on the western coast of Puerto Rico)

El Cuco: the bogeyman

él es mi novio: He is my boyfriend

el pecado: sin

El Rey de Café: the king of coffee

El Riconcito del Sabor: the name of the fictional coffee shop the Sister Chicas frequent. It literally translates to: The Little Corner of Flavor; Tasty Spot.

El Yunque: Taina's mother's restaurant is named after the lush tropical rain forest in the northeastern area of Puerto Rico. El Yunque is a U.S. State Park

empanadas: turnovers with either meat, starch, or fruit filling

entiende: understand

entiéndeme: do you understand me?

entiendes: do you understand?

entre mis huesos: in my bones

es exactamente como así: it's exactly like that

es finito: it's finished

está bien; it's good; it's okay

¿estás cansada, chica?: are you tired, girl?

este fue un momento importante: this was an important moment

estilo cubano: Cuban style

estoy en serio: I'm serious

es un placer a verte, como siempre: as always it's a pleasure to see you

ética: ethics, morals, etiquette

exquisita: exquisite

Fajardo: town on Puerto Rico's northeastern coast, famous for its fishing.

familia: family

feo: ugly

festejada: celebration

fiesta: party

fiesta patronal: a saint's day party held every saint's day for each town in Puerto Rico.

finalmente: finally

flamboyán: "Flame Tree" or Poinciana, a tree found in Puerto Rico that blooms in the spring with brilliant orange-red flowers.

flan: a baked custard, with its origins in Spain.

flor de jamaica: hibiscus flower, sorrel

fracas: a disturbance; a fight

gallinas: hens

gandules: pigeon peas

Gauloises: French-made high-end cigarettes

genia: genius (woman)

gente: people

Gilberto Monroig: Puerto Rican singer from the 1940s and 1950s who performed all over the world with musicians such as Tito Puente

gracias: Thank you

gracias a Dios: Thank God

gracias, Virgencita/gracias a la Virgen: Thank you, Virgin Mother

grandote: huge one; a big guy

grasa: grease

gringa: a female Anglo—derogatory

guayabera: a creased-front button-down light cotton shirt with pockets, which is worn untucked allowing its wearer to look elegant but stay cool. Supposedly it was invented in Cuba for landowners so they could carry things in their pockets such as guavas (guayabas).

güiro: A Latin American percussion instrument made of a hollow gourd with a grooved or serrated surface, played by scraping with a stick or rod

guisado de res: Mexican stewed beef dish

hace mucho frío: It's quite cold out

¿hay una problema aquí?: is there a problem here?

hermana: sister

hermosa: beautiful

hijita: little daughter, term of affection to refer to not only biological children, but used by older adults to refer to young adult women

hijos de la indolencia: lazy children

historia y cultura: history and culture

huipil grande: a colorful woven Mexican shawl whose origins can be traced back three thousand years; was once considered a sacred enclosure for a woman's body

idiota: idiot

iglesia: church

Iglesia del Sagrado Corazon: Church of the Sacred Heart

Iglesia el Primero Sanctuario: Church of the First Sanctuary

iluminar: to illuminate

impressivo: impressive

indígena: native, indigenous woman

Isla Verde: literally, green island: a penisular tourist area in San Juan

Jarochos: *Jarochos* music comes from the Veracruz area, and is distinguished by a strong African influence. International acclaim has been limited, including the major hit "La Bamba." The most legendary performer is Graciana Silva, whose Discos Corason releases made inroads in Europe. Southern Veracruz is home to a distinct style of *Jarochos* that is characteristically lacking a harp, is played exclusively by *requinto* or *jarana* guitars, and is exemplified by the popular modern band Mono Blanco.

jíbaro: country folk

joven: youth

joyecita: little gem, term of endearment

jugo de papaya: papaya juice

jurutungo: slang for "the boonies"

la casa de tus abuelitos: the house of your grandparents

la cocina: the kitchen

la deliciosa; the delicious

La Divina: The Divine

la farmacia: the drugstore: pharmacy

la gracia: grace

la intimidad entre nosotros: the intimacy between us

la isla bonita: the beautiful island—a common phrase used for Puerto Rico

La Raza: literally, "the race." Term meaning "the people," coined during the seventies and eighties by the Chicano movement.

La Reina Borinqueña: The event hall is named the Puerto Rican Queen. "Borinquen" was the indigenous people's name for Puerto Rico.

las bromas: jokes

las flores: flowers

Latinidad: Latin-ness

Librería Tzintzuntzán: Tzintzuntzán bookstore (Tzintzuntzán is an ancient Aztec village whose Nahautl (Aztec) name means "the place of the hummingbirds")

libro: book

lista: ready

literatura: literature

lo siento: I'm sorry

lo siento por todo: I'm sorry for everything

luna: moon

Luquillo: a pristine beach town on Puerto Rico's northeastern coast.

Machito: Cuban musician who emigrated to America in 1937. Once in the U.S. he went on to record with Latin bandleader Xavier Cugat. Machito was a founder of the Afro-Cuban jazz movement in 1940. This style of jazz was a seminal musical genre after World War II. He died after suffering a fatal stroke while playing at a club in London in 1984.

Madre de Dios: mother of God

maestra: teacher

Mami: mother, affectionate

mantecaditos: almond shortbread cookies

máquina: machine

margaritas: daisies

mariachi: As the most well known regional musicians of Mexico, mariachi bands became common in Jalisco around the beginning of the twentieth century, originally playing at weddings. The earliest known appearance of this term in reference to music is from 1852. It is said that General Porfirio Díaz, in 1907, ordered a mariachi band to play for the United States secretary of state, only if they wore *charro* suits, which were worn by the poor musicians' bosses. This is the source of traditional dress for mariachi bands, and is considered the beginning of modern mariachi. By the turn of the century, mariachi was popular across Mexico. Rural subgenres have largely died out, and urban mariachi from Mexico City has dominated the field since the 1930s. It became known as the national music of Mexico after the 1910 Mexican Revolution, and was subsidized during the term of Lázaro Cárdenas. Cornets were added to mariachi in the 1920s; they were replaced by trumpets ten years later.

Mexican immigrants in the United States made Los Angeles the mariachi capital of the USA by 1961. Mexican music was popularized in the United States in the late 1970s as part of a revival of mariachi music led by performers like Linda Ronstadt. One of the most well known examples of Mexican music (at least in the United States) is "La Cucaracha" and the Mexican Hat Dance ("El Jarabe Tapatío").

The golden age of mariachi was in the 1950s, when the ranchera style was common in American movies. Mariachi Vargas played for many of these soundtracks, and the long-lived band's long career and popular acclaim has made it one of the best-known mariachi bands.

marquesina: covered driveway or carport

marranitos: gingerbread cookies shaped like pigs

masa: corn dough made from finely pulverized meal

más tarde: later on

mavi: a root beer–like drink made in Puerto Rico and in some U.S. communities

Mayaguezana: a woman from Mayagüez, a town on the western coast of Puerto Rico

Mayagüez Indios: Indians from Mayaguez: the name of a Puerto Rican baseball team

medianoches: literally, midnight: Cuban sandwich of toasted ham and cheese

¿Me entiendes?: do you understand me?

me entiendo: I understand

merengue: Dominican rural dance and music that has close links to African forms, now a very popular form of Latin dance all over the world.

mi amor: my love

mi cielito: my little heaven: a term of endearment

mi india: My India—a term of endearment, literally, having indigenous Meso american roots.

mi'ja: short for "*mi hija,*" or "my daughter." A term of endearment.

mi madre que está en el cielo: my mother who is in heaven

mi maestro: my teacher

<u>Mi Mamá, La Cartera;</u> one of the first bilingual children's books, *My Mother the Mailwoman,* written by Inez Maury.

míralo, chica: look at him, girl

mis cuentos: my stories

mis obras: my works

mis padres: my parents

mis reinas: my queens—a term of endearment

moda de niños: fashions for children

mofongo: mashed, fried green plantain

mojito: a classic Cuban cocktail that is made from rum, lime, sugar, and fresh mint

muchísimas veces: many times; a lot

mujer: woman

música tradicional: traditional music

muy bien: very good

muy sabrosísimo: very delicious

negro: black

"*Negro bembón*": a *plena* song about the murder of a thick lipped (*bembón*) black man

nena: child—term of endearment

Nicolas DeJesus: Printmaker, painter and graphic artist, born December 6, 1960, in the indigenous Nahua region of Guerrero, Mexico. His work reflects the spectrum of his experiences, from his origins in a traditional Mexican village to the problems of the Mexican migrant in the United States and his concern for preserving his cultural identity.

ni lo puede decir: not able to say

niños: children

no llores: don't cry

no más: no more

no me digas: you don't say? Don't tell me.

no seas enojado: don't be mad

novio/a: boyfriend/girlfriend, betrothed

nuestra literatura: our literature

Oaxaca: Mexican mountain city

obra del día: work of the day

obsidiana: obsidian

ofrenda: Offerings or gifts set out for the dead, which can be a table onto itself, or a shelf within the family home, as well as a freestanding actual altar in the cemetery where loved ones are buried. To welcome the dead as honored guests, families in Mexico create *ofrendas* or memory tables with personal effects, food, and drink that the departed enjoyed during their time on earth. The *ofrendas* unite family and loved ones to reflect about their own lives.

oreja: a crispy cookie also called an elephant's ear

óyeme: listen to me

panadería: bakery

pan de agua: bread

pan dulces: Mexican sweet buns

Papi: father, affectionate

parque: park

pasteles: a tamale-like dish made of plantains stuffed with meat and raisins. usually made during the Christmas holidays.

perdóname: pardon me

pescaderos: fishermen

piragua: traditional snow cones sold from carts, and served by vendors in Puerto Rico. Made with large blocks of shaved ice, served with flavored syrups poured on top.

Plaza de Armas: literaturally Plaza of Arms/Weapons; a popular plaza in Old San Juan where the Spanish colonial City Hall is located

plazoletas: public squares or town centers

plena: a genre of Puerto Rican folk music and dance usually associated with the southern coast of the island. The *plena* is a narrative song describing life on the island, and the dance is done in pairs.

pobrecita/o: poor little thing

pollo: chicken

por favor: please

por siempre: for always

preciosa: precious—a term of endearment

prima: female cousin

primavera: spring

princesa: princess

promesa: promise

puertorriqueña: Puerto Rican

pues, está planchado: well, it's ironed out then; it's settled

punto: period

puta: prostitute

¿qué dices a mi?: What are you saying to me?

qué exajerada: what an exaggeration

¿qué haces?: what are you doing?

qué has hecho:

qué locura: what lunacy

qué pasó: what happened? What's going on?

querida/o: dear—term of endearment

qué's eso: short for *Qué es eso:* what is this

qué tipo de color: what type of color?

que vergüenza: what a shame

¿que te pasa, niña?: what's the matter, honey?

quinceañera: a young woman's fifteenth birthday celebration, a coming-of-age ritual in which she claims her identity in the community.

recuerdos: memories

responsibilidades: responsibilities

retablos: A small painting, often on metal, offering thanks to the Virgin or a particular Christian saint for misfortunes escaped. Also called *ex-voto* paintings, they sometimes depict both an event and salvation from it.

riquesísimos tamales: delicious tamales

Robi Draco Rosa: One of the original members of the popular Latin boy band Menudo, he has written most of Ricky Martin's hits. Robi Draco Rosa went on to develop a solo career that mixes the romantic pop sound and his darker Goth style, making him the ideal musical choice for Leni.

rosas: roses

Rufino Tamayo (August 26, 1899–June 24, 1991) was a popular modern Mexican painter. He was a Zapotec Indian and was born in Oaxaca, Mexico. In his paintings, Tamayo expressed what he believed was the traditional Mexico and departed from the strictly politically based paintings of many of his contemporaries such as José Clemente Orozco, Diego Rivera, and David Alfaro Siqueiros.

sabrosísimos: very delicious

sabrosos: mouthwatering

Sagrado Corazón: Sacred Heart

salonista: hair-/nail stylist

salsera: salsa dancer

San German Atléticos: Puerto Rican baseball team

santa: saint

secretos de amor: secrets of love

señoritas: misses; young ladies

siéntate: sit down

sin vergüenza: shameless one

sobrina favorita: favorite female cousin

Sombras y Sol—Memorias de Cuba: Shadows and Sun: Memories of Cuba

somos familia: we are family

Son huasteco: Son huasteco music, a style developed by Mexico's Huastec people, is a genre that has been gaining in popularity in recent years. Two guitarists sing in a falsetto with accompaniment by a violin. Improvisation is common. Los Camperos de Valle and Trio Tamazunchale are especially influential performers.

sonido tropical: tropical sound

nuestra gente y nuestra tradiciones: our people and our traditions

tacones: high-heeled shoes

Taino/a: A subgroup of the Arawakan Indians (a group of American Indians in northeastern South America), the Taino Indians were the indiginous inhabitants of the Caribbean obliterated by Spanish colonizers, other tribes, and disease. Remnants of Taino culture exist and are woven into modern Caribbean culture

tapetes: coverlets

taquerías: Mexican restaurants

tatuajes: tattoos

telenovela: television soap opera

te lo prometo: I promise you

tenemos sed también: We're thirsty too

te quiero: I love you

tesoros de tu gente: treasures of our people

timbal: instrument; percussion; drum. Typical salsa drum set consisting of two tuneable drums (different in pitch), two cowbells (*campanas*), cymbal(s) and possibly a woodblock. Played with two sticks.

toma: take

tomatillos: small green tomatolike fruit used in salsa and cooking *torta de guayaba*: guava tort

tortillas hecho a mano: handmade tortillas (flat nonleavened corn bread)

tostones: flattened fried green plantains

tranquila: calm; tranquil

tremendo: tremendous

tres leches: literally "three milks": A *tres leches* cake is a white or yellow pound cake that is pierced with a fork once it's baked, then saturated with a three-milk syrup.

triste: sad

tú eres mi hermana: you are my sister

un ataque de corazón: a heart attack

un día increíble: an incredible day

un divertido: a diversion; fun

un papi chulo: a cute guy

una sorpresa: a surprise

válgame a Dios: bless my soul/heaven forbid. Save me, God *(literally)*

vals: waltz

vamos/vámonos: let's go

vatos: men; guys; dudes

váyanse, mis cariños: go, my dear ones

ven acá: come here

ven conmigo: come with me

verdad: truth/right

virgen en el cielo: Holy Mother in heaven

ya, déjala: leave it already

ya lo sabe: he/she knows it

yanqui: Yankee, American

yo lo sé: I know it

yo no he visto una cosa mas fea: I've never seen anything so ugly

Yo no te mandé a comprar un traje: I did not tell you to go buy a dress

yuca con mojo: yucca sauteed in olive oil and chopped garlic. Yucca is a white, starchy root vegetable.

zanahoria: carrot

Zapotec: an ancient Mesoamerican civilization, with one of its major centers located in Mexico.

zempasuchitl: marigold; significant flower to ancient Aztecs, representing the sun. Traditionally, on Día de los Muertos altars, marigolds are placed prominently in order to bring sunlight to beloved ancestors and newly dead.

Recipes

TAINA'S FAVORITE FUN FOODS

These are some of the recipes my *mami* made for me when I got home from school. The *guanabana* drink and *tembleque* were always refreshing additions on a hot summer day. In Puerto Rico you can get these codfish fritters in *quioscos* on Luquillo Beach on the eastern side of the island. But usually I got them homemade. I always had great fun sitting on a kitchen stool watching *Mami* fry these cod fritters up in a thick black iron pan. So whether you're watching them being made or cooking them up yourself, these *antojitos* are always fun to eat!

Bacalaitos

1 package of bacalao *(salt cod), deboned*
1 cup of flour
1 pinch of ground black pepper
Water
Vegetable oil for frying

Soak salt cod in a bowl of water for 5–6 hours, changing water twice (this removes excess salt from fish). Using fingers or a fork, flake fish into a small bowl. Add pepper and flour, mixing all the while. After dry ingredients are combined, slowly add water and stir until paste is formed. Scoop a spoonful of mixture and drop into hot oil. (Spoonful of mix should bubble.) Fry circles of *bacalao* till they are golden brown on each side. Set aside on paper towels. Serve hot.

If you can't get *bacalao* (salt cod), then follow this simple recipe:

  1 box of Goya's Bacalaito *mix*
  1 cup of flour
  Water
  Vegetable oil for frying

In a medium size mixing bowl, combine mix and flour. Add water until a creamy paste forms. There shouldn't be any lumps in the paste. Drop one spoonful into hot oil. Fry until golden brown, turning each side every so often. Set aside on paper towels. Serve hot.

DESSERT

Tembleque (Coconut Jello)

  1 box of gelatin (flavorless/colorless)
  1 can of Coco Lopez (creamed coconut)
  1 cup of fresh coconut milk (strained carefully)
  1/3 cup of sugar
  one pinch of cinnamon

Mix all ingredients, stirring slowly. Fill into a clear cake pan. Cover with plastic wrap and cool in refrigerator for four hours or until solid. Remove from refrigerator. Sprinkle with cinnamon and cut into squares. Serve chilled.

DRINK

Guanabana (sour sop) Smoothie

Guanabana *fruit (if not available, use canned sour sop)*
1 cup of sugar
3 cups of whole milk
Ice
Sprig of fresh mint leaves, for decoration

Remove seeds from *guanabana* pulp. Drop pulp into blender.
Add sugar, milk, and ice. Blend (ice should have the consistency
of crushed ice). Serve in tall glass with a sprig of mint.

GRACIELA'S FAVORITE COMIDA

You've probably already guessed what's on this menu. I bring
you one of my mother's many masterpieces, *bien sabroso y exquis-
ito.* I only wish you could see the *genia* that is *Mamá* in the
kitchen, but this the next best thing. ¡*Buen provecho*!

Agua de Jamaica

A noncarbonated "soft" drink from Mexico made with hibiscus
flowers, also known as *flor de jamaica,* or sorrel. It's also popular
in the West Indies, Jamaica in particular.

Makes: 5–6 1-cup servings

2 cups (2 ounces) jamaica flowers
½ cup granulated sugar (or more as desired)

Bring 6 cups of water to a boil, then add the flowers and the
sugar and stir continuously while the mixture boils for one
minute. Pour into a noncorrosive bowl and steep for 2 hours.
*Note: this flower will stain; avoid using a plastic bowl. Strain the

mixture through a sieve, pressing on the flower solids to extract as much liquid as possible. Taste for strength and sweetness. If it is too strong, add water, or if too tart add more sugar. Cover and refrigerate until time to serve.

Tortillas Using Maseca

Ingredients for
1 pound masa:

2¼ *cups dry masa harina (Quaker, Maseca, etc.)*
½ *teaspoon salt*
1½ *cups warm water*

Combine all ingredients in a bowl, then turn the dough out to knead on a flat surface. The dough will be quite sticky, but will become smoother and more pliable as it is kneaded.

After being kneaded with moistened hands for about 5–10 minutes, the dough will form a smooth, nonsticky mass. When it can be pressed between two fingers, it has been kneaded sufficiently.

Let the dough rest for 5 minutes before using it in a recipe for tortillas or other masa-based dishes.

Tortillas

Once you have acquired your tortilla press and a *comal* or griddle, all you will need is some waxed paper, cut into squares to fit the dimensions of the tortilla press, to keep the dough from sticking. Although tortillas are baked on a dry surface, a little oil can be applied to the griddle or *comal* with a paper towel if the tortillas stick to the surface at first. After your *comal* or griddle has been used a few times, it will become seasoned, and you should not have to use any oil after that. Always dry your *comal* over heat to prevent rust from forming. Incidentally, the side of the tortilla that puffs up as it is baking is called the *pancita*, and should face inward when rolling the tortilla around a filling.

1 pound corn masa (use either this recipe, or your own favorite)
warm water as needed

After the dough has been kneaded until smooth and nonsticky, and allowed to rest for 5 minutes, heat a well-seasoned or non-stick griddle or *comal* until drops of water sprinkled on the surface evaporate.

Pinch off a 1½–2-inch piece of dough for each tortilla and place the dough between the waxed paper squares lining the tortilla press. Push down on the lever, flattening the dough.

Carefully remove the tortilla by peeling it away from the waxed paper. If the tortilla has cracked around the edges while being pressed, the dough is probably too dry, and a little warm water will have to be added and kneaded in.

Toss the tortilla back and forth from one flattened palm to another a few times to aerate it. (This does not have to be a big, spinning pizza-dough throw, but a few small, gentle tosses.)

Place it on the hot griddle or *comal* and bake for 30 seconds. Turn it over and bake for 1 minute. Turn again and bake for another 30 seconds. Dark spots on the tortilla indicate that the cooking surface is too hot.

As the tortillas are removed from the heat, they should be stacked inside a clean, dry cloth, such as a tea towel, and at serving time brought to the table in the cloth or tucked inside a covered basket.

Makes 12 medium-large tortillas.

Caldo Tlalpeño

This soup is a Mexican classic, and though it is said to have originated in Jalisco, it is found on menus throughout the country. This version is hearty enough to serve as a one-dish meal. The ingredient that gives this soup its distinctive flavor is the chipotle chile.

1 4-pound chicken, cut into serving pieces
1 medium white onion, peeled and chopped
2 large cloves garlic, peeled and chopped
2 dried chipotle chiles (see note)
1 sprig cilantro
salt to taste
6 quarts water
½ pound carrots, peeled and cut into chunks
1 pound green beans, sliced
½ pound zucchini, sliced
2 ears corn, each cut into 4 pieces
1 large avocado, sliced

Place the chicken, onion, garlic, chiles, cilantro, and salt to taste in a large stockpot with 6 quarts water. Bring to a boil, lower flame, cover, and cook over medium heat for 1 hour or until the chicken is tender.

Add carrots and cook 10 minutes. Add remaining vegetables and cook another 10 minutes.

Place a piece of chicken, a piece of corn, and some of each vegetable in a soup bowl with the broth and garnish with sliced avocado.

Serves 6.

Note: If a milder taste is desired, add the chipotle with the vegetables, during the last 10 minutes of cooking.

Flan de Vainilla

Considered one of the classic Mexican desserts, flan takes on a far more distinctive character when prepared using fragrant vanilla beans. This dessert should be made one day ahead of time and stored, refrigerated, in the mold in which it has been prepared.

1 quart milk
2 vanilla beans, split lengthwise
¾ cup sugar
4 lightly beaten egg yolks
2 lightly beaten egg whites

In a medium-size saucepan, heat the milk with the vanilla beans and ½ cup of the sugar, stirring frequently, until hot and slightly thickened.

Cover, remove from heat, and allow to steep for 20 minutes. Remove and discard vanilla beans. When the mixture is cool, add the egg yolks and whites and stir until well combined.

Meanwhile, caramelize 6 deep individual custard cups or a flan mold by dusting with remaining sugar and placing in a 350° F oven until the sugar has melted and begun to caramelize. Move the molds so that the inner surfaces are coated with the caramel.

Pour custard into the molds and place in a pan of water.

Lower the oven temperature to 300° F and bake for an hour, or until a knife inserted in the center comes out clean. Allow to cool, then chill in the molds in the refrigerator overnight.

Unmold just before serving time by running a knife around the edges and inverting the flan onto dessert plates.

Makes 6 servings.

LENI'S FAVORITE MEAL

Here it is, my favorite meal in the world. I always like *Abuela's Chili Con Carne*, but I also like it 'cause it's the only meal I can cook! I make it for Mom at least once a month.

Coquito is the Caribbean answer to eggnog. This is a special holiday drink that can be prepared without alcohol. I always thought it was named for Puerto Rico's cute tree frog, the *coquí*, but I think it is actually after a small coconut. (Now that I think of it, who wants a drink named after a frog, anyway?) This is Myrta's famous recipe.

And I got the guava cake recipe from Concha Dávila, the owner of my new favorite bakery. Okay, so it blocks your arteries just looking at it, but take it from me, it is *good* and totally worth it! Enjoy . . .

Abuela Elena's Chili Con Carne

1 pound ground beef
1 can red kidney beans
1 medium onion
½ fresh green pepper
1 small can tomato sauce
olive oil
fresh garlic
dried red pepper
1 teaspoon oregano
salt

Chop onion and green pepper, and sauté in olive oil. When soft, add tomato sauce, and garlic, red pepper and salt to taste, and 1 teaspoon oregano. Set aside browned veggies (*sofrito*).

In fat in pan, brown 1 pound ground beef. When brown, add *sofrito* (browned veggies) and drained red kidney beans (save liquid). Simmer on low fire until it thickens. Add leftover liquid from beans if it gets dry. Serve over white rice.

Myrta's *Coquito*

1 can cream of coconut
1 can condensed milk
6–8 oz. white rum
¼ teaspoon cinnamon
¼ teaspoon ground cloves
⅛ teaspoon nutmeg
1 teaspoon vanilla extract

Mix all the ingredients in a blender, and blend at very high speed for over a minute. Chill in the refrigerator for 1 to 2 hours. Shake well, and serve with a sprinkle of nutmeg on top. Serve in small glasses. ¡Qué rico!

Concha's *Torta Imperial*

½ pound butter (melted)
2 cups of sugar
4 eggs
4 cups flour (cake flour) sifted
½ 12-ounce can guava paste

Slice thin pieces of guava paste.

Mix sugar, eggs, and butter (cooled) for one minute. Add flour in three stages. Grease pan with butter.

Pour half of batter (will be thick like bread dough) in bottom of pan. Place ½ of guava slices on top of batter with pieces arranged evenly. Then spread remainder of batter (carefully) over top, and arrange remaining guava slices on the top.

Bake at 325°F for 35–45 minutes.

¡BUEN PROVECHO!

QUESTIONS
FOR DISCUSSION

1) Which of the three main characters, Taina, Graciela, and Leni, do you relate to the most? Why?

2) Describe the girls' relationships to their families. How do they differ from one another? How does that relationship relate to your own experiences?

3) List three things that you admire about Taina, Graciela, and Leni, and why.

4) Do any of the characters remind you of someone you know?

5) What do you think were the big turning points for the main characters?

6) Of all the characters in the book, who would you like to get to know, and why?

7) In what way have each of the girls changed by the end of the novel?

8) Who are the characters who had the most effect on each of the girls, and why?

9) What's your impression of Don Ramiro?

10) How would you describe each of the girls' mothers in the book? How would you describe their relationships with each of their daughters?

11) How does the friendship between the girls affect one another throughout the course of the book?

12) What role does creativity play in each of the girls' lives, and how is that linked to the world around them?

13) What does friendship mean at the beginning of the book? What does it mean by the end?

14) What do think of Jack and Graciela?

Taina and Yusef?

Leni and Carlos?

15) What are the different ways that Taina reconciles with her personal and cultural history?

16) Toward the end of the novel, Taina begins to see her mother in a new light. How did this change or affect their relationship?

17) How does Taina's poetry respond to her view of the world or her impression of her life?

18) How do each of the Sister Chicas evolve through their relationships with their parents, their love interests, and their friends?

SUGGESTED READING

Julia Alvarez, *How the Garcia Girls Lost Their Accent*
Maria Arana, *American Chica: Two Worlds, One Childhood*
Sandra Cisneros, *Caramelo*
Sandra Cisneros, *Loose Woman*
Sandra Cisneros, *My Wicked Ways*
Lucille Clifton, *Blessing the Boats*
Maryse Conde, *Desirada*
Edwidge Danticat, *Breath, Eyes, Memory*
Julia de Burgos, *Songs of the Simple Truth: The Complete Poems of Julia de Burgos*
Rigoberto Gonzalez, *So Often the Pitcher Goes to Water Until It Breaks: Poems*
Sandra Opoku Jackson, *The River Where Blood Is Born*
Danielle Legros, *Maroon*
Aurora Levins Morales and Rosario Morales, *Getting Home Alive*
Aurora Levins Morales, *Remedios: Stories of Earth and Iron from the History of Puertorriqueñas*
Maria Mazziotti Gillan, *Things My Mother Told Me*
Maria Mazziotti Gillan and Jennifer Gillan, eds., *Identity Lessons: Contemporary Writing About Learning to Be American*
Nicholasa Mohr, *El Bronx Remembered*

Pat Mora, *Agua Santa/Holy Water*

Pat Mora, *Aunt Carmen's Book of Practical Saints*

Pat Mora, *House of Houses*

Pat Mora, *My Own True Name: New and Selected Poems for Young Adults*

Pablo Neruda, *Pablo Neruda: Selected Poems*

Pablo Neruda, *Twenty Love Poems: And a Song of Despair*

Achy Obejas, *We Came All the Way from Cuba so You Can Dress like This?*

Judith Ortiz Cofer, *Silent Dancing: A Partial Remembrance of a Puerto Rican Childhood.*

Elena Poniatowska, *Ready to Buy? Here's to You, Jesusa!*

Elena Poniatowska, *The Skin of the Sky*

Kenneth Rexroth, ed., *Women Poets of Japan*

Luis J. Rodriguez, *Music of the Mill*

Luis J. Rodriguez, *My Nature Is Hunger*

Nelly Rosario, *Song of the Water Saints*

Esmeralda Santiago, *When I Was a Puerto Rican*

Michele Serros, *Chicana Falsa*

Michele Serros, *How to Be a Chicana Role Model*